I0708793

Unorganised Crime
Jamie C. Richter

Plan C Publishing

First published in 2026 by Plan C Publishing

ISBN 978-1-7641049-2-0 (hardcover)
ISBN 978-1-7641049-0-6 (paperback)
ISBN 978-1-7641049-1-3 (ebook)

A catalogue record for this book is available from the National Library of Australia

Dedicated to my wife and daughter, whose patience and love
have been endless.

"The Australian criminal underworld is a totally unbelievable, blood-soaked, insane, comedy of errors. It is filled with the most unrealistic, nuttiest collection of murdering, drug running, movie-watching Walter Mittys you will ever find."

Mark 'Chopper' Read

Chapter One

A Tree Falls the Way It Leans

Jack Perkins always figured that if the Gold Coast was going to do him in, it would be at the hands of a jealous husband or a dodgy late-night kebab from Cavill Avenue, not a half-baked arson job with his best mate. Yet, here he was, standing in the empty car park of the Hackston Tavern, heart pounding, nostrils stinging from the stench of petrol fumes rising from a boot full of jerry cans. The kind of acrid smell that clung to your skin like regret. Christ, loan sharks were supposed to be the ones torching your stuff, not forcing you into doing their dirty work. But hindsight had a cruel sense of humour. For most, it was the luxury of looking back with a clear head, piecing together where things went wrong. For Jack, hindsight was a gut-punch, the exact moment he realised he had well and truly fucked it up. And now, as he toyed with the cigarette lighter in his pocket, one thing was certain: no one was getting out of this unscathed.

"Come on, Hung. Move those dainty feet of yours."

"I'm moving as fast as I can—" Hung replied.

This was the early noughties, a time when 'Little Johnnie' Howard held court at the Lodge, the halcyon days of Aussie alt-rock were at an end, and smartphones were … well, not-so-smart, yet infinitely smarter than most locals, especially those of the criminal persuasion. The one constant was the Gold Coast. The Goldie never changed. It was always a heady mix of sun-soaked beaches and shady deals, where the heat came not only from the sun, and getting burned could mean more than just forgetting your factor fifteen.

Hung Van Thanh, a short, youthful-looking Vietnamese man whose face had not quite caught up to his thirties, grunted as he wrestled two jerry cans of petrol out of the boot of Jack's pride and joy, his powder-blue Datsun. The cans were bulky and awkward, sloshing precariously as he staggered across the empty car park. With each laboured step, it felt as if gravity was poised to claim victory, threatening to send him face-first into the asphalt. Despite his distinctly Asian heritage, the moment he opened his mouth, his thick Strine accent was as familiar as a Friday night meat raffle.

"How about picking up the pace?" Jack said.

"How about cutting me some slack?" Hung shot back.

"Slack? You want slack, mate? Call me precious, but I've got a burning desire to leave the Goldie with only the holes I was born with. So do us both a favour and hurry up."

Jack watched from outside the rear door of the pub, a mix of annoyance and amusement etched across his stubbled face. Tall and unconventionally handsome, with tousled dark hair framing a sharp jawline, Jack looked like he had just walked off a construction site, though his attire suggested otherwise. An unbuttoned red-and-black chequered shirt hung loosely over a faded music festival T-shirt, paired with well-worn jeans that had seen better days. A hint of mischief sparkled in his deep-set brown eyes, and a sardonic smirk tugged at the corners of his mouth, as if he could not help but find the dark humour in their precarious situation.

"You realise these are heavy, yeah?" Hung said.

"So? Harden up," Jack fired back without even glancing Hung's way, too busy fidgeting with the door handle.

"Sorry, but my arms are getting really—"

"Whinge, whinge, bloody whinge," Jack replied.

As Jack's hand gripped the handle, his eyes landed on a handwritten note taped to the door. The message was blunt: Closed until further notice. He recognised the frantic scrawl immediately: it was his own, hastily scribbled on the back of an envelope with a Keno pencil. In that instant, a flood of memories surged through him, disjointed moments spiralling out of control. Time slowed. It was a rare moment of clarity amid the chaos, a fleeting heartbeat where he could pinpoint the exact moment he had fucked everything up. That moment: meeting Magdalena Black. The mere thought of that withered cunt made the air around him crackle with tension.

Frustration mingled with resignation as Jack ripped the note from the door, crumpling it into a tight ball before tossing it onto the asphalt. That small act of destruction felt oddly cathartic: a minor rebellion against the chaos that had overtaken his life. Until recently, Jack Perkins' existence had been blissfully uncomplicated. That was before the madness began, before he found himself ensnared in a whirlwind of ruthless loan sharks, bent detectives and a motley crew of crims, both foreign and domestic. Not to mention the meddling pensioner with a hard-on for vengeance. Back then, Jack had been barely a blip on the criminal underworld's radar: a nobody pulling fifteen-hour days at the pub he co-owned with his best mate.

But now? Fast-forward one week, and Jack teetered on the edge of doing something utterly insane to escape an equally insane situation. Absurdity had become his new normal; chaos was the only constant in his life. He had long since crossed the line from mundane to madness, leaving any semblance of sanity in the rear-view mirror, fading into the distance like a long-forgotten memory.

"Are you going to open that door?" Hung asked, his arms trembling as he carried a jerry can of unleaded in each hand.

Jack glowered over his shoulder. "Hold your horses, yeah?" he muttered, yanking a bulky keyring from his jeans pocket. He thumbed through the jumble of keys, his fingers moving with practised ease until he found the right one. Sliding it into the lock with a satisfying click, he turned it sharply, then shot Hung an incredulous look as he tugged on the handle.

Like a pisshead at last drinks, it refused to budge. He muttered under his breath and yanked again. Still nothing.

Hung placed the jerry cans on the ground with a clank, eyeing the door with concern. "Is the handle jammed again?" he asked, brow furrowing. "Maybe it seized up because of all the rain the other night. Have you tried wiggling it?" His suggestion carried a casual, almost playful tone, as if he were oblivious to the fact that their lives were balanced on a razor's edge.

"What?" Jack replied, barely containing his frustration.

"Try wiggling the handle a little ... then yank it."

"Wiggle it? How about I give your neck a wiggle?"

When facing the sharp end of a gangland execution, beggars could not be choosers. Jack was open to any suggestion, no matter how absurd. He gave the handle a wiggle, then a hard yank, just as Hung had suggested, but the useless thing held firm like it had something to prove. Hung shrugged apologetically, his expression already shifting as the gears in his mind began churning, racing to devise a new plan of attack.

Jack had finally had enough. He scanned the car park, hoping their bickering had not drawn the attention of any smackheads, the kind who stumbled in for a quick leak against The Hackston's back passage before shuffling off to the local methadone clinic. The coast was clear. Jack inhaled deeply, steeling himself. Squaring his shoulders, he raised his foot and delivered a powerful kick to the door. *CRUNCH!* His boot connected with a deafening thud that echoed through the quiet car park, sharp and explosive in the stillness. The door buckled, wood splintering, rusty hinges groaning as it gave way in a burst of dust and debris. With a final crash, it flew open, collapsing in a chaotic spray of shattered timber, screws pinging across the concrete like shrapnel.

Jack stood over the wreckage, breathing heavily, a triumphant grin spreading across his face. "Now that's how you open a fuckin' door!" he exclaimed, adrenaline coursing through him.

Bam! The stench of stale beer, sweat, and cigarette-soaked carpet smacked Jack in the face, as sharp as any left jab from Lionel Rose. It was the kind of funk that could curl a mortician's toes. Despite its persistence, clinging to the air like a foul demon that refused to be exorcised, Jack had long convinced himself he would get used to that daily assault on the senses. However, he never did. Hung had dubbed it the "bouquet", the unmistakable perfume of every pub, in every town or city. To Jack, though, it was more than that. It smelled of freedom. It smelled like everything that made Australia fucking great. After all, this was not just any putrid den of inebriation; The Hackston was their 247-square-metre slice of paradise.

"Right, let's make this quick, like ripping off a band-aid," Jack said, his eyes adjusting to the gloom inside the pub. "And that means you, Hung. No stuff-arsing about, no trips down memory lane. Trust me, if we start thinking, we might just get emotional and do something we might regret." He stepped over the splintered remains of the rear door, heading straight for the security panel on the wall. "Remember: in and out, mate, like a couple of Japanese racing snakes."

Hung frowned, still loitering by the door, jerry cans in hand, his arms aching under the weight. "Uh, like a what now?"

"What I mean is, don't do anything stupid."

Hung raised an eyebrow. "Stupid? Look around, Jack. We're about to torch our own pub. I reckon we're already," he glanced at the jerry cans, "what, forty litres of petrol past stupid o'clock?"

Jack let his partner's words hang in the air as he turned away, his mind drifting while he absently hummed a playful tune. His fingers tapped in the eight-digit security code: '19870202'. His niece's birthday. Not that he was sentimental, but somehow that date had lodged itself in his mind, burned in like a safety net amidst the chaos. Maybe it was the one thing he could cling to, a reminder that despite the wreckage his life had become, there was still a thread of normality, of family, buried beneath the ashes.

A green light flickered as the security system disarmed.

"You don't sound particularly cut up," Hung remarked.

"And what makes you say that?" Jack replied.

"The fact you're humming one of your little tunes."

Jack shot Hung an incredulous look and snatched a jerry can from him. The irony of humming Sinatra, a singer with alleged mob ties, was lost on them as they prepared to commit arson to escape the clutches of the Gold Coast's own brand of organised crime. It was a dark, twisted symmetry. Yet somehow, in that moment, it felt like just another absurdity in the chaos they were navigating.

"You know crooners aren't my 'thing'," Hung said.

"Neither's good taste, it seems," Jack retorted.

The pair made their way through the mostly barren storeroom, deeper into the rabbit warren that was The Hackston. "You wouldn't say that if you knew how incredible the final movement of Sibelius' *Symphony Number 2 in D minor* was," Hung grumbled as they pushed through the heavy door leading into the front bar.

The atmosphere shifted sharply. The dimly lit space enveloped them, thick with the familiar, now almost suffocating stench of stale beer and cigarette smoke. Worn wooden floors groaned underfoot, while neon signs flickered weakly against cracked plaster walls, casting an eerie glow over scattered tables and mismatched chairs. Framed photographs of patrons and local legends adorned the walls, a testament to the pub's storied, and somewhat chequered, past.

As painful as it was to accept, if Jack and Hung were ever to reclaim any semblance of normality, their pride and joy, this nearly century-old pub, steeped in the memories of countless publicans, was fated to become a pile of smouldering rubble by sunset. Jack took one last look around, his gaze settling on the back wall, where a black-and-white lithograph overlooked the beat-up pool table. It depicted none other than Hollywood icon Humphrey 'Bogie' Bogart, trademark trench coat and hat, his hangdog expression paired with an era-appropriate cigarette dangling from the corner of his mouth. It was a ghostly reminder of a time when larger-than-life legends walked the earth, unburdened by the notion of toxic masculinity.

What would Humphrey Bogart do? he wondered.

The man had a remarkable ability to portray intelligent, playful, and reckless characters, each one anchored by a steadfast moral code, striving to navigate a corrupt world. Perhaps that was why Jack felt such a profound affinity for him. He gazed into Bogie's apathetic eyes, seeking guidance in the quiet intensity of the lithograph.

Burn the place to the ground, kid. Burn it all.

Jack nodded, the weight of the decision settling in. "You take the bar, Hung. I'll take the office," he said, his voice steady, a sense of purpose ignited by Bogie's silent encouragement.

The Hackston's office exuded all the rustic charm of a prison cell, with the dimensions to match. The walls were a patchwork of cold, exposed concrete, the kind that swallowed any hint of warmth. Muted grey tones dominated, giving the space a suffocating, institutional feel. It was missing only the essentials: a steel cot bolted to the floor, a grimy toilet squatting in the corner, and a few lewd images of women plastered to the walls with the kind of homemade glue a person did not ask questions about. The place felt less like an office and more like solitary confinement for a white-collar criminal.

If their final gamble went belly-up, the best they could hope for was that their cramped office would serve as an introduction to a five-to-ten stretch in one of Queensland's illustrious correctional facilities. The worst-case scenario? An involuntary swim in a pair of cement Dunlop Volleys just off the break at Surfers Paradise.

"Bugger me," Jack muttered, taken aback by how the normally barren office was now overflowing with columns of haphazardly stacked cardboard boxes, shrinking the already claustrophobic space to the point of suffocation. The room, once sparse and lifeless, felt choked by the weight of unspoken misery. The boxes were utterly nondescript: unmarked, identical in size, and disturbingly ordinary. Yet their presence pricked the air, like a coiled Eastern Brown, its muscles tense and ready, poised to strike with lethal precision.

Truth be told, neither Jack nor Hung had any idea what the boxes contained, and, given the circumstances, neither man wanted to know. All they knew was that those boxes belonged to someone dangerous. Someone whose reputation made curiosity not just reckless, but 'bullet-to-the-forehead' fatal.

Accepting that it was time to grow a pair, Jack shimmied his way through the cardboard maze, aiming for his desk, which sat dead-centre in the room, just a smidgen to the right of the freestanding safe in the corner. With a bit of contortion and a lot of cursing, Jack's lanky frame eventually navigated its way to that rectangular oasis of reclaimed timber. He set the jerry can down precariously on the last tiny scrap of vacant space, catching his breath before tackling the safe.

The Hackston had been haemorrhaging cash so regularly that opening the safe had become pure muscle memory. The last time Jack had checked its contents, there had been close to thirty grand tucked away, give or take. But now? The safe was about as empty as a politician's promise.

"Hey, Jack, are you still in there?" Hung's muffled voice came through the cinder-block wall, accompanied by the faint slosh of liquid and the unmistakable sound of someone exerting themselves far too hard. "Uh, sorry to bother you, but do you have a few seconds?"

"Huh? Say that again, mate?" Jack replied.

"Have you got a few seconds?" Hung repeated.

"Given the seriousness of the situation, do I seem like the sort of bloke who has a few seconds?" Jack shot back, stuffing the contents of the safe into his jacket before slamming the door shut. In that instant, a wave of liberation washed over him, like a brief bout of amnesia cleansing him of all his sins and doubts.

The simple act of closing the safe felt like shutting the door on a chapter of their lives. Soon, all the chaos and bullshit of the past twenty-four hours would be behind them. Thousands of kilometres behind them.

"How's it going out there, anyway?" Jack asked, bracing himself for the inevitable stupid question.

"Ah, pretty good, I suppose," Hung replied, breathless.

"And what do you mean by 'you suppose'?"

"Uh, that's kind of what I wanted to ask you, Jack." Hung hesitated, his voice faltering. "Like ... how do I know if I'm doing this right? I mean, is there really a 'right' way to commit arson? I've never exactly dabbled in this sort of thing before. Well, more specifically ... the optimal distribution of accelerant," he admitted.

Jack chuckled, a dry, weary sound that echoed off the walls. "The optimal-fucking-what now?" he muttered under his breath, shaking his head in disbelief. Of all the things Hung could have been worrying about right now, like, say, getting caught or blowing them both to pieces, he was on the other side of the wall, obsessing over the 'art' of burning the place down. Typical Hung. He always overthought the smallest details, even when they were knee-deep in the shit.

"You wanna know something?" Jack said.

"What's that?" Hung replied, his tone cautious.

"You're a deadset friggin' nerd, mate."

It was finally time to rip off the metaphorical band-aid. Jack sighed, popped the top off his jerry can, and began pouring with sharp, violent jerks. Torrents of foul-smelling petrol gushed from the nozzle, drenching the desk and soaking the surrounding cardboard boxes. For a man with zero experience in the 'optimal distribution of accelerant', he was certainly giving it a red-hot go.

Jack admired his partner's handiwork in the front bar; it was impossible not to pause and appreciate the sheer artistry of it all. The neat trail of petrol snaked along the counter, its shiny surface glistening under the dim lights with a quiet menace. It wound across the dance floor, leaving a faint sheen that sharply contrasted with the worn timber boards before circling the pool table, where a few stray balls lay abandoned. The trail stopped just millimetres shy of the office he had recently vacated, an ominous barrier that seemed to taunt him with its proximity. He had to hand it to Hung for his meticulous attention to detail; this was not merely a masterpiece of destruction but also a testament to their audacity, so much so that Jack could not help but feel a flicker of pride at the sight before him.

"I reckon you missed your calling, mate. You could've been an artist or, I don't know, one of those TV presenters." Jack smirked as he tossed his empty jerry can onto the ground. "How about *The Joy of Arson*, with Hung Van Thanh? You know, have a little catchphrase like, 'There are no mistakes, just happy insurance jobs'."

Hung blinked, unsure of how to respond. "Uh ... thanks?" he muttered, a strange sense of accomplishment blooming across his deceptively innocent features. A backhanded compliment was still a compliment, after all. He glanced at Jack, sensing an unusual openness in him, especially considering they were standing in what would soon be a colossal bonfire. Maybe now was the time to ask.

Clearing his throat, Hung shifted his weight slightly. "Jack," he began cautiously, "have you stopped to ... uh, think about it?"

Jack raised an eyebrow. "Think about what?"

Hung hesitated for a moment before pushing forward. "You know, everything. The pub, Magdalena Black, the Koreans ... how we ended up in this mess? The whole kit and caboodle."

Jack sighed, his eyes narrowing. "What? Between dodging attempted murders and ... well, whatever the hell's going on in that office back there? Yeah, I've probably thought about it more than I care to admit." He scanned The Hackston, his expression hardening. "We were just a couple of blokes trying to make an honest living, but somewhere along the line, things got a little, uh ... messy."

"Messy's a bit of an understatement," Hung replied.

Jack paused, frustration creeping into his tone. "Hell, maybe once this all blows over, if it ever does, we can buy one of those fancy corkboards, yeah? Run bits of red string between all the bad guys and piece it together like they do on those cop shows." A weary look etched lines into his long face. "But right now, Hung? I dunno. I just want to get this over with and put as much distance between us and Magdalena Black as we can, while we bloody can."

That was a long-winded way of saying Jack did not want to talk about it, especially with the pungent stench of petrol thick in the air, its sharp fumes clawing at their throats. In the enclosed space, the smell quickly became unbearable, leaving both Jack and Hung lightheaded, their eyes beginning to water. Yet, it still failed to address Hung's burning question.

"Okay, but are you absolutely certain?" he asked.

"Huh? Why do you keep asking me that?" Jack retorted. "What, you think I'm going to have a sudden change of heart?"

"I just need to know this is what you want," Hung pressed.

"Want?" Jack laughed, shaking his head. "What either of us *wants* doesn't even get a look-in, mate."

The men had nurtured The Hackston from a rundown dive into ... well, a slightly more upscale dive. The kind of place where an addict could confidently leave their underage kids to roam unsupervised while they pumped their dole payments through the pokies. Life was far from perfect, but it had been semi-comfortable. Suppliers were mostly paid on time, there were enough regulars to keep the doors open, and all the trappings of a typical Aussie pub were in place. But then, as always, shit happens. Now, they were about to embark on a path that, just a few days ago, would have seemed unconscionable to both men. Surrounded by the stench of petrol, beer, and stale body odour, burning their beloved pub to the ground felt like the only logical conclusion: a punchline to a twisted joke.

But as they say, needs must when the devil drives.

"Right, whatever we have left to do, man ... can we just get on with it?" Hung spluttered, burying his nose in his sleeve as the fumes overwhelmed him. "I'm feeling ... a bit ... dizzy."

Jack took a final, fleeting glance around, his eyes settling on the lithograph of Bogie that hung prominently on the wall. His partner noticed and nudged him subtly, suggesting he should take it as a souvenir. Jack contemplated the request for a moment before dismissing the idea. "It'd make a nice memento, but my gut tells me it would be a prick to fit into our carry-on, especially considering where we're headed," he said, exchanging a knowing look with Hung.

The two men stood in silence, tension hanging between them. Jack raised an eyebrow at his partner.

"Any words of wisdom before we do this?" he asked.

Hung shrugged, still unsure of what to say.

"Jesus, remind me never to ask you to write my eulogy," Jack said with a snort, pulling a disposable lighter from his pocket. He flicked it a few times before holding it aloft. "Well, here's to the good times ... and to fuckin' it all up," he said as he sparked it. Nothing. Just a few stubborn clicks and no flame. The pair shared a defeated chuckle, the lighter's refusal carrying an odd, unspoken weight. Jack gave it a shake, tapped it against his forefinger, and tried again. This time, a brilliant orange-red flame flared to life, dancing in the draught from the busted rear door. They stood there for a beat, eyes locked on the flickering flame, the weight of the moment hanging heavy.

Eventually, Hung spoke, shattering the silence.

"Should I ask you one last time?" he said.

Jack shook his head, a heavy sense of finality settling over him as he thumbed the cigarette lighter, contemplating the destruction of everything he and Hung had built. Where had it all gone wrong? Ordinary law-abiding citizens did not end up in situations like this unless they had messed up somewhere along the way. Maybe it was fate. Or perhaps it was just rotten luck. Maybe one of Jack's ancestors had kicked a burning puppy into an orphanage, and now inter-generational karma had finally met him halfway.

"This entire ordeal reminds me of this Zippo my old man used to have," Jack said, staring into the flame. "Brought it back from when he was a NASHO over in ... well, you know." If anyone knew about the Vietnam War, it was Hung. "It was one of those proper old-school ones too, none of this disposable crap. All dinged up to hell with a US Army insignia on it. It always fascinated me as a little tacker. Hmm. Kinda wish I knew where it wound up in the end."

Hung, eyes locked on the naked flame, barely blinked.

"Maybe he lost it torching a pub?" he said drily.

Jack winced as the heat licked at his fingertips. "Nah, my father wasn't that stupid." He shrugged. "Either way, it doesn't matter. Point is, there was this, uh, old proverb engraved on it. Something like, 'A tree falls the way it leans.'"

Hung frowned, trying to make sense of it. "I don't get it."

Jack stared at the flame, a glimmer of realisation crossing his face. "Never understood it myself," he replied. "At least, not until today."

Chapter Two

That Necessary Inconvenience

Forty-eight hours earlier.

'Queensland: Beautiful one day, perfect the next.'

Each Australian state and territory prided itself on its tacky tourism slogan. Typically, they were just that: tacky, bordering on self-aggrandisement. However, today, the Sunshine State not only matched but exceeded its boastful reputation. The birds chirped merrily, the sun radiated in all its melanoma-inducing glory, and a gentle sea breeze wafted in from the east. As far as the eye could see, hardly a cloud marred the azure sky. It was another perfect day in the state's crime capital: perfect in the sense that it felt like an inside joke that a Higher Power would bless such a glitzy, self-absorbed wasteland of kebab shops and vanity licence plates with impeccable weather. Of course, little of this concerned the powerful individuals who loomed large above the ne'er-do-wells and scantily clad tourists in their towers of glass and steel.

Magdalena 'Maggie' Black was one of those oblivious individuals: oblivious to the state of the weather or how merrily the birds chirped on this fine day, and oblivious to the struggles of common people. Instead, she was completely engrossed in the hunt. The apex predator stood vigilant on her penthouse balcony overlooking the golden stretch of sand known as Surfers Paradise, a flip phone in one hand and a pair of binoculars in the other.

She cut an alluring figure in her beach attire. Her slim frame was wrapped in black designer Italian swimwear, a two-piece complemented by a floral silk sarong tied securely around her hips. A pair of pink platform sandals, embellished with tiny daisies on the buckles, perfectly matched her nail polish. The ensemble was completed with sunglasses perched atop a wide-brimmed hat that concealed her thick auburn hair and alabaster complexion, hinting at an unspoken English lineage. She possessed the beauty and grace of a Hollywood starlet left to wither under the harsh Queensland sun, a grace instantly shattered the moment she opened her mouth and barked profanities with the ease of a seasoned dockworker.

"Fuck you! Don't make me—" Magdalena paused mid-tirade, granting the voice on the other end a fleeting reprieve. Truth be told, her focus had drifted to the bikini-clad jailbait cavorting on the beach below. "—don't make me waltz into your station, Detective, and give you an impromptu colonoscopy with my fucking stiletto."

Within the upper echelon of Gold Coast underworld figures, Magdalena Black stood just shy of divinity. Depending on who you asked, she ranked comfortably in the top five of the exclusive Who's Who of scumbags, often nestled between Sammy 'The Turk' Golob and Sammy 'The Leb' Farkas. For reasons beyond her, or anyone else's, understanding, the city seemed to harbour an inordinate number of gangsters named Sammy. Perhaps it was mere coincidence, or some statistical anomaly tied to Middle Eastern children born in Australia during the late seventies, but it was something nobody could quite wrap their heads around.

Despite inheriting the lion's share of her wealth from her late father, Magdalena's lavish lifestyle, complete with beachside penthouses and designer swimsuits, was largely sustained through loan sharking, a practice notorious for its exorbitant interest rates among the more unsavoury circles of society. Still, any underworld figure worth their salt was expected, if not required, to own at least one legitimate business to launder their ill-gotten gains. Whether it was cafes, laundromats, construction firms, or the occasional legal practice, the latter serving as a cheeky middle finger to the criminal justice system, the choice of fronts varied. Magdalena's front was the exclusive BLACK, recently winning the 'Most Energetic Bartenders' award at the Annual Nightclub Gala. Proof, if proof were needed, that there was an award for everything nowadays.

"Whooptee-fucking-doo! So, every time some local miscreant ends up with a bullet in the back of their head, the police make a beeline for my front door? Christ, Detective, the ink has barely dried on the last warrant they served," Magdalena said, her voice laced with mock indignation. "Surely, even a dolt like you can see how that might be construed as inconvenient for someone in my line of work?"

She continued to scan the beach with her binoculars for exceptional specimens of the fairer sex, deftly deflecting excuses from the disembodied voice on the other end of the line. Magdalena spotted a six-out-of-ten, a four, and a generous two before her gaze fell upon a blonde temptress frolicking in the surf. She paused and executed a less-than-subtle double-take. The woman was barely a day over eighteen, her lithe body clad in a red string bikini that may as well have been hand-forged from Satan's discarded dental floss.

"And what of it? The fact that I had most of them offed is neither here nor there." Magdalena pursed her lips, ogling the beauty for a few moments longer. "Please do not misunderstand the root of my frustration, Detective. It's not that I don't appreciate your tip-off about the upcoming raid. Far from it. My issue is that I pay you and your colleague a lot of money, and I stress, a *lot* of money, to ensure that these visits do not eventuate in the first place."

Magdalena waited for a reply, the silence deafening.

"Are you still with me, Michael?" she asked.

Angered by the lack of snappy back-and-forth, Magdalena tightened her grip on the handset. Her fury simmered, punctuated only by the faint breaths of a garden-variety idiot. Enough was enough. She *slammed* the phone against the wall, once, twice, three times for emphasis, her rage almost primal. After a deep breath to compose herself, she put the battered phone back to her ear.

"Give me something to work with! Anything. Is this not exactly what I pay you for? To keep my name out of the newspapers? I'm certainly not paying for your scintillating conversation." No reply came in the time it took Magdalena to draw breath. With a frustrated sigh, she tossed the binoculars onto the nearby cane lounge. Without looking back, she headed inside, her mind already racing ahead to the next move. "You and your fat friend had better start delivering results. And fast. Because, let me tell you, if you were a lame horse, I would've had you put down long ago." She paused at the sliding door that separated the balcony from the living room, peering in at the figure sprawled across the leather lounge; sordid details were best kept outside. "Detective, are you familiar with how unsavoury types deal with an underperforming racehorse? And I don't mean the knacker's yard. I'm talking about the kind of creative solution that doesn't raise eyebrows when an insurance claim is lodged."

It was safe to assume the answer was 'fuck no'.

"You make the death look like natural causes. Colic or something equally mundane. No poisons. No torching stables in the dead of night. None of those Phar Lap shenanigans. All you need is a regular electrical extension cord straight from your odds-and-ends drawer. Cut off the plugs, slice it down the centre to expose the wires, and then, here comes the crafty bit, wrap the ends of the wires around a couple of alligator clips. Do you see where this is going? Clamp one to the horse's ear and the other to its rectum, plug the cord into the wall, and hey presto! Two-forty volts straight up the back passage."

Magdalena slid open the door and entered the room.

"Now, I don't want to give the impression that I'd ever do anything so unsavoury to one of God's creatures. Nor am I being cute in implying such a fate could befall you or your colleague. Nothing of the sort. I'm simply sharing an anecdote my dearest daddy once told me. You are familiar with Harold Black's legacy, are you not, Detective? But unlike daddy, I am a lover of all creatures, great and small, horses especially. So, believe me when I say I'd never harm such a majestic beast. But if push came to shove, I would reluctantly employ a professional to handle it. Do I make myself clear?"

The figure sprawled across Magdalena's leather lounge was Becky, an attractive blonde in her mid-twenties, with sun-kissed hair cascading over her blue bikini top and skimming the small of her back just above her frayed denim cut-offs. Plucked from the very sands surrounding the penthouse, Becky was a testament to Magdalena's talent for scouting prospects through the lenses of her high-powered binoculars. They say that gentlemen prefer blondes, but so do the often marginalised demographic of female loan sharks with a penchant for offing underperforming racehorses.

"Where do I find these morons?" Magdalena muttered, half to herself, her hand resting loosely over the receiver so the other party could hear. Becky, of course, was too distracted to care.

"What are you watching, anyway?" she asked, pressing her hand firmly over the receiver; she had given up on making any sense of the idiot on the other end. From a quick glance, it looked like one of those convoluted American soap operas where characters returned from the dead about as often as Lazarus with a mortality complex.

Silence hung in the air. Magdalena snapped her fingers, hoping to jolt Becky out of her daytime trance. Nothing. At this point, the odds of engaging in some banter with one of those lifeless soap characters seemed better than with the mute sprawled on the lounge. With a sigh, she returned the phone to her ear, only to be bombarded by the verbal diarrhoea of a man desperate to save his skin.

"Shut up!" she snapped. "I'm sick of your constant excuses, Detective. Just sort something out, because I have better things to do than flap my gums at you—" Magdalena hovered her thumb over the disconnect button. "—so, as they say in the classics, 'off you fuck'."

Magdalena mashed the button with satisfaction as she paced the spacious living room, her mind churning with schemes, footsteps sharp and furious. Before she could wear a furrow into the Persian rug beneath her or, more critically, provoke the ire of the young woman sprawled on the lounge, she hurled the burner phone at the mahogany coffee table, shattering it into a dozen pieces.

"Mark, get your arse in here!" she shouted.

A toilet flushed in the adjacent room. The man-mountain known as Mark 'The Cane Train' Campbell emerged from the bathroom with such urgency that the last thing to follow him out was the upward yank of his fly.

Campbell was a walking, talking slab of muscle, six foot two and built to intimidate. His cropped brown hair did little to conceal decades of self-abuse: a nose permanently crooked from too many bar fights, ears swollen into the telltale shape of cauliflowers, and scars crisscrossing his body like back roads on a cheap service station map. He was a born brawler; for him, "How about we take this outside?" was more than just a serving suggestion. It was practically a mantra.

"Please tell me you washed your hands," Magdalena said with a sigh, shaking her head at the unsavoury thought of her enforcer skirting even the most rudimentary of hygiene practices.

"My hands, boss?" Mark blinked, feigning confusion.

"Yes, your hands, you big galoot! The ones you should've washed before you came charging out of my bathroom not five seconds ago. Please, at least humour me, Mark. Tell me you washed them!"

Mark was the brawn to Magdalena's brains, perfectly suited to deliver a message when her acerbic tongue failed. Despite looking like he had been through a meat grinder, face first, the bloke was all chest and shoulders straining against a beat-up leather jacket. His blue jeans hugged tree-trunk legs, while a black T-shirt stretched taut over the frame beneath. With Mark, what you saw was what you got: tough, dependable, and if brains were dynamite, he would scarcely have enough to blow his nose.

"Uh, yeah, I ... washed 'em," Mark replied, his tone lacking conviction as he ran a hand through his hair, stopping at the jagged scar above his right temple. "Come on, Maggie. Give me a break, yeah? You called for me like I was a friggin' ambulance."

"An ambulance?" Magdalena shot back.

"You know, those things that go 'weeeooo!'"

Magdalena scowled, rubbing her forehead in exasperation. "Jesus wept. I know what an ambulance is, Mark, you twit. And last I checked, even ambos wash their dick-beaters on occasion."

Mark glanced at the carpet, guilt etched on his face. "Sorry, boss," he muttered, quickly shifting gears. "So, what's doing?"

Magdalena levelled a cold, indifferent stare at her enforcer. Before cementing his place as her right-hand man, everyone's favourite galoot had been a professional rugby league player for a string of floundering clubs up and down the east coast. His nickname, 'The Cane Train', stemmed from his imposing size, his Rum City roots, and the fact that his football career had started at the promptly defunct South Queensland Crushers. While few would deny the linear path from being criminally overpaid to crack skulls on the football field to being criminally underpaid to crack skulls for an underworld figure, the fact that Mark Campbell was now in the employ of a notorious loan shark suggested his lack of success in the former.

"What's doing?" Magdalena repeated, mock incredulity dripping from her tone. "My goodness, Mark. Now, I'm no Rhodes Scholar by any stretch, but that's not even remotely an intelligent response. 'What's doing?' I swear they must hand out frontal lobotomies the moment one of you Neanderthals signs an NRL contract. Either that, or stupidity is contagious. Tell me, how many times were you on *The Footy Show* with that red-headed dropkick, 'Fuzzy'?"

"Uh, you mean Fatty? I dunno, boss. The first time would've been the '96 Origin preview with … " Mark trailed off, realising he was the only person in the room who gave a frog's freckle.

Magdalena's eyes narrowed. "How. Many. Times?"

"A few," Mark muttered, realising it was a trap.

Magdalena grinned. "A few? Be specific."

"Three … maybe four? Dunno. Why's it matter?"

Magdalena's tone grew more indignant with each reply. Like the *RMS Titanic* barrelling toward a massive fuck-off iceberg, it became clear where this conversation was headed. Mark, knowing better than to speak, wisely kept his trap shut, refusing to take the bait.

"So, four times then?" Magdalena started, her tone icy. "Part of me suspects you couldn't count to four if your life depended on it, but I know you can. Want to know how I know? Because yours truly was running a book on the '98 semi-final. You remember that match, don't you, Mark? The one your team should've romped in?"

Mark stared at the floor, counting the threads in the rug.

"Who in their right mind goes for a field goal from fifteen metres out on the fourth tackle? Down by three, with twenty seconds left on the clock, and you were fifteen bloody metres from the line!" Magdalena's long manicured nails sliced through the air with each exaggerated story point. "What in God's, or Vishnu's, or Zeus's name possessed you? Honestly, pick one, because I'm dying to know."

Mark grimaced. "I don't recall, Maggie."

"Hmm. Well, I'm no expert on that ridiculous game of yours, Mark, but I know one thing for certain: forwards should never take field goals. They lack the, how should I put this, the cognitive capacity to do anything but charge headlong into other meatheads running in the opposite direction. And you know what else forwards shouldn't do? Attempt a field goal when their team is trailing by three!"

Every man had his trigger, a switch that, once flicked, unleashed a torrent of incendiary rage. This was Mark's trigger. In that very moment, at the crossroads of time and patience, it took all of Mark's self-control to holster not only his tongue but also the sledgehammers attached to the ends of his wrists. Magdalena Black had given Mark a second chance at life, a purpose. And while he would always be grateful, somewhere in the darkest recesses of his mind, the hulking ex-footballer found grim satisfaction in imagining her face reduced to mincemeat, a fate not far removed from what awaited anyone foolish enough to rib Campbell about the result of the '98 NRL semi-final.

Mark's jaw clenched, his hands balling into fists inside his pockets. Desperate to change the subject, he grasped for a distraction. Anything to steer the conversation away from the unwelcome trip down memory lane. "By the way, Maggie, you still have those two blokes sittin' in your office," he said, striving for a casual tone. "They've been waiting since—"

"Forget those pricks," Magdalena cut him off, draining the last of her enforcer's patience. "So, did you even crunch the numbers, Einstein? You get one point for a field goal. Three minus one is ... ?"

"Uh, that'd be two, yeah?" Mark guessed.

"Correct. So, even if you had made that kick, your team still would've lost! Why not go for the try line instead?"

Despite his brief absence for a call of nature, Mark had the distinct impression that whatever had been said during Magdalena's recent phone call on the balcony had lodged itself firmly up her hoity-toity backside, forcefully and without the aid of lubrication.

"Sorry, but what's this all about, anyhow?" Mark finally asked, desperate to put an end to the relentless barrage. "You called me in here as if the building was burnin' down or something, Maggie. And for what, exactly? To talk footy? It was a brain explosion, boss. Ancient history. I don't even think about it anymore, honest."

That was a lie. His former life haunted him every day.

"That's your problem, Mark. You never think," Magdalena scoffed, shaking her head with a bitter laugh. "Thanks to your little stunt that afternoon, I nearly had a brain explosion of my own, courtesy of none other than Johnny-fucking-Hammersmith." She let the words hang in the air, watching Mark wince as he braced for impact.

Hammersmith was the loan shark to end all loan sharks, a grey-haired mongrel, mad as a cut snake and twice as unpredictable. While unpredictability was common among those practising the algebra of the morally flexible, the principle itself was as old as time: a loan shark, Hammersmith, in this case, expected to recover the money lent, plus interest. If a client could not, or would not, pay, then, and only then, did the threat of violence come into play. But Johnny-fucking-Hammersmith had few principles and respected even fewer. With half a century of broken bones to his name, and more money than God, sharking had become as passé as a Sunday roast. By the end of his reign, the old boy from Swansea lived for one thing, and one thing only: the pure, unadulterated thrill of physical violence.

"There I was, all of twenty-seven," Magdalena continued, her voice flat but steely. "Kneeling on the floor of some filthy petrol station bathroom, soaked in my own amber fluid. I'll never forget it: the grimy green tiles, the stench of cheap cleaning product. Oh? Or that Welsh prick looming over me, a revolver pressed to my temple, repeating, 'Never run a book on borrowed money, sweetheart,' like a broken bloody record."

Becky sat up, watching the tension simmer between Mark and Magdalena; their dysfunction was more captivating than any soap opera. As Mark fumbled for a comeback, the silence between them stretched, thick and heavy. Becky's voice sliced through the stillness like a scythe. "Well, that makes two of you, huh?" she said.

Magdalena scowled. "Two of what?"

"Two broken records," Becky replied, unfazed.

"What in the world are you jabbering about?"

"Don't you tire of repeating that story?" Becky asked, her tone as steady as a rock. "It was years ago, and Mark has already said he's sorry, like, a dozen times. Just let it go already."

"Let it go, my dear? I was a bee's dick away from getting killed—" Magdalena gestured with her thumb and forefinger to approximate the size of male bee genitalia. "All because some meandering knobhead fancied himself the next Diego Maradona?"

"But it wasn't personal, Maggie," Becky shot back. "Give it a rest, yeah? Stop being such a cranky pants."

Magdalena sneered. "A cranky pants?"

"You heard me," Becky replied, unwavering.

Mark struggled to suppress the smirk tugging at the corners of his mouth. For a lowly shitkicker like him, having Becky around was not only a welcome reprieve from Magdalena's relentless verbal sparring; her free-spirited audacity also came as a refreshing change from the apathetic strays his employer had collected over the years.

"I suggest you keep your opinions to yourself, young lady," Magdalena said, her voice dripping with venom. "What Mark and I discuss within these four walls is not open for your comment or consideration. Understood? That's especially pertinent when those opinions come from someone who spends most of their day glued to my lounge, devouring corn chips and watching *The Bold and the Bedridden*. Devouring corn chips on my twenty-thousand-dollar, Italian, handmade leather lounge, might I fucking well add."

Magdalena Black: confirmed cranky pants.

Becky chuckled. "Twenty-thousand-dollar lounge this, three-thousand-dollar suit that," she replied, brushing a tuft of blonde hair from her face. "You know what? You could've just popped down to the op shop and got something similar for, like, two hundred."

Magdalena sighed. "In full-grain Nappa leather?"

"Does it fucking matter?" Becky shot back.

"Bah. I don't recall any objections about my money when I let you chauffeur your friends around in my BMW." Magdalena paused deliberately, giving Becky a moment to object. The silence was deafening. "Exactly. I covet the finer things in life and work hard to acquire them. This penthouse. That giant television you spend hours staring at. You're familiar with the concept of *work*, right? It's that necessary inconvenience for funding a person's lifestyle."

Magdalena conveniently neglected to mention the sizeable inheritance she received after her father's passing. As the only child of a standover man with a creative accountant, she was set for life, never wanting for anything, least of all Italian leather lounges.

"Piss off. I have been looking for work," Becky said.

"Oh, I just bet you have," Magdalena replied.

"Yeah, I have. But the market's tricky at the moment," Becky continued. "Anyway, I still don't get why you won't give me a job at your club. Like, how hard is it to flash a little cleavage and sling overpriced shots to yuppies?"

At the mention of her nightclub, Magdalena's gaze drifted to the diamond-encrusted timepiece on her wrist. As the seconds slid by with Swiss precision, it occurred to her she had overlooked a crucial detail: running her business. She glanced at her enforcer and tapped the watch. Mark nodded in stoic acknowledgement, having already reminded her of the pressing issue of the two guests unsupervised in her penthouse office.

"Well... uh... perhaps we can discuss the pros, and considerable cons, of that arrangement another time," Magdalena replied, fully aware of the golden rule when it came to mixing business with pleasure: never shit where you eat.

"But you never want to talk about—" Becky began.

"Here, take this," Magdalena interjected, waving a credit card in Becky's direction. "Phone a few of those jobless wonders you call 'friends' and spend the afternoon shopping or something. Get your hair done. Drop in a job application at Macca's. I don't give a fuck what you do. Just remove yourself from my vicinity for a few hours."

Becky pried herself off the lounge and stormed over to Magdalena, her face like thunder. She snatched the credit card from Magdalena's hand and headed toward the bedroom, casting a quick nod toward Mark as she passed. Mark grinned and returned the gesture while Magdalena silently counted down, bracing for the inevitable response, predictable as clockwork.

"You know what you can go do, Maggie? Eat my arse!" Becky shouted, slamming the bedroom door hard enough to rattle the artwork on the adjacent wall with a violent jolt.

That was young-woman code for 'conversation over'.

Chapter Three

The Khyber Pass

Magdalena Black's office exuded the affluence one would expect from a rich kid turned loan shark: imported European furniture, walls adorned with landscapes by prominent Australian artists, and bookshelves overflowing with unread first editions. Like its owner, the office was striking and intimidating, yet ultimately dead behind the eyes. A closer look revealed the absence of personal touches one might expect in a space occupied for any length of time: no knickknacks, no souvenirs, no family photos. Even 'dearest daddy' was conspicuously absent. It was as if Magdalena had perused *Australia's Richest List*, picked a wealthy wanker at random, and instructed her decorator to replicate their office down to the last curated detail.

"Look sharp, boys," Mark Campbell said, opening the door.

Magdalena drifted into the room, still in her beach attire, offering neither acknowledgement nor apology. She gave a brief nod to her enforcer before settling gracefully into the executive leather chair behind the desk. Mark returned the gesture, closed the door, and swaggered across the room to take up position behind Magdalena's guests. The man-mountain always kept within arm's reach in case a meeting went pear-shaped. Not that these two posed a threat to anyone with a tinker's chance of knuckling their way out of a wet paper bag. And knuckle, Mark most certainly could.

"Apologies for the interruption," Magdalena said, giving her guests a quick once-over; her poker face revealing little of the machinations behind her piercing green eyes. After a pause that drifted somewhere between mild contempt and amusement, she leaned forward and unleashed a grin worthy of a cunning wolf. "You know what they say about women: can't live with them, can't kill them."

There was a moment of awkward silence, followed by a smattering of uncomfortable chuckles from across the desk. When an individual found themselves seated in the inner sanctum of an underworld figure, laughing at their witticisms, no matter how tasteless, typically ensured that said individual had a better-than-fifty-fifty chance of leaving alive. 'Typically' being the operative word.

"Alright, gentlemen. I'm eager to wrap this up, as I need to get down to the club," Magdalena started, her tone laced with urgency. "I swear, I cannot leave that place for five minutes without something going off the rails, but I'm sure you both know the feeling. Running a pub in your neck of the woods? That must be like trying to run a brothel in Baghdad. One minute, it's all happy endings; the next, you're dodging hand grenades just to make it through happy hour."

Seated opposite were the owners of those aforementioned uncomfortable chuckles: a couple of down-on-their-luck publicans by the name of Jack Perkins and Hung Van Thanh. In hindsight, this was their gut-punch moment of clarity. The exact point when Jack and Hung realised their dream had slipped through their fingers. The Hackston, once brimming with the chatter and clinking glasses of loyal patrons, was now a ghost of itself, its barstools empty, the beer-soaked air thick with unpaid bills and dashed hopes. Business had all but evaporated, and now their creditors were pounding at the door, demanding money they simply did not have. What else could a couple of ordinary blokes do to save their slice of the Great Australian Dream? In desperation, they turned to Magdalena Black.

"Before we continue, did my associate make you feel at home during my absence?" Magdalena asked, feigning interest.

Jack sighed and glanced at his business partner.

About ten minutes earlier.

"Waltz … station … colonoscopy with my stiletto … "

Jack and Hung sat in Magdalena Black's office, awaiting her return after she had stepped out to take an urgent call on the balcony. Dwarfed by the imposing mahogany desk, they fidgeted in their seats like schoolboys summoned to the principal's office, exchanging anxious, sidelong glances. Nearby, Mark Campbell stood watch, arms folded and shoulders tense, just within their periphery. His looming presence radiated silent disdain, as though their mere existence were an affront. The weight of his gaze, layered over the thick silence, made the atmosphere almost unbearable.

"Local miscreant … beeline … my front door … "

With his head cocked just so, Jack caught random snippets of Magdalena's conversation. A word here, a phrase there. Out of context, they seemed mostly harmless, yet the weight in her tone painted a picture of a woman far from pleased. Hung, meanwhile, appeared to make a bold choice: he set about pissing-off the most dangerous man in the room, tapping his index finger on the armrest in time with an inaudible Latin rhythm. His fidgeting clashed with the heavy silence, eliciting a slow, menacing look from Mark.

"Oi, Charlie! Give it a bloody rest!" Mark snapped.

Charlie. Victor Charlie. VC. Military slang derived from the NATO phonetic alphabet to refer to Communist forces during the Vietnam War. Oblivious of the slur, whether out of nervousness, choice, or sheer ignorance, Hung continued tapping away to a rhythm only he could hear. Grumbling, Mark shifted, angling his frame into Hung's line of sight. "Mate, I suggest you stop that. Now. Otherwise, I'm gonna snap off those dainty little digits of yours and shove 'em fair up your Khyber," he said matter-of-factly.

"*Natural causes ... mundane ... Phar Lap ... *"

Jack shot his partner a look that could freeze the ninth circle of hell. Message received, loud and clear. Hung stopped tapping and sank deeper into his chair, leaning toward Jack with a conspiratorial look. "What's my 'cyber'?" he whispered, covering his mouth.

"Your Khyber. The Khyber Pass," Jack replied.

Hung shrugged; geography was not his forte.

Jack smirked. "It's your friggin' arse, mate."

"Oh ... uh, oh!" Hung exclaimed as the realisation struck him. He shot upright in his chair, hands neatly folded in his lap. Having his fingers forcibly removed and shoved up his 'Khyber Pass' was definitely not on Hung's bucket list.

"So, Jack, did Mark here make you feel at home in my absence?" Magdalena leaned in, her gaze razor-sharp as she repeated the question. "Please, tell me you knuckleheads didn't just sit here in complete silence the whole time I was out on the balcony?"

"No, Mark was, uh ... " Jack fumbled for the right word, mentally cycling through his vocabulary. "He was very ... hospitable."

Magdalena chuckled. "Hospitable? Old Bugalugs here?" She raised an eyebrow. "I've always found him to be a rude bastard, if I'm being honest. But there you go. Maybe he blossoms in the company of strangers." It was bullshit, and everyone knew it. Mark only confirmed as much by nodding and flashing a gap-toothed grin that looked more like a war trophy than a smile.

"Anyway, Jack and ... " Magdalena continued, snapping her fingers as if summoning a waiter.

"The name's Hung," Hung replied, with a faint sigh.

His name had been Hung twenty minutes ago when Magdalena had failed to remember it, and it had been Hung the five times before that. If the kid had any sense of self-awareness, he might have taken her forgetfulness as a slight. However, in the grand scheme of things, being utterly forgettable could be considered a perk when dealing with people to whom you owed sizeable sums of money.

Magdalena smirked. "Your name's Hung?"

"That's correct, Miss Black," he replied, keeping his tone steady despite the obvious hint of amusement in her voice.

Hung Van Thanh's parents were among the first wave of immigrants who arrived after the Vietnam War, long before the term "boat people" became a fixture in the Australian vernacular. To an outsider, Hung might seem like a kid hopelessly out of his depth. But Hung was sharp. A true academic, book smart, if not streetwise. In mathematics, computing, or dissecting the avant-garde compositions of American theorist John Cage, Hung was an idiot savant. Yet when it came to business, common sense, or the basic art of human interaction, Hung was, to put it bluntly, a regular fucking idiot.

"Enough of the pleasantries," Magdalena said, flipping open the red handwritten ledger on her desk. "Now, Jack," she began, "the goal of a moneylender, namely myself, is that when they lend money to a client, namely yourself, they expect to get it back at some point. With a healthy dose of interest, naturally. It's a fairly simple concept, one I learned the hard way from individuals far scarier than I am. It's really not that difficult to grasp, is it?"

"Uh, well ... " Jack leaned forward, fidgeting with his wristwatch as he carefully weighed his response. He let the silence stretch, knowing the wrong words could have real consequences. "No. It's not that difficult, really," he began. "The thing is, though—"

"It's not like we're talking quantum mechanics?"

"Uh, no, Miss Black. But I don't—"

"Or the baffling popularity of the band Oasis?"

"Oasis? No, but you've got a fair poi—"

"Magnets, Jack?" Magdalena interjected.

Jack blinked and shrugged. "Huh? What abou—"

Before he could finish, Magdalena sprang from her chair, *slamming* her palm onto the desk with a bone-crunching thud of finality. "So why on God's green earth are you sitting in front of me asking for another fucking loan when you can't even pay back the one you already fucking-well owe me?" She glared daggers across the desk. "Well, Jack? Harry? Anyone? Somebody had better explain themselves, and fast, because I don't have all damn day!"

Jack floundered for an answer. Or more precisely, the answer Magdalena had been waiting for since these two numbskulls first stepped into her office. Her eyes burned with fury. Jack sank lower in his chair, bewildered at how a delicate woman, clad in a two-piece swimsuit and pink platform sandals, could put the fear of God into a grown man. Beside him, Hung sat frozen. Wide-eyed. Mouth agape. Paralysed. The tension in the room cranked up to a solid ten. Eleven, when Mark's massive paw landed on Jack's shoulder.

"Ah, yeah, well … we're getting back on our feet," Jack replied, a nervous edge in his voice. "The pub's been practically dead for months. Couldn't even get near the place with all the roadworks. Honestly, I'm tempted to give the council a piece of my mind."

"A brief exchange, no doubt," Magdalena quipped.

"But … uh, it's all complete now," Jack continued, brushing off the insult. "Business has picked up. We just need a little runway to tackle some debts. Suppliers, for one, and a few repayments to the bank. Hopefully, everything should turn around by Christmas." He sighed. Given more time and less pressure, he could have crafted a more coherent explanation. "Honestly, we're good for the money, Miss Black. It's just a matter of—"

Magdalena raised a finger. "Zip it, Jack. I doubt either of you could manage a piss-up in a brewery, let alone run a public house that actually serves the swill." She sat back in her chair, a sigh escaping as she levelled them both with a calm, unwavering stare. "I always thought owning a pub was a licence to print money. Every morning, a lineup of degenerates out front, practically ready to suck the chrome off the doorknob just to get inside." Her gaze drifted down as she flicked through the ledger, her tone growing almost reflective. "But maybe that's the appeal for you, Jack. Misery sells?"

Misery sells? That was a tad hypocritical, especially coming from a loan shark who thrived on misery like bogans thrived on budget flights to Bali. Sensing the deescalation, Mark withdrew his hand from Jack's shoulder, and both men straightened instinctively. Resigned to their fate, they kept silent as Magdalena continued to thumb through her ledger, each page turn heavy with foreboding. Finally, her finger came to rest on a particular entry with unnerving precision, causing both men to shift uneasily in their seats.

"Here we are, Jack Perkins and Hung Van ... whatever," she began, barely glancing at the scrawl in front of her. "Hmm. From the looks of things, it appears you two already owe me a neat fifty thousand." Jack nodded, knowing full well that any attempt to dispute the number, truthful or not, would make no difference to its author. "So then, how much are you and your friend after this time?"

"Another forty," Jack replied, trying to sound casual.

"Forty?" Magdalena narrowed her eyes slightly.

Jack gulped. "Uh, yes, Miss Black."

"Hmm. Why not an even fifty instead?"

To be fair, it was a reasonable question.

"Well, we kind of figured forty is enough to settle up with, uh, just about everyone we need to get square with."

"Maybe so. But why settle for square, Jack, when you could get ahead? Besides, fifty thousand is easier to remember, don't you think?" Magdalena leaned in and flashed a sly grin. "Fifty's a nice, round number. And since it is nearly the weekend and I'm feeling generous, I can do it for you at ... twenty points."

'Points' was sharking parlance for percentage interest.

"We appreciate the offer, Miss Black. Truly, we do. But forty thousand was the figure we had in mind." Jack hurried to get ahead of the upsell. "Besides, I doubt Hung or I will have any trouble remembering that we owe money to Magdalena Black," he added, forcing a polite smile. Beneath the surface, however, his heart hammered like a hamster huffing on a crack pipe, pounding so violently he feared she might hear it from across the desk.

"So, what's this pub of yours called again, Jack?"

"The Hackston Tavern. It's on the corner of—"

Magdalena raised a finger. "I didn't ask for directions," she said, then glanced over at her enforcer. "What's this place like, Mark?" Her tone was more perturbed than inquisitive. "Sell me on it, especially since I'm about to outlay more money to keep it afloat. How's the atmosphere? The clientele? Are the bathrooms clean? Nothing is worse than visiting the ladies' only to find some filthy mole has scrawled her Master's thesis on the wall in her own excrement."

Mark shrugged. "How should I know, boss?"

The loan shark clenched her jaw, rubbing her temples as if trying to massage away the pain of stooping to Mark's level of stupidity. "Are you kidding me?" she said. "You used to play professional rugby league. If I were a betting woman, and I am, I'd wager you've been banned from more pubs than I've had twenty-firsts."

"Sure, when you put it that way," Mark replied. "Can't really comment on the sheila's crappers, boss, but I drank there a couple of times when Big Mal was still running the joint, and it was a fuckin' dive back then. And I've got my suspicions it's still a fuckin' dive now." Mark paused, scratching his head, uncertain if he had met the brief. "What else do you wanna know, Maggie? It's in a dodgy part of town, rundown, and chock-a-block full of bogans and wankers."

The assessment was blunt, yet undeniably accurate.

"Full of bogans and wankers?" Magdalena asked.

"Yeah. Absolutely crawling with 'em, boss."

"Surely you must've felt right at home, then?"

Hung chuckled at the retort, prompting Mark's immediate response, a meaty slap to the back of the head.

Delighted by the self-orchestrated chaos, Magdalena grinned and turned toward a concealed panel in the wall behind her. It was not so much hidden as cleverly designed to seem less important than it actually was. In a room adorned with rich list wank, a little misdirection was hardly an arduous task. With a fluid motion, she slid the panel aside, revealing a flush-mounted safe. Olive green and industrial, it was the kind that would look right at home in a commercial bank. She spun the wheel and gave it a solid heave; the door opened without the need for any pesky combinations.

What kind of criminal failed to lock their safe?

The answer: an incredibly cocky one.

Jack and Hung stared wide-eyed at the contents. Everything inside was meticulously arranged across three shelves, each serving a chillingly precise function. The top shelf held brick-sized bundles of Australian currency, stacked with a banker's precision, the crisp edges of various denominations practically screaming 'crime'. The middle shelf gleamed with antique jewellery, its opulence interrupted by sealed envelopes, their contents whispering secrets that dared to be uncovered. But it was the bottom shelf, ominously dubbed "the toy shelf", that stole their breath. A ballistic pick-and-mix of hardware, potent enough to topple any tinpot regime, or even New Zealand, if one was feeling cute on a lazy Sunday afternoon.

Magdalena plucked two wads of cash from the safe and turned to face her guests, who were still busy picking their jaws off the floor. "Twenty. Forty," she counted aloud, tossing each rubber-banded brick onto the desk with a satisfying thwack. "I trust you boys are good for this. Otherwise ... " She nodded toward Mark, who stood in the corner grinning, cracking his knuckles for emphasis. "You'll have to deal with my rather large friend here. And believe me, he's considerably less ... shall we say, 'personable' than I am. Understood?"

Jack and Hung nodded in unison, perhaps a touch too eagerly, as if their synchronised response might be enough to buy them a sliver of goodwill. Forty grand cash, sure, it was enough to answer their immediate prayers, but in the flesh, it looked surprisingly unsatisfying. The Hollywood fantasy of bloated briefcases stuffed with loot was just that, a fantasy reserved for wannabe wise guys. In the shady underbelly of society, cash moved in tattered envelopes and plastic sandwich bags, minus the sandwich. For a boring bloke like Jack, a bulging jacket pocket did the job just fine, letting him slip under the radar with a small fortune riding comfortably at his hip.

"So, are we all done, Jack?" Magdalena asked.

"Uh, yeah, I guess so," he replied.

"Good. Because I have a proposition of my own."

And when a woman like Magdalena Black made a proposition, it was typically the kind of proposition one could not refuse.

Chapter Four

Mister Birdie

Later that morning.

Eyes buried in a dog-eared textbook, Charlotte 'Charlie' Watson failed to notice Jack and Hung's covert entrance via The Hackston's rear car park. With her Developmental Psychology exam just days away, every stolen moment to cram felt like a lifeline. These impromptu study sessions had become routine, squeezed between pulling the occasional beer and keeping the riffraff in check. It was an unspoken perk of the job, especially given The Hackston's dwindling patronage ever since the council began tearing up the nearby intersection.

A quick headcount of the crowd landed at four, five, if you included the walk-in who came to take a dump before visiting the podiatrist next door. Factoring in wages and operating costs, there were barely enough bums on seats to justify remaining open, a decision made even harder to defend when the collective IQ of those bums struggled to scrape room temperature.

"… so the black fella turns to the copper and goes, 'No thanks, brudda. That sounds pretty dodgy, eh? I think me and Morton here will put these witchetty grubs back in our pockets and keep on pushin' these bikes down the road. Catch ya, blokes!'"

Charlie peered over her textbook as the peanut gallery erupted in raucous laughter. "Really, Conrad?" she asked, deadpan.

The Hackston's most regular of regulars, or, more precisely, as regular as his fortnightly Centrelink payment allowed, Conrad never missed a beat when it came to being an insufferable shit. Every second Friday, rain, hail, or shine, he would roll in at opening, claim his barstool, and stay put until he had pissed away every cent of the taxpayer's dollar. Short and shifty, with a mop of ginger hair and skin like sun-beaten leather, Conrad was a walking, talking cautionary tale for why blood relatives should never give in to their baser instincts. Clad in his signature red flannelette shirt and threadbare trousers, with nicotine-stained fingers that attested to a lifetime spent punching darts, Conrad exuded an aura that made you instinctively check your wallet, even if he had never strayed within cooee.

"Come on, love," the creature rasped, his voice reminiscent of gravel being dragged across concrete. "Can't take a joke?"

"There are two things in this world that I can take, and one of them is most definitely a joke," Charlie replied, as her hazel eyes returned to the wordy realm of her textbook. "I enjoy a laugh as much as the next girl, but, come on. You've got to cut the racist shit, Conrad. The days of the White Australia Policy are over. The world has changed, yeah? Society's changed. Hell, maybe if you took your beady little eyes off your drink once in a while, you'd notice that."

"Bah, changed when?" Conrad shot back.

"When those 'black fellas' earned the right to vote."

A sneer tugged at Conrad's lips. "Yeah, and it was the worst thing we ever did. Right up there with letting you sheilas vote."

Despite the masculine nickname, Charlie embodied the archetypal woman that lonely, delusional old men convinced themselves they had a fleeting chance with. At just twenty-two, she was tall and slender, with long raven hair and a playful smile capable of disarming even the most heartless of bastards. While most patrons came to The Hackston to drown their sorrows, and others for the 'atmosphere', or lack thereof, some came solely to vie for the attention of Jack's niece. Why? Because that was what lonely, delusional old men did when the high-octane world of casual bigotry and negatively geared investment properties lost its charm. Intelligent and fiercely independent, Charlie much preferred an evening with a glass of red wine and her West Highland Terrier to the company of any man, especially one desperate enough to haunt a dive like this.

"So, what's the second thing?" Conrad asked.

"What do you mean?" Charlie replied.

"You said there were two things you could take."

Charlie hesitated. "Oh? No, it's kind of silly."

"Aww, come on. No point bein' shy now, love."

"You sure?" Charlie began. "It's a little—"

"A little *what*?" Conrad pressed, leaning in closer, his curiosity burning brighter than the neon XXXX sign above the bar.

Charlie's voice dropped. "Well, it's a little ... uh, filthy."

A faint blush spread across her cheeks, her lips twitching with a barely contained grin. Conrad leaned so far forward on his barstool it was a wonder he had not toppled over, his eyes wide and fingers gripping the counter in anticipation of Charlie's next words.

"Hmm. Maybe forget I said anything," she muttered.

"What? You can't leave us hanging like that!"

"Okay, okay." Charlie paused, letting the silence build as everyone within earshot, all four of them, waited for the inevitably salacious revelation. "So, the first thing I can take is a joke, right?" She let the moment linger, her grin widening. "And the second thing?"

Conrad leaned in further, barely breathing.

Charlie's tone sharpened, and her grin turned venomous. "The second thing I'd love to take is my foot … and shove it RIGHT UP YOUR ARSE if you don't cut the racist shit!"

The peanut gallery erupted again as Conrad's face turned beetroot red, his retort dying in his throat. Charlie's amusement, however, was fleeting. Her expression darkened, shifting from playful to pissed as her gaze locked onto two familiar figures attempting, and failing, to slip past unnoticed. Her scowl deepened, and she raised a finger in Conrad's direction, the universal sign to stick a pin in it. Bewildered, he turned, following her line of sight over his shoulder.

"Jack Francis Perkins," Charlie began, her voice slicing through the din like a whip. "Tell me, what could've been so important that you needed me to cover for you this morning? Three days before my closed-book Developmental Psychology exam, no less?"

Jack and Hung froze in their tracks, locking into that timeless pantomime of guilt, eyes darting around the room as if searching for the source of the vaguely familiar yet unmistakable voice, all the while knowing exactly where it came from. They exchanged a brief, guilty glance before Charlie stormed out from behind the bar, her footsteps echoing in the dimly lit corridor leading to The Hackston's office.

"What, you didn't get Hung's *thingie*?" Jack replied.

"You mean his SMS? The one you had him send me at seven this morning, asking if I could cover you, with no explanation?" Charlie shot back. "Yeah, I got it. Otherwise, the lights'd be off and the doors locked. You know I need to study, Uncle Jack. I don't have the time or the inclination to babysit this place … or you two, for that matter."

The Hackston would have descended into chaos if not for Charlie. Fortunately for Jack, his niece needed a flexible part-time job to help her through university, and Jack required someone who could tolerate his constant bullshit. It was a win-win situation.

"So, what's with all the Secret Squirrel shit lately?" Charlie asked, arms crossed, her tone sharp and demanding.

"Nothing you need to worry about," Jack replied.

"Yeah? Well, guess what?" Charlie shot back.

Jack shrugged casually. "You're mad, and I'm not?"

Charlie rolled her eyes, shaking her head in frustration. "Seriously? I'm not five anymore, Jack. How about having an adult conversation about what's going on around here?"

Jack grunted noncommittally, his focus fixed on the office as he made a beeline for it, clearly more intent on depositing Magdalena Black's money than addressing his niece's concerns. Without so much as a backwards glance, he left his business partner to face the full brunt of Charlie's piercing stare. And what a stare it was: a volatile mix of expectation and frustration, underscored by her tightly crossed arms, as though they were the only thing holding back the storm brewing behind her sharp gaze. Hung shifted awkwardly under the weight of her scrutiny, the silence between them growing heavier with each passing second. He fidgeted, his eyes darting between the sticky, beer-soaked floor and Charlie's face, as if stalling might somehow conjure the answers she was waiting for.

"Really? That's the best my uncle can manage? Grunt like a Neanderthal and stomp back to his cave?" Charlie said, the rhetorical bite cutting through the silence. "Christ, the male role models in my life have a genuine talent for avoiding confrontation, don't they?"

"Um, well, you see ... " Hung trailed off, his eyes drifting nervously to the closed office door. "Jack's, ah, kind of—"

Before Hung could finish his bumbling reply, Charlie thrust a seemingly random piece of paper under his nose.

"What's this?" he frowned, tilting his head.

"It's an invoice," Charlie snapped, stabbing the page with her finger. "See those big red letters? 'UNPAID'. Ring any bells? Or are we holding out for the Braille edition to really hammer it home?"

"No, I realise that," Hung protested, "but—"

Charlie huffed in exasperation. "I found about a dozen more of these buried in a desk drawer in the back office," she began, her tone razor-sharp. "Now, normally, I don't go snooping through people's shit, but while you two were off gallivanting around the Goldie, one of your wholesalers rang and absolutely ripped me a new one. A lovely Greek gentleman by the name of 'Petros', I believe?"

"Oh, right ... Petros," Hung replied reticently.

"So, you know him?" Charlie asked. "Anyway, yeah ... between his creative bursts of profanity and generously peppering the conversation with the 'c-word', Petros made some pointed threats about debt collectors before slamming the receiver down in my ear. Now, naturally, this was the first I'd heard about any of this. So, you can probably appreciate my, ah ... surprise, when he called."

Hung nodded slowly, as though he were carefully constructing a response that might keep him from digging the hole any deeper.

"The obvious takeaway here," Charlie continued, "is that my uncle needs to keep me in the loop. Neither of you seem to realise I've been practically running this place solo for the past month!" Her voice rose, sharp enough to cut glass. "And if it's not obvious, I've had an absolute gutful. I have enough on my plate already without copping abuse from irate Grecian wholesalers. Got me?" She paused, glaring at him, her frustration radiating like heat. "I'm only here because Jack is family. If he wasn't, I would've told him to stick the job ages ago."

"Okay ... I'll talk to him," Hung eventually replied.

"Do that, because Jack's never going to listen to me, let alone clue me in on what's really going on around here. And you? You're not much better. Always covering for him, but never with a straight answer." Charlie folded her arms, her gaze unwavering. "Let me take a stab in the dark here. You two are up to your necks in debt because of all the roadworks?"

Hung remained deathly silent, either unwilling or uncertain how to respond. It hardly took a psychology undergrad to see that Hung scored off the charts in agreeableness: kind, altruistic, and compliant to a fault. While these traits made him a great friend, they were less useful as a business partner. Charlie knew she would need to ramp up the pressure if there was any hope of Hung developing the requisite backbone to have a serious conversation with her uncle.

"Either way," she continued, "you're the only person Jack listens to, Hung. I've tried, but I can't get through to him. That means you're going to have to step up and take a swing at it."

"I hear you, Charlie. I'll take care of it when I can."

"Yeah, but you keep saying that, and nothing changes."

"I will, just ... when the time's right. Okay?"

Charlie grabbed Hung by the shoulders, spinning him to face the office. "Well, the time is now! March in there, talk to him. Come on, you're thirty-five and you still act like Jack's errand boy!"

"Huh? I'm only thirty-four," Hung muttered.

"Whatever," Charlie shot back, unimpressed. "It doesn't change the fact that you're standing out here like a shag on a rock while Jack's holed up in there. You're supposed to be business partners, Hung. This pub's as much yours as it is his, so how about acting like it?" Her tone shifted, softening as she caught a glint of recognition in Hung's eyes. "Whatever my uncle's going through, he shouldn't have to carry that burden alone. Speak up. Let him know you're here for him. God knows I've tried, but he's so damn ... insular."

Hung nodded, recognising it was time to step up.

"Attaboy," Charlie said, her tone lighter now. She urged him forward with a flutter of her fingertips, coaxing him out of his hesitation.

Several minutes later.

"Any chance you could unlock the door, Jack?" Hung called out, rapping on the frame with his knuckles. Through the frosted pane, he could make out Jack's slumped silhouette at the desk. "I know you're probably busy with, uh, whatever, but it's kind of important."

Jack pinched the bridge of his nose and exhaled a long, weary sigh. He was not in the mood for another tirade about the temperamental drinks fridge or Charlie's suspicion that Conrad was swiping beer coasters from the pokies room. Lately, every interaction felt laced with urgency, yet none of it ever seemed to matter in the grand scheme of things. What truly mattered was keeping The Hackston afloat, by any means necessary.

For Jack, that meant borrowing just enough to stave off disaster, always hoping they could shovel through the mounting pile of shit before it buried them completely. Five thousand dollars here. Another ten thousand there. That was how Magdalena Black sank her claws in: not with a single crushing debt but through a relentless trickle of "just enough". Death by a thousand cuts. And no matter the sum, it was always precisely enough to keep their heads above water, until the next dreaded invoice left them gasping for air all over again.

"Jack? It's Hung. Mind letting us in, please?"

Us? Jack straightened in his chair, forcing himself to refocus. "Of course I know who it is. Can't you tell I'm busy?" Muffled whispers and the shuffling of feet seeped under the office door, suggesting Hung was not alone. Jack's scowl deepened. "If that's my niece coming to whinge about that busted fridge again, I'll kick off."

There was a faint murmur of more hushed conversation. The second voice lacked the soft tones of a woman, carrying instead the deep, resonant baritone of a man. Definitely not Charlie, nor Hung, for that matter. Perplexed, Jack pushed back his chair, rose, and unlocked the door. As it creaked open, the broad frame of Mark 'The Cane Train' Campbell filled the doorway. Grinning like a Cheshire cat, Mark cradled a nondescript cardboard box under his bulging left arm. Shit. While his visit to The Hackston was neither unexpected nor impromptu, it was much earlier than they had agreed upon.

"Well, well, well. Fancy runnin' into you again, Jacko," Mark said, his grin the kind that never quite reached his eyes. "Don't tell me I caught you enjoyin' a bit of alone time in there?" He peered into the office, giving Jack a disdainful once-over. "I'm happy to wait a tick if you need to hide the hand lotion and tissue box, mate."

Jack's eyes widened. "Huh? No, it's nothing like—"

Mark cut him off, unfazed. "Speaking of boxes, where do you want these?" he said, patting the cardboard variant under his arm. "Got a ute load out back, courtesy of Maggie."

Hung popped his head around the corner, his voice cheerful and completely oblivious to the tension in the room. "Mark's here with the boxes, Jack!" he announced, as though revealing earth-shattering news. Jack and Mark exchanged a puzzled glance, their eyes rolling in perfect unison, as if they had rehearsed it a hundred times before. Hung stood there for a beat, looking from one to the other, still oblivious to the silent exchange. "Where is Miss Black, anyway?" he asked curiosity, as if the awkward pause had never happened.

"Huh?" Mark replied, arching a brow. "Maggie doesn't concern herself with the small shit, and if you know what's good for ya, neither should you. That goes double for you, Jackoff." He jabbed a meaty finger in Jack's direction before pointing at the box under his arm. "Well? I'm not getting paid by the fuckin' hour, boys. The only thing you pricks need to know is where we're gonna dump these."

"Uh, okay … " Jack scanned the office. Aside from the desk and the freestanding safe in the corner, the room was about as spartan as they come. "How many boxes are we talking?"

"What? You want an exact figure?" Mark scoffed.

"It'd help us figure out where to put them," Jack said.

"Alright. There's just enough to work up a sweat."

"And you're still not, uh, gonna tell us what's inside?"

Mark refused to dignify the question with an answer. In the realm of hard-hitting underworld types, there was an un-spoken distinction between pushing your luck and pushing up daisies. One wrong move, one ill-timed remark, and you might find yourself transitioning from the former to the latter with alarming ease.

"Fine." Jack raised his palms skyward, a gesture that some-how conveyed both exasperation and a half-hearted attempt at goodwill. "I'm just … I'm not entirely sure about Magdalena leaving a bunch of random boxes in our office for safekeeping. I mean, I'm not trying to be funny, Mark, but I'd kinda like to know what's in them first."

Given that Jack and Hung were now nearly a hundred grand in the hole with Magdalena Black, it was a textbook case of the old adage: beggars cannot be choosers. Jack's concern, however, was less about the request itself and more about whether it might tarnish The Hackston's reputation. What little reputation it had. After all, the pair prided themselves on running an entirely above-board operation.

"Promise that there's nothing dodgy in those boxes?" Jack asked, squinting at Mark like he was trying to read fine print in dim light. "Level with us, it's not, uh, Giggle Weed, is it?"

Mark scowled. "Giggle ... fuckin' what now?"

"You know, drugs." Jack's voice dropped to a conspiratorial whisper. "The Ganja? Ice? Crystal Meth? Scooby Snacks? Bombay Blue? Horse? Black Tar? Purple Haze?"

Mark pinched the bridge of his nose with a heavy sigh.

"So?" Jack pressed. "Absolutely no drugs, then?"

"None. Scout's honour," Mark replied flatly.

"Good, because we're uncomfortable with drugs."

Hung nodded. "Yeah, we're uncomfortable with drugs," he echoed, as if the gesture lent Jack's statement an air of authority.

"Jesus Christ. No. It ain't drugs, you knobjockeys," Mark snapped, his steely blue eyes scanning the room as if sizing up a pair of particularly dense opponents. "Oh? And for the record, Jack, I don't give a rat's rectum what you reckon you're comfortable with, alright? Magdalena Black will be the judge of your comfort level. She's the one you made the deal with. Comfortable, uncomfortable, doesn't matter to me. I'm just the cunt who makes the sausages."

With that, he thrust the cardboard box into Hung's arms. The sudden weight almost sent him crashing to the floor, his knees wobbling like a newborn giraffe on a pair of roller skates.

Jack and Mark stood frozen, amused expressions fixed on their faces, watching the ungainly spectacle unfold in silence.

Ten minutes and twenty-one cardboard boxes later.

The three men stood outside the office door, peering into what had once been a sparsely furnished space, now engulfed in a sea of cardboard and stale sweat. Twenty-one boxes might not sound like much, but when crammed into a room barely big enough to swing a cat, they had transformed the small office into a claustrophobic maze that could put the willies up even the most hardened professional spelunker.

"Told ya they'd fit," Mark said, a smirk of accomplishment tugging at the corners of his mouth.

"Dunno why we ever doubted you," Jack replied.

"Because you're a proper couple of pricks, that's why." Mark's tone was as flat as the look he shot them. He gave his wristwatch a quick glance and huffed. "Right, I've got two more stops to make, so pay attention. And I ain't in the mood to repeat my-fucking-self, so consider this the gospel, from Maggie's lips to your Noddys."

Jack exchanged a quick glance with Hung, brow furrowed. "Fire away," he said, bracing for the inevitable lecture.

In hindsight, that choice of words might have been a touch prophetic. Mark, without so much as a hint of irony, opened his jacket, revealing a .45 pistol tucked snugly into the waistband of his jeans. Chrome-plated and glinting under the dull office light, the piece was adorned with a flying eagle engraved on a mother-of-pearl handle. The weapon looked hilariously out of place, as though it had been pried from the cold, dead hand of a Texan oil tycoon.

"Three rules," Mark began, his tone sharp enough to slice through the growing tension. "They're a piece of piss, so even you turkeys shouldn't cock this up. Rule number one: touch any of these boxes, and you'll be answerin' to Mister Birdie." Jack and Hung's eyes darted nervously between the gun and Mark, their heads twitching with restless energy. "Rule number two: open any of these boxes and guess what? You'll be answerin' to Mister Birdie." Mark leaned forward slightly, his grin razor-edged. "And last but not least, rule number three: if either of you so much as thinks about opening any of these fucking boxes, you'll be … " He let the sentence dangle, eyes shifting between the two men, waiting for a reaction.

Jack shifted uncomfortably, clearing his throat as if about to speak, but then immediately thought better of it. Despite his humble suburban upbringing and limited knowledge of firearms, it hardly took a genius to figure out that the piece tucked into Mark's jeans was likely the "Mister Birdie" in question. After a long pause, he swallowed hard and ventured, "We'll be … answering to Mister Birdie?"

Mark's face lit up with mock delight, snapping his fingers like a game show host rewarding a correct answer. "Bingo! You aren't nearly as dumb as you look, mate. Maybe I'll let you keep your kneecaps." He grinned, clearly relishing their discomfort.

This was how loan sharks got you by the short and curlies. Once they found something worth exploiting, the entire dynamic shifted from what the loan shark could do for you to what you could do for the loan shark. It always started small. Little favours to test the waters. Here, it was something as harmless as storing a 'few' cardboard boxes for safekeeping.

"And what about you, Chinaman?" Mark growled, spinning sharply to fix his glare on Jack's partner. "Did you have your listenin' ears on, or were you too busy noddin' along like a bloody bobblehead?"

Hung, conspicuously silent, shifted uncomfortably, his unease betraying the tension in the room. Mark's gaze dropped to where Hung's hand rested, far too casually, on one of the rectangular harbingers of death. The sight was like a red rag to a bull, sparking a flicker of anger that quickly blazed into a full-blown glare.

"Oi! Hand off the box," Mark barked, swatting the offending appendage away with a force that brooked no argument. "Fuck me, mate. What part of that spiel didn't make sense to you?"

Hung hesitated. "Uh, I think I caught most of it."

Mark's glare sharpened. "Which part didn't you catch?"

Hung shrugged, his expression halfway between nervous and oblivious. "Who in the world is this 'Mister Birdie' guy?"

Chapter Five

That Little Prick

"He's an absolute shonkster, Barry. I bought this heap of junk a week ago, take a butcher's." From the passenger seat of his squad car, Detective Sergeant Michael 'Mick' Hughes brandished a gold ladies wristwatch from his pocket as if it were Exhibit A. His frustration was palpable as he jabbed a finger at the offending timepiece. "Look, the bloody minute hand's just rattlin' around in there rooted."

His long-suffering partner remained silent.

"What's wrong, big fella? Not interested in anything your sarge has to say?" The sawn-off redhead drawled, his voice carrying that unmistakable undertow of 'Westie' twang. Proof positive that you could take the morally questionable boy out of Sydney's Western Suburbs, but you could not take the Western Suburbs out of the morally questionable boy. "Christ, I'd bet my hairy left nut that if I mentioned lunch, you'd be all over it like a seagull on a hot chip."

Not even a nibble. Detective Barry Gamble's face was etched with concentration as he navigated the narrow, potholed stretch of misery known as Hackston Street. Every movement behind the wheel was deliberate; he crept along, the speedometer barely cracking double digits in a sixty zone. His sharp gaze darted between the treacherous road ahead and the fresh roadworks, scanning for their person of interest with hawk-like precision. Unfortunately, their glacial pace was anything but inconspicuous, as evidenced by the rising cacophony of car horns and the colourful array of hand gestures from the irate drivers piling up behind their unmarked Commodore.

"Come on, take a squiz," Hughes said, thrusting the wristwatch dangerously close into his partner's line of sight.

"Piss off," Gamble replied, eyes fixed on the road.

"Aww, come on, it'll only take two seconds."

"No, Mick. I'm trying to bloody drive."

"What? You can't spare two seconds?"

"Even if I could, does it seem like I care?" Gamble asked, letting out a sharp exhale, his patience thinner than Hackston Street's pothole-ridden bitumen. "Honestly, Mick, what do you expect from a counterfeit you scored out of a car boot?"

"I expect my money's worth," Hughes replied.

"From what? All of twenty bucks?" Gamble shot him a fleeting, incredulous glance. "Between that knock-off watch, those aviator sunnies, and that imitation leather jacket, you look like ... I don't know ... like one of those bad guys of the week from an '80s cop show."

"Nothin' wrong with a little *Miami Vice* on the Goldie." Gamble scoffed, his gaze shifting to the footpath.

"What?" Hughes asked, sceptically.

"It's just ... people talk, Mick. That's all I'm saying."

"And who's talking, exactly? Fat bastards like you?"

Gamble shot his partner a withering look. Despite his broad shoulders and unnatural height, a shade under six-foot-five when he was not hunched over the wheel of the squad car, years of night shifts, takeaway lunches, and desk duty had taken their toll on the former junior sportsman's physique. The cheap, off-the-rack suits he now poured himself into did little to disguise the evidence of a life spent largely sedentary, their strained buttons and pinched seams only accentuating the spare tyre he had stashed away.

"What's up your arse, anyway?" Hughes asked, tugging on the collar of his imitation leather jacket. "You've obviously got some sort of problem with me. Let's hear it."

"Nope. There's no problem here, Sarge."

"Bah, don't bullshit me," Hughes shot back.

Gamble muttered something into the collar of his crumpled grey suit, the words indistinct but dripping with a lack of enthusiasm. His partner, sensing that something was brewing in the driver's seat, decided there was no better time to get to the bottom of it than now.

"If you've got an issue, Barry, real or imagined, I suggest you spit it out," Hughes continued. "Because, and I didn't want to say anything earlier, but you've been shirty all day, mate."

"Shirty?" Gamble echoed, amused.

"Yeah, fuckin' shirty," Hughes repeated. "You've been giving me looks dark enough to knock a buzzard off a shit-wagon."

Gamble took a measured breath and dropped the car into second gear with a shriek of the transmission. Short of diving from a moving vehicle, there was no practical way to escape his partner's line of interrogation. With a deep sigh, he gave in, figuring it was time to bite the bullet. "Well, okay, it's just that you always—" he began.

"I always what, Bazza?" Hughes pushed.

Gamble sighed. "Don't take this the wrong way, but—"

He paused, gathering his thoughts. Starting a sentence like that was usually, pardon the pun, a gamble; no matter what came next, the person on the receiving end almost always took it the wrong way.

"You're the one always telling me to stay calm, right?"

Hughes chuckled. "What brought this on?"

"*You*, Mick. *You* brought this on," Gamble replied. "I'm not sure if you've noticed, but you've been flying off the handle at every little thing lately. Case in point: the old bloke outside that B&E in Southport yesterday. The one who flicked a lit cigarette at your feet, yeah? If I wasn't around, you would have sparked him out, then and there."

Hughes scowled. "Well, he shouldn't have done it."

"Maybe so, but decking a pensioner isn't exactly standard QPS operating procedure, is it?" Gamble retorted. "I know your home life isn't ... ideal ... right now, Mick, but come on. Having a go at me for being shirty? Don't you think that's a bit h-hypo-hypocritical?"

Gamble had a tendency to stammer under stress, an affliction Hughes met with his trademark absence of compassion. Not that Hughes had much compassion for anything or anyone. Whatever reservoir of patience he might once have had was as shallow as a tinker's bath and dried up completely the moment they were out of earshot of anyone capable of filing a formal complaint.

"F-f-f-fuck off, mate," Hughes replied, mimicking Gamble's stammer. "You're practically Porky Pig with a warrant card. And for the record, what you saw yesterday was what the pencil-pushers in the Police Media Unit call 'positive public relations', yeah? That old prick flicked a lit ciggie at my feet. An attempted assault on an officer of the law, Barry. He got off easily. What I should've done was tackle the coot to the ground, drop a couple of well-placed knees into his kidneys, then write him up for whatever struck my fancy. You know, all that pre-CJC malarkey coppers used to get up to back in the day. But instead, I let him off with a verbal warning, in effect savin' Johnny Taxpayer the cost of unnecessary paperwork and overtime. And, most importantly, I upheld the exemplary image of the Queensland Police Force."

Hughes' mental gymnastics deserved a gold medal.

"If you reckon that was me losing my shit, Barry, then you're very much mistaken. You reckon my shit isn't together? My shit is forever together. You'd do well to remember that."

His colleague huffed with disinterest. Disinterest that bled into curiosity the moment Gamble's gaze snagged on something promising about fifty metres down the street. His bottle-green eyes narrowed against the midday sun, straining for confirmation.

"Your hunch might've paid off, Sarge," Gamble said.

Hughes leaned forward. "You've clocked him?"

"See that car up ahead?" Gamble asked, nodding toward a lone vehicle parked at the end of the street. "Look familiar?"

Hackston Street had a natural southeast to northwest slant, starting with a gentle incline at the fashionable end, where upmarket boutiques, shoe stores, and cafes once lined the street. But as it descended sharply at a near 45-degree angle, the vibe shifted: seedy tattoo parlours, adult shops, and dingy drinking establishments took over. It was the perfect embodiment of the adage that shit rolls downhill, and unsurprisingly, the low end of the street was where this particular wheeled nugget had come to rest.

"What did I tell you, Barry?" Hughes said, a grin creeping across his face. "It's dole day. Knew he'd be jerking off 'round here somewhere." He sat forward, excitement sparking in his eyes as he nudged his aviators down the bridge of his nose. "Say what you want, but that little prick's nothin' if not predictable."

The 'little prick' in question was none other than a pitiful specimen known to the local constabulary as Conrad Manfred Fenstermacher. Conrad was to the noble pursuits of dole-bludging, chain-smoking, and general pissheadery, as Madonna was to popular music or Cher to modern mummification. When not nursing a rum at his favourite watering hole, The Hackston Tavern, Conrad moonlighted as a small-time fence, peddling anything a scumbag could steal, plunder, or pilfer: electronics, mobile phones, jewellery. You name it, he had it. And if he did not have it, well, he would happily steal it for you. That was Conrad's 'Five-Finger Guarantee'.

"How do you want to play this?" Hughes asked his partner. "Go in all cat-like, or the old-fashioned way, loud and proud?"

Gamble shrugged. When you danced to the devil's tune, it was in one's best interest to avoid treading on his hooves. If he had his way, he would be back at his desk in the air-conditioned bullpen with a cup of Earl Grey and a mountain of paperwork. Anywhere but in this squad car, especially when their little sojourn felt more like one of Hughes' personal vendettas than actual community policing.

"It's your barbecue, Mick," he eventually replied.

Hughes paused, weighing up the options.

"Alright then. See those two parked cars up ahead? I want you to slide in between them, all sneaky style."

Gamble wrinkled his porcine-like snout and scoped the lay of the land. If you ignored Conrad's vehicle parked at the end of the street, the stretch of asphalt between the Detective's creeping Commodore and their target was barren, save for a nondescript white sedan and a sporty convertible, two cars separated by a solitary space.

"Get stuffed. I'm not parking in there," he said.

"Huh? What's the issue?" Hughes asked.

"There are dozens of empty spaces closer by. Why not here?" Gamble asked, pointing at an alternative spot behind the BMW.

"Because I said 'between', yeah. Not 'behind', Barry."

"What? Come on, now you're just taking the piss."

"No, Fat Boy, it's called being inconspicuous. Stealth. Getting the drop on the perp." Hughes glanced at the line of disgruntled drivers stuck behind them, a grin tugging at the corners of his mouth. "Put into practice all the skills you learned at the Academy. I'm assuming you passed the driving component, yeah? Otherwise, they wouldn't let you within an Irishman's dick of an actual cop car."

The piss was now most definitely being syphoned.

"Sorry, Mick. But I'm onto your head games."

"Games?" Hughes asked, feigning innocence.

"Yeah. It doesn't take a genius to see what you're doing," Gamble grumbled. "You're going out of your way to make me parallel park just so you can have a laugh when I stuff it up. You're a bully, like my father-in-law. We can do a round trip in silence, but the second we pull into that driveway, he's gotta put in his two cents. 'You were a bit hot on those brakes, Barry? You'll wear out the pads'. Blah, blah, blah. And you're exactly like him, Mick. A First Class cun—" Gamble dangled his toes over the precipice of dropping the magic word.

Hughes' ears pricked up. "I'm a First Class what?"

"A First Class ... carrot," his partner replied.

Hughes suppressed a snort of laughter behind his typically stoic facade. Despite years of rolling with some of the most foul-mouthed, misogynistic shit-talkers to ever button up a blue uniform, Gamble still clung to a faint shred of his Catholic school upbringing, his conscience evidently not as hardened as his partner's.

"While your statement may hold water, Barry, you seem to be forgettin' one thing," Hughes continued, his tone oozing mock sincerity. "I've got 'Detective Sergeant' in front of my name." He clapped his hands with magnanimous authority. "Now, chop chop!"

"You really are a jerk," Gamble muttered.

"And proud of it," Hughes replied, flashing a grin.

Conrad shuffled toward his car, a rolling monument to neglect and despair, identifiable only to the most obsessive of motoring enthusiasts. Once, it might have flaunted a respectable pedigree, but the passing decades had stripped away every shred of its dignity. It now wore a constellation of dents and scratches, a distinct lack of badges or insignia, and an oppressive coat of grime that clung to it like a second skin. Its colour, a dreary, unflattering walnut brown, only solidified its image as a figurative turd on wheels.

He popped the boot, leaned in, and began rummaging through its chaotic contents, much like a mangy dog digging through garbage at the local tip. Inside lay a haphazard assortment of electrical goods, a smattering of cheap jewellery, and a variety of odd paraphernalia that seemed plucked straight from the graveyard of late-night *As Seen on TV* infomercials. Conrad's boot was less a storage space and more a barely mobile emporium of dubious wares. A veritable cornucopia of contraband more likely to have "fallen off the back of a truck" than to have been acquired through any legitimate means.

BANG! The boot slammed down onto Conrad's noggin.

"Wha ... what the ... " he muttered, dazed.

KA-THUNK! The second blow followed quicker and harder, cutting through his confusion like a hammer through glass. It was the kind of cheap shot straight out of a *Looney Tunes* short, one that should have left a perfect Conrad-shaped dent in the offending boot and a halo of twittering birds circling above his head. Shaken and perplexed, Conrad staggered back, hands instinctively raised in front of his face, determined to catch even the faintest glimpse of the prick who was giving his coconut such a savage working-over.

As the boot lifted, it revealed Detective Sergeant Hughes, his smug grin matched only by the audacity of his fingers, still wrapped around the handle, poised for another blow. Conrad bellowed something unintelligible, half fury, half confusion, as he squinted through the blinding midday sun, just in time to spot a second figure: Detective Gamble, a few paces back, lazily waving his arms with a passive authority that screamed, "nothing to see here, folks."

In truth, there was plenty to see. At least a dozen onlookers gawked at the spectacle of Hughes trying to reeducate a bogan with a car boot, not once, but twice. Fortunately for the detectives, that bastion of journalism, *A Current Affair*, was on hiatus, leaving little chance of their failed 'low profile' approach making headlines.

"Connie. Long time, no see," Hughes said smugly.

"Aww, shit, it's you," Conrad groaned.

"Shit indeed." Hughes seized Conrad by the collar of his red and black flannelette shirt, twisting it in his fist. With a swift, violent pirouette, he slammed Conrad against the side of the car, the metallic *thud* echoing down the street. "How's life treating you, brother?"

The men were not brothers in any biological sense, far from it. To claim otherwise would have been to suggest a grievous failing in Detective Hughes' bloodline, one he would never entertain. Conrad was, in fact, Hughes' former brother-in-law. Every family had its black sheep. Those no-hopers and malcontents whispered about at gatherings from behind palm-covered mouths. And for two years and seven months, right until

Hughes' sister's ill-fated marriage was dissolved via Decree Absolute, this five-foot-nothing sack of manure was probably as black and as sheepish as they come.

"I ... I ... can explain," Conrad stammered.

"Oh, can you just?" Hughes shot back.

Conrad nodded vigorously, his grogginess momentarily forgotten as he scrambled to regain control of his faculties.

"Something tells me you don't even—" Hughes began, but before he could finish, Conrad exploded from his grip like a greased pig on amphetamines. With the suddenness of a jolt of electricity, the shaggy little runt tore down the street, moving faster than anyone would have expected. His legs pumped like pistons, arms churning in perfect sprinting form, face as red as a Moscow sunset. For a bloke with only twenty percent lung capacity, courtesy of a lifelong habit of smoking backyard 'chop-chop', the bastard could move when his freedom depended on it, usually straight for the nearest pub.

"Well, Barry?" Hughes pivoted, shooting daggers at his partner. "You just gonna stand there lookin' pretty, or are you gonna make like a caterpillar and get a wriggle on? Go chase our little mate down."

"But ... we know where he's heading," Gamble replied.

"So? You could still use the exercise, Barge-Arse."

Hughes crashed through the front door of The Hackston, just behind Conrad and seconds ahead of his partner, his boots thudding heavily on the worn wooden floor. A handful of patrons at the bar froze mid-swig, eyes widening as they locked onto the unexpected intrusion, drinks still gripped in their hands. Hughes scanned the room, his posture hunched, hands planted on his hips, as he inhaled the thick, stale air of the pub, eyes flicking around for his quarry. It had been too long since he had engaged in an old-fashioned foot chase; pursuits were usually left to the suckers in uniform. But with the 'off the books' nature of their enquiry, it was a burden he had to take on the chin.

"Where'd that scruffy prick go?" Hughes asked, his voice slicing through the beer-soaked silence. The patrons remained frozen, wide-eyed stares locked on him, lips sealed tighter than the pub's doors on Christmas Day. Straightening to his full height, an unimpressive five foot eight, Hughes let his icy glare sweep the room, daring anyone to look away. "I bet all of you parasites know Conrad, so don't even think about protecting him."

A ripple of unintelligible glances passed through the patrons, a flock of turkeys more invested in the amber depths of their schooners than in the rising tension thickening the room. The silence stretched, bloated and awkward, until someone cleared their throat, breaking the spell.

"Looking for daddy, little boy?" Charlie asked, peering over the top of her textbook with a practised air of disdain.

Hughes chuckled, the sound low and dismissive.

"Just tell me where he's hiding, love," he said.

"Depends who's asking, doesn't it?" Charlie replied, her gaze sweeping over him, pausing pointedly on his gaudy Hawaiian shirt. "Though, judging by that fancy dress outfit of yours, I'd wager you've got a badge in one pocket and a sizeable grudge in the other."

Hughes flashed his badge with a smug grin. "Bingo! Detective Senior Sergeant Hughes at your service, Miss," he said, leaning forward to ensure his presence could not be ignored.

Charlie barely spared him a glance, her fingers idly flipping through her textbook. "Brilliant, well, Detective Senior

Sergeant," she replied, her tone dripping with sarcasm, "unless you plan on asking your question with a bit more civility, or you're chasing a drink, gin and tonic's on special, by the way, I suggest you move along."

Hughes let out a nervous laugh, his gaze lingering on the spirited brunette as if sizing her up for sport. His hand drifted to the holster on his hip, a gesture that teetered awkwardly between an attempt to assert dominance and a clumsy bid to catch her attention. Whether he aimed to intimidate or impress was anyone's guess, though the effect was about as subtle as a bull in a ballet recital.

"Guessin' you don't know my reputation?" he asked.

"Should I?" Charlie replied without so much as glancing up, the casual dismissal cutting sharper than any insult she could have voiced. "Though, based on your demeanour, Detective, I'm guessing that gin and tonic's a touch too sophisticated for your palette."

Before Hughes could muster something suitably pithy in response, his partner Gamble barrelled through the front door, his sizeable frame crashing into the nearest wall like an errant wrecking ball, shaking the building's very foundations. The timing, as it turned out, was impeccable, since Hughes had been perilously close to having his arse handed to him by a bar wench with an acid tongue.

"Well, if it ain't Mr Athletics," Hughes sneered.

Gamble paused, hands pressed against his knees as he fought to catch his breath, his chest heaving beneath the weight of his exertion. "So ... where is he?" he asked.

"Dunno, Baz, but the young lady here reckons I ought to brush up on my manners if I wanna find out," Hughes replied.

Gamble shrugged. "Maybe she's got a point, Mick."

Hughes narrowed his eyes. "What's that mean?"

"Well ... you could work on being nicer, Sarge."

"Exactly!" Charlie chimed in, her tone dripping with mock sweetness. "Kindness doesn't cost a thing." She set her textbook down with deliberate ease, fixing Hughes with a pointed stare.

Hughes' lips twitched in the beginnings of a smirk, as if waiting for the punchline to land. His eyes darted between Gamble's nonchalant shrug and Charlie's unwavering stare, certain that they had to be winding him up. But as the seconds stretched on, the smirk faded. She was not joking. Her gaze was steady, almost daring him to argue the point, the raised eyebrow now a silent challenge.

"You're serious, aren't you?" he asked flatly.

"Absolutely serious," Charlie replied.

"Uh," Hughes began. "Where's that prick, Conrad?"

Charlie shook her head. "Sorry, try that again."

Hughes exhaled sharply, pinching the bridge of his nose in frustration. "Could you please tell me where Conrad is?"

Charlie did not skip a beat. Like a cricket umpire signalling a boundary, she gestured toward the nearby pokies room. "See? How difficult was that, Detective?" she sneered, her grin wide as she basked in her small but satisfying victory.

Chapter Six

Blind Freddy

The Hackston's pokies room was packed with as many machines as the space could accommodate: one row of ten along each wall, two rows of twelve cutting through the middle, and a tattered red swivel chair in front of each. A single door served as both entrance and exit. There were no potted plants, no windows, and no trace of the outside world; only an outdated portrait of Queen Elizabeth II above the door and a smattering of obligatory anti-gambling posters slapped onto the rusty-orange walls. Clocks were conspicuously absent, allowing patrons to easily lose track of time and perhaps forget how long their children had been left unattended in the car while they pissed away their money inside. To say the room threw the tenets of interior design out the window would be fair, especially since there were no windows to throw them out of.

The detectives moved in tandem, their eyes methodically sweeping the room. Gamble's broad frame cast long shadows under the lighting as he trailed along the left wall, inspecting every nook and cranny. Hughes took the right, his footfalls muffled by the threadbare carpet. He paused at a row of machines, peering underneath them.

"Any signs of life, Sarge?" Gamble called softly.

Hughes shook his head. "Not unless you count this prick," he said, gesturing toward a lone gambler hunched over a machine nearby. "And even that's debatable." The dishevelled figure seemed to savour the ritual of feeding coins into the slot with almost meditative precision. *Clink, clink, clink.*

"Do me a favour, get his attention," Hughes said.

Gamble approached the brain-dead husk in the swivel chair and flashed his warrant card. Whether it was the way the badge caught the light or the gambler mistook the glint for a handful of change, the effect was immediate. The creature straightened up with a grunt, snapping out of the one-armed bandit's Medusa-like trance.

"Apologies for dragging you away from whatever it is you're wasting my tax dollars on, but I'm Detective Sergeant Hughes of the Gold Coast CIB, and that stout individual there is my colleague," Hughes gestured toward his partner, "Detective Senior Constable Gamble. We're going to need to cordon off this room. Police business, yeah. So, don't take this in the wrong spirit, mate, but could you do us a kindness and politely, er, fuck off?"

A string of unintelligible grunts and clicks followed, the kind that could have been mistaken for rudimentary Morse code. Or, more fittingly, a primitive dialect reserved for stick insects and football players. It was likely some feeble attempt by the gambler to enquire about proceedings, but judging by the lack of humour in Hughes' tone, the detective did not give a single solitary shit.

"Well then? On your bike, champ," he added.

The gambler clicked a few more times in frustration.

Hughes glanced at his partner, quizzical for a moment, before shrugging and turning back to the gambler. "ON YOUR BIKE, YOU FUCKIN' GOBLIN!" he bellowed at the top of his lungs.

Before the spittle could dissipate into the air-conditioned ether, the gambler scurried from the room, clutching fistfuls of gold coins. The detectives tracked his every move, from seat to exit, with Gamble locking the door behind him in a theatrical flourish. As the pair let the dust settle, their ears strained for the faintest sound. Conrad had to be hiding somewhere, but where? Ever the optimists, the detectives waited, the silence thick with anticipation. After a beat, it became obvious Conrad had made his choice. In the time-honoured tradition of criminal scumbags everywhere, he was exercising his right to remain silent in the absence of legal representation.

"Just come on out, Connie," Hughes began, meandering through the row of pokie machines, arms outstretched, tapping buttons as he passed: *tap, tap, tap*. "There's no escape. Barry's got the exit locked up tighter than a fish's arsehole, so save us the hassle, yeah? It's a corker of a day outside. I could think of a thousand things I'd rather be doing than playing hide and seek with a low-rent deadshit."

Tap. Tap, tap, tap. Tap, tap. Tap, tap, tap.

The detective reached the halfway point of the room.

"Listen to him, Conrad," Gamble urged, trying to expedite the situation. "Cooperate, and maybe Sarge'll go easy on you."

It was the classic good cop/bad cop routine.

Suddenly, a faint *ka-thud* echoed from the farthest corner of the room. A space once occupied by a broken machine but now repurposed as a hiding spot for a low-rent deadshit with a surprising touch of agility. The detectives froze, exchanging a brief flurry of hand signals that could generously be described as improvised.

Hughes' instincts kicked in, his focus zeroing in on the source of the sound. With a sharp, deliberate motion, he yanked his former brother-in-law out from the shadows, slamming him against a nearby machine and pinning him by the scruff of his collar. The fugitive let out a whiny, pathetic whimper, his bravado vanishing faster than the man himself when it was his turn to shout the next round.

"What ... the? I ain't done nothin'," Conrad protested.

"You don't say, mate?" Hughes replied, glancing over at his partner, then back at Conrad. "So, what? You just make a habit of randomly running away from the cops?"

"I do when they bash me with a friggin' car boot!"

The detectives exchanged glances; he had a point.

Hughes seized the moment to frisk Conrad, his hands gliding over the man's grimy, cigarette-stained torso with all the enthusiasm of someone dragging a cat into the deep end of a swimming pool.

"If this is about that Rolex I sold—" Conrad began.

With a sneer, Hughes abandoned the search, reached into his jacket, and retrieved the timepiece. He held it aloft, the gold-plating glinting mockingly under the harsh pokies room lights.

"She's a real beaut, ain't she?" Conrad said.

"A beaut? Cut the horseshit," Hughes sighed, his frustration bubbling to the surface. "I've got a good-for-nothing wife, a mortgage, and two dogs that hate my guts. Dogs. Man's best friend, right? Even they don't want a bar of me." He paused, letting the sheer weight of his words settle like a heavy fog. "Oh, and let's not forget, I'm up to my eyeballs in debt. So, don't piss on my leg and tell me it's raining. We both know this piece of junk ain't fair dinkum. I know it. You know it. Hell, even Blind Freddy over here knows it."

The fact "Rolex" was spelled with two L's probably should have raised alarms, even for the most amateur of horologists.

"The only person who didn't know it was fake was my missus. You remember Deb, right?" Hughes continued. "Gave it to her for our anniversary. Everything's good for a few days and then guess what? The minute hand falls clean off." He rattled the watch inches from Conrad's face. "So, you know what Deborah did? She was so shit-scared, thinking she'd broken her anniversary present, that she took it to the jeweller's to get it repaired. And ... well, I bet you can probably work out how this little story of mine ends?"

"Oh, shit," Conrad muttered under his putrid breath.

"Oh shit, indeed. The jeweller took one look at it and laughed her out of the store. Called security and everything. Deb was in tears!" Hughes glared at Conrad, the veins in his neck visibly tightening.

"Christ, I'm sorry abo—" Conrad began.

"Shut the fuck up!" Hughes barked, cutting him off. He leaned in closer, his face inches from Conrad's. "Any idea how that made me look in front of the missus?" Hughes did not wait for an answer, jabbing a finger into Conrad's chest for emphasis. "I'll tell you how that made me look. It made me look like a proper cunt!"

"But ... " Conrad hesitated, his words faltering as he braced for the inevitable verbal smackdown. Yet, to his surprise, no interruption came. He glanced at Hughes, expecting the fury to erupt any second. Despite the detective's riled-up appearance, marked by the throbbing carotid artery in his neck and his heavy, uneven breaths, Hughes was waiting, his eyes boring into Conrad with simmering expectancy.

For the first time, Conrad realised he had been handed the floor. An open invitation to spew whatever ridiculous garbage popped into his head. He should have used the pause to reconsider or, better yet, said nothing at all. But caution had never been his strong suit, and the silence was too tempting to resist.

"To be fair," he began, his lips curling into a shit-eating grin, "you didn't need a watch to make you look like a cunt."

The words hung in the air like a lit fuse. Conrad's grin faltered almost instantly as he saw the shift in Hughes' expression. It was subtle. Too subtle for the untrained eye, but to Conrad, it was a ticking time bomb. He could almost hear the slow *tick-tick-tick* of his own downfall. His only recourse was to close his eyes, tense his facial muscles, and brace himself for the detective's rebuttal.

"Restrain the suspect, Barry," Hughes said calmly.

Conrad opened an eye to scope the situation.

"What? Are you serious, Sarge?" Gamble replied.

"Don't second-guess me, Constable. Restrain the suspect! And don't stand there umm'ing and ahh'ing about it like a sheila, either. Pull your head out of your arse and get it back in the game."

Gamble sighed, a sound heavy with reluctant complicity, and lumbered toward his partner. Everything about his body language screamed that he wanted no part of what was about to unfold. His large frame moved with deliberate slowness, each step burdened by the resignation of a man already bracing himself for the worst.

"But ... but ... I ain't done nothing," Conrad pleaded.

"Really? Normally, I'd look the other way while you pedal your Chinese knock-offs down back alleys like the shithouse rat you are," Hughes said, his voice cold and cutting. "But not this time. Not when your bullshit bleeds into mine. That, and you're getting a bit too familiar, like that outburst just now. Or when you call me Mick ... rather than addressing me by my rank and surname. Something tells me you've forgotten your place in the food chain around here."

Conrad shook his head. "I ain't. Believe me, Mic—"

Before he could finish his sentence, Gamble had Conrad on the ground in a textbook police-issue arm lock: high and tight against the centre of his back, firm enough to suggest that his humerus was a muscle twitch away from snapping like a chicken bone. Conrad's breath hitched as his body slammed into the floor, his face mashed against a carpet that reeked of piss and poor life choices.

"Watch it, you ten-foot fuck!" Conrad snapped, his voice brimming with defiance as Gamble hoisted him back to his feet effortlessly.

"Best get used to bein' tossed around like a rag doll, Connie, 'cause if you get pinched one more time, it won't be old pencil dick here you ought to be worried about." Hughes' tone was cruel, his grin widening as he eyed the now-restrained Conrad. "Remember all those Islander boys in Woodford, Connie? Fists like anvils, dicks like drainpipes. Get sent back again, and it won't be six months and out. It'll be a three-to-five stretch this time. Guaranteed." He leaned in closer, his voice low and dangerous. "And while you're there, I'll make sure they stick you in a cot with big Johnny Buttafuko over in Cell Block 4. I know a few of the screws there. I'm sure they'd happily turn a blind eye while Johnny went about greasin' your tailpipe."

Conrad's face drained of all colour as the full weight of Hughes' words pummelled him. He opened his chapped lips to speak, but his throat was drier than a New Zealander's sense of humour.

"What ... what do you want?" he eventually asked.

"Compensation," Hughes replied flatly.

"What? You want your twenty bucks back?" Conrad asked. "I, uh, don't have it on me, but I'll have it next week. Soon as my dole cheque clears." He paused, eyeing Hughes' expression. It was not the face of a patient man. "How about a couple of those, er, new fruit phones instead? Apples, pears, whatever. Consider 'em yours. Heck, I'll even throw in one for Deb," he added with a strained grin.

"Sarge can barely send a fax," Gamble interjected.

Hughes, seizing on the shift, stepped in closer. The faint scuff of his boots against the floor cut through the tense silence, sharp and deliberate. He leaned in, his eyes boring into Conrad's. "What else have you got?" Hughes asked, his tone low and edged with menace.

Money was a no. Merchandise was out. Conrad wracked his brain, scrambling for anything else of tangible value.

"How about, uh, information?" he mumbled.

"Information?" Hughes replied, raising an eyebrow.

"The juicy kind. Straight from a bloke I ran into last week ... " Conrad began, his voice trailing off as his brow furrowed, struggling to stitch together the details rattling around in his aching head.

Somewhere, sometime last week, 'allegedly'...

"I'd be givin' it away for anything less than five hundred," Conrad said, his hands clasped in front of his chest with all the flair of a snake oil salesman. Only instead of peddling miracle cures from a horse-drawn wagon, Conrad was busy hawking a DVD player to a customer who, in the dim light of the parking garage, bore a striking resemblance to Magdalena Black's enforcer, Mark Campbell.

The grizzled ex-footballer crossed his thick, muscular arms and cocked his head, his expression a mix of disbelief and disdain.

"Five hundred, for that? Piss off," he replied.

"Uh ... four hundred then," Conrad countered.

"Two hundred," Mark shot back. "Final offer."

Conrad's face twitched. "You know what these go for in the shops?" he asked, his tone equal parts indignation and incredulity.

"Does it look like we're in a bloody shop?" Mark growled. "Nah. We're standin' in the middle of a parking garage like a pair of plonkers." His eyes scanned the dimly lit space, briefly landing on a janitor shuffling near the western entrance with a squeaky cart. Seeing nothing amiss, Mark's focus returned to Conrad. "Two hundred, mate. No more," he began, jabbing a finger toward the orange ute parked under a flickering fluorescent light. "Two hundred, and I'll hop in my sexy car over there feelin' sore but not like I got completely bent over. That way, we both leave with a shred of dignity." Mark leaned in, his size and presence doing most of the talking now. "Sound like a plan, pipsqueak?"

"But … but it's got all the latest whizzbang features. Shit, I heard it even looks smick with that new Finding Nero movie all the kids are into." Conrad smiled and nodded, praying his wafer-thin knowledge of kids and their cinematic habits would pass muster.

Mark chuckled. "It's Nemo, not Nero, ya knob."

"Yeah? *Finding Nemo*. What did I say?"

"Finding Nero. Nero's that crazy cock who torched Rome," Mark said. "Nobody's gonna make a kid's film about him, are they?"

The two men stood in tense, uneasy silence, each vehemently convinced the other was a stone-cold fucking idiot.

"Bugger it. It's now one-fifty, or nothing," Mark said.

The price was dropping faster than his patience.

"Huh? Weren't you at two before?" Conrad asked.

"I had a sudden change of heart," Mark replied.

"A change of heart? On account of what, mate?"

"On account of havin' to deal with an absolute fuckwit."

Before Conrad could make his counter-offer, Tina Turner's 90s rock anthem, 'Simply the Best', bellowed from Mark's jeans. "Christ. Hold on a tick, mate," Mark muttered as he pulled out his phone, squinting at the caller ID before lumbering out of earshot.

Or at least what he thought was out of earshot.

"What's doing, boss?" Mark said into the receiver.

Over his shoulder, Conrad feigned interest in the DVD player, his eyes skimming it as though it held the secrets of the universe. All the while, he strained to catch snippets of the nearby conversation. In his line of work, keeping an ear to the ground was a professional necessity. Relieving someone of their possessions became infinitely easier when you knew they were otherwise occupied.

"What day's the Korean arrivin'?" Mark asked, his focus locked on the voice at the other end of the receiver as he fished a small notebook from his jacket. The dainty object looked almost comical, swallowed by his meaty fingers. "Yeah, I'm lookin', boss. I wrote his flight number down the other day."

Mark thumbed through a dozen or so pages, pausing only when he found the right one. Upon doing so, he shot a glare in Conrad's direction to ensure he was not getting too nosy. Undeterred, Conrad maintained the pretence of being an avid electronics enthusiast.

"Nah ... but if I can't, whoever we go with is gonna need to keep an eye on him. Shit, the last thing we need is some stooge leaving him at the airport, files in one hand, old fella in the other. The way I see it, boss, everyone's gonna want to get their hands on that intel."

Mark snapped his notebook shut with a sharp flick, then swaggered back toward Conrad, the conversation clearly winding to an end. His grip on the phone tightened, his tone soft-ening to something almost cordial. "Anyway, I'll see what I can do. The ute hasn't had a decent run into Brissie in a while," he said, ending the call with a curt nod before returning the phone to his pocket.

"Right," Mark said. "So where were we, little man?"

"I was tryin' to sell you a DVD player," Conrad replied, his face twisting into an expression of weary disdain as the re-alisation hit that he was still mid-haggle with the impersonal man-mountain.

"We agreed on one-fifty, yeah?" Mark asked.

"Er, no. We agreed on five hundred."

"Pig's arse we did," Mark said. "One-fifty. Tops."

"Uh, three hundred then. That's my final offer."

Mark closed the gap between the two men. "Enough of this shit. I'm gonna make you my final offer, and dependin' on how you respond might just determine whether this is the last offer you ever receive." Conrad nodded and locked eyes with the giant enforcer. "How 'bout I give you one hundred for the DVD player, yeah, and I lose the sudden urge to beat you to death in this parking garage?"

Conrad gulped. "You've got yourself a deal."

Hughes furrowed his brow. "You expect us to buy that, Con-nie?" he said, his tone thick with scepticism. "A random Korean bloke's flying in with some sort of intel, and what? Planning to flog it? Here, of all places?" He let out a sharp laugh, giving his partner a playful jab in the shoulder. "This is the Goldie, not a Bond film. And sorry to break it to you, champ, but you're no Roger-bloody-Moore either."

"It's the God's honest truth," Conrad replied.

Despite there being a better-than-average chance Conrad was telling porkie pies, the currency the detectives could gain by passing that intel to one of the local crime outfits far outweighed the misery of enduring another five minutes within the stifling radius of Conrad's armpit stench. Truth be told, scouring South East Queensland for a phantom Korean sounded far more appealing than chasing leads on bikers cooking bathtub crank in derelict rentals. With the sweltering heat and bikers' well-documented disdain for law enforcement, the choice was an easy one to make.

"I don't trust you, Connie. Not as far as I could throw you ... but fuck it, I'll play along," Hughes replied, his voice sharp with irritation. He turned back toward Conrad, his eyes narrowing. "So, any idea what kind of information your chink mate plans on selling?"

Gamble shifted uncomfortably, his face tinged with embarrassment. "You can't say that anymore, Mick."

"What, 'chink'?" Hughes asked, rolling his eyes.

"Er, yeah ... that one," Gamble replied.

"Fine. 'Oriental' then, if that keeps HR off my back." Hughes leaned in closer. "I just wanna know what this prick's flogging. Names? Addresses? Pol Pot's Christmas card list?"

Conrad shrugged like an idiot, the kind of shrug that broadcast his utter lack of self-preservation and awareness in equal measure.

"And you've never seen him before?" Hughes pressed.

Conrad blinked. "Who? This Korean fella?"

"No. The bloke you sold the bloody VCR to!"

"It was a DVD player," Gamble interjected helpfully.

Hughes shot his partner a look that could wither a cactus.

"Hard to say if I recognised him," Conrad said, running a hand through his mop of red hair. "I yarn to that many people that they all sorta melt into one another, like a big bowl of Neapolitan ice cream." He scoured his aching brain for the finer details. "He was a big boy. Cropped brown hair. Scars. Fortyish? Looked as if he'd copped a few busted noses, too. Dunno. That garage was pretty dark."

"So, Frankenstein's monster?" Hughes quipped.

Realising that Hughes' history with Conrad was clouding their enquiry, Gamble decided it was time to take control. "Alright, so we've established he's no male model," he said, keeping his tone casual as he worked to steer the conversation back on track. "But we'll need more. Was there anything else distinctive about this bloke?"

Conrad thought for a moment before responding.

"Well, he struck me as the serious type, Detective Gamble. Steal-from-his-own-grandmother type of serious. Definitely not the sort of fella I'd wanna run into in a dark alley."

Dark alleys were out of the question, but a poorly lit parking garage seemed like a perfectly acceptable meeting place? Gamble shook his head in bewilderment, realising it was just another one of Conrad's contradictions. But instead of dwelling on it, Gamble pressed on, hoping that a few of these contradictory pieces might just fit together to generate a lead worth following up on.

"Come to think of it, he did look kind of familiar," Conrad added. "Like I'd seen him somewhere before."

"That's how familiarity works," Hughes muttered.

"Yeah, yeah. Alright, I know," Conrad shot back.

What Conrad failed to appreciate was that he had just described ninety percent of the perps they chased down regularly. If he had told them the guy was Lebanese and drove a pimped-out Subaru, he would have nailed the other ten.

"Stuff it. Let him go, Barry," Hughes muttered, casting a resigned glance at his dishevelled former brother-in-law.

"What?" Gamble replied, disbelief clear in his voice.

"You heard me," Hughes said. "Let the turd go."

Puzzled by his partner's change of heart, Gamble released the arm lock on Conrad and gave him a firm nudge toward Hughes. Ever the showman, Hughes caught him with mock civility, smoothing out Conrad's rumpled attire with exaggerated precision. The act was theatrical, but the intent was clear. Hughes was determined to leave no inconvenient questions about police harassment.

"You're lettin' me go?" Conrad asked, a hint of trepidation in his gravelly voice. "Just like that? No tricks?"

Hughes formed a three-finger salute. "Scout's honour."

"But ... what about the watch? I can still pay you."

"Eh. Just piss off before I change my mind."

Conrad looked like the cat who had eaten the canary.

"You're a saint, Detective," he said. "That goes for you too, Detective Gamble. Shit, if anyone around here ever says a bad word about either of you, I'll set 'em straight." He skirted around Gamble and made a beeline for the exit. "Don't you worry about that."

Worried? The detectives were anything but. In polite society, the ringing endorsement of a career criminal was about as useful as an inflatable dartboard. As they watched the hairy weasel scurry toward the door, a bee's dick away from making a clean getaway, Hughes had another sudden but calculated change of heart.

"Oi! Hold up a second there, champ," he called.

Conrad froze in his tracks, glancing over his shoulder, then back at the door, then back over his shoulder again. The fluorescent green exit sign beckoned like a siren from some old myth. It was so close, he could almost taste The Hackston's stale pub air seeping in from underneath the door, lapping at his mismatched pair of thongs.

"Out of interest, Connie?" Hughes said. "That watch?"

"Yeah, what about it, Detective?" he replied.

"It's completely shock-resistant, isn't it?"

Conrad stood there, puzzled by the question. Behind his back, Hughes methodically wrapped the faux-Swiss timepiece around his fist, transforming it into a crude pair of brass knuckles. Oblivious to the threat, Conrad turned to face Hughes, still clueless about what was coming. Gamble, however, recognised the signs all too well and dropped his gaze to the gaudy maroon carpet underfoot.

CRACK! Before Conrad even realised what had hit him, quite literally, Hughes' horologically augmented fist slammed into his right eye socket with a bone-jarring thud. The precision and sheer force of the blow sent him crashing to the floor in a heavy, sprawling heap.

"Western Sydney Junior Featherweight Champ, '89 through '91, motherfucker! Don't you ever forget that," Hughes said, as he flailed his hand around to dispel the all-too-familiar sting of pugilistic exertion. "Who's the fuckin' cunt now, you … uh … cunt?"

Gamble sighed, his head hanging low as a wave of shame washed over him, the echo of the impact still ringing in his ears. Hughes, unfazed, stepped over the crumpled heap on the floor and inspected his throbbing fist. The prognosis: it hurt like a son-of-a-bitch, but nothing a bag of frozen peas could not fix. The wristwatch, however, had not been so lucky; its faceplate lay in ruins, and with it, any likelihood of it actually being shock-resistant.

"Geez. Was that n-n-necessary?" Gamble asked.

Hughes grinned. "N-n-no. But it felt fuckin' good."

The reality was grim: two of the Gold Coast's finest holed up in a dingy pokies room, a member of the public sprawled unconscious on the floor, sporting police-inflicted head injuries. All it would take was one curious soul to unlock the door or pull the CCTV footage, and the Crime and Misconduct Commission would be so far up the detectives' arses that all they could taste was polished boot leather.

"Shouldn't we ... help him or something?" Gamble asked, casting a concerned eye over Conrad's limp body sprawled on the ground. "Maybe grab him an ice pack from out front?"

"Eh. The prick'll be right as rain come tomorrow."

Gamble raised an eyebrow at the prognosis.

"Well ... can we at least get out of here?" he added.

"Why? You got somewhere else to be, Barry?"

"Uh, no. Not exactly, Sarge, but it's—"

"Good. Because if old mate here is tellin' the truth, someone important out there has to be keen on getting their hands on that intel, yeah? And what do important someones usually have in spades? Money." Hughes stuffed the shattered wristwatch back into his pocket, his gaze lingering on the flashing lights of a nearby pokie machine. "But that's assuming Conrad's being straight with us. And given recent history, well, that's quite the leap of faith."

Gamble sighed. "I'm not sure about this, Mick."

"Really? Well, use your *big boy* voice, Barry."

"Okay. It's just ... " Gamble frowned, his voice trailing off. "Something about this smells fishy. Koreans? Parking garages? Honestly, we're better off leaving it well enough alone."

Gamble worked to sow the seeds of doubt, his motives more self-serving than they appeared. It was not just about avoiding a potential international incident; he had no intention of being dragged into yet another of Hughes' chaotic escapades. Unbeknown to his partner, Gamble had long since outgrown his role as sidekick to the CIB's most detestable arsehole. His sights were firmly set on a transfer to the Child Protection Unit, a position he hoped would demand less moral compromise and come with fewer headaches. After all, working with Hughes was not unlike dealing with a toddler. Except, occasionally, you could reason with a toddler.

"It's definitely got a stink on it, Barry, but Magdalena Black's got us by the balls over this warrant on her penthouse tomorrow. And hell, I figure if we play our cards right, we might just wriggle back into her good graces. That, and make it worth our while. Two birds, you know?" Hughes gave a sly grin. "Let's do some digging around and see if we can confirm this story of his. Then next time we see Maggie, we let slip what Conrad here told us. Make it look like we're being proactive. Most importantly, we might stand to pocket a little coin."

"Er, maybe we should run it past her first," he said.

"Maggie? What'd be the point?" Hughes asked.

"A phone call might save us a lot of trouble, Mick. That's all I'm getting at," Gamble said, glancing at Conrad's crumpled body and letting out a breath of relief as he spotted the faint rise and fall of his chest. "Nothing gets past Black on the Gold Coast, especially something this sophisticated. Maybe, you know, reaching out to her first is the prudent move here?"

"Nah. No need gettin' her involved," Hughes replied.

Chapter Seven

Arterial Red

The Hackston Tavern drifted toward slumber after another lacklustre day of trade. The odour of stale bodies and spilt beer hung thick in the air, a heavy reminder of failure that clung to everything and everyone. Somewhere within that inky void, amid the hum of refrigerators and the intermittent chirp of a dying smoke alarm, a solitary light waged war against the darkness. The vigilant bulb flickered, as though ravaged by an unseen moth, its feeble glow weaving mischief among the rows of upturned chairs, casting demonic silhouettes across the feature wall behind.

Encased in that ring of light, silently cheered on by a crowd of empty schooners, Jack and Hung sat like punch-drunk combatants on the verge of a decisive twelfth round. Their egos, battered and bruised, mirrored the stoic expressions on their faces as they sat at opposite ends of the alcohol-soaked table, each man poised for another beating. But this was no prestigious title bout; this was an Irish street brawl masquerading as The Hackston's finances.

"Is that necessary?" Jack asked sharply, sensing movement in his periphery. He looked up from the ledger, his face dark with anger, and fixed his gaze on his partner, who was fidgeting restlessly.

"Is *what* necessary?" Hung replied with a wiggle.

"That! Whatever the hell it is you're doing," Jack snapped, his patience wearing thin. "I find this hard enough without you sitting there doing the bloody Nutbush in your chair. Just stop!"

"Sorry," Hung replied. "But I can't get comfortable."

"Really? Well, for your health and my sanity, try to."

Hung sat motionless for a moment before arching his back and letting out a long, exaggerated groan. "Have you ever actually *sat* in one of these chairs, Jack?" he asked with exasperation. "Like, *properly* sat in one? They're absolutely terrible. It's no wonder people hate it here. Can't we at least use part of Maggie's money to buy some decent chairs? Ones that aren't medieval torture devices?"

"Jesus. For the tenth time, no," Jack replied flatly.

"Come on, man. It's like sitting on concrete."

Jack glowered across the table, his irritation simmering just beneath the surface. The chairs were just one item on the ever-growing laundry list of reasons the average punter despised The Hackston. In truth, most of the furniture was shithouse. Apart from Jack's prized Humphrey Bogart lithograph, which hung proudly above the toilets, the pub's décor was a chaotic mishmash inherited from its previous owner, a disgraced local politician who had exited public office in the least dignified manner possible: in handcuffs.

"I won't argue with you about the seating, Hung," Jack said, running a hand through his stubble. "But we wouldn't be out here if our office wasn't stuffed to the brim with cardboard boxes, would we? You can thank your mate, Mark Campbell, for that." He let the moment linger for a beat before turning his attention back to the financials. "And besides, you know as well as I do, new chairs aren't exactly a luxury we can afford right now. This place is barely breaking even. So, for the love of God, just drop the subject, yeah?"

Hung pouted and sipped his diet sarsaparilla while Jack continued to crunch the numbers. After a few moments of furrowed brows and muttered frustration, Jack dropped his pencil onto the table and spun the ledger toward Hung. The mathematics guru tackled the figures with steely-eyed focus, his finger darting across the page like a seismograph needle tracking a magnitude-ten earthquake.

"That, there. That's definitely wrong," Hung declared, tapping an erroneous figure at the bottom of the page. His pickup was almost instantaneous. "And that over there." Jack's eyes followed Hung's finger across the page. "That should be seventy-five."

Jack's gaze fell, his expression souring as the mistake became glaringly obvious. He groaned, dragging a hand down his face.

While Hung appreciated Jack's 'roll up your sleeves' attitude, especially when it came to tackling grunt work, his staunch refusal to abandon pencil and paper did little to ease the challenges of running a modern business. At best, it meant double-handling; at worst, it opened the door to costly human error. And with a queue of rabid debt collectors already breathing down their necks, the last thing they needed was an open invitation for friendly fire.

Jack made a few quick adjustments before grimacing and spinning the ledger back around, silently praying it would be for the last time. Hung's brow furrowed momentarily as he scanned the page, his finger darting forward to pinpoint yet another glaring error.

"That should be a two instead of—" Hung began.

"Oh, for fuck's sake, mate," Jack cut him off.

"What?" Hung asked, his tone defensive.

"Contain your pulsating hard-on for a second and focus on the important part of the story." Jack jabbed a finger at the balance. "You clocked that enormous number at the bottom of the page yet?"

Hung glanced at the total and nodded with reluctance.

"There's what? Thirty-five grand there, give or take. And that's just our costs to keep the lights on each month." Jack's intense gaze drilled into the table. "That doesn't include what we owe Magdalena ... let alone the twenty percent interest she expects on top of that."

The truth, when laid bare at a beer-soaked table nearing midnight, felt staggering, but it was hardly a revelation. They knew it, of course, but admitting it was another matter entirely. The two men shared a concerned glance before Hung finally broke the silence.

"So, how are we supposed to make ends meet?" he asked.

Jack sighed. "Short of a bloody miracle, we're not."

"What, so you're just going to chuck it in, then?"

"Chuck it in?" Jack shot Hung a look, running a hand over his face. "Listen, I'm not waving the white flag just yet, yeah? But you know the books better than I do. The ends are so far apart right now, I reckon even the Hubble Telescope couldn't pick them up."

Before either man could dwell on the gravity of that remark, a sudden stir of activity erupted behind the bar, movement any seasoned bartender would instantly recognise: the unmistakable sound of a lowball glass on a timber countertop. Both men leaned in, eyes narrowing as they peered into the inky black void.

"Astronomy was never a passion of mine," a familiar feminine voice replied from the murk, catching them both off-guard. "However, if you boys play your cards right tomorrow ... well, maybe I could be of assistance in bringing those ends significantly closer."

Ushered in by the click of a switch, the fluorescent lights above the bar sputtered to life, their hum punctuated by a stuttering flicker. Any hope the mysterious figure had for a dramatic entrance was thwarted by a faulty starter. *TICK* ... *TICK* ... *TICK* ... After what felt like an eternity, the bar was finally bathed in harsh luminescence, revealing none other than Magdalena Black behind the counter, pouring herself a slug of The Hackstons' moderately priced Scotch whisky.

Gone was her casual beach attire. In its place was a uniform more befitting a woman of her standing: a black Giorgio Armani single-breasted velvet jacket and matching pants, paired with a plunging white silk undershirt and a subtle silver pendant necklace. She was all curves, class, and command. Her enforcer, Mark Campbell, lingered at the edge of the bar, his finger still hovering over the light switch. Unlike his employer, his fashion sense leaned toward the casual end of the spectrum: white T-shirt, black leather jacket, and blue denim jeans. His 'bad boy' starter pack rounded out with his trademark scowl and a weapons-grade case of halitosis.

The men muttered quiet curses under their breath.

"Magdalena? How ... how long've you been standing there?" Jack asked with a strained chuckle, his mind racing to replay the last few minutes of their back-and-forth, searching for anything that might have cast the woman before them in a less-than-flattering light.

"Long enough," Magdalena replied, wafting the glass under her nose before tossing back its contents in a single, fluid motion. Jack opened his mouth to respond, but stumbled over his words, leaving a string of half-formed syllables hanging in the air. Magdalena silenced him with a raised finger, her eyes closed and lips pursed as she savoured the fruity, smoky flavour, letting the dry finish linger with an air of indulgence. "Surprisingly complex for a drop from the Eastern Highlands," she added, scrutinising the empty glass as if it owed her money. "I never really shared my late father's reverence for the Devil's drink. But then again ... " She paused, a smile curling at the corners of her lips, a quiet hint of something darker beneath. "I also failed to share his reverence for consorting with prostitutes instead of attending my doting daughter's grade eleven dance recital."

"Um ... okay. That's ... handy to know," Jack replied, his voice trailing off as he shifted uncomfortably in his seat.

What had begun as a routine late-night bookkeeping session had spiralled into, well, whatever the hell this was. It was hard to believe that the loan shark had committed criminal trespass just to wax poetic about Scotch whisky and her father's infidelity, especially at 11:46 pm on a Friday. Magdalena should have been holed up at her nightclub, relaxing in her luxurious beachside penthouse, or enjoying one of her many other lavish properties scattered across the Gold Coast.

Yet, somehow, The Hackston had captured her interest.

"Reviewing the finances, Jack?" the loan shark asked as she poured herself another drink. "Well, I say 'reviewing', but it looks more like you're fucking them, and your little Vietnamese friend here is reinforcing racial stereotypes by dutifully ... unfucking them."

"Er, I guess you could say that," Jack replied.

"In that case, don't let us interrupt you." Magdalena ran a finger across the bar, inspecting the thin layer of grime clinging to her fingertip with faint disgust. "It's always fascinating to see how the other half lives. Please, carry on and pretend we're not here."

Easier said than done. Especially for Jack, who wrestled with performance anxiety even when it was just Hung scrutinising the numbers. Now, with an audience, he felt like a trained monkey under a spotlight. The pair sat in tense silence for a moment, until Hung shot Jack a pointed glare, his expression practically pleading for him to confront the eccentric figure now commanding the room.

Jack placed his pencil down. "No, we're finished."

"Oh? Are you sure?" Magdalena replied, her tone laced with playful scepticism as she relished their palpable discomfort.

Jack silently closed the ledger and pushed it aside.

"Fantastic," Magdalena said, setting her empty glass on the counter as she stepped out from behind the bar. Tired of playing the world's most selfish bartender, she decided it was time for an impromptu tour of The Hackston Tavern. Without missing a beat, Mark fell into step behind her, a looming shadow as she navigated the dimly lit establishment toward Jack and Hung.

Magdalena's gaze swept the room in one calculating motion, taking in every grimy detail of her surroundings. She paused, allowing the weight of her verdict to linger. "Hmm, you were right about this place, Mark. It really is a shithole," she said, her tone flat but sharp enough to cut through the thick, stale air. "Nothing that another loan or three couldn't fix, I suppose." She gestured lazily at various features of the pub, her critiques as effortless as they were brutal. "That pathetic excuse for a dance floor? Tear it up. The Christmas lights strung above the bar? Tacky beyond belief. And my lord," she added, her voice climbing into mock horror, "the corrugated iron nailed to the wall there? The less said about that, the better."

Mark towered over Magdalena's shoulder, his tree-trunk arms folded, a warped grin like a November jack-o'-lantern on his face. It was a silent endorsement of her brutal assessment.

Jack, meanwhile, fought to hold his tongue. She was not wrong, especially about the corrugated iron feature wall, but the relentless barrage of criticisms, delivered with rapid-fire precision and dripping with condescension, was almost impossible to let glide through to the keeper.

"What's your overarching theme?" Magdalena continued, as if she were the ineffectual host of a prime-time reality show, where hapless contestants showcased their complete ineptitude for interior design.

"Our theme?" Hung echoed, genuinely curious.

"Yes. The underlying idea that runs through your venue."

"Uh? It's a pub," Jack interjected. "That's our theme."

"Well, you need better branding, then," Magdalena quipped. "Or any branding, for that matter, because this place screams 'spit-and-sawdust joint', minus the sawdust." She glanced around, her expression twisting in exaggerated disdain. "If it were me, Jack, I would gut this entire space and start from scratch. Something stylish. Youthful. Modern. Though the location … " She wrinkled her nose. "Not much you can do about that. Unless, of course, you're considering a charitable act of arson to raze the suburb."

That was one way to boost property values. Of course, it did little to address the elephant in the room.

"Sure. So, ah, I don't want to sound forthright," Jack began cautiously, "but was there something specific you wanted, Miss Black … y'know, before you and your walking erection here materialised in our pub? It's just … it's been a long day, is all."

Magdalena glanced at her enforcer, sensing he was itching to put Jack in his place. With a brief, measured look, she issued a silent command to stand down. Her piercing gaze sliced through his simmering frustration. Still, Mark's hulking frame edged closer, pacing a slow circle around the table. The sheer weight of his presence pressed down on Jack, heavy with unspoken menace.

"I come offering a … lifeline," Magdalena replied.

"What sort of lifeline?" Jack asked cautiously.

"The kind that would ease your financial burden."

Jack's brow furrowed. "Like the easing that occurred when you had old Bugalugs here fill our office with cardboard boxes this afternoon?" he asked, his voice tinged with exasperation.

Magdalena fixed Jack with a stern glare, pondering whether leaving him in Mark's capable hands might be more satisfying than enduring this inane questioning. The tension in the room thickened, and Jack felt the fragile ice beneath him begin to crack. His tone had fallen short of the respect Magdalena demanded, and he knew it was only a matter of time before someone called him out on it.

"I'm here with a one-time, mutually beneficial proposition, Jack. One-time, as in, never to be repeated," Magdalena replied smoothly, leaning back slightly, her posture an embodiment of controlled elegance. "To circle back to your question about my presence, I've learned that the Gold Coast CIB will be visiting my penthouse in the morning." She glanced at her wristwatch. "Court-issued search warrant in hand."

"Oh? My, er … condolences?" Jack offered.

"If only I believed they were sincere," Magdalena replied coolly. "But no, it's just the boys' club indulging in the harassment of a legitimate businesswoman. A minor inconvenience, nothing more."

The crucial detail Magdalena conveniently omitted was that the local constabulary had recently taken a keen interest in the murder of a drug dealer named Jimmy Jacobsen. That was not to suggest the loan shark or her enforcer were guilty, but court-issued search warrants were rarely granted without reasonable suspicion.

"So, what's this got to do with us?" Hung asked.

"I require your assistance in handling a delicate matter."

Jack smirked, slipping into his best Jimmy Cagney impression. "Oh, I get it. You want us to whack some coppers for ya, see?"

Magdalena groaned, rubbing her temples as she contemplated which of these two morons was supposed to be the brains of the operation. If this were a competition, it was shaping up to be a race to the bottom. She shook her head, casting the men a scornful look that suggested she would not trust either of them to whack Mark's plonker, let alone a bunch of Homicide detectives. Not that Jack nor Hung had the testicular fortitude to play the role of trigger men.

"Good lord, Jack, there will be no 'whacking', as you so elegantly put it. Nothing so morbidly clichéd or barbaric," Magdalena replied. "What I require, however, are a couple of responsible individuals, such as yourselves, to run an errand for me tomorrow while—"

"The police search your penthouse?" Hung interjected.

"Bingo," Magdalena said, tapping her temple.

And with that, Jack began nodding slowly at first, then faster, as the big picture snapped into focus. A flicker of annoyance crossed his face, partly at himself for taking so long, but mostly because Hung had beaten him to it. As the picture sharpened in his mind, like someone fine-tuning an old television, the inevitable follow-up question formed. Before he could voice it, however, Magdalena stepped toward him, slicing through his train of thought.

"Undoubtedly, you are wondering, 'Why us?', Jack?" she purred, leaning in so close her devilish grin hovered mere inches from his face. The crisp, tantalising scent of green apple and bergamot clung to the air, a disarming contrast to her standoffish demeanour.

Jack gulped. "The thought had crossed my mind."

At the far end of the table, Mark burst into the men's periphery without warning or provocation. A towering force of raw aggression. In one fluid, lightning-fast motion, he wrenched a pistol from his belt and jammed the cold barrel against Hung's temple. The sheer speed of the move was breathtaking, catching both men off guard.

"Surely the fact I asked nicely should suffice?" Magdalena said, her tone sharp and deliberate. "Besides, you weren't my first choice, so set aside any illusions of grandeur. Truth be told, it's the eleventh hour, and I need ... anyone ... to handle this errand. And you and your friend, Jack," she continued, her piercing gaze unwavering, "strike me as men who know how to follow orders, especially when provided with the right ... motivation."

Mark pressed the barrel harder against Hung's temple, the unyielding metal branding his skin with a chilling precision. Hung winced, his head shifting just enough to catch sight of the square-jawed brute hell-bent on merging a bullet with his brain.

"Consider them motivated, boss," Mark said, a bee's dick away from redecorating the walls with a fresh coat of arterial red.

Perhaps it was the primal, reptilian part of his brain kicking in. The same irrational grey matter that inexplicably made Southerners find VB palatable. But something snapped, thrusting Jack into a state of restless urgency. A voice in the back of his mind goaded him to act, to do *something* rather than sit there like a stunned mullet. His breath quickened, fists tightening as his thoughts spiralled out of control, each scenario more reckless and idiotic than the last.

Mark, sharp-eyed and coiled with anticipation, noticed the shift immediately. His finger hovered near the trigger, ready for the first flicker of a foolish decision. Jack, after all, was unremarkable in every sense: six feet tall, eighty kilograms of nothing special. But desperation had a way of turning anyone into a fool.

And fools, by their very nature, were dangerous.

"Come on, Miss Black! This isn't necessary," Jack pleaded.

"Oh, really?" Magdalena's smirk was all knives and venom. "Then perhaps you should take your concerns up with my colleague."

Jack glanced at Mark, who grinned back with predatory intent, then shifted his gaze to Hung. Hung's look was sharp and deliberate. A silent warning: *do not do anything stupid*. Jack locked eyes with him, holding the stare for half a heartbeat, his clenched jaw betraying the storm brewing inside. Hung gave a subtle shake of his head, firm but pleading. A last-ditch effort to rein Jack in.

"Shit," Jack mouthed, barely more than a breath, as he did the only sensible thing and surrendered to self-preservation.

"Cured of your little hero complex?" Magdalena asked.

Jack gave a slow nod and forced a shaky smile.

As the tension eased, Magdalena made a playful come-hither gesture toward Mark. The hulking man reluctantly capitulated, muttering something under his breath. He lowered the gun, tucked it into the waistband of his jeans, and rummaged through his pockets. Pulling out a folded piece of paper, he thrust it toward Jack, his eyes burning with disdain.

"And what's this supposed to be?" Jack asked.

"A piece of paper, dickhead," Mark replied.

"Oh, right? I thought it was an abstract sculpture."

Magdalena chuckled with amusement. "Now, now, play nice, boys," she said. "That piece of paper, Jack, contains everything you need to know. And I do mean *everything*." Her tone shifted, hardening as she laid down the law with unmistakable clarity. "Do not misplace it. Do not show it to anyone. And do not make any copies of it. Fail to follow instructions, and the forensic pathologist at the morgue will be busy making copies of your dental records."

It was clearly more than just an ordinary piece of paper.

Jack unfolded the page with shaky, adrenaline-fuelled hands and studied its contents. It featured a black-and-white photograph of a man in his early twenties, accompanied by a list of vital details: a name, flight number, airport terminal, and, last but not least, a local contact telephone number. Judging by his appearance, Jack pegged the mystery man as likely Korean or Thai. Years of pulling beers had given him a pretty keen sense of where people hailed from.

"So who's the kid?" he asked, his curiosity piqued.

"That's unimportant," Magdalena snarled. "You're not required to know anything about him beyond what's on that piece of paper. And don't worry, Jack. There's no closed-book exam at the end of this. Except, perhaps, the one with Saint Peter outside the Pearly Gates, should either of you cock this up."

Jack swallowed hard, his eyes skimming the sparse details on the page once more. The confusion only deepened. What the hell were they being asked to do here? Kidnap the guy? The thought gnawed at him, an icy knot of dread tightening in the pit of his stomach.

"Right. But what's he got to do with us?" he asked.

"I was on the precipice of explaining that, Jack, before I was so rudely interrupted," Magdalena replied, her tone dripping with impatience. "The young man in that photograph is the errand. Collect, babysit, and deliver. Collect him from the airport in the morning, and then while he's in your charge, babysit him for a few hours somewhere out of the way. A location where there's no chance of him interacting with the public ... perhaps, here?"

"Okay. And what about the delivery?" Jack asked.

"Simple. After the police have finished snooping around my penthouse, then and only then will Mark call you using the telephone number on that page to arrange a drop-off at my club. Collect, babysit, and deliver. It's an extremely straightforward proposition."

Nothing in the criminal underworld was ever truly straightforward, nor should anything ever be taken strictly at face value. Everyone seemed to know that, except, apparently, for Hung Van Thanh.

"So, we're chauffeuring a tourist around?" he asked.

Magdalena nodded. "Something like that."

The two friends exchanged a sideways glance, both fully aware that they were long past the theoretical point of no return. Rejecting Magdalena's offer now would only increase the likelihood of Mark introducing fifteen grams of hot lead to their frontal cortices.

"So, what? If we do this ... 'errand' tomorrow, pick the kid up from the airport, look after him, drop him at your club, you'll waive our debt?" Jack asked, scepticism heavy in his voice. "Just like that?"

"Part of it, Jack. Just like that," Magdalena replied.

"Only part of it? Not the whole thing?" Jack pressed.

"Exactly. You don't get far as a moneylender by just waiving debts willy-nilly? Where's the business sense in that?"

With a swift, almost theatrical flourish, Magdalena produced a business card from her jacket, holding it aloft between her slender, impeccably manicured fingers. The card was a masterpiece of minimalist sophistication: 'BLACK' etched in bold white font against a sleek black background, with the address discreetly embossed on the reverse. Magdalena smiled, a glint of mischief dancing in her eyes, before flicking the card onto the table like a spent match. It sliced through the air with effortless precision, spinning on the table as Jack and Hung watched, transfixed, until it slowly came to a stop.

Magdalena checked her wristwatch, her gaze never leaving the men. "The errand's flight from Korea lands in under six hours," she said, a smirk tugging at her lips. "Best get your beauty sleep."

Chapter Eight

The Errand

About six hours later.
Brisbane International Airport.

Jack witnessed a scene that had played out countless times before: waves of dishevelled long-haul passengers flooding the arrivals lounge, like bipedal, suitcase-dragging rats fleeing a sinking ship. Human flotsam surged forward, eager to claim any familiar object or unclaimed patch of *terra firma* in their path. For many, that anchor was a waiting friend or family member armed with flowers and hugs, a balm for the travel-weary soul. For the less fortunate, the ones nobody gave two shits about, familiarity was found in the dull comfort of a watered-down drink at the nearest airport lounge.

Perched beside a bank of orange payphones, Hung decided his energy was better spent admiring a procession of exotic-looking stewardesses sauntering past. Dressed in sleek navy jackets and tailored dresses cinched with red sashes, they radiated effortless poise. The moment unfolded in slow motion, each step stretching out as if it held sway over time and space itself. Unable to resist, Hung raised a feeble, boyish wave, entranced by the parade of plump pouts and immaculate hairdos as they made a beeline for wherever the beautiful sought refuge from the unsightly and unappealing.

"Where do you reckon they're from?" Hung asked.

"Huh?" Jack grumbled, his patience wearing thin as he scanned the crowd, still searching for their elusive passenger.

"Those stewardesses? They must be French, right?"

Jack shot his partner a dark look. "Not to burst your bubble, but you heard what that crazy bitch said last night, right?" Without skipping a beat, Jack held up the page from Magdalena Black, jabbing a finger at the image of a young Korean man with shoulder-length black hair. "Maybe you missed it, seeing as it was around the time Mark shoved a gun to your head ... but Maggie made it clear what'd happen to us if we fuck this up. So Paris, Germany, Timbuktu. It doesn't matter. As stunning as those girls might be, right now, I couldn't give a tinker's toss where they're from."

Hung pouted. "Sorry. I was only trying to—"

"For the record, they were definitely French," Jack said, his eyes scanning a group of middle-aged businessmen. He hoped a young man with long, shaggy hair, probably dressed in civvies, had somehow got lost in the crowd. "Hell, if they were any more French, they'd be carrying baguettes under their arms and tooting clouds of Chanel No.5 from their derrières as they floated on by."

"See? I told you," Hung replied with a grin.

The men watched, transfixed, as the beauties melted into the crowd, their grace fading like a mirage in the chaos of the terminal. Their movements, fluid and seemingly choreographed to a rhythm only they could hear, left behind a trace of perfume and poise that lingered just a beat too long. It held them in a brief trance until reality snapped them back to the bustle, and more importantly, to Magdalena's errand.

Brisbane Domestic Airport.

At the same time Jack and Hung waited for their international arrival, two men loitered in front of a small information kiosk across from the baggage carousels in the domestic terminal. One was young, the other considerably older. Both had matching tan duffle bags slung over their shoulders. The younger of the two was Cyrille, a strikingly handsome man in his late twenties with olive skin and a strong jawline that hinted at a European ancestry. His muscular build was a testament to hours spent in the gym, and his dark eyes held a glint of quiet intensity. He flicked through a stack of 'Discover Queensland' brochures, neatly arranged along the front counter. The images depicted couples cavorting on golden beaches, grommets hanging ten on perfect waves, and children with koalas perched precariously on their arms. The usual sun, surf, and saccharine bullshit that The Sunshine State was all too eager to propagate to the world.

"Fuckin' Queensland," the older man muttered.

"You really hate it here, don't you?" Cyrille replied.

"Queensland's a bit like incest or line dancing," the older man said, his lips curling into a grimace. "It's something you try once, and when you do, it's best not to go blabbing to your mates about it."

The older of the two men was Donald 'The Diamond' Jacobsen, a giant of a man with bulging forearms capable of powering a locomotive and a head of ivory hair fashioned into a military-issue buzz cut. Jacobsen earned the nickname 'The Diamond' on account of the fact that he was harder than a butcher's dick. After two tours of Vietnam with the Royal Australian Artillery in '68 and '71, Donald returned home and found his true calling with Melbourne's notorious Painters and Dockers Union. The same union that the Costigan Commission pinned for taxation and social security fraud, theft on a grand scale, extortion, the handling, and importation of drugs and armaments, along with all manner of violence and murder. And despite The Diamond having a digit in many of those pies, he soon found himself as the go-to when it came to the aforementioned charge of 'all manner of violence and murder'.

"A little sun might do you wonders, Don," Cyrille said.

"This state, and its sun, can politely go fuck itself, lad."

Donald's travel companion sighed and muttered under his breath as he stuffed an assortment of travel brochures back into their respective slots. It was becoming increasingly clear that Cyrille could forget any notions of maintaining his tan while visiting the state that so enthusiastically worshipped the burning sphere in the sky.

"Excuse me, love?" the ivory-haired giant said in a booming voice as he leaned against the counter. Donald's attempt at a conversation starter was directed at a brunette seated behind a terminal.

The young woman stood up, smiling through gritted teeth as she tapped her name badge with a cherry-red fingernail, clearly counting down the seconds until the ordeal reached its merciful conclusion.

"It's Francesca," she replied. "How can I help, sir?"

There was silence, almost as if Donald was in the midst of processing what to do with a seemingly useless piece of trivia such as the woman's name. He looked across at his travel companion, shrugged, and then continued with his enquiry.

"The young blood and I are after some lodgings," he said.

"As in accommodation? Sure, I can help with that." The attendant's piercing gaze swept over Donald's companion in a slow, salacious once-over. He had just the right mix of tall, dark, and handsome to turn the head of anyone with two eyes and a heartbeat. "Any preferences on location or budget, sir? There are plenty of upmarket hotels in the CBD, many just a stone's throw from the casino."

Donald screwed up his face. "Eh? How's that?"

"I beg your pardon?" the attendant replied.

"How's that, then?" Donald repeated, raising his voice.

Cyrille stepped back, tilting his head with a friendly smile as he exaggeratedly pointed to his ear. The attendant's frown deepened in puzzlement before the penny dropped. She studied Donald more closely; her gaze settling on the hearing aid protruding from his right ear, a lingering souvenir of a hangfire incident with a howitzer.

"My apologies," she replied, her voice rising to meet her level of embarrassment. "Do you have a preference for where you'd like to stay while in Brisbane? Perhaps you're interested in visiting a museum? Or attending the third test at The Gabba this week?"

"Do I look I watch bloody cricket?" Donald asked.

"Er, sorry," the attendant replied, quickly realising any response could be a misstep. "I was just trying to get a sense of your plans. If I knew more about what you're hoping to do while you're here, I could point you toward more suitable accommodation. Apologies if I came across as too forward. That wasn't my intention, honestly."

Despite The Diamond's very presence in the state being enough to raise red flags with local law enforcement, keeping quiet about his proclivities to a humble kiosk attendant still seemed excessive. Then again, after dodging more than his fair share of bullets, both literal and figurative, caution had become second nature.

"We just need something cheap and cheerful," he said.

"Alright, let me take a look," the attendant replied.

"Preferably near ... what's it called?" Donald muttered.

"The, uh … Gold Coast," Cyrille added.

The attendant nodded and rifled through a tray of haphazardly organised pamphlets, as if the filing system were some arcane knowledge possessed only by a select few. The men used the lull to scan the terminal for anything out of the ordinary: law enforcement, shady characters, reasonably priced food and drinks. But nothing jumped out at them. For all intents and purposes, it appeared to be a regular, fully functioning domestic terminal. As they turned back, a green pamphlet was thrust toward Donald, who plucked it from the attendant's manicured hand without a moment's hesitation.

"And what's this then, sweetheart?" he asked.

"Accommodation in and around the Gold Coast, courtesy of the tourism board," she replied, eye-fucking Cyrille from across the counter. "Truth is, we're not supposed to show any favouritism or make recommendations, just provide information. Code of ethics, and whatnot. But that's where these lists act as a bit of a loophole. Listings are ordered by average price per night. Of course, prices will vary during peak seasons and special events, like school holidays or, uh … the cricket, but for the most part, they're pretty accurate."

"I see. Define 'pretty accurate'?" Donald asked.

"Updated biannually," the attendant replied.

Donald nodded as he fumbled for the reading glasses in his top pocket. "Hmm. Let me see if I've got this right? Pricier places up top, cheaper ones at the bottom, yeah?" he asked. The attendant nodded, her expression impassive, as though she had delivered this information countless times before. Donald slipped on his glasses and stared at the page for a few seconds, as if trying to decipher a long-dead language. With an anguished grunt, he ran his thick finger to the bottom of the list and tapped the last entry: The Cockatoo Inn. It was so far down the page that the printer had all but given up about three-quarters of the way through the line. Cyrille shot Donald a knowing glance, as if he expected more, and then it came. Donald flipped the pamphlet to check the other side. A brief, unmistakable wave of disappointment washed over him when he saw the back was entirely devoid of text. As far as dubiously named flophouses went, The Cockatoo Inn was as cheap as they came.

"It seems we've got ourselves a winner," he said.

"Wow! That was quick," the attendant replied.

"You know what they say? A quick one's a good one."

The brunette's face contorted as she tried to assign some form of non-sexual context to what was likely a well-known Australianism. When nothing coherent sprang to mind, the attendant did what any rational person might in such a situation; she took a half-step back and silently hoped for an escape from the awkward exchange.

"Um, okay. So, was there anything else I could assist with today?" she asked, trying to keep things strictly professional.

"Depends. Can we keep the pamphlet?" Donald replied.

The attendant gave a small nod of confirmation.

"Then there'll be nothin' else, love," Donald said with a shake of his head, handing the list to his travel companion. Cyrille tucked it into his pocket, flashing Francesca a cheeky, if somewhat apologetic, wink. She returned a bright, albeit puzzled, smile. Before the rosy glow could fully fade from her cheeks, the two men were swept away by a stream of short-haul arrivals, all rushing toward franchise-branded lattes and wanky foreign rental cars.

"So, what's our next move, Don?" Cyrille asked.

Donald grunted. "If I were you, I'd hop on the blower and book us a room at that Cockatoo joint, the cheapest one," he said, pocketing his reading glasses. "And none of that separate room caper, lad. Twin share. Ask about cash discounts too. Tell 'em I'm ex-service."

"Why? Got a touch of jet lag?" Cyrille teased.

"After three hours inside a chunder tube?" he replied. "Nah. I just figure if I spend any longer around these XXXX-drinking mouth-breathers, I'm liable to flip my cart and throttle someone. And as God is my witness, Cyrille, I've got no intention of getting pinched before we have a yarn with the cunt I came here to kill."

Still lingering in a quiet corner of the arrivals lounge, Jack tapped impatiently on the back of a nearby seat, his growing frustration impossible to disguise. The endless parade of unfamiliar faces only amplified his nerves. Beside him, Hung leaned casually against the wall, arms crossed, though the sharp sweep of his gaze betrayed a similar tension. The longer they waited, the more their collective fear took hold. What if they had already missed their man?

Then, just as Jack's anxiety threatened to tip into full-blown panic, a figure emerged from the thinning crowd. Familiar enough to spark a flicker of recognition, yet not quite enough for complete certainty.

"Oi, Hung. Reckon that's him?" he asked, nodding toward the approaching figure with a mix of hope and uncertainty.

"The guy in the Bruce Lee shirt?" Hung replied.

"No, the toddler in the pyjamas. Who do you think?"

The men scrutinised the approaching traveller, their eyes narrowing with focus as they silently assessed every detail: his gait, his posture, and the faint familiarity of his features. They did so with the fervent optimism of a parched man eyeing a shimmering oasis.

"I'm pretty certain that's him," Hung said.

"How certain are we talking here?" Jack replied.

"As in, *almost certain*. Like, ninety-nine percent."

Hung did not deal in ambiguity. His world allowed no room for shades of grey. No margin for error. Everything was black or white, yes or no, one or zero. The notion of "almost certain" simply did not compute in a universe governed by binary absolutes. Jack compared the grainy photograph against the stranger making his way into their line of sight, his eyes flicking back and forth between the image and the man in front of him. This was the closest match in over an hour of people-watching, and right now, Qantas Airways flight QF106 was running low on candidates. It was do or die. Jack had no intention of returning to Magdalena Black with the stench of failure clinging to him. Failure, as Magdalena herself had made abundantly clear, made for an exceedingly uncomfortable existence.

"You know what we should've done?" Hung said.

"Not borrow money from a loan shark?" Jack replied.

"No. Well ... yes," Hung paused, shaking his head. "I mean, what we should have done was make one of those little signs with his name on it. You know, like limousine drivers have in the movies when they're waiting to collect somebody famous from the airport. Heck, I could have broken out the arts and craft supplies."

"Any excuse to get ya glue stick out, huh?"

It was hard to say which was sadder: that a grown man was packing a stash of arts and crafts supplies like a bloody kindergarten teacher, or that nobody had thought of it beforehand. Regardless, their man was edging closer, and with each passing second, the window of opportunity grew smaller. It was now or never. Jack shot a quick look at his partner, checked the name on the page, and took a few measured steps toward the approaching figure, hoping against hope that he was not about to make a colossal dick of himself.

"Excuse me? Are you Chul-Moo?" he said.

There was a visible twig of recognition. Jack repeated himself, this time softening his tone. The traveller paused, cocked his head, and scanned the vicinity. Jack gave a wave to catch his attention. Contact. Chul-Moo smiled and returned a knowing nod. It was confirmation that they had finally found the right man. Like awkward teenagers on a first date, the two men approached each other, the air thick with tentative curiosity as the Korean extended a hand.

"G'day, mates!" he said with boyish enthusiasm.

"Once again, Detective, I must apologise for being such an ineffectual host. Who could have possibly predicted that the ducted air conditioning would fail mere moments before you issued your search warrant?" Magdalena Black mused, her voice laced with calculated charm as she perched on the edge of the lounge. In one hand, she swirled a glass of gin, the ice clinking softly; in the other, an antique Japanese folding fan, which she flicked open with practised ease. She wielded her words like a finely honed weapon, directing them at the sweaty, moustachioed detective supervising a uniformed officer who was clumsily fumbling an irreplaceable Russell Drysdale landscape. Beside her, Becky radiated indifference, reclining with her long legs draped across the loan shark's lap, idly inspecting the police officers scrutinising Magdalena's prized collection of Australian art. Meanwhile, Mark Campbell, the hulking enforcer, loomed nearby, shadowing the dozen-or-so officers as they combed through the luxury apartment. "Try as I might, I was unable to secure the services of an electrician on such short notice. And since the windows are sealed shut up here, well, I guess we'll all just have to suffer through this stifling summer heat together."

The detective maintained his long-running Marcel Marceau impression, now veering into the uncanny, as he silently dabbed the perspiration from his brow with a handkerchief. For a moment, it seemed as if he might speak, but instead, he turned his head, his eyes drifting back to the worker bees buzzing around the room.

Mark gestured at him. "Is your mate always like this?"

"The strong, silent type?" Magdalena replied drily.

"Oh, is that what we're callin' it these days, boss?" Mark smirked. "I always figured 'strong and silent' meant a bit of, uh, brooding menace. Y'know, like Clint Eastwood in those midday Westerns." He cocked his head. "This prick here? Christ. If he were any more silent, someone might just mistake him for a fuckin' coat rack."

Magdalena chuckled and sipped her gin lazily, as if the intrusion was nothing more than a minor disruption to the art of looking effortlessly glamorous. She took another slow sip, set the glass down, and let the silence do its work. Killing the air con was just a petty way to twist the knife, not that it mattered. There was nothing in the penthouse to tie her to anything illegal, real or imagined. Sergeant Hughes' tip-off had seen to that. This was all about making the Gold Coast CIB sweat like a Catholic priest eating a saveloy. The heat kept them motivated, eager to rush through their warrant. And the sooner they tore the place apart, the sooner they would realise they had found two things, Jack and shit, and everyone could get back to their dull little lives.

"By the way, all the relevant paperwork for those paintings is in my safe," Magdalena said smoothly, amusement curling at the edges of her voice. "And besides, Detective, I would be mortified if you found your smoking gun, literal or figurative, behind one of my Drysdales. Doubly so, given my legal counsel, who is en route as we speak, has made it abundantly clear that I have no knowledge of, ah ... ?"

"Jimmy Jacobsen," her enforcer chimed in.

"Yes, this Jimmy Whats-his-face character," she said with an airy wave of her hand. "And any insinuation to the contrary would be tantamount to slander. I'm a legitimate business-woman, Detective, not some street thug offing people like it's suddenly en vogue."

Regardless, the detective's search warrant bore the signature of a respected Supreme Court judge with a liberal-enough interpretation of the Police Powers and Responsibilities Act. As long as there were reasonable grounds to suspect a crime had been committed, or would be within the next seventy-two hours, the search of Magdalena's penthouse was entirely legitimate. Objections be damned. All the trio could do was sit back and watch the spectacle unfold: a theatre of procedure laced with thinly veiled hostility, as the uniformed officers toiled in the stifling Queensland heat.

And then, without warning, all hell broke loose.

Ring ding ding ding ding ding ...

Ring ding ding ding ding ding ...

Ring ding ding ding bem bem bem ...

"Fuck me with a pawpaw. What's that racket?" Mark grimaced as a grating, high-pitched revving sound tore through the lounge room, followed by an off-key, manic yodel: equal parts demented cartoon and synthesised war crime. It was so shrill, so obnoxiously persistent, it could make a man confess to sins he had not yet even considered committing, just to make the god-awful torture stop.

Ring ding ding ding ding ding ...
Ring ding ding ding bem bem bem ...

The entire universe seemed to come to a screeching halt. Everyone froze, their attention snapping to Magdalena: the constables halted their meticulous combing, the detective abandoned his Marcel Marceau impression, Mark stopped his shadowing, and Becky? Well, Becky stopped doing whatever it was she so frequently did ... which, to the untrained eye, was utterly imperceptible.

Ring ding ding ding bem bem bem ...
Ring ding ding ding ding ding ...
Ring ding ding ding bem bem bem ...

Mark scanned the room, his brow furrowing as the ghastly noise persisted. The cacophony seemed to emanate from Magdalena herself, drawing collective confusion, except for Becky, who stifled a snicker into a nearby cushion. The unmistakable twang of a novelty ringtone, sharp, jarring, and wildly out of place, filled the air.

Magdalena shot a withering glance at the cackling blonde draped over her lap before muttering something indecipherable. The source of the racket became painfully clear: it was blaring from her own jacket pocket, discarded over the back of the lounge in defiance of the heat. She winced, shaking her head. For a woman who revelled in being the centre of attention, she was turning redder than the drought-stricken landscape in one of her beloved paintings.

Ring ding ding ding bem bem bem ...
Ring ding ding ding ding ding ...

"I told you never to touch my telephone, did I not?" she said. "This is a business tool, Becky, not some Fisher-Price toy."

Becky continued to cackle into her cushion.

Magdalena brushed Becky's legs off her lap with an irritated swipe. Her patience, already paper-thin, was on the verge of snapping. "Mark, keep an eye on our guests while I take this call out on the balcony. We both know how the police operate around here. Let your guard down for a second, and they'll plant a kilogram of narcotics in your unmentionables drawer. Eagle eyes, yes?"

The henchman gave an exaggerated thumbs-up.

Ring ding ding ding ding ding ...

Ring ding ding ding bem bem bem ...

Magdalena tossed her folding fan onto Becky's lap and rose from the lounge, gin still in hand. Retrieving her phone from her jacket pocket, she departed the room with the unhurried grace of a seasoned catwalk model. Her tight, well-rehearsed smile barely masked the simmering irritation beneath her composed exterior. As she glided past a cluster of officers, they instinctively parted like the Red Sea, not without enduring her biting remarks about their apparent enthusiasm for romantic entanglements with livestock, all delivered with her trademark cutting nonchalance.

Reaching the sun-bleached balcony, Magdalena slid the glass door shut behind her, blocking out the chaos inside. Without so much as a glance at the million-dollar views stretching to the horizon, she let out a pensive sigh and brought the phone to her ear.

"Uh ... hello? Miss Black? Is that you?" came a familiar voice, hesitant yet unmistakable. "It's, uh, Jack Perkins ... "

"Jack Perkins?" Magdalena repeated, eyebrow raised.

"From The Hackston Tavern," he added.

Given that Magdalena was using a burner phone, one only Jack had the number for, introductions seemed unnecessary.

"Oh shit," Jack muttered. "We're not supposed to—"

"Not supposed to what?" Magdalena cut in, her tone sharp.

"You know … use our real names on the phone."

The loan shark shook her head. "It's a bit late for furtive acts of self-preservation now, don't you think, 'Jack Perkins from The Hackston Tavern'?" The words slipped out before she could remind herself just how far down the list of candidates she had to go to end up with the idiot on the other end of the line. "So? You've come this far, Jack. Spit it out. What is it you so desperately need to talk to me about while the police are executing a search warrant on my penthouse? And it better be important. Because between that cow yucking it up on my lounge and that fucking Crazy Frog, I've been made to look like a right turkey in front of the local constabulary."

Jack paused for an inordinate amount of time, presumably struggling to process the menagerie of animal-based follies that had befallen Magdalena's pristine existence.

"There's a crazy … turkey?" he replied, baffled.

"A crazy turkey? What? No. Jesus Christ."

"Huh? Sorry, but didn't you just say—"

"No, forget about fucking turkeys, Jack!"

Magdalena sighed and pressed the phone to her forehead, stepping closer to the balcony edge. She peered over it, weighing whether hurling herself off would be less agonising than enduring another second of this mind-numbing conversation. Her gaze flicked between the two-hundred-metre drop below and her shoes, then back again. She sighed, deeper this time, contemplative. Suicide was one thing, but condemning a pair of Christian Louboutin open-toe pumps to such an undignified fate was an entirely different matter.

"I have little doubt you were a product of the public education system, Jack, so I shan't waste time asking how robust your French is," she began, "but, in keeping with the French tradition of making existential despair sound sexier than a Brigitte Bardot film festival, they coined this transcendentally poetic phrase: *l'appel du vide*. It translates to 'the call of the void', but at its core, it encapsulates those fleeting, self-destructive impulses: the sudden urge to swerve into oncoming traffic, step off a high-rise, or, worse, vote Labor, despite having no real suicidal intent."

Jack took a moment to let that factoid sink in, wondering if it would be on tomorrow's exam. After a beat, he opened his mouth to say something, anything, but faltered. His words dissolved into an awkward silence. His mind grasped for a thread, any thread, but without the gift of clairvoyance, none presented itself. What, in the name of all things holy, did any of this have to do with the price of eggs in China ... or more importantly, some kid from Korea?

"So, do we have a problem?" Magdalena asked.

"Er, what?" Jack replied, still floundering.

"Do we have a problem?" Magdalena repeated.

"Well ... no. Not really, it's just that—"

"Then what is the purpose of this call? This number was not provided to you for idle chitchat whenever the mood strikes. You were advised to wait for Mark's call." Magdalena pinched the bridge of her nose and exhaled slowly, rubbing her forehead as if trying to massage away the mounting irritation. She silently counted to three, her patience hanging by a thread. "What do you want, imbecile?"

"Uh ... just to see ... if, uh—" Jack stammered.

"See what? For the love of God, use your words!"

"To ... see ... to see if anything's changed."

"To what exactly, Jack? A simple three-point plan devised no more than eight hours ago?" Magdalena replied, her tone biting. She glanced through the sliding glass doors, where uniformed officers were rummaging through her meticulously curated collection of first-edition books. The sight alone was enough to make her blood boil, but she maintained her composure. Turning away, she took a deep breath to steady herself. "Nothing has changed," she said firmly. "I instructed you to wait for a call from Mark. And Mark only. All existing stipulations stand: the Korean is not to speak to anyone, he is not to call anyone, and he is not to leave your sight. Absolutely no deviations."

Later that morning, Jack's powder-blue Datsun rattled down the Pacific Highway, swallowed by the shimmering asphalt stretching endlessly ahead. Traffic crawled, the mid-morning heat seeping into the car's interior despite the windows being cranked down as far as they would go. Sweat clung to the back of Jack's neck, his grip loose on the wheel, fingers drumming idly on the gear stick. His expression lingered somewhere between boredom and irritation, eyes shifting between his cargo, the sluggish traffic, and the warped horizon.

Beside him, Hung sat with his arms folded, gaze locked on the road ahead, suspiciously silent. In the back seat, Chul-Moo had his head on a swivel, taking in the sporadic clusters of houses and petrol stations that broke up the long, sunbaked stretches of bushland. Compared to the towering glass monoliths and relentless energy of his native Seoul, this no man's land between Brisbane and the Gold Coast must have looked like the arse-end of the universe.

Jack made the mistake of glancing at the rear-view mirror just as Chul-Moo did the same. The Korean's face split into a bright, disarming smile, his body language practically screaming with eagerness to break the silence. Maybe if Jack ignored him, the kid would take the hint. His grip tightened on the wheel, jaw clenched. He flicked a glance at Hung, then back at Chul-Moo. Shit. This was exactly what Magdalena had warned them against. Nobody, absolutely nobody, was to talk to the Korean. And as far as Jack was concerned, that directive applied to them, too.

"May I bother you?" Chul-Moo asked casually.

Jack cleared his throat. "Uh … sure," he replied.

It was hard to deny the kid an audience; he had the effortless good looks of a movie star and a smile that could turn the tide. Maybe Chul-Moo was some B-list celebrity on a whirlwind tour, promoting Magdalena's nightclub. Then again, Jack had his doubts, especially when she had them chauffeuring the kid around in such a clandestine manner. But how was Jack supposed to know? He was just a beer-slinging troglodyte with zero interest in pop culture, hardly the target demographic for a *Women's Weekly* subscription.

"How much farther to our destination?" Chul-Moo asked, glancing at his wristwatch as if he had somewhere more important to be.

"Um, another twenty or so minutes?" Jack replied.

Normally, the drive from the airport to the Gold Coast took about 45 minutes, give or take. But with South East Queensland's never-ending love affair with roadworks, the trio would be lucky to reach The Hackston any faster than if they had hoofed it.

"Why's that?" Jack asked. "Keen to take a slash?"

Chul-Moo blinked. "Er … taking a … slash?"

"Uh, yeah. I mean … you know? Havin' a piss."

The blank stare suggested otherwise.

"Shakin' hands with the wife's best friend?"

Chul-Moo's brow furrowed. "I … do not unders—"

"Pointing Private Percy at the porcelain?"

Not even the faintest hint of comprehension.

Realising his toiletry interrogation had been lost in translation, Jack quickly looked away and refocused on the road ahead. Until now, the trip back to civilisation had been spent in relative silence, save for a mixtape nearly as ancient as Jack's ride. Recorded straight from Triple J in an era before youth radio devolved into hip-hop bullshit, it was two reels of Gen-X bliss, encapsulating the halcyon days of Aussie alt-rock: Spiderbait, Grinspoon, Silverchair, Regurgitator, The Superjesus.

It was not until halfway through TISM's seminal 1986 masterpiece, 'Defecate On My Face', that Hung finally abandoned his self-imposed silence. He locked eyes with Chul-Moo in the rear-view mirror, his expression shifting from disinterest to intent, like a Pulitzer Prize-winning journalist about to pounce on a scandal.

"I don't get it," Hung began. "Why fly all the way here to meet Miss Black? Like, you could've just messaged her, right? That's what my cousins and I do. Every Sunday night, we hop into a chatroom and catch up. Seems like it would've been simpler than ... all this."

Before the words had even settled, Jack shot daggers at his partner, as if he had just committed the cardinal sin of roundhousing a pregnant woman at a baby shower. Hung had not merely crossed the line, he had tripped, face-planted, and skidded ten feet past it.

"You don't have to answer that, mate," Jack replied.

"No, it is fine, really," Chul-Moo said calmly.

Jack shook his head. "It's very much not," he pressed, his gaze a warning to Hung: either change the subject or, better yet, shut it.

Hung scowled for a moment before his mind shifted into overdrive, preparing his next ill-advised question. Jack could almost hear the gears grinding in his friend's jug-eared head as he sifted through a mental catalogue of conversation starters, each one more likely to get them killed than to earn them a lasting friendship. Jack doubled down, hoping a piercing glare might help stave off the inevitable. But, like most things in his life lately, it failed spectacularly.

"Any idea what your name means?" Hung finally asked, his tone innocent, yet tinged with something more probing.

Jack exhaled sharply, barely keeping his anger in check. Short of tossing his partner from a moving vehicle, it seemed like this getting-to-know-you session was going to happen whether Jack liked it or not. All he could do was try to limit the damage.

"I assume they do the whole etymology thing in Korea," Hung continued, scratching his head as he fumbled for the right words. "See, my family moved to Australia toward the end of the war. You know, back in the seventies. And since I was the first of my siblings born here, in their new adoptive country, my parents named me 'Hung'. It means 'courage' in Vietnamese," he added with a small smile. "It's just one of those ... I dunno ... Eastern traditions from back home. Most names have some kind of meaning behind them."

"Even the Western ones?" Chul-Moo asked.

"Even the boring Western ones? Like 'Jack' here."

Jack: a diminutive of John that originated in the Hebrew language and meant 'man who bought a pub with an idiot'.

Chul-Moo's bilingual brain lingered on the origins of his name, a faint curiosity gnawing at him. He had never really considered it before, but now, as Hung spoke, he found himself wondering if there was more to it than just a legacy passed down through generations. "I see," he began, pausing for a moment.

"Chul-Moo is a very old name. The meaning may vary depending on the hanja characters used, but in your English, I believe the translation to be 'iron weapon'."

"What? Like a sword or something?" Hung asked.

"Axes too," Chul-Moo replied matter-of-factly.

Hung let out a low whistle. "Geez, that's cool," he said, stroking his chin as he reflected on his own parents' far less fearsome approach to naming. "Did you catch that, Jack?"

The question dangled in the air, but Jack refused to take the bait. His knuckles tightened around the wheel, eyes darting between the road and the rear-view mirror. A massive B-double loomed beside them, its giant frame swaying unpredictably as it inched forward, forcing Jack to cling to the left lane. His focus sharpened, not on the conversation, but on the truck that could reduce them to an unkempt roadside memorial with a single wrong move.

"Got that outta your system?" Jack finally muttered, just as the B-double thundered past, its roar fading into the distance.

Hung grimaced. "Got what out of my system?"

"The stupid bloody questions," Jack replied.

Insulted, Hung crossed his arms like a sulking toddler, his gaze fixed on the passing landscape as Jack's mixtape blared, now loud enough to make it clear the driver was not in the mood for any more questions. Sun-scorched fields and scrubby bushland blurred past the windows, the horizon stretching endlessly ahead, a shimmering mirage of heat and dust as they pressed on homeward.

For a few peaceful minutes, silence stretched between the trio, thick and unyielding, mirroring the highway ahead. Hung sat stiffly, arms crossed, his gaze fixed on the blur beyond the window. Every so often, his lips parted, only to press shut again, as if the words had second thoughts. Then, out of nowhere, he let out a deep, reluctant exhale, half frustration, half surrender, and finally turned to Chul-Moo in the backseat.

"What's with the whole North versus South thing, anyway?" he asked. "Which one's the 'bad' Korea? I can never remember."

Jack reflexively elbowed his partner in the ribs. Idle chit-chat was one thing; delving into the complexities of Southeast Asian geopolitics was another matter entirely. Chul-Moo smiled through his obvious confusion as Hung leaned across to Jack, lowering his voice.

"What the hell was that for?" Hung asked.

"You know damn well what that was for," Jack muttered, his voice low enough to be swallowed by the alt-rock soundtrack. "No one talks to that kid, yeah? And I mean no one. Not even us. So, no more prying into why he's here, no more waffling on about swords, none of that. And absolutely no more political crap either. Got it?"

"But ... it's not like he's a serial killer or any—"

"Am I speaking bloody Swahili here?" Jack shot back, eyes flicking to the road. "I don't give a rat's rectum if he's Harold-bloody-Holt and just crawled out of Cheviot Beach with a midget sub hanging out of his clacker. Not our circus, not our monkeys. Everything about that kid is on a need-to-know basis, and guess what? We don't need to friggin' know. That's straight from Magdalena Black herself."

"But can't we just find out—" Hung started.

"No! Eyes on the road, mouth shut!"

Hung scowled and turned to the window, his jaw tightening as he glared at the passing scenery, racking his brain for a witty comeback. Something sharp, something that would shut Jack up for once. But nothing came. So he just sulked in silence, staring out at the road.

Detective Constable Barry Gamble stood watch beside the mailbox of a rundown house in an equally rundown neighbourhood. The fibro and cinderblock façade was pockmarked with years of neglect, its walls stained with grime and weathered to a dull grey. The roof sagged under the weight of time, a few tiles missing, exposing the raw timber beneath. The front yard, more a wild tangle of weeds than grass, was littered with the skeletal remains of rusted play equipment and broken furniture. A once-loved trampoline had been reduced to a jagged frame, its fabric long shredded and blown away. A torn, faded curtain fluttered from an open window, barely clinging to its rod, as if it, too, were struggling to hold on.

In real estate parlance, it was a real 'fixer-upper'. To everyone else, it was two spoons and a candle short of a crack den.

Sprawled across the overgrown lawn was Neville, an unconscious drug dealer in his late twenties, his wiry frame twisted where it had landed. His face was a ruin of fresh bruises and split flesh. One eye was already swelling shut, his bottom lip split wide open. A trail of blood leaked from his nose, pooling in the grass beneath him. Glass shards clung to his clothes and bare arms, catching the early-morning sun like flecks of shaved ice. His once-white tank top was smeared with crimson, a grim mosaic of brutal violence and questionable life choices. The shattered bedroom window above him stood as a silent witness to the chaos that had just unfolded moments earlier.

"That fucking ... fuck ... cunt!" Detective Sergeant Mick Hughes bellowed, booting the tattered flyscreen door open in a fit of rage. He stormed outside, his right hand clenched in a claw-like spasm. Pain tugged at the corner of his mouth as he lumbered forward, the dull throb of his recent misdeeds pulsing through his knuckles.

"Was that n-ne-necessary, Sarge?" Gamble asked, flicking a quick glance over his shoulder for any witnesses before wading in for a front-row seat to the shitshow of the century.

"Which part?" Hughes said, feigning innocence.

"The part where you launched Nev here through a plate-glass window in full view of the neighbourhood."

Hughes shrugged. "When you put it like that, it probably was a tad excessive," he said with a grin, clearly anything but remorseful.

Gamble sighed and paced the patchy, overgrown lawn, hands on his hips, exhaling sharply through his nose. The morning heat pressed down, thick with the smell of damp earth and something faintly chemical. He could feel the neighbourhood's eyes on him, peering through tattered curtains and half-closed blinds, drinking in the spectacle like a pisshead flogging a bar tab at a work Christmas function. Meanwhile, his partner crouched over the battered drug dealer, rifling through his pockets with the casual efficiency of a man who had done this a thousand times before, completely indifferent to who was watching. Looking for leads? Probably. Cash? More likely.

"Did he say anything at least?" Gamble asked.

"Eh. Nothin' worth a pinch of shit," Hughes muttered.

"Come on, the bloke must've said ... something."

Hughes finished rummaging and got to his feet. "Well, nothing about any Koreans, anyhow," he said, eyeing the pulverised, mullet-sporting lump at his feet as he tucked a few baggies of something questionable into his sock. "Soon as I stepped inside, he started blubbering about that Jacobsen kid getting clipped last week. Poor prick must've been hitting the glass barbecue so hard this morning he thought I was the Grim fuckin' Reaper himself."

"Jacobsen? As in Jimmy Jacobsen?" Gamble asked.

Hughes nodded his head slowly, picking at his teeth with the indifference only a man who gave zero shits could muster.

"And get this, he reckons we did it," he replied.

"What?" Gamble asked, raising an eyebrow.

"Yeah. The gospel according to fuckhead here was that Jimmy's uncle used to be some big swinging dick with the unions. Down Melbourne way. No idea what that's got to do with us, but as you can see, our mate wasn't exactly in the sharing mood."

Gamble's head swam as he tried to connect the dots.

"He thinks ... *we* ... killed Jacobsen?" he asked.

"The royal 'we', you cock," Hughes replied.

"But still, the police? As in ... the Gold Coast police?"

"Well, I doubt he meant Sting and Stewart Copeland."

Hughes eyed his partner, waiting for a chuckle. Or at the very least, some sign that his quip had landed. Nothing.

"Of course, none of that work of fiction makes any sense, especially since Flannery's team already has Maggie in the frame for that one," Hughes continued. "Hell, they're probably still tossing her joint as we speak. Fucker plays his cards close to his chest, Baz, like he doesn't trust me. And rightly so."

Gamble turned his back on the chaos, running a hand through his curly black hair. None of the usual suspects had the foggiest about the extracurricular activities of any Koreans, and the longer that missing piece remained out of reach, the wider Hughes' trail of destruction grew. It was time for Gamble to rein in his superior. Or, at the very least, steer him away from any more local miscreants in need of a little wristwatch-induced attitude adjustment.

"This is all getting messy, Sarge," he began. "I know you're keen on getting back into Maggie's good books, but we're scraping the bottom of the barrel when it comes to leads on this tourist. And from what we've seen in the last few hours, I'd say that barrel's pretty much bone dry. Heck, we've had more leads on the Jacobsen shooting than on whatever story Conrad sold us. Let's face it, this whole thing's been a wild goose chase from the get-go."

"Bullshit. We're getting close," Hughes replied.

"Are we though?" Gamble asked as he straightened his tie. "I'm not trying to be funny or anything, but I don't see any Koreans around here. Do you? And I definitely don't remember spotting any Koreans at the three other houses we hit this morning. In fact, nobody we've talked to knows a damn thing about any Koreans. Just admit it, Mick, either that bloke lying at your feet deserves a Gold Logie for playing dumb, or, well, your former brother-in-law was … "

"Talkin' out of his fucking arse?" Hughes said.

Gamble nodded. "Your words, not mine."

Detective Hughes paused, retrieving his aviators from his collar as he surveyed what remained of the neighbourhood. It looked like a twisted version of his childhood stomping grounds, thousands of kilometres away and two decades removed. Where once there had been neatly manicured lawns and picket fences, only overgrown grass and rusting car bodies remained. Chalk drawings on footpaths had long since given way to graffiti on abandoned houses. The sounds of children playing had all but faded into memory, replaced by an oppressive silence that could never be unheard.

This once-pristine suburb had been transformed by shifting demographics, and any holdouts, those too brave or foolish to sell their homes years ago, now found themselves trapped in a claustrophobic maze of methamphetamine and indifference.

"Barry, is your mum's VCR still on the blink?" Hughes asked, the sudden change of subject catching his partner off guard.

"Huh? Uh ... I think so. Why?" Gamble replied.

"Because there's one name left on my list of villains."

"Oh yeah? Who, Sarge? My dear old mum?"

Gamble took a moment to piece it together. When the realisation finally hit, a shiver crawled up his spine, slithering from the base of his neck to the small of his back. The discomfort was immediate, undeniable. Hughes, ever the opportunist, seized on it in an instant, flashing him a smug, knowing look of satisfaction.

"Sorry, big fella," Hughes said, his apology thick with insincerity. "I know how much you hate stepping foot in that shop of his, but like you said, we're spinning our wheels here. Granted, The Pom might not be in the same league as Magdalena Black, not like his old man used to be, but he's definitely got his finger on the pulse of what's going down on the Goldie, that much is for bloody sure."

Gamble sighed and bit his lip before responding, his voice low and measured. "Maybe so. But that shop ought to be condemned."

"Come on," Hughes said with a smile. "It ain't that bad."

"It's not exactly that good either, is it, Mick?"

Hughes shrugged. "Bah. All adds to the charm."

Charm? The monstrosity known as The Exchange, aka Irish's, aka The Pom's, was one stiff breeze away from caving in, sagging under its own weight. The water damage had left stains on the ceiling that looked like abstract art gone wrong, each drooping sag a silent promise of impending collapse. It crawled with cockroaches, and black mould thrived in every corner, thick and stubborn, as though it owned the place. If that was what Hughes considered 'charm', then Dame Edna Everage was the Queen of bloody England. Gamble muttered to himself, pacing a few steps around the scene, the weight of the situation pressing down on him. His eyes flicked back to the drug dealer, now conscious and shifting weakly on the lawn. Ragged breaths rattled from the man's chest, each exhale a struggle, and his sluggish movements only highlighted the pain he was clearly in.

"Oi. Don't even spare that joker the time of day," Hughes said, his tone low and flat. With the exception of a few curious onlookers still peering through drawn curtains, the commotion of a deadshit being throttled within an inch of their life and then thrown through a window barely raised an eyebrow in this neighbourhood anymore. "Doubt anyone around here's gonna call uniform, but just in case, I suggest we skedaddle. It might all look a little, uh, *Fight Club* if we rock up and start taking statements for a crime we committed ourselves."

"A crime *you* committed, Sarge," Gamble interjected.

"You. We. Me. Potato, fuckin' potahto, mate."

Hughes chuckled, turning away as he walked off, as if this kind of public clusterfuck was second nature to him. Gamble, however, hesitated, a flicker of conscience tugging at him. His steps slowed, reluctant, and his gaze drifted back to the groaning figure on the lawn. This was light years away from why he had joined the force, and right now, he would have happily put another million between himself and the jumped-up little arsehole calling the shots.

"P-po-police ... br-brutality ... " a voice spluttered.

The detectives stopped dead in their tracks.

"That's p-police brutality," the voice rasped again.

Neville's bloodied face glared up at them from the tangle of overgrown weeds and shattered glass, eyes glazed but still locked defiantly onto Hughes. For a moment, the detective lingered. A bigger man might have let it go, might have walked away, but Mick Hughes was rarely the bigger man, in either temperament or stature. Before his partner could talk him down, the diminutive redhead had already closed the distance, striding back across the nature strip with building intensity. He knelt beside the dealer, his next move all but decided.

"What the fuck'd you say?" Hughes growled.

"You h-he-heard me, arsehole," the dealer replied.

Hughes grabbed a fistful of Neville's greasy mullet, yanking it back as far as the human body would allow. "Nah, didn't catch it," he said. "I was too busy thinking about how this used to be a quiet street. A street full of decent, hard-working folks just trying to make a living. Families. Kids in the park, frying meat ants with magnifying glasses. Carefree abandon. Basically, just a bunch of boring pricks going about their day without having to worry about shitheels skulking around, trying to sell their ankle-biters a few grams on the sly."

The dealer spluttered something vaguely incoherent, his words mangled by a mouthful of broken teeth and claret-soaked vowels, each syllable a garbled mess of muted pain and defiance.

"What's that, Lassie? Timmy's trapped in a well?" Hughes leaned in closer, his breath hot and fetid against the dealer's ear. "Nobody gives a fuck what you've got to say for yourself, cunt." He wrenched the dealer's head around, forcing him to take in the nearby houses. "Go on, have a good look. See anyone rushing out to help? Nah. Didn't think so. Truth is, no one gives a single solitary shit about some slimy ice-slinger finally getting what's coming to him."

As the detective spat his rebuke, flecks of saliva peppered Neville's face like a fistful of buckshot. The rancid stench of his breath, stale coffee and rot, clung to the humid mid-morning air, thick enough to taste. But before it could settle, the dealer met Hughes' gaze, eyes glinting with the promise of a retort.

"Copper ... how about you g-g-go—" he began.

"Go what?" Hughes prompted, anticipating the punchline.

"G-go ... go ... fuck yourself," Neville stammered.

Without a moment of conscious thought, Hughes yanked Neville's head back, a shit-eating grin spreading across his face before ... *CRACK!* The sickening hollow sound of cranium hitting *terra firma* echoed down the street, sharp and brutal. The dealer's body jerked violently, a guttural wail ripping from his throat as blood surged from deep within, staining the ground beneath him.

CRACK! Another blow landed, its echo slicing through the air with sickening precision. Hughes' voice, low and venomous, followed, dripping with malice. "You're a fuckin' parasite!"

CRACK! The third strike hit, louder, a violent punctuation to his words. "A steaming turd on the footpath of society!"

CRACK! A fourth sickening blow, the force savage enough to rattle bones and make the earth itself tremble. "If I stepped in you walkin' down the street, I'd go burn my fuckin' shoes!"

With a savage growl, Hughes tightened his grip, Neville's neck a brittle twig in his hands. A sinister grin spread across his face, eyes blazing with sadistic anticipation, as he prepared for what could very well be the final act in his brutal, blood-soaked house call.

"Christ, enough already!" Gamble barked, stepping forward, his hands jerking to a halt like they were caught in a stop-motion frame, stiff and unnatural as they reached out in a desperate bid to intervene. "Keep it up, Mick, and you're gonna kill the bloke!"

Hughes froze, his eyes narrowing into slits as he turned to glare at his partner. The look was primal, like a lion staring down a trespasser ballsy enough to snatch an antelope from its jaws.

"And who'd give a fuck if I did?" Hughes growled.

"I'd give a fuck, Mick. That's who!" Gamble replied.

Mr Catholic School had dropped the F-bomb. This was serious. So serious, in fact, that the mere utterance short-circuited Hughes' baser instincts. With a thud, he released the dealer's hair, letting his head flop onto the blood-soaked concrete, then wiped the greasy residue on his pants. As he rose to his feet, the detective could feel the eyes of the entire neighbourhood searing into him.

Hughes had their full, undivided attention. He was the conductor of his own symphony of chaos, orchestrating each violent note with chilling precision. Every footstep, every beat, every breath was part of his performance; a twisted dance of brutality and dominance. The quiet of the suburban street, interrupted only by the dealer's groans, gave way to a heavy tension, as if the entire block was holding its breath, waiting for the next movement in his ruthless composition.

And then came the sickening finale ... *CRUNCH!*

A brutal stomp to the dealer's head knocked him out cold.

"Now *that's* police brutality!" Hughes sneered.

Chapter Nine

The Cardinal Rule

Later that afternoon.

The Cockatoo Inn was the archetypal roach-infested motel on the outskirts of the Gold Coast, although calling it *roach*-infested was arguably generous, given the cockroaches had long since been overthrown by a more aggressive bedbug regime. Wedged between the hinterland and the city's gaudy sprawl, the place was cheap, quiet, and most importantly, out of sight. It was the kind of no-questions-asked establishment where two, or even three, like-minded individuals could rent a room by the hour and indulge in whatever consensual activities floated their collective boats.

Not that there was anything wrong with that.

The complex comprised five self-contained cabins, each about as spacious as a tinker's shoebox, with a white demountable manager's office tucked behind a comically oversized car park. The lot was so ambitious it made the place look permanently deserted. Between the cracked expanse of asphalt, guests who preferred not to be seen within a bull's roar of such a shady shithole, and the complete lack of a working pool or gym, despite what the signage claimed, The Cockatoo Inn had a serious image problem.

"An absolute dive"—4WD Travel Magazine.

In the middle of that comically oversized car park, Donald 'The Diamond' Jacobsen leaned against their rental car, soaking up all the creature comforts fifty-five bucks a night afforded. Sure, it did not look like much, but for a pair of colourful characters trying to stay off the radar, it ticked enough of the right boxes. He waited patiently as his offsider strolled back from the manager's office, twirling the room key around his finger like a roided-up cowboy with a six-shooter.

"Which room did you snag, lad?" Donald asked.

Cyrille grinned and held up five meaty digits.

Tucked at the very end of the complex, cabin five offered the pair a tactical trifecta: fewer nosy neighbours, a clear sightline to the road, and a quick escape route if things went tits-up. Cyrille had chosen it in honour of the wisdom Donald had drilled into him over the years. Control your exits. Never give the enemy more angles than necessary. And, if possible, sleep with your boots by the door.

"Fine choice," Donald said, a flicker of pride in his voice.

"Thanks, Don. But, uh ... yeah," Cyrille muttered.

"But what? You ask about any pensioner discount?"

"Yeah. I asked. Just ... mind if I speak freely?"

The question hung in the air, unanswered. Given the state of the old man's hearing, it was entirely possible it had slipped through to the keeper. Just as Cyrille was about to repeat himself, a gravelly grunt cut through the silence. It was apathetic enough to be mistaken for disinterest, but close enough to pass for actual consent.

"Uh ... okay," Cyrille continued, nudging a discarded cigarette butt with his foot as he gathered his thoughts. "I know we're supposed to keep things on the down low. I get that, Don. Really, I do. But ... shit, I'm just gonna say it. This place sucks."

Donald surveyed the immediate surroundings while Cyrille rattled off a laundry list of grievances with The Cockatoo Inn, everything from a dead rat out front of the manager's office to used condoms strewn across the car park. And as for the filthy pair of jocks flapping on the roof of cabin two, well, the less said, the better. Donald sighed and nodded along, feigning interest, despite not giving the aforementioned dead rat's arse. Sure, the place could have used a lick of paint and a little TLC, but it had four walls and a roof. And right now, that was all he needed. Everything else was a luxury.

"And don't start me on that *thing* in the manager's office."

"What? You mean the manager?" Donald replied.

Cyrille scowled and nodded enthusiastically.

"You know how I feel about slobs," he said. "Like, bud, show your body some respect. How hard is it to do an hour of cardio each day? Cut out junk food. Eat a salad. Drink lots of water. Hell, try running a bloody comb through your greasy hair while you're at it."

Donald remained silent, one eyebrow raised. If not for the buzz of a nearby fluorescent sign, the chirp of crickets might have filled the void. With a grimace, he pushed himself off the side of the sedan. There was no point in getting comfortable. The longer he stayed still, the harder it was to shake the rust from his old bones.

"I just mean," Cyrille continued, "if he keeps his motel anything like he keeps himself ... well ... Jesus, I don't even—"

"Hmm. Are you just about finished?" Donald asked.

"Huh? Finished with what, Don?" Cyrille replied.

"Your constant bloody whinge-talking, for starters."

Cyrille grumbled under his breath and popped the boot. The hinges let out a tortured groan, as if even the car had second thoughts about being there. He stared at the two olive-green duffle bags inside, quietly cursing himself for ever opening his big mouth. For the supposed muscle, Cyrille spent a suspicious amount of time hauling luggage and making tea. Not that the old codger needed backup. Short of all-out warfare erupting on their doorstep, there was little an old campaigner like the Diamond could not handle on his Pat Malone. And if it came to all-out warfare? Nothing screamed human shield quite like a meathead in a singlet and a pair of ADIDAS trackpants.

"Mind the mess," Jack said as he opened the door to their humble flat above The Hackston, ushering Chul-Moo inside with the sheepish smile of someone revealing an embarrassing secret. "We weren't exactly expecting company, so, er, please don't go home thinking the average Aussie lives in a hovel over a pub. It's just a, uh ..."

"A temporary arrangement," Hung chimed in.

"Yeah, exactly. At least until we're back on our feet."

What both men had carefully avoided mentioning was that their so-called "temporary" arrangement was anything but. In truth, they had spent three excruciating years living in each other's pockets. The space was the very definition of utilitarian: a multipurpose lounge room, a pokey kitchen, an even pokier laundry nook, a single bedroom (which Jack had claimed), a toilet, and a musty utility room that doubled as Hung's makeshift boudoir. The air hung heavy with the stale stench of cigarettes, and the walls, once white, had taken on the jaundiced hue of decades' worth of neglect and nicotine.

"You have a pleasant home," Chul-Moo said.

Jack blinked. "Uh ... thank you? I think?"

Chul-Moo's eyes lingered on every detail of the flat. It was not curiosity born of polite obligation, but a genuine interest, as if he were trying to decipher the stories woven into the mismatched op-shop furniture and retro-sixties charm. He took in the faded floral curtains, the dirty dishes, and the tattered lounge with an almost clinical gaze, as though the space held some kind of provenance.

"Grab a pew," Jack said, motioning toward the entertainment-cum-dining room. "Just avoid that cushion on the left ... well, not unless you fancy getting a spring up the clacker."

The Korean raised an eyebrow, still trying to make sense of Jack's words. Now was not the time for a crash course in Aussie slang. Jack gestured toward the lounge again, and after a pause, their guest took the hint, easing into the seat with a reluctant wince. Jack and Hung followed. The silence stretched, thick and awkward, until Jack's long-dormant publican instincts finally kicked in.

"You must be thirsty," Jack said. "Want a cold beer? Maybe a scotch? Or if you're off the hard stuff, we've got orange juice on tap."

Chul-Moo smiled and politely shook his head.

"Come on. You've gotta be parched?" Jack pressed.

"I do not wish to be any trouble," Chul-Moo replied.

Jack grinned, a knowing glint in his eye. "Trouble?" he said. "We're sitting above a pub, mate. Really, it's no trouble at all."

Pleasantries aside, there was Buckley's chance Chul-Moo was leaving without a drink in his hand. It was bad enough the men were already deep in Magdalena Black's servitude, the kind of depth that involved babysitting randoms, but letting the kid die of something as preventable as dehydration would be a whole new level of discomfort.

"Hung?" Jack said. "Get Chul-Moo some water."

"Uh, alright. But he didn't—" Hung began.

"Not from the tap, either. Grab him a bottle."

"What? From downstairs?" Hung asked, his voice hitching with nerves. "But ... what if Charlie catches me down there?"

"Well, make sure she doesn't," Jack said firmly.

Hung let out a long sigh and trudged toward the stairs, muttering under his breath. Jack shot him a sarcastic thumbs-up, a grin tugging at the corner of his mouth. Hung rolled his eyes, but Jack's smirk only grew as he watched him leave the flat and head downstairs.

The door *slammed* shut with a deafening thud.

"Sorry about my mate," Jack said, tone apologetic. "He's got this habit of, uh … well, let's just say he's a bit *special*. Don't get me wrong, Hung's a good bloke. He'd give you the shirt off his back if you needed it." He fished the television remote from beneath a pile of unopened mail on the coffee table and handed it to Chul-Moo. "Right, I've got a quick phone call to make, but the telly's all yours. There's bound to be a movie on. If you get stuck, I'll be over in that … eh, that little rectangle back there that's supposed to be a kitchen."

Jack waited for a nod of recognition and left the room.

Alone at last, Chul-Moo took another run at studying his surroundings. At first, he surveyed the space with the same quiet scrutiny he had shown earlier, searching for clues, trying to make sense of the chaos. But the intrigue faded fast. Whatever puzzle the flat had offered was not worth solving. With a glance at his wristwatch and a sigh that betrayed mild defeat, he gave in to the lack of stimuli, sank into the tattered lounge, and flicked through channels until the novelty of Australia's four major television networks wore thin.

Click. Click. Click. Click. Click. Click. Click.

The Korean stopped on a news bulletin with the ominous headline 'GANGLAND SLAYING UNRESOLVED'.

'Gold Coast detectives are appealing for witnesses after alleged drug dealer James Arthur Jacobsen was gunned down near a popular nightspot on Friday.' The bulletin cut from a generic blonde newsreader to archival footage of uniformed officers

combing through a nondescript alleyway for evidence, all the while being overseen by the two legends in their own lunchtime, Detectives Mick Hughes and Barry Gamble. As was customary for officers of their seniority, neither party looked particularly interested in getting their hands dirty. *'Preliminary information indicates the 43-year-old Bundall man, nephew of reclusive Melbourne crime figure, Donald Jacobsen, was seen talking with an unknown party near the BLACK nightclub around 12:30 am when a utility or pickup stopped nearby. The occupant exited the vehicle and, following a brief altercation, the 43-year-old sustained gunshot wounds to his torso, before the driver retreated to the vehicle and drove off'.* The bulletin cut back to the newsreader doing her best to look increasingly serious. *'Police believe the incident to be targeted, and that there is no threat to the public. Detectives are appealing for anyone who may have witnessed the incident or has relevant CCTV footage to contact Crime Stoppers'.*

The Diamond, Magdalena Black, and the detectives?

It really *was* a fucking small world, after all.

"You seen the state of that sink?" Cyrille asked.

There was silence from the adjoining room.

"Did you hear me, Don?" The muscle exited the bathroom clutching nothing more than his toothbrush and a strategically placed towel. "There's black gunk all around the plughole and mould up the shower curtain. It's gross. I told you this place was a dump."

Prior to the semi-naked bodybuilder's sermon about bathroom cleanliness, The Diamond had been perched on the edge of his king single, trying to decipher the same local news bulletin with the ominous headline 'GANGLAND SLAYING UNRESOLVED'. Between The Cockatoo Inn's isolation and its

Cold War-era television with cheap digital set-top box, the signal was like having a front-row seat to Tetris pieces fornicating furiously inside a kaleidoscope.

"Guessin' you caught the latest, then?" Donald asked.

"About Jimmy? No, when was this?" Cyrille replied.

"During your customary half-hour shower," Donald said, his tone laced with disdain. "Oh, silly me. Here I was thinkin' you might've overheard the blonde piece on the news mention it. You know, while you were in the bathroom probably havin' an Uncle Hank."

Cyrille dismissed the accusation with a shake of his head.

"Either way, seems we're in luck, lad. The locals know as much as we do," Donald began, as he reiterated the police talking points. "Jimmy got clipped near some club in the city. The shooter drove a ute. They're still appealing for witnesses. Blah, blah, friggin' blah."

Cyrille chuckled. "So they've got bugger all then?"

"Spot on. Hell, even yours truly got a mention."

"You, Don? On the news?" Cyrille replied.

"No. On the bloody roof," Donald said, tossing the television remote aside. "Of course, on the news. Some clever cookie down in the bowels of the *Channel Nine* archives must've put two and two together and figured Jimmy and I were related. Fair play to 'em."

Unbeknown to Cyrille, Donald had once been a regular fixture on the news back home, at least for a solid three months, thanks to one Teddy Wheeler. Wheeler was an ex-cop turned security guard, unceremoniously drummed out of the Victorian police for harbouring an unhealthy interest in underage boys. Short on cash and long on debt, old Teddy decided it would be a stroke of genius to stage the robbery of his own armoured truck.

And not just on any day, but on the busiest day of the year: the first Tuesday in November.

So where did The Diamond fit into all of this?

That armoured truck just happened to belong to a security firm with ties to Melbourne underworld figures. Long story short, those figures did not take kindly to being robbed by a kiddy fiddling ex-cop. Especially one who could barely lie straight in bed. With guilt apportioned and no one eager to involve the local constabulary, men of a certain moral flexibility were tasked with making sure Wheeler paid the price. The result: three days of torture involving a power drill and a hypodermic needle filled with battery acid. And thanks to a botched police chain of custody that saw the trial dismissed, Donald Jacobsen was *allegedly* one of those morally flexible men.

"So much for keeping a low profile," Cyrille said.

"Eh. It was bound to happen, lad. It's not every day that a bone-fide celebrity makes their way up to this neck of the woods, do they?" Donald replied, followed by a hearty chuckle. "Regardless, the plan remains unchanged. All we've gotta do is stay off the radar for a few more days, at least until we've accomplished our objective."

"And when are we starting on that, Don?"

Cyrille shoved his toothbrush back into his mouth.

"All in good time. My first order of business is to have a kip. And while I'm stuck into that, I'd recommend you whack on a pair of dacks and give Mandy a call, yeah? I spied a payphone a click-or-two back down the road. Let her know that her favourite uncle's in town and he's expectin' a cuppa and a biscuit."

"What do ya mean, *nothing*?" Mark Campbell asked.

Jack pried the phone from his ear and poked his head into the pass-through that divided the kitchen from the living room; Hung and Chul-Moo were engrossed in one of the myriad of seventies Hollywood extravaganzas filled with square-jawed Americans going toe-to-toe with the Third Reich's most blonde and blue-eyed of bastards. Jack stared at the cigarette-stained ceiling and grumbled under his breath as he held the receiver at arm's length.

"I mean, he's doing *nothing*," he eventually replied.

"*Nothing*? Define 'nothing'," Mark pressed.

"Why? In case our definitions somehow differ?"

Jack took another look. The situation report was identical to the one from moments earlier: the Korean was still wedged between Hung and a busted cushion, both of them watching a decades-old war movie. The only observable change was Chul-Moo taking a sip of water during one of Clint Eastwood's squint-laden monologues.

"*Nothing*. As in, the 'watching a movie' sorta nothing."

Mark growled at the vagueness. "How's old mate holding up, at least?" It was a last-ditch attempt to confirm his boss's investment was still in one piece and the plan had not been compromised. "Does he look healthy? All his fingers and toes accounted for?"

"Fingers? I've got no idea what—" Jack began.

"Does he still have all his fuckin' digits?"

"Can't say I've counted 'em. Was I supposed to?"

There was muffled chatter at the other end of the line.

The silence that followed was a yawning chasm, wide enough to conga a herd of elephants through. Jack's brain was going like the clappers as he scrambled to make sense of Mark's cryptic line of questioning. Fingers? What the hell was that even about?

"Right. You're clear to drop *it* around," Mark said.

"Oh? You mean … the, uh, 'package'?" Jack replied.

"The package? Hmm. Clever. Yeah, alright then. Permission to deliver the 'package' at your earliest convenience. See? You might just have the nous for this cloak and dagger shit after all, mate."

Jack exhaled and shook his head. He had no idea what had just gone down, but he hoped desperately that he had not broken the cardinal rule of dealing with the criminal underworld: never prove yourself more useful than absolutely necessary.

A maze of roadworks and missed turns later …

Jack's powder-blue Datsun was parked opposite the rendezvous point, the trio inside the only sign of life within a two-block radius.

"I thought this place was popular?" Hung said.

"That's what I've been led to believe," Jack replied.

"Okay. So, uh, where is everybody then?"

The imaginatively titled 'BLACK' was a discrete affair that catered to the upper-echelon of Gold Coast society; individuals who had more money than sense and had transcended the notion that their best fishing shirt and a pair of acid-wash jeans constituted appropriate evening attire. Painted struck-match black, save for the nightclub's name emblazoned across a marquee in large white lettering, the only evidence that this former abattoir was anything but came in the form of an opulent red carpet that snaked its way up the front stairs and abruptly disappeared beneath an imposing steel security door. Soviet-era Magnitogorsk steel. Complete with rectangular viewing slit, it was an impenetrable piece of nineteenth-century engineering that would have looked equally at home in a gulag: presumably so that the meathead on the other side could give potential guests a quick inspection before politely suggesting that they bugger off.

"Where is everyone?" Jack repeated, amusement in his tone. "I know neither of us got any sleep last night, Hung, but you've gotta be taking the piss?" He glanced at the Korean in the rear-view mirror before turning back to his partner. "It's a bloody nightclub, mate. When was the last time you took a Captain's at your watch?"

Hung shrugged and made good on the suggestion.

"It's nearly lunchtime. So what?" he said.

"And nightclubs, by their very definition, operate *when*?"

"Uh ... well, typically at night?" Hung replied.

"Bingo. It's all in the name, you friggin' Gumby."

Despite the surrounds being a veritable ghost town, once the sun slipped behind the horizon it became an absolute nightmare getting within two blocks of where they were parked. BLACK was the hottest ticket in town, and invariably, the closer one parked to the entrance, the greater the opportunity to show off that shiny red Italian marvel of engineering, or the bottle-blonde trophy wife with bolt-on tits that typically accompanied a life of unbridled opulence.

Of course, such style-over-substance was not everyone's cup of tea. That sentiment held especially true for an uncomplicated specimen like Conrad Fenstermacher, who was parked around the corner, out of sight. Puffing on a homemade cigarette, he observed the Datsun's occupants through a pair of children's novelty binoculars he had lifted from an unattended schoolbag earlier that week.

Unbeknown to Jack and Hung, The Hackston's favourite purveyor of stolen goods just happened to have been seated at the end of the bar, nursing a cold beverage and a nasty black eye, when they slipped out the side passage. Having clocked the publicans' sneaky exit with a man of Asian persuasion in tow, a persuasion that seemed to be all the rage with Gold Coast detectives lately, Conrad figured it was his duty as a concerned citizen to keep an eye on proceedings.

"Well, well, well. What are you silly sausages up to?" Conrad said as he watched the trio exit their vehicle and make a beeline for a maintenance door in the nearby alley. "Nobody believed me. I told 'em there was some Asian fella sniffin' around the Goldie, yeah? Just wait until Mick gets a load of this."

Like a rat up a drainpipe, Conrad sprang from his shitbox and popped the boot. With a cigarette still jutting from the corner of his mouth, Conrad rattled off a string of profanities as he rummaged through his collection of mobile phones in search of an operational device: namely one that had yet to be reported stolen and still had enough juice to make an outbound call.

No. No. Broken. No. Nope. Wait …

You little ripper, the phone had a dial tone.

He punched in a number and held the phone to his ear.

"Come on, answer ya prick."

Chapter Ten

Unorganised Crime

Jack, Hung, and Chul-Moo were herded into the nightclub's office by Magdalena Black's enforcer, Mark Campbell, with all the warmth of their previous interactions, which was somewhere between fuck all and none. Unlike the opulent office in her beachfront penthouse, this space was stark and minimalist, dressed in dark, muted tones to match BLACK's carefully curated aesthetic. The only hint of personality came from a framed piece of memorabilia above her desk and a few signed photographs of B-list celebrities who had either graced the venue or, more often, disgraced themselves in it.

"Chul-Moo? As I live and breathe," the loan shark said, rising from behind her desk with a bright smile and a firm handshake. "It's a pleasure to finally put a face to the name, as they say."

The Korean nodded. "Likewise, Miss Black."

"Spare the formalities," Magdalena replied with a dismissive smile, gesturing to the empty chair opposite. Chul-Moo took the hint, stepping away from Mark with a touch of awkwardness. He sat, placing his hands in his lap like a parishioner bracing for a sermon. "Anyone who's pulled ten hours on the red-eye from Seoul just to see little old me has more than earned the right to skip straight to first names. 'Miss Black' is impersonal. Please, call me Magdalena."

Chul-Moo offered a practised smile and a respectful nod, while Jack and Hung exchanged glances, still unsure what the meeting was really about or why it was important enough to warrant a summons under threat of summary execution. Not that they expected to be let in on the details. Odds were, whatever was about to go down, they would be on the other side of the door when it did.

And to be fair, that was probably the safest place to be.

"First things first, Chul-Moo. I must apologise for the change in schedule," Magdalena said, tracing a perfectly manicured finger along the edge of a leather binder. "As you can no doubt appreciate, some conflicts in business are, regrettably, unavoidable."

Chul-Moo nodded. "That is okay," he replied.

"No, it's not. But thank you for feigning politeness," Magdalena said, her smile cordial but tight. "Uncertainty is not a tenet upon which I conduct business. Still, you could not have been in better hands. I trust every need of yours was seen to while I was indisposed?"

This was the moment of truth. Magdalena's gaze snapped to Jack, her expression unreadable but sharp enough to cut through any lie. If her eyes were anything to go by, the boys were one mediocre review away from joining Queensland's long list of missing persons.

Chul-Moo hesitated, mouth open, searching for words.

"Jack and Hung treated me, uh ..." he began.

The pause dragged on long enough to make Jack sweat.

"They treated me ... well," he said at last.

The publicans let out a collective sigh of relief.

Well was adequate. *Well* was satisfactory. And, with a bit of luck and depending on Magdalena's most recent flirtation with prescription benzodiazepines, *well* might just qualify as a passing grade.

Magdalena shot them a sceptical glance, the kind that suggested she was disappointed not to be fitting them for matching graves.

"Mark," she said with a sigh, "kindly escort Jack and his friend downstairs while Chul-Moo and I discuss the finer points of business. Have Pablo fix them a couple of drinks while they wait. Nothing top-shelf. I'm not running a charity."

Mark snarled and rested a giant hand on his hip, somewhere in the vicinity of the .45 tucked into the waistband of his jeans.

"You absolutely sure about that, boss?" he asked.

Chul-Moo might have been thousands of kilometres from home and about as threatening as a case of gingivitis, but protocol dictated that the man-mountain be present at any face-to-face meeting with potentially untrustworthy individuals. That was an edict straight from Magdalena herself. Mark locked eyes with his boss in a silent plea to be spared, but she dismissed it just as wordlessly. Mark was going to have to sit this one out, and that killed him. The added insult of having to babysit Bill and Ben only twisted the knife. It was more grief than any reasonable person should be expected to bear, and Mark Campbell was anything but reasonable.

"Right. You floggers heard Miss Black," he said with a smattering of disdain, marching Jack and Hung from the room with the same lack of fanfare that had marked their arrival. At the door, Mark paused and glanced back at his boss, as if checking she was sure about sending him away. But Magdalena was too busy flashing polite smiles at her new Korean friend to even notice.

The room fell silent as both parties sized each other up.

"So," the loan shark began, her tone light but deliberate as she attempted to break the ice. "How are you enjoying Australia?"

It took all of five seconds for Magdalena to wheel out one of those cardinal sins locals loved to commit when speaking to anyone from north of Cape York: asking what they thought of the country.

"I have not seen much, but it looks ... *nice*."

"*Nice?*" Magdalena repeated, a wounded expression creeping across her face. "Coming from someone who lives downwind of a dictator with his finger hovering over the big red button, that response seems ... rich. Sure, this might not be the Amalfi Coast, but if my other option was living under the constant threat of all-out war, I'd say that our humble little nation was akin to God's country. God, Buddha, Allah. Whatever or whomever happens to be your deity of choice."

Chul-Moo shook his head. "I belong to no god."

"Oh? Another card-carrying member of the world's most distrusted minority? And here I was thinking you could not possibly rise any higher in my estimation." Magdalena picked up the phone and pressed it to her ear. "How about we toast our shared spiritual liberation with a drink? Our resident mixologist, Pablo, does a splendid cocktail called *The Agnostic Archbishop*: four parts Champagne, two parts vodka, a splash of cranberry juice, and a dash of egg white, served in a chilled martini glass."

Chul-Moo held up a hand in polite refusal, once again wondering what it was with Australians and their obsession with forcing alcoholic drinks onto complete strangers. If he did not know any better, he might have taken it as a not-so-subtle hint to lighten the fuck up.

"Are you sure? It's one of Pablo's own creations."

"I am … okay … for now, Miss Magdalena."

There was a hint of distraction in Chul-Moo's voice. Magdalena could tell his attention had drifted to something behind her.

"Admiring the anniversary gift from my former husband?" she said, as she placed the receiver down and turned her attention to a framed copy of the 1969 novel *The Godfather*, that overlooked her desk. "I know, I know. Under normal circumstances, I should have incinerated every remnant of our union. However, I made one exception. First edition. Signed by Mario Puzo himself. Normally I would be loath to admit this, but my former husband had exceptional taste when it came to trinkets and trophies." Magdalena smiled, a smile that involuntarily twisted into something more like a rictus grin as she recalled her former husband's fondness for barely legal dental assistants. "Besides, Chul-Moo, the very thought of burning a perfectly serviceable book feels so … authoritarian. Does it not?"

Australian criminals had an inexplicable hard-on for the gospel according to Vito Corleone. It was not uncommon to spot some low-level gronk with a dog-eared copy of *The Godfather* jammed in their back pocket as if it were a playbook, just as the real Cosa Nostra obsessed over *The Art of War* by Sun Tzu. What a possibly fictional Chinese general from five centuries before Christ could teach a bunch of spaghetti-slurping mafiosi, who would not piss on you unless you could trace your Sicilian bloodline back three generations, about loan sharking or slinging gear was anyone's guess.

"Ever read *The Godfather*?" Magdalena asked.

Chul-Moo gave a small shrug and shook his head.

"Really? You're missing out." Magdalena opened a desk drawer, rifled through it, then shut it with a sigh. "There's a paperback in the Beamer's glovebox. Consider it yours. It's in

English, not whatever it is you speak, but it might help kill time on the flight home."

It was an offer Chul-Moo could not refuse.

Magdalena turned back to her guest with a smile that balanced charm and calculation. "And while we're on the topic of professional organisations, I must express my gratitude to you and yours," she said. "Travelling all the way from Seoul for a face-to-face meeting? That's the kind of commitment sorely lacking in this country."

"Thank you, Miss Magdalena. I will pass that—"

"Magdalena is fine," she said, cutting in gently.

The Korean offered a small, apologetic nod and smiled.

"Commitment and organisation, Chul-Moo. I need not remind you how essential those traits are when conducting business. Especially the latter." Magdalena nodded toward the prized possession on the wall behind her. "Maybe it's our convict DNA, but Australians have never been much for either. Organise a piss-up at the park? Sure, we'll do that at the drop of a hat. But anything involving actual effort gets tossed aside as too hard. Perhaps Australians should stick to what they do best: 'unorganised' crime."

Chul-Moo nodded along, having long since lost the thread of Magdalena's rambling monologue. Her tangents on Aussie crims and half-baked punchlines would have tested even a native English speaker.

"Anyway, enough of me pontificating," the loan shark said, chuckling to herself, clearly amused by the sound of her own voice. "Before we begin, Chul-Moo, there's one question that's been running through my mind, and I do hope you take it in the good-natured spirit it's intended. Otherwise, things might get a little ... awkward."

"Oh? Please. Continue," Chul-Moo replied.

"So, how did you smuggle *it* into the country?"

"*It?* Ah, I do not understand—" Chul-Moo began.

"The information. Perhaps I've read too many spy novels, but you never arrived with a briefcase or anything of that sort."

The Korean reached into his pocket and pulled out a black rectangular device, roughly the size and shape of a packet of gum. He slid it across Magdalena's polished mahogany desk, where it came to a stop just inches from her. She studied it briefly. Then she gave it a poke with her pen, hesitant and curious, like a crime scene investigator inspecting a suspicious piece of evidence.

"I have no idea what this is," Magdalena said earnestly, "but judging by that look on your face, please tell me you didn't do something barbaric like, ah, smuggle it in via the old bot-bot."

"The bot-bot?" Chul-Moo asked, puzzled.

"You know? Did you shove it up your bum?"

The Korean politely refused to incriminate himself.

Chul-Moo sat hunched over a flamingo-pink laptop emblazoned with sticker-fied wisdoms like *I* ♥ *Cats* and *Bartenders Shake It Nightly*, a loaner from Pablo, the nightclub's resident mixologist. Hovering over his shoulder, Magdalena watched in awe as the Korean navigated the desktop with a volley of lightning-fast keystrokes and erratic mouse clicks. Behind her stood the recently un-exiled Mark, the only other person on Magdalena's payroll, aside from Pablo, who had even the faintest clue about computers. It was a case of the inept overseeing the clueless, especially given that Mark's expertise extended to a very niche repertoire of internet searches: hunting down celebrity sex tapes, checking the odds at the local turf club, and obsessively poring over his NRL career stats.

"This is all rather fascinating," Magdalena said.

Chul-Moo continued to tap-away on the keyboard.

"While I must confess I have little idea what's going on with all the, er, double-clicking, it's rare that I find my curiosity piqued," the loan shark continued, her eyes glazing over as she chased the cursor around the screen. "How are your curiosity levels, Mark?"

"Consider 'em equally piqued, boss," Mark replied.

"In fact, this entire arrangement has been unorthodox," Magdalena continued, more than likely babbling just to fill the silence. "And it becomes even more so when the primary stipulation involves dispatching a courier all the way from South Korea to hand-deliver the files. Is this what you do, Chul-Moo? Travel the globe selling classified information? Here I was under the assumption that you hacker types relished anonymity."

The Korean paused just long enough to glance over his shoulder before returning to his ritual of clicks and keystrokes. A subtle shift in his posture betrayed his growing weariness with the constant barrage of questions and condescension from the peanut gallery. Perhaps this was the moment everyone's favourite hacker could have launched into a spiel on the many and varied methods used to acquire the data, but considering Magdalena and her enforcer barely grasped the basics of what was happening in front of them, any explanation would have only ricocheted off their tanned foreheads.

The frenetic clicking and double-clicking continued.

Magdalena turned to her enforcer, giving him a look that all but summoned a response. Mark shrugged, offering little more than muscle-bound confusion. She gave a small cough, then posed her most burning question in a seemingly roundabout way.

"Chul-Moo, this information you're selling ..." she began. "Mark and I were talking and, uh ..." For the first time in a long while, Magdalena seemed at a loss for words. "He mentioned a few concerns about the price. And while I assure you we're still good for the wire transfer tomorrow, half a million dollars isn't exactly 'fell behind the couch cushion' money."

Mark shot his employer a cold, hard look that made it clear he did not appreciate being thrown under the bus.

"You have money concerns?" Chul-Moo asked.

"No. What I'm driving at is, I need assurance."

Chul-Moo stared at Magdalena blankly for a second.

Magdalena sighed. "An assurance is like a guarantee, Chul-Moo. I need some sort of guarantee that the information I'm purchasing from your organisation is worth my time and money. After all, I'm the one seemingly absorbing the majority of risk in this arrangement."

The Korean mulled it over, nodded thoughtfully, and attacked the keyboard with the frenetic energy of a Jack Russell on a kilo of Colombian marching powder. Judging by his enthusiasm, he clearly had an ace up his figurative sleeve, presumably in the form of the haphazard collection of files now congregating on his screen.

"And what exactly am I looking at?" Magdalena asked.

"That, Miss Black, is assurance," Chul-Moo replied.

"Really? Looks more like commie gobbledygook to me."

Chul-Moo sighed and continued. "Profiles of every registered police informant in Queensland." *Click.* "Details of active undercover operations and task forces." *Double-click.* "Decrypted department emails and correspondence." *Click.* "Police service records." The Korean paused, letting the image of a random warrant card speak for itself. "So? Are you satisfied with the supplied information?"

Magdalena feigned disinterest, brushing imaginary lint from the lapel of her black Armani suit as she casually made her way back behind the desk. Like muscle memory, the man-mountain that was Mark Campbell resumed his post behind her, bulging arms crossed, face like a bulldog licking piss off a nettle. It was Underworld Negotiation 101: maintain the illusion you could take it or leave it, ideally the latter. Show too much enthusiasm, and you were already halfway to being bent over the bargaining table.

"How old is this information?" Magdalena asked.

"Less than one month," the Korean replied.

That was as specific as things were going to get.

"My apologies, Chul-Moo, but even a week could mean the difference between sipping Agua de Valencias on a beach in Majorca or chugging toilet moonshine in a Supermax at Her Majesty's pleasure." The Korean stared back blankly. He had facilitated enough of these deals to discern between genuine curiosity and a thinly veiled attempt to knock a few bucks off the asking price. "Business is mercurial. The Gold Coast may appear laid-back, lots of sexy people wearing bikinis and shit-eating grins, doing what amounts to fuck all, but a lot can happen here in a week. One week may as well be one month. And, as I'm sure that you can appreciate from a business standpoint, I am hesitant about paying a premium for information that may already be past its best before date."

"And as you can appreciate, time was needed."

"What do you mean by that, Chul-Moo?"

"It means you were not the only bidder, Miss Black."

The loan shark chuckled. As Magdalena's offshore account in the Marshall Islands would soon attest, this was no one-sided affair but a fierce bidding war.

"During negotiations, time was needed to deal with interested parties," Chul-Moo continued, his normally cheerful demeanour tinged with frustration. "And once legitimate parties were separated from those who were not, we provided those parties with sample information. Information to, as you say, give assurance." He double-clicked on a file within a folder marked 'CI' and a black and white mugshot of dealer-turned-informant Jimmy Jacobsen leapt onto the screen. "Having viewed your local television, it would seem that somebody found the sample we provided ... satisfactory."

Magdalena shot Mark a fiery look as she came to the realisation that she had been snookered by what amounted to sheer coincidence. What were the odds that Chul-Moo was up to date with the local news cycle? Nevertheless, Magdalena had been caught sampling the wares in the most public of forums, namely snuffing-out a police informant who had been flying a little too close to the sun.

The Korean unplugged the USB and closed the flamingo-pink laptop with a sense of finality. Was he miffed, or was this simply how business wrapped up south of the 38th parallel? Magdalena tried to read the room as the silence lumbered into a third beat. Maybe she should just power through like nothing had happened. Best case, she could bluff her way past the awkwardness. Worst case, she could take a page from the great Australian playbook of monumental cock-ups and chalk it up to a "cultural misunderstanding".

"So, what happens next?" Magdalena asked, choosing to power through as she watched Chul-Moo pocket the USB with the kind of focus usually reserved for loaded guns or large sums of cash.

"I need nothing more from you," Chul-Moo replied.

Magdalena gave the Korean a cryptic look.

"We are finished with our initial meeting," he continued. "I must now contact my superiors to make sure the credentials for the money transfer tomorrow are correct. I will place that call tonight from my accommodation once I have had time to rest."

Magdalena breathed a sigh of relief. "Oh? Excellent," she replied. "I'll have Mark here collect you in the morning, Chul-Moo. Expect him parked outside your motel room at precisely eight o'clock sharp, engine idling. A two-hour head start should be more than enough to battle traffic on the M1." So far, so good, on the bullshitting front. Magdalena eyed the USB-shaped bulge in Chul-Moo's pocket and decided to push the boat out further. "This may be testing the friendship, Chul-Moo, but there is always the option to leave that ... stick ... of yours in the safe here overnight. Assuming that is agreeable, of course. It has to be infinitely more secure than one of those rinky-dink motel room safes. Mark here would probably be familiar with the type I'm referring to."

"Yeah. I know 'em well, boss," Mark replied.

"The little safes with the keypads on the front?"

Mark nodded. "You wouldn't catch me keepin' a dead dog's dick in one. I remember watching old Merv bust into one once. Took him two seconds flat with a metal file and a hammer."

Chul-Moo tilted his head. "With a hammer?"

"Yep. And for what it's worth, my mum used to be a maid at a hotel up in Mackay. Reckoned stuff was always going missing outta the safes. Thieving pricks everywhere these days, mate."

"Precisely," Magdalena said. "And it would be a shame if the data were to fall into unscrupulous hands at such a crucial stage of the deal ... especially prior to the money transfer in the morning."

What the loan shark and her lackey had failed to account for, or even recognise for that matter, was the biometric scanner on the underside of the device. With its contents only accessible via Chul-Moo's unique thumbprint and protected with 448-bit military-grade file encryption, the USB was little more than a glorified trinket in the hands of any light-fingered motel maids.

The same applied to the hands of Magdalena Black.

Residence of the late Jimmy Jacobsen.

Mandy, a petite, drug-ravaged brunette in her mid-thir-ties with a fashion sense that suggested she had been dragged through a St Vinnie's kicking and screaming, stood in the cir-ca-1970s kitchen sobbing. Tears cascaded down her cheeks and onto the broad right shoulder of Donald 'The Diamond' Ja-cobsen. Like the emotionally detached misanthrope he was, Donald appeared paralysed by the display of grief. Should he hug her back? Pat her on the head? Whisper a comforting 'there, there'? He was utterly lost.

The honest truth was that men of The Diamond's ilk rarely set out to be miserable old cunts. Few miserable old cunts ever did. That illustrious title simply came with the shit-smeared diploma that life thrust into their hands after graduation from the often cited but rarely attended School of Hard Knocks.

"I'm so bloody sorry, love. I truly am," he said.

"Huh? Sorry for what, Don?" Mandy replied.

"For missin' my own nephew's funeral, for one."

"Bugger off. You've got nothing to apologise for," Mandy replied as she wiped away a tear and broke off their hug. "Jenny phoned us and explained everything, so quit thinking that you let everyone down. Yeah? Especially Jimmy. He'd have under-stood. He knows ... fuck. I'll never get used to saying that ... uh, Jimmy *knew* how important Denise is to you."

"Eh. Maybe so, Mandy. But it doesn't change the fact."

Ronnie, a middle-aged, stocky, pony-tailed lackey of Mandy's late spouse, nodded and took a seat beside Cyrille at the kitchen table. The juxtaposition between him and the clean-cut, clean-living Mr Universe appeared borderline comical. Dressed in a natty Hawaiian shirt, Ronnie looked like the stereotypical scumbag that one would expect to be peddling gear to children and the long-term unemployed, which, funnily enough, was precisely how Ronnie earned a crust.

"So, how's she doing?" Mandy asked.

"Pardon, love?" Donald replied.

"Denise. How's she holding up after the fall?"

"The missus? She's, uh, had a rough couple of months, but she's takin' it in her stride. One day at a time, and all that. But hey, we didn't travel all this way to burden folks with my domestic dramas back home." Donald paused and gestured toward the very visible baby bump protruding from beneath Mandy's flannelette shirt. "The young blood and I came here to pay a visit to you and that little peanut in there. See how you're going without, ah … Jimmy around."

Mandy frowned. "You're not gettin' out of it that easily," she replied, her voice taking on the unmistakable tone of a disgruntled schoolteacher. "Come on, talk to me. Please."

"What do you want to know?" Donald asked.

"Christ, you're making it sound like I asked you to move heaven and earth? I was just lookin' for a little human interaction. You know? With someone other than Ronnie here. It's not a lot to ask for? To die happy knowin' there's at least one bloke in the Jacobsen clan who can open up and tell a person what's going on in their heart."

Adversity was part and parcel of growing up in post-war Australia. A doting father lost in the war. A mother who beat him mercilessly with little to no provocation. A Vietnam veteran with two tours under his belt. Blah, blah, fucking blah. What was another poker in the fire?

"My troubles are just that, love. Mine," he said.

"But they aren't," Mandy replied. "What's the old saying? 'A trouble shared is a trouble halved'? Yeah? So how about we try this again? Hello, Don. How's Denise doing at the moment?"

It was like teaching social niceties to a toddler.

The Diamond figured that there was no way to dodge this bullet without seeming excessively rude or insensitive. He capitulated and exhaled at the realisation that he was going to have to sing like a grizzled, world-weary canary.

"We're thinking she must've fallen while gettin' off the toilet. Blacked out and caught her cheek on the door handle so hard it looked like she went twelve rounds with Cassius Clay. But she's back home now, at least. We've got Jenny staying with her while we're up here, but the docs, they, uh, keep pushing me to shove her into one of those aged care places. Especially after this latest tumble."

"Seriously? Are you for real?" Mandy asked.

Donald nodded. "God's honest, love. They reckon I'm getting too old to fulfil my husbandly duties. It's funny because the pricks wouldn't know me from a bar of soap. Too old? Bugger off. That's what you get these days. It's about regulations and ticking boxes, rather than what's in the patient's best interest."

He had a point. If one was to remove Cyrille from the equation, purely on account of the fact that no sane person should ever feel the need to devote most of their waking lives to appeasing the gymnasium gods, then the old bull was unquestionably the hardiest prick in the room by a country mile.

"Have you looked into alternatives?" Mandy asked.

"Alternatives? Like what?" Donald replied.

"Like, I dunno. Hiring a live-in nurse, maybe?"

There was a brief silence while Mandy waited for a response. Donald wandered over to the window, his gaze sweeping across the overgrown backyard with an eye more accustomed to mowing down rivals than tending to six hundred square metres of bindi-infested buffalo grass. After all, violence was a familiar comfort. Vulnerability, foreign territory. As he pondered the future, Mandy closed the gap between them, gently placing a hand on his shoulder.

"As much as you wanna look after her, Don, you're not a doctor. Neither's Cyrille. Denise needs professional care."

"I dunno, love. It's just that—" Donald began.

"Why? What's the matter?" Mandy asked.

"Eh, death do us part and all that." The Diamond grimaced at his unfortunate turn of phrase. "One minute, she'll be right as rain. Sitting there smilin', telling stories about her brother Clancy like it happened only yesterday. The kid's been dead for forty years. Ten minutes later, she won't have the foggiest about who you are or where she is."

"Jesus, Don. I don't know what to say."

"What's there to say? Dementia's a proper cunt." Donald turned his head and made a covert attempt to wipe a well of moisture from his eyes. "Anyway, I didn't come here for tea and sympathy. Now I know my word probably isn't worth a pinch of shit lately, on account of missing Jimmy's funeral, but Cyrille and I both know what it's like to grow up without a father figure. It ain't easy. So, when that kid's old enough to either beer or bleed, I want you to do me a favour."

"Ah, okay. And what's that?" Mandy replied.

"Let 'em know that their Uncle Don cared enough to square the ledger. Yeah? Forget all the other bullshit going on. That's what Ronnie's here for, the day-to-day stuff. All I need from you, love, is for you to believe me when I tell ya that

Cyrille and I are going to track down the prick that killed Jimmy. We're gonna find him, and we're gonna make him hurt. And the moment he begs and pleads for a quick, merciful death, then and only then will this prick truly understand the folly of messin' with a bloke's family."

Donald's sentiment was enough to elicit the waterworks.

With Mandy mid-bawl, Cyrille figured that now was the time to take to his feet and thrust a tattered yellow envelope into her trembling hands. She stared at him quizzically through puffy, tear-stained eyes for what felt like an eternity. "A gesture of goodwill from Don and all the crew back home," he said, as he pointed toward the wad of assorted fifties and hundreds.

Donald shook his head and eyeballed the kid.

"It's for you and, uh, the bub," Cyrille added.

"Really? Oh, my God. Thank you both."

Mandy tearfully embraced both men.

"No worries, love. And there'll be more envelopes like that one, every month, for the foreseeable future," Donald said, shooting a sideways glance at Ronnie. "At least until you're back on your feet."

Ten thousand dollars was a generous gesture, especially considering that James 'Jimmy' Jacobsen, a low-level dealer with all the business acumen of a cinderblock, rarely cleared even a tenth of that in a good week. Not that anyone would have guessed it, judging by the state of their home. Most of Jimmy's profits had a habit of disappearing through the business end of a hypodermic needle.

"I really dunno how to thank you both," Mandy said.

"Like I always say, love, we take care of our own."

A pall of silence descended over the kitchen as Mandy took a seat at the table and picked at the edges of the envelope with a chewed fingernail. The men stared at one another, unsure of what to do. A full minute passed before Donald decided to fast-forward through the grieving in an attempt to expedite the manhunt. Besides, with the formalities done and condolences expressed, there was little left to do but let The Diamond do what he did best: exact bloody revenge.

"Hmm. You're lookin' flustered, love," Donald said.

"Me? Flustered? Uh … do I?" Mandy replied.

Donald nodded. "How about you pop upstairs and rest your eyes?" he said, gesturing toward the nearby staircase. "Grab forty winks while we have a quick yarn with Ronnie here. It shouldn't take long. Once we're done talking shop, we'll pop our heads in before we go."

"Is that a promise, Don?" Mandy asked.

Donald smiled. "Yeah. Scout's honour, love."

Mandy might not have been the sharpest tool in the shed, but she knew that when blokes started tossing around euphemisms like 'talking shop', it was her cue to disappear. She gave the trio a nod and made her way upstairs without so much as a murmur.

"Poor girl," Cyrille said. "It must be rough for her."

Donald grimaced and pulled up a chair at the table.

"That's the nature of the business though, ain't it?" he said, as he took a seat across from his nephew's lackey. "The wrong decision. Indecision. A word out of place. Hell, take one wrong turn down a dark alley and … well, pardon my French, but you're fucked. Hmm. Reminds me of this saying one of the ration assassins from our regiment had: 'A man's lifespan is only as long as his luck'. And well, let's not bloody kid ourselves. Jimmy was never that lucky."

"That's a bit, uh, harsh, isn't it?" Ronnie replied.

"A drug deal went tits-up, and the lad found himself inside a pine box," Donald began, as he glanced at Cyrille before dragging a plate of biscuits into his orbit. "Lucky? Dunno about you, but that hardly suggests everything's been comin' up roses now, does it?"

"What would you call Mandy and the bub then?"

"I'd call them collateral damage, Ronnie."

The man in question began to splutter and stammer as he searched for a response to Donald's rather pointed statement.

"Dealing's a mug's game, Ronnie. And if I'm speaking plainly, it baffles me how you two dickheads managed to survive this long before one of you ended up on the pointy end of a bullet. Hell, if I were a betting man, I'd have wagered it would've been you, you fat, ponytailed prick. Not Jimmy. At least my nephew had a little nous, even if he was a worthless two-bit Queensland gear-slinger."

Cyrille nodded as if Donald's words were gospel.

"Dealers are lower than snakeshit. In fact, the only thing worse than a drug dealer is a kiddy fiddler," Donald continued, in a matter-of-fact tone. "Oh? And speakin' of which, that bloke in my regiment? The one with the whole 'lifespan as long as your luck' shtick? Know how lucky he turned out to be?"

"Uh … not very, I'm guessing?" Ronnie replied.

"Bingo. Let's just say that, ah, old mate got written up as a 'training accident' on account of a stray frag grenade taking a wrong turn into the latrines. Cut him into a pile of red confetti, just like that." Donald snapped his fingers in an attempt to remind his colleagues of the fickle, finite nature of life. "Word had it he'd been sneaking under the wire after dark. Allegedly, he liked to trek the ten clicks to the nearest village to, well, there's no pretty way to say this, mate … he had a thing for little boys. Shit. It was terrifying what a couple Seppo greenbacks and a handful of lollies could get a sick cunt over there … especially when the kid's parents were in on collectin' the money."

Cyrille recoiled. "Jesus, Don. Too much info."

"Bugger off, lad. I didn't come all this way to blow smoke up Ronnie's arse. A missus, a baby on the way, whatever. The point I'm trying to drive into this thick baboon's head is, we live or die by making our own luck. By stayin' smart and keeping a low profile."

"We were, Don. God's honest," Ronnie replied.

Donald harboured no illusions about being the inspiration behind his late nephew's chosen career path. Those old yarns that floated through the Melbourne underworld had a way of turning a bloke who had simply been luckier than most into someone seven feet tall and bulletproof. But the truth was, The Diamond and James 'Jimmy' Jacobsen were not cut from the same cloth. Jimmy had been a lost cause from the moment he evacuated his mother's birth canal. If not for a shared surname and a stubborn sense of honour, The Diamond would have been more than happy to see out his self-imposed retirement back in the land of lattes and laneways.

"Enough jawing," Donald said. "Now that Mandy's out of the equation, this is the part where we get down to brass tacks. Question and answer time. And on account of being the oldest and meanest prick here, I'll be the one asking the questions. So don't give me any of your conniving, weaselly bullshit. Straight answers only."

This was the moment Ronnie had been dreading. Mandy had been the circuit breaker in Donald's slow-burn autopsy of that fateful night. But now she was out of the picture, and Ronnie was left at the mercy of a pensioner with a knack for prising out the truth.

"It doesn't take a genius to work out what my first question's gonna be. And you better be upfront, Ronnie, because I know you've been dodging Cyrille's phone calls."

"Huh? I don't really know what you wanna hear."

"I wanna know what the hell happened!"

"Happened to who ... Jimmy?" Ronnie replied.

"To the bloody Easter Bunny. Who do you reckon?"

Ronnie looked away, his gaze immediately darting to the floor. If this were an interrogation, he would go down like a drunken, late-night kebab: greasy, messy, and undignified.

"And don't say you don't fuckin' know." Donald's stare hardened, his eyes redder than the Devil's dick. "Ignorance doesn't cut the mustard, Ronnie. Weren't you two best mates? Some sorta fuckin' mate you turned out to be. He's six feet under while you're sittin' here nursing a cuppa with your thumb up your clacker, doing your best Sergeant Schultz impression. So never tell me you 'dunno' anything, dear Ronnie, because you can go fuck right off."

"But ... uh ... I wasn't even there, Don."

"Oh? And what's that supposed to mean?"

"That night, I mean ... I wasn't there, alright?" Ronnie began. "I wasn't there when Jimmy got clipped. I wish I had been. Things might've gone differently, you know? But, ah, it ain't like we were joined at the hip." Ronnie's eyes lit up before he rummaged through a stack of newspapers on the table in front of him. "Wait! There was something in one of these. Somewhere. Something a witness saw."

"Wait. I thought the cops said there weren't any witnesses?" Cyrille replied. "Now they're coming out of the woodwork?"

Ronnie spun a newspaper around to face the men and stabbed at it intensely with a stubby index finger, as if he were trying to tunnel his way to China. Donald squinted at it for a moment and nodded. He would rather style it out than admit that he had left his reading glasses on the dashboard of their rental car. Conversely, Ronnie would rather volunteer anyone else for the job than admit to his inability to read at a level higher than that of a fourth-grader.

"So, what's the gist of the article?" Donald asked.

"Nah, Don. You've gotta read it for yourself."

"And steal the glory? I'll let you have that honour."

Ronnie cowered like a kicked puppy as he conveyed 'the gist' of the article, an act which involved reciting it verbatim and at a speed that could only be described as 'snails paced'. As fortune would have it, the lull afforded Donald time to polish off his tea and biscuits, and Cyrille time to watch Donald scoff said biscuits with dismay as he mentally tallied every calorie that passed his lips.

Four minutes and 300 calories later ...

"Christ," Donald began, "I'm usually not one to, ah, make light of a fella's shortcomings, Ronnie, but have you ever considered splurging some cash on one of those adult reading classes? I know, literacy is hardly the be-all and end-all for a creep who pedals gear to school kids but, uh, a little self-improvement wouldn't go astray?"

"Sorry, Don. I never had much schooling, is all."

"Yeah. No fucking shit," Donald shot back.

The human ponytail sighed and slumped in his chair.

"Right. So after listening to Banjo Paterson here bang on, am I right in saying that the only new info the coppers have is the fact Jimmy's killer might've been packing a wanky pistol?" The actual description was a 'polished, customised pistol', but Donald refused to let that hamper his uncanny knack for summarising a situation in 'twenty-five words or less', a skill perfected over decades of working with wordy arseholes. "Hmm. Now, I've seen more guns than you pair have had hot dinners, but I can't for the life of me put my finger on what might make one stick out like a pair of dog's balls."

"Civvies aren't fans, regardless," Cyrille replied.

"True. Even a water pistol's gonna look meaner than a junkyard dog, especially to some nonce who sips passion-fruit-flavoured beer and drives a European motor. But between this new tip-off and what we saw on the telly, the report claiming the shooter was driving a ute, well, it gives us a couple of hornet nests to stick our wedding tackle into."

Cyrille ran a hand through his hair and prayed that the remark about sticking one's unmentionables into a hornet's nest was not another of The Diamond's sordid war stories.

"That's still not a lot to go on," he replied.

"It's more than we had twelve hours ago, lad."

"True, but this ain't Melbourne. Is it, Don?"

Donald cocked an eyebrow and looked at his offsider.

"I'm just saying, and I'm not trying to be funny or anything, but finding some guy with a shiny gun and a ute on the Gold Coast is gonna be like, I dunno, finding a needle in a haystack of needles. Maybe you haven't noticed, Don, but everybody around here thrives on either being a beach bum or a yuppie. There's no in-between."

Donald had noticed a definite pattern emerging.

"At least back in Melbourne we've got the contacts. What've we got here?" Cyrille gestured in Ronnie's direction. "Some fat bloke who dresses like a date rapist on a cruise ship. Sorry, mate, no offence."

"Er, none taken ... I suppose," Ronnie replied.

Donald examined the walking ponytail with a steely gaze.

"Point taken, lad. But as we both know, experience trumps local knowledge. Plus, there's nothing we can't finesse out of the locals when using the right motivation and, ah, manner of persuasion. Yeah? Just focus on the holy trinity: money, guns and gash. They'll always lead you back to a crim." Donald paused and turned his attention to the man opposite him. "So, Ronnie, my friend, my pal, care to cast a little of that local illumination on the situation?"

Ronnie stared at Donald with vacant eyes.

"Where can we acquire some party poppers?"

"Party poppers, Don? I'm not sure I—"

"Shooters. Hand cannons. Pocket rockets," Donald replied, with a hint of whimsy. "Guns, you fuckin' cock. You know? The topic we've been talking about for the last five minutes. Find the gun, find Jimmy's killer. So what are you waiting for? A faxed invitation? Point us toward the Gold Coast's premier gunrunner and I'll see if I can, uh, 'turn on the Jacobsen charm', so to speak."

Jack and Hung stood before the nightclub's namesake like a pair of naughty students waiting to take their lumps from a headmaster with a perpetual hard-on for corporal punishment. Magdalena sighed and tapped her fingernails against the heavy mahogany desk as if pondering the fate of the two men. With each tap, the room thickened with a sinister, claustrophobic tension that could have easily passed for a prelude to an intimate firing squad. The dread only deepened thanks to Mark Campbell, who had positioned himself squarely in their peripheral vision, just in case the publicans grew bold and fancied their chances against one of the Gold Coast's preeminent villains.

"That's the third time you've asked now," Jack said.

"And I'm gonna keep on asking," Mark replied.

"What? In case the fourth time's a charm?"

Mark snarled and held aloft the paper containing Chul-Moo's flight information that he had confiscated from the pair moments earlier.

"So? Did you make any copies?" he repeated, presumably for the fourth time. "And be honest, Jacko. Because if I find out there're copies of this floating around, well, the coppers might just find a couple of turkeys matchin' your descriptions floating face-down off Snapper Rocks. Catch my drift?"

"Lovely," Jack replied. "And with what time, mate?"

"What do you mean 'with what time'?"

"Well, I don't know about you, Mark, but between filling our office full of cardboard boxes, the late-night visits, and pickin' up Chul-Moo from Arrivals at the crack of dawn, I've barely had time to scratch my arse. So yeah, I'm sorry. Sorry I didn't hand you some sort of licence to bump us off for makin' photocopies of your precious paperwork."

Chul-Moo appeared unfazed by the testosterone-fuelled theatrics, content to sit in the corner with a well-worn loaner copy of *The Godfather* in hand. With his demonstration over and the half-million all but in his employer's account, he was already counting down the hours until his flight home.

"And what about your boyfriend here?" Mark asked.

The attention shifted to the man beside Jack.

"What? Are you talking about me?" Hung asked.

"I don't see any other dung-punchers around here."

Having a monosyllabic rock ape like Mark Campbell cast aspersions about his sexuality came as a welcome change from the usual shtick of belittling his Vietnamese-Australian heritage. Hung bowed his head and eyed the black shagpile carpet underfoot like a chastised toddler. It was a shame that he was the wrong side of six-feet-nothing and lacked the intestinal fortitude required to stand-up to a bully like Mark because nothing would give him more satisfaction than to scale that barely literate bastard like a Nepalese Sherpa and plant a knuckle sandwich right on his kisser.

"Well? Did you make any copies?" Mark asked.

"Of Chul-Moo's schedule? No," Hung replied.

The hulking forward gave the pair a long, uncomfortable stare before producing a cigarette lighter from his pocket. With a flick of his thumb its amber flame slowly bled across the surface of the page, invariably eliminating the only physical evidence that linked Jack and Hung back to the Korean, and in turn, Jack and Hung back to Magdalena Black. With the remnants of Chul-Moo's flight schedule and the photograph now smouldering in a nearby ashtray, Magdalena decided it was time to inject herself back into the conversation.

"Cease castigating my guests, Mark," she said.

"Huh? But ... I hadn't even got that far yet. Be my pleasure, though. Just let me nip out back and grab my bolt cutters."

"What in the Lord's name are you on about?"

"Cuttin' off their cock and balls, boss."

"*Castigation*, Mark. As in, to rebuke or reprimand."

Magdalena shook her head and pondered what unimaginable horrors she might have returned to had she left Jack and Hung alone any longer with her castration-happy enforcer. Of course, it went without saying that the potential victims of said castration were both dismayed and ecstatic in equal measure, Jack in particular, who breathed a heavy sigh of relief and covertly patted the front of his jeans to ensure that his little fella was still very much intact.

"My apologies, boys. Clearly a thesaurus wouldn't go astray when it comes to Mark's Secret Santa this year," she quipped, as she leaned forward in her chair. "Regardless, credit where credit is due. Somehow, above and beyond all preconceived expectations, you both managed to follow a series of simple instructions."

The men allowed the faint praise to waft over them.

"So? I assume we're done then?" Hung asked.

"Done? In what sense?" Magdalena replied.

"In the sense of you, uh, waiving part of our debt."

Magdalena glanced at her enforcer, who shrugged and rested a hand on the pistol-shaped bulge beneath his jacket. There had been no formal talk of payment, just a vague nod toward some kind of future reciprocation.

"I'm pretty certain we discussed it," Jack added.

"Doubtful," Magdalena replied. "However, I recall the part where, well, to put this crudely, Jack, you accepted this errand on the proviso that your friend here not be murdered in cold blood. That seems more in keeping with the style of deal that I would normally broker."

"Uh, but wasn't there some—" Jack began.

"You calling my boss a fuckin' liar?" Mark cut in.

"No, I'm not, Mark. I just thought that—"

"Well, you must've thought wrong, dickhead."

"Silence," Magdalena said, raising a finger to put an end to the phallus-measuring contest. "Backhanded compliments aside, Jack and his friend did exactly as instructed. And as both of us are painfully aware, Mark, competence is a low bar when it comes to the calibre of miscreants in this city." She paused. "Right. Being the benevolent individual that I am, I'll knock twenty thousand off your tab. For services rendered. Consider it a token of my gratitude, and a humble attempt to atone for my underestimation of your ... competency."

There was that dreaded C-word: *competency.*

Competency meant being useful, and usefulness was the ultimate balancing act in the crime caper. Appear too competent, and you get singled out for more work. Drop the ball, and, as Mark so eloquently put it, a pensioner walking their

Labradoodle might just stumble across your decomposing body somewhere off Snapper Rocks.

"Oh, one last thing, boys," Magdalena said just as Jack and Hung turned to leave. "I'm sure you're eager to get going, but could you humour me with a question before you do?"

Jack hesitated. "Uh, sure. Fire away."

"Are either of you familiar with The Cockatoo Inn?"

Just when they thought they were out, she pulled them back in.

Jack, Hung, and Chul-Moo exited the nightclub and made their way to the car parked opposite. Conrad looked on intently as he jammed the mobile phone against his ear for what felt like the hundredth time.

Ring … ring … ring … ring …

Detective Hughes was still not answering.

The Exchange.

Painted an aggressive shade of yellow and filled to the brim with all manner of second-hand books, magazines, and assorted knickknacks, The Exchange stood out like the proverbial dog's balls compared to the other, more modest businesses in the vicinity. Formerly an old bank branch, this now dingy beacon of frugality was a mecca for folks who loved to riffle through mounds of worthless old crap that one could not normally give away for free. The sort of crap that carried the unmistakable stench of mildew that smacked a person square in the nostrils the moment they stepped through the door. The store's proprietor, Jarrah O'Sullivan, aka 'The Pom', leaned against the counter in the middle of the floor and kept a watchful eye on a gaggle of young men flipping through stacks of vinyl records. Barely a day over twenty-five, with a smooth, dark complexion and long shoulder-length hair, there was little that The Pom could not get his hands on without the appropriate monetary incentive. Truth be told, The Pom was about as British as the boomerang. A descendant from the original inhabitants of Rockhampton and the Capricorn Coast, Jarrah had been dubbed 'The Pom' through that admirable Australian tradition of nicknaming someone in an utterly counter-intuitive or ironic manner. So, what social faux pas had this young man committed to deserve such an incongruous moniker? He once spent the good part of a week listening to Radiohead's seminal debut album *Pablo Honey* during his formative years. The fact that Jarrah O'Sullivan had a rather Celtic-sounding surname, courtesy of an Irish grandfather who had a proclivity for getting 'hands-on' with the help at his cattle farm, made no nevermind to the brains trust responsible for the dispensation of witty nicknames. 'The Pom' it was. And for all intents and purposes, 'The Pom' it would forever be.

"I don't understand this world anymore, Barry."

"Why? What's not to understand, Sarge?"

"Take DJ Cockgobbler and The Boof Boys over there."

Detectives Hughes and Gamble loitered in the furthest corner of The Exchange and observed the same cultural holocaust being played out as the group of twenty-somethings sifted through a stack of vinyl records. The detective sergeant scowled as he observed the young men doing whatever it was that twenty-somethings presumably did, his face contorted in breathless waves of spasmodic rage.

"Look at 'em, Barry? Have you ever seen anything so unnatural in your entire life? Right down to their ever-so-perfectly cultivated facial fungus. It's like they lost some collective bet and had to superglue each other's pubes to their faces."

The pair mulled over the mental image in their minds.

"Apparently that's the style these days, Sarge."

"What? You've got to be friggin' kidding me?"

Gamble nodded and shrugged his broad shoulders.

"Since when did going out of your way to look like a kiddy fiddler suddenly become the height of fashion?" Hughes asked as he scratched his head in bewilderment. "The tight jeans. Those pork pie hats and the poxy beards. Buzzing around old Leo Sayer records like flies on shit. Honestly, if I didn't bloody know better, I'd almost reckon that somebody was havin' a lend of me, Barry."

Despite being a seemingly self-aware parody of a police officer, right down to his reflective aviator-style sunglasses, Mick Hughes struggled to accept the existence of the retro-kitsch lovechild of Generations X and Y, affectionately known as the 'hipster'. How dare a bunch of individuals who felt alienated from mainstream culture decide to make a statement by dressing differently or taking pleasure in long-forgotten hobbies? The concept was so repugnant to the societal watchman and purveyor of all things ocker that he was aggrieved by the fact that nobody had intervened earlier, preferably through the act of a four-hundredth trimester abortion.

"Just face it, Mick. We're not *with it* anymore."

"Huh? Like you've ever been *with* anything, you fat—"

Before Hughes could critique Gamble's own sense of style, his mobile phone began to belt out a familiar AC/DC riff; the detective yanked the device from his belt and cast an eye over the incoming number. He immediately mumbled and stabbed at the disconnect button as if it had been responsible for kicking his dog.

"Plan on answering that, Mick? What if it's a CI?"

"Name me one informant who's awake before noon?"

"Uh, well. Hmm? There's—" Gamble began.

"Exactly, Baz. Plus, it's an unrecognised number."

"So? What's that got to do with anything?"

"Well, if it was a call from someone I gave a toss about, their number would already be in my phone. Wouldn't it, shit-for-brains?"

Nudging Hughes in the direction of anything that even remotely resembled the duties of a police officer was an exercise in frustration.

"I just think we should get back to focusing on our actual caseload, Sarge. At the moment, we're running around like headless chooks trying to get a bead on some Korean who we aren't even sure exists. All we've got to go on is, uh, something your ex-brother-in-law claims to have overheard in a parking garage," Gamble said, as he straightened his clip-on tie and draped it over his belly. "I know you're trying to smooth things over with Magdalena Black, but if the Inspector finds out we've been playing hooky all morning instead of doing our jobs, he's going to tan our hides."

"And how's he gonna find out, mate?"

"Dunno. But what if he does?" Gamble asked.

"Bah, MacKenzie can suck my hairy plums," Hughes replied. "Let Super Cop here worry about the Inspector, yeah? I just need you to shut your trap and follow my lead. And hey, if nothing eventuates, then we'll make an appearance at that B&E over on Cavill. That's a guarantee. Hell, maybe we'll make a day of it and grab one of those sloppy Yank burgers you love so much on the way?"

"A double-chilli cheeseburger?" Gamble asked.

The mention of food was enough to pacify his partner.

"Uh, sure. If that's what it takes to shut you up."

The detectives began the slow and arduous approach from the rear of the store to the front counter through a series of narrow goat tracks carved between mountains of second-hand goods. Their journey made even more treacherous by the columns of cardboard boxes stacked from floor to ceiling that prevented sections of water-damaged roofing panels from collapsing in on themselves, a crude reminder that this was indeed the land that workplace health and safety had forgot.

"Well, if it isn't little Detective Hughes and his not-so-little mate," The Pom said, flashing a toothy grin as he leaned into the counter. "Let me take a wild guess. Some old dear had her pearls pinched last night, yeah? And before the crime scene's even cold, you two are straight into the squad car to harass the blackest fella you know."

"Piss off. I've got freckles darker than you, mate."

The Pom chuckled. "Maybe if I were a few shades lighter than your freckle, Detective, you might actually make an effort to catch those school kids nickin' my merchandise, eh?"

The detectives scoped the length and breadth of the store. If there was any quality merchandise secreted somewhere within the bowels of The Exchange, then The Pom was doing an exceptional job of keeping that fact on the down low.

"Theft? That sounds more like a *you* problem, Jarrah. Besides, I highly doubt anybody in their right mind is interested in your so-called 'merchandise'," Hughes replied. "All we're after is a little info."

"And who says I'm in the information business?"

"Cut the shit. We've been pretty lenient with you until now, mostly on account of your old man droppin' dead. But what do you reckon, Barry? Maybe it's about time we ripped those training wheels off?"

Hughes took a step forward and cast an eye over the colourful assortment of knickknacks that littered The Pom's counter, a legacy from his father's time at the helm. The detective's gaze landed on a small plastic Alsatian dressed in a police uniform beside a sign that read, 'Smile. You're on candid camera'. A faint grin licked at the corners of Hughes' mouth. He picked up the toy and examined it briefly before thrusting it toward his partner and giving it a satisfying squeeze. The familiar sound of a squeaky toy reverberated throughout the store, drawing the attention of nearby customers. Content with his small-scale attempt at upsetting the apple cart, the detective placed the toy back on the counter and continued with his diatribe as if nothing out of the ordinary had occurred.

"You're probably too young to remember, son, but there was a time when I used to come in here on the regular. Back when I was in uniform," Hughes said. "Your old man would call me a ginger-haired cunt. I'd call him something equally colourful. We'd do our little dance, and he'd slip me the occasional lead in exchange for, well, let's just say I took a more, ah, lenient approach to that *other* merchandise of his." The detective winked and cocked his head toward the building's rear. Judging by the way The Pom bit his lip and retreated into his own skin, Hughes must have been flying above the target. "Something tells me you know exactly what I'm talking about."

The Pom scoured the vicinity for curious ears.

"Come on. Keep it down, alright. I'm listening," he replied.

"You'd better do more than listen, Jarrah, because a satisfactory answer now is gonna shape the course of any relationship we might have goin' forward. Slip us a wrong one and, well, we might just decide to ... I dunno? Maybe we'll have a squiz at the paperwork for those DVD players over in the corner there? My gut feeling tells me they're hotter than a Cape York Christmas."

Detective Gamble nodded and shifted his weight.

"I'm just trying to run a business here, detectives. The legitimate sort. So whatever you reckon my old man was into, well, that's not my problem. Is it? Sins of the father, and all that nonsense they brainwash you whitefellas with at Sunday school. So, if you've finished giving me the third degree, time is money. And right now I don't have either the time, the money or the inclination to spare, especially if that means standing around here actin' like some sorta bush telegraph for the boys in blue."

Detective Hughes nodded toward the group of hipsters.

"Sure you wanna get into this here, Jarrah?"

"There's nothing to get into, Detective? And if there was, well, I suggest you pair of overpaid public servants go have a yarn with my legal representative."

"Hear that, Barry? Old mate's got a lawyer."

"Guess we ought to pack it in and go home, Sarge."

Feigning defeat, Hughes winked at his partner and turned to head for the exit. Before he could take a step, he returned only to waggle an accusatory finger in The Pom's direction.

"Out of professional curiosity, Jarrah, does your 'legal representative' know what's in that old bank vault out back?" he asked. "The fifty-odd counts of, uh, what's it called, Baz?"

"Possession of an unregistered firearm, Sarge?"

Hughes nodded and picked at his front teeth.

"Pfft. I don't have a clue what you're—"

"Give it a rest, Jarrah. Every man and his dog knew Merv had enough boomsticks out back to start World War Three. Need a gun on the Goldie? Go see Merv. It was the worst-kept secret in town."

"Don't always believe what you hear, Detective."

"Yeah? And when you hear something often enough?"

Despite old Sir Joh being six feet under and the Fitzgerald Inquiry little more than a footnote in the pages of history, not much had changed in Queensland. Sure, the faces were different, but the same old vices remained: drugs, prostitution, extortion. And then there were entrepreneurs like The Pom. Why take gun traffickers out of circulation when you could bleed them for all they were worth? Or better yet, allow them to carry on with their bloody trade, no questions asked. As long as their weapons wound up in the hands of ruthless shitheels who, in turn, used them to thin out the population of less favourable shitheels, it made sense to turn a blind eye to the chaos.

"And supposin' any of that were true?" Jarrah asked.

"What? About your stash?" Hughes replied.

The Pom closed his eyes and nodded solemnly.

"Well, I'm no barrister, mate, but I'd reckon you could forget about goin' on a walkabout any time soon. And that's before the good-time boys in Forensics slip their sweaty little digits in and have a poke around. Hell, something tells me that even those cockwombles could manage to link at least a few of your father's guns back to most, if not all, of the unsolved crime committed on our patch."

"Especially after Jimmy Jacobsen," Gamble added.

"Too right, Barry. Thanks to that hairy scrotum, our inspector has a real hard-on for gun crime at the moment."

The back-and-forth grew heated enough to catch the ear of any nearby vinyl aficionado. The Pom grimaced, leaned over the counter, and cut through the noise with a single, icy glare.

"Okay. What's a bloke gotta say to get you off his back?"

"Oh? Now you want to cooperate," Hughes replied.

The Pom scowled and mumbled something unintelligible.

"Good. So, me and Lard-arse here are trying to track somebody down. An overseas tourist. And, well, seeing as you get all sorts through this place, I figured—" Hughes began, moments before his mobile phone chimed in with another face-melting rock 'n roll riff. "Really? For fuck's sake, I've had an absolute gutful of this."

He thrust his index finger skyward as if to press pause.

"Detective Michael Hughes. This better be good."

"I found your Asian," came the reply, the voice gravelly and low.

Chapter Eleven

A Well-Maintained Revolver

Later that afternoon.

Jack Perkins made idle chit-chat with The Cockatoo Inn's manager, Maximilian 'Max' Stedkole, inside the motel's demountable office. Standing five feet tall and nearly as many wide, the local celebrity known as "Sleazeball" leaned forward in his chair with an ungodly groan and scratched at a tuft of wiry chest hair sprouting from the neckline of his stained white singlet. Pushing fifty, with a thick woolly moustache and a greasy clump of hair ravaged by male pattern baldness, Max ticked just about every box marked 'no fucking thanks' on the long list of undesirable masculine qualities.

"So, how do you know the Matron of Mirth?" he asked.

"Who? Magdalena, you mean?" Jack replied.

"Oh, already on a first-name basis then, are we?"

"Uh... yeah. I *suppose* you could say that."

Max grinned. "Let me guess. You two're rooting?"

Jack groaned and waved the accusation away dismissively.

"What? You mean to tell me you'd knock her back if she asked politely? Bullshit. Maggie might be a cold-hearted bitch, but she's still got urges like the rest of us. Hell, I bet she goes off in the sack."

Ordinarily, Jack would have avoided small talk with anyone connected to Magdalena Black. Unfortunately, she had insisted he do the opposite, even hoping they might strike up some kind of friendship. There was not a Buckley's chance of that happening. Jack resisted every opportunity to get to know this slimy prick, instead using the lull in conversation to run an eye over Max's office.

The space was almost as charmless as its owner: dented filing cabinets, a scratched-up desk and plastic chair, piles of faded, hand-labelled VHS tapes whose contents were best left a mystery, and a black-and-white television permanently tuned to the greyhounds at Albion Park. Jack could not quite put his finger on it, but the room exuded something quietly malignant, almost sinister, like stumbling across a freshly drilled glory hole in a hospice lavatory.

"Know what Magdalena reminds me of?" Max asked.

"Oh, and what's that?" Jack replied, playing along.

"Those Amazonian vampire fish," Max began. "Saw a doco about 'em recently. Little bastards live in freshwater lakes out in the forest. One day you're just swimming, minding your own beeswax, and then BAM! Outta nowhere, one shoots straight up your dick eye."

Jack grimaced and felt a sudden tightening in his gut, followed by an even sharper one further south of the equator.

"Not that there's anything wrong with objects going up your old fella," Max continued, fixing Jack with an unnerving snicker. "Just depends on whether it's entirely consensual."

"And ... *she's* a vampire fish?" Jack asked.

Max grinned, eyes gleaming. "Mate, Magdalena Black's *the* vampire fish. Slips in when you're not looking, and by the time you realise it's too late, you're gettin' rid of her by amputating your tackle."

Crude as the analogy was, Jack had already arrived at a similar conclusion. They exchanged a knowing nod before Max spun around in his chair and gazed out the window at the bushland surrounding the motel. It was a dense tangle of ferny undergrowth, punctuated by towering eucalyptus trees and the occasional golden flare of wattle. It was thick and unforgiving, the kind of terrain where a person could vanish without a trace. And given the sordid reputation of The Cockatoo Inn and its clientele, there was a better-than-average chance more than a few bodies were already out there.

Jack cleared his throat to regain Max's attention.

Max swivelled in his chair, granting his guest permission to speak with all the pomp of a greasy king perched on a plastic throne.

"Why'd she insist we bring Chul-Moo here?" Jack asked.

"And what's wrong with *here* exactly?" Max replied.

"Uh ... well, it's just that there, ah—" Jack began.

Max chuckled. "I'm having a lend of ya. I know this place is a dump," he said. "But there's no mystery why she loves it here, Jack. Just take a look around."

At first, there seemed no good reason for someone with Magdalena Black's resources to stash a valued guest at The Cockatoo Inn. But the more Jack thought about it, the clearer it became that a morally flexible motel manager could be useful for all kinds of dirty work, especially when the place sat smack in the middle of nowhere, a good twenty minutes from the nearest police station.

"Let me guess," Jack said. "You owe her money too?"

Max just had that look about him, like someone who had taken a cheeky leak in the Amazon and returned with more than just memories. Before he could launch into his tale of woe, a sharp knock on the nearby window shattered the moment. Hung's face appeared in the doorway a second later. Jack and Max exchanged a glance, eyes narrowing as they waited for the interloper to speak.

"Chul-Moo's all settled," Hung said, giving a thumbs up.

Could it be? Jack and Hung were finally … free. Jack exhaled hard, his shoulders sagging as if someone had just cut him down from a noose. They had collected the Korean from the airport, chauffeured him to his meeting, and delivered him to The Cockatoo Inn. Six hours of white-knuckled servitude to a ruthless loan shark, and not a single thing had gone wrong. It was over. Lady Luck had taken pity on them for once. They were in fucking the clear!

If Jack had an ounce of energy left, he might have danced a jig or belted out a heartfelt rendition of *Am I Ever Gonna See Your Face Again* by The Angels. Instead, he made a silent vow to honour the first deity that came to mind with a cold beer, a sloppy kebab, and twenty-four hours of dead-to-the-world unconsciousness.

"But … there is one minor issue," Hung said.

Jack's jaw clenched at the word 'but', his brief moment of victory evaporating quicker than piss on the Devil's pavement.

"There's a weird smell coming from his cabin."

Max raised an eyebrow and leaned forward with a fleshy thud as his bulbous gut slapped the edge of the desk. "A weird smell?" he repeated. "How weird are we talkin' here?"

"Uh, like … someone died in there. Recently."

Max barely blinked. "Define 'recently'."

Donald and Cyrille sat in their rental car across from The Exchange. While the former checked his wristwatch, the latter gazed wistfully out the driver's side window at a barber shuttering his shop. It was bang on five o'clock, that magic hour when ordinary punters began the commute back to their McMansions and statistically average 2.4 kids. Or, for the childless and mortgage-free, it marked the shift change between white-collar commerce and the kind of carefree, neon-soaked debauchery that made the Gold Coast famous.

"Ever wonder what it's like, Don?" Cyrille asked.

"Working an ordinary nine-to-five?" Donald replied.

"Yeah. Like old mate Giuseppe over there."

The pair watched as the man in question flipped the 'Open' sign to 'Closed' and vanished into the inky darkness of the barbershop.

"Dunno, lad. In all my previous, uh, occupations, there was always a decent chance of gettin' your head blown clean off. Best I can figure? Workin' that hard for that little's gotta be disheartening. But hey, when's the last time some poor bastard got stuffed in a 44-gallon drum and set on fire for givin' a bloke a dud haircut?"

Out of nowhere, a young, dark-skinned man appeared and wrapped a knuckle on the passenger-side window. Both men jumped a little in their seats. Like a curious emu inspecting the contents of a termite mound, The Pom craned his head into view and gave the occupants of the rental car one of his trademark cheeky smiles.

Cyrille scowled and rolled down his window.

"Piss off. We don't need our windscreen done," he said.

The Pom laughed. "No one's ever accused me of bein' a windscreen washer before. A crackhead, sure, but never a bloody windscreen washer," he said. "So? Who've we got here? I presume one of you punctual fellas must be Don?"

"That'd be me," the man in question replied.

The Pom poked his head through the open window, giving the men a thorough once-over, his gaze lingering on the muscular figure in the driver's seat. Cyrille met his stare, returning the favour with a chimpanzee-like grimace of unmodulated indignation.

"And who's your mate, Don?" The Pom asked.

"Smiley here? Lad travels with me," Donald replied.

"Yeah? He's a big unit, isn't he? What's he get up to when he's not tagging along? Guessing he's a boxer or something?"

Donald glanced at Cyrille and shook his head.

"Nah. Just a flog who spends too much time at the gym."

"Figures. Too pretty to be a pugilist. Still, I wouldn't wanna go twelve rounds with him. Nor with you, Don," The Pom said.

"Me? I'm more of a lover than a fighter. But if anything kicks off … " He leaned in, grinning. "I've got the guns. *Big* guns. And plenty of 'em."

While Cyrille silently wished they would stop talking about him as if he were some third-person proposition, The Pom squinted down the street, scanning for anything out of the ordinary: cops, tails, meter maids. Aside from a few dejected businessmen hustling toward the nearby bus stop, the trio had the area to themselves. Considering he was a black man dealing in black-market firearms, chatting to a couple of gangsters with rap sheets as long as their arms, avoiding public scrutiny was probably a wise choice.

"So, is Smiley gonna be any trouble?" The Pom asked.

"Not unless I need him to be," Donald replied.

The Pom shrugged and slapped the roof of the car.

"Well, in that case, you boys better come inside."

The trio made their way toward the rear of The Exchange through a maze of goat tracks littered with secondhand knick-knacks and worthless junk. By Donald's count, they had passed at least half a dozen security features on the way to their final stop, a reinforced steel door that could have swallowed a ballistic missile whole and still gone back for seconds. While the store's beefed-up security was probably just precautionary, anyone who had dealt with eccentric types knew there was a fine line between caution and outright paranoia. And in the case of the Donald's new friend, he had likely crossed that line with all the grace of a man in full sprint.

"I need you fellas to do me a favour," The Pom began. "In the interest of safety, specifically *mine*, I'll need you to plant yourselves, arms at your sides." He produced a small black box no larger than a packet of cigarettes, a telescopic antenna protruding from the top. "No sudden moves either. That goes double for you, Smiley."

Cyrille glanced at the device with a hint of trepidation.

"Not until you tell me what *that* does," he replied.

"My gadget? Righto. Well, you see this bulb?"

The Pom pointed to an LED on the top of the device.

"If that starts flashin' red, or the unit vibrates, then you and Don here can consider yourselves uninvited. Nothing personal, yeah? Ronnie might've vouched for ya, but I really don't appreciate doing business with coppers of the undercover variety."

The Pom held the device up, waving it at Cyrille with a sly smirk before grinning devilishly as he slowly swept the unit over his guests. Every second stretched with tension as the men eyed one another. Would it flash red? Would it vibrate? Would they falter at the first hurdle?

It was as quiet as a church mouse.

"You passed the first test," The Pom said. Satisfied that neither man was wired for sound, he slipped the device back into his pocket. "Now, one last little thing before I let you enter."

"What? The rubber glove treatment?" Donald replied.

"Nah, nothin' that impersonal. A simple yes or no."

The men waited for the inevitable follow-up.

"Are either of you fellas carrying?" The Pom asked.

"Carrying what, champ?" Cyrille said. "Guns?"

Donald cocked an eyebrow. "Sorry, but why in fuck's name would we already have guns when we came all this way with the express intention of buyin' guns from you?"

The old man had a point. The Pom shrugged and pulled a red swipe card from his front pocket. He ran it through the keypad beside the security door, waiting for it to blink from red to amber. Then he punched in a ten-digit code, each button press punctuated by an audible *beep*. The keypad completed its final transformation, blinking amber, then turning solid green as the magnetic lock disengaged with a hefty *CLUNK*. Just like that, the dance was done. The Pom heaved the heavy steel door open and motioned for his guests to step inside the vault.

"Welcome to the House of Guns," he said.

Encased in reinforced concrete, the twelve-by-five metre sarcophagus came complete with morgue-like fluorescent lighting and an emergency ventilation system that provided two hours of fresh air in the event of accidental lock-in or robbery. Around the perimeter of the vault were a series of black powder-coated shelves arranged three deep, each filled with an assortment of olive green equipment cases dispersed at irregular intervals. And last but not least, in the centre of the vault, where the men stood, there was what could only be described as a 'giant fuck-off' piece of machinery obfuscated under an equally 'giant fuck-off' blue tarpaulin. The eerily familiar silhouette made the hairs on the back of Donald's neck bristle. All in all, the vault had a far more regimented tone than the junk store which acted as its front. It was as if The Exchange had become the redheaded stepchild, left to fend for itself once the more lucrative world of black-market gunrunning had entered the picture.

"What'd you fellas have in mind?" The Pom asked.

The men took a moment to examine their surroundings. Aside from a rack of military uniforms in the far corner, the room had a muted, almost underwhelming sense of showmanship. Where were the bespoke corkboards lined with matte-black firearms? The rows of body armour and vintage gas masks? The Eureka Flags draped heroically across the walls? Apart from a few shelving units and the tarpaulined curiosity looming in the centre of the vault, the space felt about as cold and clinical as a proctologist's waiting room.

"So, what's the biggest weapon here?" Cyrille asked.

"The biggest? Nah. I doubt you could handle her."

"Well, I didn't come here to buy a spud gun, mate."

The Pom made an emasculating gesture with his pinkie finger and walked over to the tarpaulin-covered object. He waited until he was absolutely sure that he had the full attention of the men before tearing the tarp away, akin to a dinner-theatre magician performing some grandiose illusion. *Ta-da!* His visitors responded with a string of profanities as their eyes came to rest upon what appeared to be a partially constructed piece of military-issue artillery.

"Heh. I never tire of doin' that!" The Pom said.

Donald grinned like a besotted teenager as he approached the steel monstrosity, running a hand along the weather-beaten barrel. Known locally as the Hamel Gun, it was hardly state-of-the-art, but the fifteen-kilogram shells it fired were more than capable of silencing even its harshest critic. He slipped on his reading glasses, crouched beside the carriage leg, and gave it a once-over. The weld was rough, as though it had been slapped on by a hungover apprentice, but the overall finish was passable. Donald leaned in, squinting, as if the metal might whisper its war stories straight into his ear.

"So, how'd you get your hands on her?" he asked.

"Well, let's just say my father had friends in all the right places. Or more specifically, an engineer mate up Townsville way who could scrounge up mothballed parts. Dad'd been tinkering with it on and off since I was in high school. Shit, with another couple of years I reckon he might've gotten this big mumma operational again."

"Nice. Was your old man in the service?" Donald asked.

"Army? Nah. They wouldn't have looked at him twice."

"What, on account of him being an Aboriginal?"

"Nah. On account of him missin' half a leg."

"I'm gonna assume you two aren't big-game hunters," The Pom said with a grin, pulling an olive green equipment case from a nearby shelf. "Let's skip straight to the daily beaters, yeah?"

One by one, he held a series of weapons aloft for his customers' perusal before carefully placing them on the wire racking with an OCD-like fastidiousness. The two Melbourne hardmen exchanged amused glances as The Pom went through the motions until an eclectic assortment of lead-spitters were laid out in front of them.

"So, where should I start, fellas?" he asked, as he playfully glided his slender fingers across the line-up.

"Beginning's as good a place as any," Donald replied.

"Deadly. The Glock it is then," The Pom said.

He retrieved the first cab off the rank and pulled back the slide in order to demonstrate its silky-smooth, mercurial action.

"This here is Austria's third most famous export, right behind Arnie and, well ... that other bloke no one likes to talk about. Aside from it bein' standard-issue for the Queensland Police, the old Glock here is a personal favourite of every wannabe gangster rapper and knobjockey from Brissie through to the back o' Burke."

"What sort of specs are we talkin'?" Donald asked.

"She's a 9mm, polymer-framed, locked-breech semi-automatic. A lot of marketing mumbo jumbo, I know. The main thing you're really gonna need to remember is that she's got a fifteen-round magazine ... and I'm not gammin' ya here when I say this, but you're likely gonna need every one of those slippery little suckers."

"Christ, they're that inaccurate?" Donald pressed.

"Well, not exactly, Don. Now, I don't like to generalise, but some of these Glocks have a habit of jammin' as often as an unemployed musician. Eh? Honestly, you'd be doing me a favour by takin' this thing off my hands for, I dunno? Let's say, a neat three hundred? I'll even throw in a box of ammo just to get it out of my sight."

It was quite a sales pitch, not that one was needed. Despite their alleged tendency to jam at the worst possible moment, Glocks sold themselves. Decades of teens idolising hip-hop dickheads with lousy grammar and even lousier self-control had seen to that.

"Did I hear right? It's made of polymer?" Cyrille asked.

"The frame is *partially* polymer," The Pom replied.

"So you can, like, sneak it through airports?"

"Yeah, nah," The Pom said. "There's no such thing as a plastic gun, Smiley, despite what ya might've seen in the movies. Eighty-odd percent is still regular ordnance steel, like the barrel and slide for starters. And the parts that *are* made of plastic use a special X-ray visible polymer. So, no. You ain't getting through any metal detectors with this stuffed down the front of your Levi Strauss."

Donald chuckled to himself, then chimed in.

"What you're overlooking is the ammo, lad. Even if the weapon were entirely plastic ... or polymer ... or whatever the fuck, how in God's name are you supposed to sneak a box of brass through an X-ray machine?" he said, in no uncertain terms. "Anyway, not to interrupt the spiel here, but, uh, plastic guns weren't exactly what we had in mind. The young blood and I are in the market for somethin' a bit more, er, how should I put this? A fraction more ... shiny."

"Shiny? Like chrome-plated?" The Pom replied.

"As in, the sorta hardware that would make a bloke cream his shorts the moment you whip it out. The, uh ... fancy shit."

It physically pained Donald to drop the F-word: *fancy*. Drawing undue attention to oneself was the very antithesis of everything he stood for. But if he was going to get any leads on who had killed his nephew, he would need to step outside his comfort zone.

"Ah! From the moment I laid my big brown eyes on you, Don, I could tell you appreciated craftsmanship. Wait there." The Pom turned to a nearby case and retrieved an exquisite, nickel-plated .357 Colt Python. "You wanted fancy?" he asked, opening the revolver before snapping it shut again with a satisfying *CLICK!*

Donald examined the weapon with a wolfish grin.

"Beaut, ain't she? You can't look past a Colt when you're chasin' accuracy and stopping-power, especially with that four-inch barrel and gorgeous nickel finish. But I doubt I need to sell you on the virtues of a Colt." Donald shook his head as The Pom gently tossed the weapon back and forth between the palms of his hands in some sort of misguided attempt to demonstrate weight distribution. "What's that old mantra? 'God created men. Colonel Colt made them equal'."

Donald nodded. "It certainly fits the brief," he replied.

"Yet, I'm sensing a 'but' here?" The Pom said.

"But what's to say it's not gonna explode in my hand?"

The Pom chuckled. "Reputation, Don. My old man, Merv, maintained every firearm that passed through this place. He wasn't in the habit of selling paperweights, and neither am I. Blokes like us don't last long in this business if we do. One unpleasant experience and the customer's back on your doorstep the next day, tryin' to force-feed it to ya, barrel-first … if you catch my drift."

The Pom retrieved a green box of ammunition from inside the case and placed it on the shelf beside him. He opened the cylinder, placed a round in one of the six empty chambers, and then snapped it shut again. Cyrille looked uneasy. He stole a quick glance at Donald, who appeared unfazed by the recent development. The Pom spun the cylinder and, reluctantly, placed the barrel against his temple.

"Oi! What the hell are you doing?" Cyrille asked.

"Don't you worry, big fella," The Pom replied.

"Worried? You're about to friggin' slot yourself."

Donald remained suspiciously quiet, reminded of another old mantra: "Never interrupt your enemy when he is making a mistake". Or in this case, never interrupt a gunrunner when he is about to top himself. Best case, they walked away with a free shooter. Worst case? The merchandise was a dud.

The Pom nervously exhaled and cocked the hammer.

"Don? Wanna say something here?" Cyrille said.

"It's, uh, perfectly safe," The Pom replied. "Load a single round into the chamber of a well-maintained revolver, spin the cylinder, and the one with the round in it will *almost certainly* fall to the bottom. Trust me. Dad swore by it. Called it his ... guarantee of quality."

'Almost certainly' hardly sounded all that certain.

The Pom went to squeeze the trigger. His finger-work was shaky at first, trepidatious, but the longer he sat on the precipice, the more that heady mix of fear and intent billowed behind his eyes. Was this kid really going to go through with it? Donald had seen enough. He cleared his throat, signalling an end to the macabre sales pitch.

"There's no need for any of that shit," he said.

"Phew! Thank the fuckin' Rainbow Serpent for that," The Pom replied. "I might be crazy, but I'm not that bloody crazy. Oh? And for future reference, Don, decent folks usually stop me long before I begin squeezin' the bloody trigger, yeah. What the heck were you waiting for? A bloke could've done himself a real mischief."

"Ah well," Donald said. "You live, you learn."

Under normal circumstances, he might have let the lunatic follow through, then turned the place over hoping to find a list of customers. But not here. Not at The Exchange, a colossal shithole run by a paranoid wreck. The chances of dredging up any records in a timely fashion were next to nil. Besides, only an overly enthusiastic salesperson would jam a loaded firearm against their temple without first establishing a price. And as anyone with five minutes of customer service experience could attest, enthusiasm was a finite resource. The more Donald saw of The Pom and his methods, the more obvious it became that this kid still had his L-plates on when it came to wheeling and dealing in the world of black-market firearms.

"So, how much for that revolver?" Donald asked.

"Uh ... eight hundred," The Pom replied, still flustered. "Usually they go for over two grand, but I'll give it to you at mate's rates."

"Mates already, are we? That was quick."

"Buy a few more guns and we'll be best friends."

Donald chuckled. "Sorry, what was your name again?"

"Jarrah. But folks 'round here call me The Pom."

The Melburnians exchanged a sideways glance. The Pom? There was sweet bugger all about this kid that screamed 'English'. Even if they could look past his flawless smile and positive demeanour, his tan was too impressive for any Englishman they had ever met.

"So eight hundred, Jarrah?" Donald asked. "Hmm. Feels steep, especially for something I'm just going to drop to the bottom of Davy Jones' locker when it's done talking."

"How about something more budget-friendly then?"

"What? Like that Glock you had a minute ago?"

Despite the obvious merits of one firearm over the other, The Pom sensed that Donald's actions were driven purely by the perceived damage to his hip pocket. In other words, the man was tighter than a duck's farter. It was an observation that would have been handy to clock well before he pulled the whole revolver-to-the-head stunt.

"How much was on that Glock again?" Donald asked.

"Three hundred, cash," The Pom said, turning to the shelf. He set the revolver down and went to reach for the Glock.

"Actually, was that three with or without ammo?"

The Pom paused. "With ammo," he replied.

"And as far as the slide goes? Stock or aftermarket?"

The Pom hesitated, hand hovering halfway to the Glock. The relentless back-and-forth was feeling like a tennis match, if tennis were played by morons and the prize was a migraine.

"Stock, Don. It's completely 'as is', no need—"

"On second thought, let me just feel the Colt again."

The Pom sighed and handed the revolver back to Donald, who in turn mimicked the gunrunner's palm-to-palm toss from moments earlier. The balance was perfect. A few grams heavier than expected, but there was a valid reason for that. He opened the cylinder to confirm his suspicions. Bingo. Donald glanced back at The Pom with a devilish grin and then snapped the cylinder shut again with a quick, almost indistinguishable flick of the wrist.

"Oh shit. There's still a—" The Pom began.

"A round in the spout?" Donald cut in.

The gunrunner exhaled and nodded solemnly.

In between all the back-and-forth and Donald's changes of heart, albeit with the intent to sow confusion, The Pom had forgotten that there was still a live round in the revolver. A revolver that was now in the capable hands of a standover man who was short on leads, and possibly soon to be even shorter on material witnesses.

"Like I said, Jarrah. You live, you learn."

"And what about our Asian friend, Sarge?"

"Tucked up in his cabin, snug as a bug, Baz."

Obscured behind the safety of a nearby culvert, Detective Hughes observed the comings and goings at The Cockatoo Inn through a pair of comically large binoculars from the passenger seat of their unmarked vehicle. Unsurprisingly, the ledger consisted entirely of goings and no comings. Gamble sat behind the wheel, while Conrad stretched out across the backseat, devouring the last remnants of the detective sergeant's double-chilli cheeseburger with all the relish of a man unfamiliar with nourishment beyond a yeasty liquid lunch.

"Did I do good or what, fellas?" Conrad asked.

"*Good* is a relative term," Hughes replied.

Conrad straightened and leaned between the front seats, wedged between the detectives. Hughes swatted him away like an oversized, odorous mosquito as flakes of partially chewed hamburger rained down on everything within an immediate one-metre radius.

"Relative to what, Detective?" Conrad asked.

"Relative to me not busting you the next time I catch you flogging stolen gear out of your car boot. But only on one condition, Connie. That you kindly fuck off back to wherever you came from."

Conrad nodded and hurriedly scooped up the remnants of his burger before exiting the car, not bothering with another word to either man. The detectives exchanged a look, their eyes following the flannelette-wearing goblin as he scurried across to the other side of the culvert, where his pathetic excuse for a car was parked.

"Okay. So, uh, what's the plan?" Gamble asked.

"Don't blow your wad too early, Barry. The blokes in the blue Datsun only just left," Hughes replied, watching Conrad's car ease onto the highway and vanish in the rear-view mirror. "Let's give our little mate more time to settle in. Then, when he's sitting on the bog, old fella in hand ... that's when we catch him unawares."

"And ... I can't possibly talk you out of this, Mick?"

Hughes scowled. "Not unless you wanna walk home."

"Any idea of who I am, lad?" Donald asked The Pom.

The Pom shrugged and shook his head.

"I'm Donald Edgar Jacobsen. Name ring a bell?"

Silence. He focused his aim on the gunrunner's kneecap.

A firearm aimed centre mass, the point at which most of a person's vital organs happily congregated, was a telltale sign of a simple business transaction; an unspoken tip of the hat from one crim to another to imply that there was no malice intended. However, when that aim travelled south of the border, that once simple business transaction morphed into something very painful, very prolonged and very personal. And when it came to The Diamond, there was nothing more personal than family.

"How about my nephew then?" Donald asked.

The Pom stared at his interrogator blankly.

"Jimmy Jacobsen?" Donald continued. "You must've heard of him. He was the unlucky prick who got clipped in an alleyway last week and was left to bleed out like a stuck pig."

The Pom's eyes lit up as he realised that this was not the first time today that somebody had dropped the name 'Jimmy Jacobsen' in impolite conversation. The first instance had been Detective Hughes and his dogged attempt to acquire information on an Asian tourist. The second, and clearly the more life-threatening instance, were these two crims out to purchase a 'fancy-looking' firearm. 'Fancy-looking' being their words, not his. The Pom was curious about the connection, if only for the fact that something big was going down on the Gold Coast and, for once, he was out of the loop.

"I don't know anyone called Jimmy," he replied.

"Hmm. You absolutely sure about that, lad?"

The Pom nodded like his life depended on it.

"Well, a little birdie told us your old man used to be the King Dick of under-the-table firearms around here," Donald began. "And by extension, I'm guessing that now makes you

Little Dick. So yeah? I mightn't be a gambler, Jarrah, but I reckon it's a safe bet the shooter used to kill Jimmy was from outta this vault. Supply and demand."

"But ... you're missin' something," The Pom said.

"Oh? And what would that be?" Donald replied.

"Maybe, ah, put the gun down first, eh? Then we talk."

Donald sneered. "The gun stays put. You talk."

"Shit, eh? Well, like I said, my father's long gone. Ya nephew dyin' is real sorry business and all, but Don, a bloke's not responsible for what happens with his merchandise once it leaves the store." The Pom paused to concoct an analogy. "That's like saying, I dunno? I drive to Bunnings to buy myself a hammer. And then, hey? I use that same hammer to cave-in somebody's brainbox."

"Huh? What the heck are you on about, Jarrah?"

"Well, it's hardly Bunnings' fault now, is it?"

Donald looked The Pom square in the eye and gave the cylinder of the revolver a hefty spin. The solitary .357 cartridge did its merry-go-round of death with a daunting *CLICK-ETY-CLACK* before settling wherever chance or perhaps fate willed it. A generous one-in-six shot at a cranial suppository, odds that made even stone-cold killers reminisce about their abusive childhoods.

"What was that theory of yours, Jarrah?" he asked.

"Uh, I ... huh? What theory?" The Pom replied.

"When a round's placed in the chamber of a well-maintained revolver, and spun, that round will almost certainly fall to the bottom? That one. I remember you using the words 'almost certainly' like you were on Mount Sinai readin' from the Ten Commandments."

Donald took a menacing half-step toward The Pom.

"Come on now, Don. I don't know anything!"

"That's unfortunate then," Donald said. "Because if your theory holds up, that round should be ready to rock on the … third trigger pull? So, mathematically speaking, that gives you the luxury of two wrong answers. Three, if you're as lucky as a dog with two dicks."

The arithmetic sounded solid enough, but given the current circumstances, it was unlikely that anyone was going to correct Donald while he was in possession of a loaded firearm. Donald reached into his shirt pocket and retrieved a newspaper article given to him by Ronnie earlier that day; its torn edges and smudged print spoke to the truth that it had been harvested with complete disregard for the existence of scissors. He looked The Pom in the eye as he shook open the folded page and passed it to his offsider.

"Go ahead and read that, lad," Donald said.

Cyrille shrugged and scanned the article in silence.

"Christ. Try reading it aloud, you numpty!"

"Sorry, Don. Uh, let's see. 'An eyewitness reported the assailant carried a chrome pistol with a mother-of-pearl handle, with an image of an American bald eagle engraved in the centre of the handle'."

The gunrunner stared up at the flickering fluorescent lights, realising this was no longer a robbery. That was the frustrating part. He would have happily let them walk out of the vault with as many guns as they could carry. But Donald was not here for the merchandise. He was after answers.

"Come on, fellas. Merv sold a shitload of guns out of here," The Pom began. "Do you really expect me to remember the name of every Tom, Dick, and skinhead he'd ever dealt with?"

"No. But surely he kept notebooks?" Donald asked.

"Hardly. It was all up here," The Pom replied, as he pointed to his head. "He never recorded anything. If there's nothing on paper, then there's nothing for the cops when they kick your door down."

"Mmm. And what about the guns *you've* sold?"

The Pom let out a nervous chuckle.

"What's so bloody funny, lad?" Donald asked.

"Can I be completely honest?" The Pom replied. "I haven't, ah ... I haven't sold a single item out of here since Dad passed. Zip. Zilch. Zero. Not even so much as a stray bullet. And shit, it's not for a lack of tryin'."

"Bull," Donald said. "No one's buying that, Jarrah."

"Well, guess what, Don? No one's buyin' my guns either. No matter what I do ... the Russian Roulette demonstrations, putting on this whole blackfella persona ... the locals only wanna deal with Merv. And frankly, I would've preferred it that way, but, hey? He dropped off the perch and left us with a mountain of debt."

The Melburnians were on the verge of restlessness.

"How about gettin' to the point?" Cyrille said.

"Point is, you'd probably never tell by lookin' at me, but I've got a Master's in Chemical Engineering. Flogging guns isn't me. Truth is, fellas, I deplore guns. And I deplore all the palaver that goes with 'em. I'm just moving the rest of Merv's stock so we can keep the lights on and fix that roof before it collapses in on itself."

That would explain The Pom's eagerness to meet.

"A Master's in Chemical Engineering?" Donald said, impressed. "So, I'm guessin' you must be halfway clever?"

"Well ... I wouldn't say clever exactly, but I—"

Donald grinned and squeezed the trigger. *CLICK!*

A wave of relief crashed over The Pom. Relief, and a sudden involuntary dribble of piss, as his body betrayed him in the aftermath of panic, finally processing the reality of his near-death experience.

"Right. That's chance number one, mate!" Donald said.

"Okay! Okay!" The Pom replied, hands raised in front of his face in a futile defensive gesture. Futile in the sense that an eight-gram jacketed hollow-point travelling at over four hundred metres per second was hardly going to stop and ask for permission before it sliced through his paws like a hot knife through butter.

"The gun ... in the article? It came in a pair."

"Huh? A *pair* of guns?" Donald replied.

"Yeah. A pair. As in, there were two of them."

"Oh cheers, prick. I passed Grade One maths."

"Sorry. It's just, I remember Merv sellin' a pair of handguns a few years back with carvings on the handles. One had an eagle perchin' on a hand grenade ... or maybe it was a bomb? I dunno. The other had a dove, sat on one of those peace signs." The Pom held aloft the classic 'V sign' hand gesture. "I remember 'em clearly because it's not every day something like that comes through here."

"And you saw them with your own eyes?" Cyrille asked.

"Nah. Just what I heard," The Pom replied. "Funny thing is, no one ever came looking for 'em. Makes me think they were nicked from down south and written off on insurance."

There was a twisted irony in the notion that the weapon used to murder Jimmy may have originated in the Melburnian's own backyards. That revelation aside, at least the men had made progress with their investigation. The Pom distinctly remembered the firearm in question; now it was just a matter of linking said firearm to the local miscreant who had purchased it from his father.

"You positive it was a dove and an eagle?" Donald said.

The Pom again nodded like his life depended on it.

"Mmm. Sounds pretty wanky, if you ask me."

"Not when you think about it, Don," Cyrille replied.

"And how do you figure that, young blood?"

"The carved motifs on the handles … they're an obvious play on the duality of man. The eagle? That's a manifestation of man's masculine, warmongering nature. And the dove? Man's peaceful, passive nature. Ying and yang shit."

Donald stood there dumbfounded. That was possibly the most intelligent thing ever to pass Cyrille's lips, and it was completely wasted on a fellow crim and a black-market arms dealer held at gunpoint in a disused bank vault. Donald shook off his disbelief and refocused on the more pressing matter at hand.

"My original enquiry still stands, Jarrah," he said. "Got a name for the bloke who bought these Freudian firearms?"

"You know I can't tell you that," The Pom replied.

"Why? Did you sign a non-disclosure agreement?"

"Nah, 'cause he'd fuckin' kill me. That's why."

Donald sighed and replied with a squeeze of the trigger.

The hollow *CLICK!* of the revolver's hammer striking dead air resonated through The Pom like the mellifluous sweet-nothings of a flock of angels descending from the heavens. He whimpered and snatched a lungful of air as the adrenaline surged through him.

"That's chance number two," Donald said.

"And the third time's the charm," Cyrille added.

Somebody Is at the Door

Later that night.

Max Stedkole, the moustachioed manager of The Cockatoo Inn, sat hunched over his desk, demolishing a packet of corn chips, eyes glued to the One Day International between Australia and the West Indies. Max found the gentleman's game about as riveting as a case of genital warts, but when Magdalena Black gave explicit instructions to keep an eye on her special guest, it was in his best interest to feign interest, if only to stay awake. As the locals' defence grew more hopeless with each passing ball, Max used the lull in play to glance out the window toward cabin three, a loaded hunting rifle resting across his lap. He had never needed to brandish the old World War II-era relic for anything more than deterrence, but when push came to shove, he was more than capable of putting the 'find out' into anyone foolish enough to 'fuck around and find out'.

Chul-Moo sat on a complimentary bath towel draped across the edge of the bed, absorbed in a rapid-fire phone conversation in his native tongue. The scratchy fabric offered little protection from the sordid history steeped into the soiled duvet beneath him, a silent testament to the indiscretions of previous guests. The air reeked of stale cigarette smoke and sweat, the stench curling in his stomach and making it difficult to focus. Perhaps if the windows actually opened, he might have attempted to air the place out. But clearly, Magdalena Black had spared no expense on his accommodation, just as The Cockatoo Inn's housekeeping spared no effort beyond removing the sex toys and trinkets left behind by the pay-by-the-hour clientele.

Gwangju, Jeollado Provence. South Korea.

The voice on the end of Chul-Moo's receiver belonged to Yoon, a rotund, balding crime boss. He sat behind a lavish mahogany writing desk, his gaze fixed on the page as he scribbled furiously onto a sheet of lavender-scented stationery. Yoon's stoic demeanour and measured tone exuded quiet authority and absolute control. Flanking him on either side were two bodyguards, imposing figures with dead eyes and a reputation as fuckers tougher than microwaved steak. Known as *jopok*, members of an organised crime syndicate, they were easily recognisable by their signature *gakdoogi* haircuts, shaved sides with a tuft of hair up top, and vibrant, full-body tattoos. But it was the tailored black suits that truly sealed the deal, like something plucked straight from a Quentin Tarantino-approved wet dream.

"What do you make of this woman?" he asked.

"Miss Magdalena?" Chul-Moo replied.

Yoon nodded, the corner of his mouth quirking into a faint smile. "As my father used to say, 'Never conduct business with those who bleed'." He paused, placing his fountain pen with deliberate care in the ornate silver holder on his desk. "While I am aware that such thinking may seem archaic to young men like yourself, his point stands. Are we to shackle ourselves to a woman who, through her very biology, is temperamental and prone to inconstancy?"

Chul-Moo took a slow breath before responding. His boss' crude take on women aside, he had seen enough of the Gold Coast loan shark to know she was damn near impossible to read.

"She appears ... genuine," he said finally.

"But can we do business with her, Chul-Moo?"

"Magdalena Black can be ... how would you say ... eccentric?" he began. "But I believe she intends to honour our transaction. She raised concerns about the price when we met, although it seemed more like opportunism than hesitation. As we both know, that is to be expected when dealing with Australians."

Yoon paused, taking a long, deliberate sip of tea.

"And what time will the transfer take place?" he asked.

"Mid-morning," Chul-Moo replied confidently. "Magdalena has already obtained a copy of the account information, and the decryption software is on the USB drive, all set for deployment." There was a brief pause before he continued. "The arrangement is for Magdalena's head of security to drive us to her club. From there, we will conduct the final wire transfer. All things considered, I should easily be back at the airport for my eight o'clock departure."

"Very well," Yoon said. "Do you anticipate problems?"

As Chul-Moo pondered the five-hundred-thousand-dollar question, a loud, sharp *knocking sound* reverberated through the telephone, bringing their conversation to an abrupt halt. It was so vivid, so sudden, that it almost seemed to originate from Yoon's own office.

The mob boss sat forward, his features tightening with concentration as he strained to identify the source.

"Chul-Moo? What was that?" he asked.

Chul-Moo's eyes scanned the cabin for anything out of the ordinary. He had expected no visitors, especially not at this late hour. This was supposed to be a covert business visit, in and out, with absolutely no room for any unforeseen interruptions. Suddenly, there was another sharp *knock* at the door of cabin three. The noise startled Chul-Moo. He did his best to suppress the creaking of the rusty mattress springs as he cautiously rose from the bed, all while still keeping the telephone receiver pressed against his shell-like ear. He peered through the gap between the window and moth-eaten curtains, searching for the source of the knocking.

"Somebody is at the door," he whispered to Yoon.

With Jack and Hung presumably back at The Hackston, Chul-Moo was left to contemplate the identity of the mysterious visitor. The logical conclusion was that it must have been The Cockatoo Inn's manager, Max, but it seemed unlikely that he would deliver fresh towels or bedding at this hour. Or at any hour, for that matter. Chul-Moo hesitated, unsure of whether he should answer the door or wait to see if the visitor would simply leave of their own volition.

"Hello?" he said, his voice barely above a whisper.

There was a faint shuffling from outside, but no response.

He waited a few seconds before repeating, "Hello?"

The *knock* came again, more insistent this time. Chul-Moo's heart raced with a sense of apprehension. This was not what he was cut out for. He was not one of Yoon's battle-tested henchmen, merely a shitkicker who was handy with a laptop and a modem.

"Who is there?" he asked, his voice more forceful.

Again, there was nothing but silence.

With the current line of questioning appearing to be fruitless, Chul-Moo peered through the peephole in the door, the telephone cord perilously stretched to its limit. His heart pounded in his chest. The peephole was one of the few luxuries at The Cockatoo Inn, and it had saved many a guest from being caught in a compromising situation. Despite Yoon's pleas not to answer the door, Chul-Moo's curiosity got the better of him. He inched closer, pressing the telephone receiver firmly against his chest. He peered through the peephole, squinting to make out the figure on the other side. The darkness made it difficult to discern any features, but it was obvious from the silhouette that it was of a male figure standing with his back to the door. The way he stood, with an air of anticipation, suggested that he was waiting for something ... or someone.

Out of nowhere, a size nine boot appeared!

CRUNCH! The door exploded off its hinges, sending Chul-Moo hurtling backwards onto the shagpile carpet below, and the telephone receiver back into the wall like an obese English tourist at the end of a bungee cord. The brutal impact rendered Chul-Moo unconscious. As he lay there amidst the splintered debris, motionless, a familiar figure limped through the door frame sporting a fetching olive green balaclava and a crooked smile.

"My fuckin' foot," Detective Hughes mumbled.

He hoisted Chul-Moo from the floor and dragged him feet first through the door to the waiting car outside. The detective's muscles strained as he hurled the Korean's limp frame into the open boot, body flopping awkwardly with the effort. After a moment's pause to catch his breath, Hughes dashed back into the motel room, scanning the space frantically for any clues to the victim's identity. His eyes darted from corner to corner until he spotted the Korean's backpack teetering on the edge of the bed. Acting quickly, he grabbed the bag and rushed to the car, tossing it into the boot and slamming the lid shut with a heavy thud. The sound rang out across the desolate car park, sharp and unmistakable amid the chaos.

Maybe that was what caught the motel manager's attention. More likely, it was the kicked-in door. Or the scuffle. Or the sight of a man being shoved into the boot of a Commodore like a sack of spuds.

Whatever the trigger, Hughes spun just in time to see the barrel of Max's rifle aimed in his direction. *BOOM!* A puff of plaster exploded beside him as a round tore into the wall, showering him with debris.

"Fuck me. Punch it, Fatty!" Hughes yelled.

Gamble stomped on the accelerator of the car, causing it to fishtail through the car park. Hughes ran frantically beside it, struggling to keep pace. "Slow down!" he gasped, pounding the boot with an open palm. Gamble eased off of the pedal. The pair were now at least fifty metres away from the scene, but there was little doubt that another round from Max's hunting rifle was due for dispatch. The detective's legs pumped battery acid. His heart thumped in his chest like a bass drum. He urged himself to keep running, to catch up with the car. Just as Gamble slowed enough to allow his colleague to keep pace, the detective grabbed hold of the open rear window frame and dived headfirst into the backseat, slamming abruptly into the upholstery.

BOOM! TING! ... BOOM! TING!

Two more rounds pounded into the detective's car.

Gamble's grip on the steering wheel tightened until his knuckles turned molten white. He struggled to maintain control of the car as they barrelled through the motel's car park and out onto the connecting road as fast as their Commodore would allow. They did not know where the rounds had landed, but the faint whizzing sound slicing past Hughes' melon made it clear they were landing dangerously close. Truth be told, anywhere within the current postcode would have been far too close for comfort.

BOOM ... ... TING!

With Max's parting shot echoing in the warm summer night, he lowered his rifle and cursed a blue streak under his breath. He felt utterly useless as he watched the car disappear into the inky darkness, his heart pounding irregularly in his chest.

The telephone handset lay abandoned on the floor of Chul-Moo's cabin, with Yoon still on the other end of the line, anxiously repeating his name. He had heard everything that had transpired in the last few minutes, and to say he was "a little concerned" would have been a gross understatement.

Chapter Thirteen

Dig, Rover. Dig.

BLACK pulsed with energy as a sea of bodies moved and gyrated in time to the godawful beat of electronic music, the air thick with the heady scent of alcohol, sweat and perfume. Strobe lights illuminated the dance floor, casting shadows that danced along its obsidian walls and multi-level catwalks. As the DJ mixed tracks, the crowd's energy intensified, their movements becoming more frenzied and animalistic. Amidst the chaos, groups of friends huddled together, shouting conversations into each other's ears over the blaring music. At the bar, patrons coddled their drinks, their eyes drawn to Pablo, the nightclub's resident mixologist, a slender figure with tattoos that adorned his flesh like the intricate accoutrements of a professional wanker. Perched atop his head, a stylish fedora added an air of enigmatic charm to his brand. With effortless dexterity, Pablo showcased his seasoned expertise, gracefully concocting drinks with a practised finesse that seemed almost second nature.

It was everything that Mark Campbell despised.

Mark's imposing figure manoeuvred through the crowd like a leather-jacketed Moses parting the Red Sea, with Magdalena Black, a tempest of fury, close behind, her piercing green eyes ready to cut down anyone foolish enough to cross their path. Their exit carried a sharp sense of urgency, naturally putting someone as big and ugly as Campbell in the lead. He relished clearing the way, effortlessly shouldering aside intoxicated patrons like a freight train in full swing, a ghost of his glory days in the NRL. The reason for the urgency? Magdalena had just received the bad news: Chul-Moo was rattling around in a car boot somewhere on the M1 Motorway.

"Magdalena!" a voice wailed above the chaos.

The loan shark turned her head and saw a heavily bandaged figure emerging from the writhing masses. It was Neville, the mulleted drug dealer that Detective Hughes had flung through a plate-glass window earlier that day. Despite his injuries, he seemed to be *in*, or *on*, relatively good spirits. Magdalena muttered something undecipherable under her breath as the dealer continued to worm his way through the crowd toward her, presumably desperate for an audience with the self-proclaimed Queen of the Gold Coast. When he finally came within arm's reach, the dealer called out again.

"Hey, Magdalena!" he yelled into the void.

Mark caught a twitch in his peripheral vision and skidded to a halt. To be fair, a bloke who looked like a Hammer Horror villain fresh from a twelve-rounds with Muhammad Ali was hard to miss, even when gunning for the nearest exit. It took a second, but the dead-eyed stare and toothless grin gave Neville away.

"That's 'Miss Black' to you, Nev," Mark boomed.

"Oh. I … I just want to talk to her," the dealer replied.

"Yeah? Well, make a fuckin' appointment."

Out of nowhere, Campbell grabbed Neville by the shoulders and clocked him with a headbutt. *CRACK!* The sound rolled through the crowd, rattling teeth, buckling knees, and drawing a few well-earned gasps of disbelief. Neville flew backward, arms flailing, instantly swallowed by the writhing mob. Now was not the time to shoot the shit. Campbell straightened his jacket, nodded lazily at nobody in particular, and strode on like a bloke late for mum's Sunday roast. Magdalena thundered behind him, eyes flashing murder, and the pair slipped out through a side exit so discreet it might as well have been invisible. Behind them, the nightclub carried on, a sweaty, screaming mess of spilled drinks, flying elbows, and broken teeth.

Outside the nightclub, Donald Jacobsen and Cyrille stood in a queue that snaked around the block, waiting to enter. Donald appeared out of place amidst the sea of young, fashionable club-goers, while Cyrille seemed to blend in effortlessly. He was dressed impeccably for the occasion, sporting a sleek black silk shirt and form-fitting jeans that accentuated his muscular physique. Donald, on the other hand, stood out like a sore thumb in his faded flannelette shirt and cargo pants that looked like they had seen better days. As the two burly security guards on the door ushered in yet another group of women who had audaciously cut in line using the time-honoured 'stop and chat' technique, the pair could not help but rightly feel frustrated. However, they knew better than to cause a scene. After what seemed like an eternity, they finally reached the front of the queue, where a large Fijian with a name badge that simply read 'Bob' extended a massive hand.

"I'm sorry, gentlemen," he said in a deep voice. "The club is currently at capacity. I'll have to ask you both to step aside."

Donald and Cyrille exchanged quizzical glances.

"You're kidding me, right?" Donald replied.

"Afraid not," Fijian Bob repeated firmly, maintaining his composure. "We take fire safety regulations seriously here. Now how about you do me a favour and take a few steps *over there*?"

'Over there' being a euphemism for 'anywhere but here'.

As Donald and the security guard locked eyes, Cyrille's gaze flicked to a handsome blond man standing on the footpath, yakking obnoxiously into his mobile. He took in the tight denim jeans and polished leather boots before returning to the matter at hand. The tension on the street promised an old-fashioned punch-up, but after a few long seconds, Donald grimaced and took Fijian Bob's advice, joining Cyrille on the footpath. His grimace was not surrender, men like him never surrendered, but pragmatism. He needed a cool head. No point getting on security's radar before even stepping inside.

"So, how do we get in?" Cyrille asked Donald, giving a knowing nod to the handsome man. In response, the man returned a smile and carried on with his very loud and very public conversation.

Frustrated by the situation, Donald watched with disdain as yet another group of attractive young women slipped past security and through the front door of the nightclub with little more than a few flirtatious gestures. It was enough to make his blood boil.

"What. The. Actual. Fuck?" he muttered, pointing toward the group who had just breezed through. "You seeing this, lad?"

"Yeah, I'm seeing it, Don," Cyrille replied.

"Eh, bugger this. Enough stayin' off the radar."

Donald approached the towering security guard, adrenaline surging through his veins. His heart thumped loudly in his chest, the pounding rhythm echoing in his ears. Each breath he took felt laboured and heavy, as anticipation gripped him. The security guard, a hulking mass of South Pacific impenetrability, gazed down at Donald with a hint of amusement dancing behind his eyes.

"Oi, King Kong. What's the story?" Donald said.

"The story?" Fijian Bob replied with a sneer.

"Yeah, you and your mate here have been lettin' tarts through all night, like it's the revolving door of a knocking shop. Meanwhile, me and the young blood here have been standing outside like a couple of dickheads for the best part of, what? A good hour. And as far as I can tell, there's not even so much as a snowflake's chance of getting inside. What sort of game are you fucksticks playing?"

Fijian Bob chuckled and rolled his eyes at his colleague.

"What? We aren't good enough for your shitty club?"

"Maybe. Now take a hike," Fijian Bob replied.

The hulking security guard closed the gap and clamped a hand on Donald's shoulder. He locked eyes with the former soldier, menace radiating off him, like he was itching to snap The Diamond in half. Big mistake. In one fluid motion, Donald went to work. He seized the hand, twisted hard, drove up. A wet *CRACK!* echoed as Fijian Bob's wrist folded in on itself. Before the man had time to scream, Donald drove an open palm into the bridge of his nose. A torrent of reddish-black, iron-rich blood burst forth as the giant crumpled onto the footpath below, his broken nose contorting his face like a violent Picasso. It was a very big mistake indeed. Donald straightened, chest heaving, soaking up the euphoric embrace of that old familiar feeling. Around him, silence. Patrons froze mid-step, the other guard's jaw sagged, even Cyrille looked rattled. They were all staring at a sixty-year-old warhorse who had just dismantled a Fijian powerhouse in less time than it took to light a cigarette.

"Christ, Don. You smashed him," Cyrille said.

"You don't say?" Donald retorted, brushing himself off. "Why do I even bother bringing you, lad? Honestly, some days I reckon you're about as useful as a screen door on a submarine."

The second security guard approached cautiously, right hand raised defensively. His eyes took in the scene: his mate cradling a broken wrist and a bloody nose. Instinctively, he fumbled for the walkie-talkie at his belt, ready to call for backup. Only there was none. Half the club's bouncers were out sick with gastro. He was on his own. The guard hesitated, eyes flicking between Donald and Cyrille.

"Looks like a couple of, uh … spots just opened up," he said after a moment of quiet self-preservation, nodding toward the entrance.

"How do you lot dance to this rubbish?" Donald groaned, the first words to escape his mouth after stepping foot inside the nightclub. Cyrille rolled his eyes, bracing himself for yet another trip down memory lane with his companion. "Col Joye, Johnny O'Keefe, that Little Pattie sheila. They were real musicians. Proper singers. Not like these bloody unemployed uni students with their beeping and booping and … whatever the hell *that* is," Donald lamented.

"Really?" Cyrille replied, with a lack of interest.

"Fuckin' oath, lad. I can still remember when Little Pattie came to entertain the troops in Nui Dat. One glimpse of her thigh-high skirts and knee-high socks and our boys had their peckers back up and would be out fightin' the VC for another fortnight straight."

"Yeah? That's, uh … fascinating, Don."

The two men threaded their way through the crowd and hit the bar. Pablo greeted them with a dazzling smile and a "What can I craft for you gentlemen?" in an accent that was impossible to place. Dressed all in black, sleeves expertly rolled to the elbows, he looked every bit the consummate professional. Donald did a double-take, leaned in, and in his usual surly tone ordered two rum and colas. Pablo's smile tightened, eyes narrowing and jaw stiffening. This was a man who took pride in mixing over-priced, wanky cocktails in an overpriced, wanky nightclub. To him, slinging premixed spirits was like asking Michelangelo to paint the ceiling of an outhouse.

While Donald waited patiently for his drinks, Cyrille nodded toward the young couple gyrating provocatively on the dance floor. "I bet they didn't get up to that back in your day, Don?" he said.

Donald surveyed the scene and smirked.

"You can say that again," he began. "If her old man caught me dancin' like that with his darling daughter, he would've lopped off my tackle with a set of garden shears and mailed it to my mother." Cyrille let out a laugh while Donald continued, "At least back in my day you knew where you stood with a woman. It's, I dunno, different now. Not sayin' that's necessarily a bad thing. But now it comes off as, well, young blokes don't seem to know whether they're Arthur or Martha."

Before Cyrille could rebuke his partner's unwavering social commentary, Pablo, the bartender, returned with their drinks.

"Twenty-eight dollars," he smugly announced.

Donald turned back to face the man in disbelief and raised his voice, "Pardon?" Much like his heart, he was worried that his hearing aid might have skipped a beat amidst the thumping bass line that reverberated throughout the blackened innards of the nightclub.

"The drinks? Twenty-eight dollars," Pablo repeated.

Donald was visibly taken aback. Twenty-eight dollars for a couple of rum and colas felt like daylight robbery. Extortion, even. Still, it was exactly the kind of money-making racket he could get behind.

"Well, good thing it's the lads' shout," Donald said.

Cyrille looked puzzled. "Uh ... is it?" he replied.

With a resigned sigh, Cyrille fished out his wallet and slapped a crisp hundred-dollar note onto the bar, shrugging as if it were the only cash he had. Pablo's eyes flicked to it, irritation barely contained at having to deal with such an inconveniently generous denomination. With a sigh of his own, Pablo excused himself to fetch some change from out back, disappearing through the door behind the bar, leaving Donald and Cyrille to exchange a series of amused glances.

"So, what do you reckon?" Donald asked.

"About what? Old mate in the hat?" Cyrille replied.

"Nah. What do you reckon about this place?"

Cyrille took a moment to study his surroundings before responding. "I don't know. It's alright, I suppose. Why do you ask?" he enquired. Blissfully ignorant of the reply, Donald swallowed a mouthful of rum and cola, seemingly lost in his own head. "Why do you ask, Don?" Cyrille repeated, speaking into Donald's good ear.

The grey-haired giant quietly returned to reality.

"I've only got so much of the sandy stuff left in my hourglass, lad," he said. "I'm sixty-two. Got a wife who barely remembers what day it is. And despite what you saw out on the footpath just before, I'm very much punchin' above my weight." He took another sip, letting the thought settle. "Watching these young ones, it makes an old fella cogitate. What's the point of wealth? Well, aside from the obvious. You can't take it with you. And I never had kids. No grandkids. Nobody to leave it to. Eh, maybe it's time to put all these ill-gotten gains to use. Distribute it to the people I give a shit about."

Cyrille caught a flicker of genuine regret in Donald's voice, a rare break from their usual banter. Curious, he pressed on. "What's the plan? With your money, I mean," he asked, timing it perfectly with a lull in the music that coincided with the DJ downing a self-prescribed cocktail of disco biscuits and lukewarm caffeinated energy drink.

"*You*," Donald replied, with a nod of his head.

Cyrille raised an eyebrow. "*Me*?"

"Who else am I gonna get to run my club?"

"What? You want to buy a nightclub, Don?"

"Buy, build. Whatever. It's six of one, half a dozen of the other. What I do know is that Daffy owns a couple of those old two-story buildings on King Street, within walking distance of the casino. They're a bit of a 'renovator's delight' but I reckon we could take one off his grubby little hands for half the askin' price."

Cyrille stepped back from the bar, letting the chaos hit him like an awesome wave. He soaked it in, his mind sketching a wild, vivid picture of a future just within reach.

"Clubs are a young fella's game," Donald continued. "And before you knock the idea on the head, yeah, I know it's all new to you. But how hard could it be? Slap a lick of black paint on the walls, play some shitty music. It's practically a licence to print money. And I'm not even asking for a taste. The place'd be yours to run however you see fit. Besides, I know you could out-rogue old mate in the fedora there with his twenty-dollar drinks," he added with a grin.

Before Cyrille could respond, Pablo reappeared, dumping the notes and coins onto the bar with a practised huff.

"Will there be anything else tonight?" he asked.

"Actually, there is one thing," Donald replied.

"Sure. And how can I be of service, sir?"

"It's a bit of an odd one," Donald said, leaning in, voice dropping to a whisper. "I'm chasing a bloke who might've worked here once. Big fella, plays footy. He's not in trouble or anything. I only ask because ... well ... what do you know about Gamblers Anonymous?"

The bartender shrugged, resting against the counter.

"One of the twelve steps involves making a list of all the folks you've wronged. Ya know? Because of your addiction. Anyway, so I was about halfway through writing mine when it hit me like a ton of bricks: 'Keyboard Cat' in the third at Flemington." Donald flashed three fingers at Pablo, who now looked as bewildered as a kangaroo in a swag. "Long story short, I bumped into this bloke at the bookies a while back. Outta nowhere, he hands me a tenner and tells me to put it on a random nag while he dashes off for a slash. Alright, I thought, I can manage that. Fing, fang, foom. The race is over and lo-and-behold, Keyboard Cat sneaks home for the win. At four-to-one odds, no less. So yeah, I waited around for him to come back. Ten minutes went by. I kept waiting. Then another ten. By that point, I was startin' to wonder how long it took for big boy to siphon the python."

"Uh ... so what happened next?" Pablo asked.

"Well, me being the curious type, I checked the shitters. He wasn't there. In fact, there was no sign of him anywhere. He'd vanished in a puff of smoke. So, I did what any sane person would've done. I interrogated the manager about this fella ... not in a 'gun to the head' sorta way ... politely, but all I got was exactly what I'd told ya."

"That this man used to work here?" Pablo pressed.

"Yep. That, and he used to play rugby league."

"Hmm. And this, uh, gambler of yours never returned?"

Donald shook his head. "But I reckon I did my due diligence. By that point, I'd waited an hour for this prick to come back. In the end, I just pocketed the winnings and went about my life. Like I said, I'd completely forgotten about it until I started in the program."

"And now you want to repay him?" Pablo replied.

"Bingo. I've got a fifty with this bloke's name on it burnin' a hole in my pocket … but as you well know, that's the missing piece of my puzzle. I'm short on a name," Donald admitted with a shrug.

Pablo appeared sceptical, but it was amazing how many doors opened when a person offered to pay off a debt, even with an absolute bullshit story like that one. The bartender glanced at Cyrille, seeking confirmation, and found him nodding, clearly sold on the yarn that Donald had plucked from his arse. Pablo flicked a look back at Donald, then over his shoulder at the queue of thirsty punters, all keen for their turn at his overpriced, hand-crafted libations.

The bartender put the old man out of his misery.

"It sounds like you're after Mark," he said.

And just like that, the missing piece fell into place.

Detective Gamble brought the bullet-riddled Commodore to a halt in a secluded patch of bushland, just off the highway, a dozen or so kilometres from The Cockatoo Inn. The engine's low hum ceased, plunging the surroundings into an eerie silence that seemed to seep into the very fabric of the landscape. He reached up and flicked on the interior light, casting a dim, ethereal glow that permeated the confines of the vehicle. Outside, the night swallowed them whole, engulfing them in its velvety darkness. With no artificial lights or structures in sight, their only companions were the rhythmic chirping of crickets, the melodic symphony blending seamlessly with the vast expanse of untouched hinterland, reducing the car and its occupants to insignificant specks in the grand tapestry of nature.

"How are you faring, Sarge?" he asked.

"Nothing a change of jocks wouldn't fix," Hughes quipped from the back seat, his confidence unwavering despite the remnants of a bullet being lodged in the upholstery mere millimetres from his head.

Curiosity piqued, Gamble exited the vehicle and swung open the rear passenger door, revealing Hughes lying on his back with his signature smirk plastered across his face. Despite his dishevelled appearance, his shirt creased and his cropped hair frazzled from removing a balaclava, the detective appeared unscathed. Sliding out of the car, Hughes inspected a bullet hole in the door, his expression a mix of fascination and nonchalance as his eyes scanned the point at which the round had punched through one door and embedded itself in the door opposite. It served as a chilling reminder of how close he had come to being on the wrong end of Max's hunting rifle.

"He wasn't mucking about, was he?" Gamble said.

"Discharging a firearm at a speeding vehicle, at range, is hardly the act of a man who lacks drive or clarity. Is it now, Baz?"

"Uh, sorry. I just meant he—" Gamble began.

"Was tryin' to kill us?" Hughes stated, matter-of-factly, as if kidnapping a South Korean national and the subsequent high-speed getaway were all in a day's work for a police detective. "No shit, Sherlock. They sure as fuck weren't shots across the bow, were they? Christ. Now how about you be a sweetheart and pop that boot, yeah? Let's check on how our little investment is maturing."

Gamble surveyed the darkness with scepticism.

"Well, what are ya waiting for?" Hughes said.

"Uh, are you sure that's wise?" Gamble replied.

"Wise? Do I look like a friggin' owl, mate?"

"Ah, no, I guess. But what if he tries to run?"

"Look around," Hughes replied, gesturing with his arms, as he encompassed the darkness that surrounded them. "It's blacker than a bat's guts at dawn out here. Even *if* he made a break for it, and that's a big *if*, where's he gonna go? Shit, my money's on our friend here rollin' an ankle before he got more than twenty yards away."

The senior detective had a point. Gamble relented and pressed the button on the key fob, resulting in an audible *click* as the boot unlocked. Stepping forward, Hughes opened it, revealing the faint outline of their captive curled up in the foetal position.

"Wakey, wakey! Hand off snakey," Hughes said with a hint of impatience. There was no reaction from Chul-Moo. "Oi! You can quit bunging it on," he added. "This isn't soccer or whatever you mincers play back home."

Nothing. Hughes leaned closer, prodding Chul-Moo with his finger. There was no flinching. No visible reaction. He prodded him again for good measure. Meanwhile, Gamble, taking notice of the thin beam of light streaming through a bullet-sized hole at the rear of the car, crouched down to investigate further. Silence hung in the air, broken only by the weight of their shared realisation that something was amiss. Hughes glanced down at his fingertips, discovering something ominous coating them. In the dim light, the substance took on a dark, almost tar-like appearance, thick and viscous in consistency.

Running his hand through the glow of the taillights for a second pass, Hughes felt his stomach drop.

It was blood.

"Jesus-cunting-fuck!" he yelled, his voice filled with frustration and anger. Hughes planted his size nine into the car's tyre, his carefully cultivated demeanour eroding within the blink of an eye.

"What?" his partner replied, scrambling to his feet.

Gamble's gaze flickered over Chul-Moo's body, searching for any telltale signs of life. His chest tightened as he locked eyes with his partner. The silence in the air only amplified their anxiety, making every passing second feel like an eternity. Neither man wanted to state the obvious. It was as if acknowledging the Korean's fate aloud was going to manifest an almost certainty into undeniable reality. Hughes wiped the blood onto Chul-Moo's T-shirt and slumped against the rear of the Commodore, defeated.

"There's a d-d-dead kid in our boot," Gamble said. "Christ, Mick. I told you we should've dropped this w-whole wild goose chase the moment your brother-in-law got involved!"

"*Ex* ... brother-in-law," Hughes replied.

"The kid's dead!" Gamble said, as he tried to hold back the torrent of sorrow that lapped at the shores of his conscience. "An innocent kid, for all we know. What? Are you so callous that death doesn't even register as a blip on your radar?"

"Now's not the time for a friggin' lecture, Barry."

"Oh? Well, if now isn't suitable, when?"

"Never. Just shut your trap and let me think, yeah?"

"We killed someone, Mick! What's there to think about?"

Hughes took a few angry steps toward his partner, his frustration evident in his posture. He got close enough to convey his disapproval, but then he abruptly withdrew, instead opting to waggle a crooked, accusatory finger in Gamble's direction.

"Did *you* pull that trigger, Barry?" he asked.

"Huh? What do you—" Gamble began.

"Did *you* pull the trigger of that gun? No, and I know for a fact that I sure as hell didn't. That dubious honour falls very much on the hairy shoulders of that fat prick Sleazeball, yeah? This kid here," he said, pointing at the inanimate lump of meat in the boot, "he's in that state because of, uh ... well, I dunno. Just chalk it up to the kid bein' in the wrong place at the wrong time. Murphy's law. Dodgy bloody Feng Shui. Call it whatever the hell you want. Getting clipped back there was nothin' more than bad fuckin' luck. What? Would you rather it was one of us who played catch with a stray round instead?"

"I'd rather we weren't involved at all, Mick!"

Gamble broke away from the bickering, his footsteps echoing in the stillness of the night. He walked the perimeter of the dimly lit area cast by the car's headlights, his mind racing to make sense of the situation. Over the years, he had been involved in his fair share of questionable shit under the tutelage of his partner, bending the law to get the job done. But this? This was different. This was manslaughter. This was crossing a line he could not ignore. Any chance that Gamble had of transferring to the Child Protection Unit had now all but vanished in an acrid cloud of gun smoke, much like the pulse of the unlucky Korean in their boot.

"And what happens when Max calls in uniform?" he eventually replied. "It was a snatch and grab, Mick. There's evidence from bumhole to breakfast time. Oh, and that's not counting the b-b-blood trail that's been seeping from our Commodore all the way here."

"But he won't," Hughes said confidently.

"What, reach out to the police?" Gamble replied.

"Remember who we're dealin' with? We're the last blokes Max wants poking around his little den of depravity, especially with anything that amounts to a fine-tooth comb. You and I, Bazza, are as safe as houses. All we've gotta do is keep our cool, yeah? In forty-eight hours, this kid's gonna be nothin' more than another statistic in the long tradition of tourists absconding while on holiday in our beautiful country. Just a footnote for those jokers over at Foreign Affairs." The detective grinned, winked devilishly, and added, "Hell, who wouldn't take one look at our golden beaches and big-titted women and think, 'Bugger it, I'm not going back home'?"

Gamble shot his partner a look of disbelief. Hughes, unflinching, met his gaze, one eyebrow raised in silent reminder of the crucial step they had yet to take.

"Christ. He's not even cold, Mick," Gamble replied.

"So? He's bound to have some sorta ID on him," Hughes replied, his tone resolute. "Passport. Wallet. Hell, even a bloody train ticket. Just make sure you, uh, get up in there properly."

"Bugger off, Mick. I'm not touching him."

"Oh, really? Of all the times to grow a fuckin' spine," Hughes hissed, shoving his partner aside. He rifled through Chul-Moo's pockets. The left was empty. The right one felt equally barren until a glint caught his eye. "Hold on," he muttered, his fingers probing deeper, he fished out a rectangular piece of black plastic. "No ID," he said, holding it up to the taillight, "but there is, uh ... this."

Gamble was off with the fairies, lost in a haze of chaos. Hughes' voice snapped him back. He focused on the mystery object in his superior's hand, eyes narrowing as he tried to make sense of it.

"Huh? That ... what is that thing?" he asked.

"For once, Baz, your guess is as good as mine," Hughes replied, turning the USB over in his palm, fingers tracing its smooth edges like an ape trying to fathom Einstein's theory of relativity. As he considered its purpose, his thoughts drifted to The Pom, a man renowned for his knowledge of unusual items and, more importantly, their value. "Maybe I'll hold on to it for now," he said, slipping the device into his jacket. "You know, for our mate Justin Case."

Unbeknown to either of them, the two self-confessed Luddites were now in possession of a veritable treasure trove of illegally obtained police records. Records that could land them twenty years behind bars. The catch was they had no idea what they actually possessed, nor the slightest clue how to navigate its encrypted depths. Content with his haul, Hughes leaned into the boot and pushed aside the Korean's bloodied backpack. Tucked under a loose patch of carpet by the wheel well was an olive-green fold-up shovel, the kind American soldiers had used in Vietnam. Hughes had been gifted it for turning a blind eye to some dodgy goods sold by The Pom's old man, and in the hands of a crooked cop trying to extricate themselves from a precarious situation, it was an invaluable tool.

And this was one of those precarious situations.

"I'm glad I had the presence of mind to take his backpack," Hughes muttered as he grabbed the item in question from beside Chul-Moo's body with his spare hand and tossed it onto the ground with a hollow *thud*. "I'll have a root around through his personal effects. Whatever information he might've been carrying should be in there. Or, at the very least, somethin' we can pull a name from. Maybe we can use it to piece together why he was here."

"Uh, okay. And what am I supposed to do, Mick?"

Hughes thrust the shovel into Gamble's hands.

"Dig, Rover. Dig," he said, with a smile.

Chapter Fourteen

Percussive Persuasion

Mark Campbell stood in the floodlit car park of The Cockatoo Inn, juggling his attention between assessing the aftermath of Max's impromptu target practice and attempting to make a call on his mobile phone. His intended contact was Detective Sergeant Michael Hughes, Magdalena Black's go-to inside of the Gold Coast police. In the middle of the car park, the motel's manager, Max, stood with a perplexed expression plastered across his face. His hunting rifle rested by his side, while remnants of corn chips still clung to his bushy moustache and sweat-stained white singlet. Standing before Max, radiating authority and menace, was Magdalena Black.

"How could you allow this to happen?" she asked.

"I don't know. It was … ah, dark," Max replied.

"Dark?" The loan shark cocked an eyebrow and scanned her surroundings, which were lit up like a proverbial Christmas tree. Her gaze eventually settled on Mark, who was now crouched beside a stray shell casing. With a broken twig in one hand and the mobile phone pressed to his ear with the other, he prodded at the brass artefact, desperately trying to extract meaning from it. "Dark? What in the Lord's name do you mean by 'dark', Maximilian?" she continued, her tone laced with menace. "And let me be perfectly clear: unless you provide me with some coherent answers, and soon, my rather brutish colleague here is going to send you someplace very dark indeed.

Yes? And given your, eh, scopophilic tendencies, I suspect that particular place will not only be dark but also very, very hot."

Max was not entirely sure what 'scopophilic' meant, but given his nickname of 'Sleazeball', he figured it was probably a reference to something filthy and depraved. To risk asking would be to air his own salacious interests in public, and with Magdalena knowing the dirt on just about everyone, Max did what any self-respecting voyeur would do: he let the accusation slide off him like water off a duck's back.

"I, uh, don't usually switch 'em on," he said.

"Switch what on?" Magdalena replied.

"The floodlights, Miss Black ... out in the car park."

"Hmm. And why, pray tell, would that be?"

"Because the electricity costs an arm and a leg."

"What? You're going to stand there and imply that a couple of nobodies waltzed in and kidnapped Chul-Moo right under your bulbous nose, all because you were being frugal?" Magdalena barked, her eyes burning with fury. "Christ, Maximilian. You can't even fathom the colossal shitstorm you've unleashed on us."

Max, feeling small, stammered, "I ... I'm sorry."

"Sorry?" Magdalena replied. "Your apology is about as worthless as the snivelling miscreant delivering it. I have no interest in hollow platitudes. What I *am* interested in right now are answers."

"And you might never get 'em," Mark interjected.

The man-mountain pocketed the stray shell casing and stood up, casting a wistful glance toward the horizon. The Korean was gone, vanished without a trace. With a snarl, he made his way toward his employer, mobile phone pressed to his ear as he attempted to get a direct line to the Gold Coast CIB's most corrupt specimen.

"Nothin' in the way of physical evidence," Mark continued. "And as for getting onto our jumped-up little prick with the badge, he must be letting it ring out. Keeps getting diverted to voicemail."

"And did you leave him one?" Magdalena replied.

"Uh, no. Should I? It's just—" Mark began.

"Leave the man a damn voicemail, you galoot!"

Mark hit redial with his meaty thumb and waited as the phone rang out, only to be redirected to voicemail. Frustration rising, he unloaded into the phone, voice laced with fury. "Oi! You fucking cocksucker! Call me back ... now! My boss needs ya, and you know damn well who this is, so don't even think about fuckin' dodgin' me." With a swift motion, Mark *snapped* the phone shut, cutting the call short.

"About as subtle as a sledgehammer," Magdalena said, rolling her eyes as she flicked her auburn hair over her shoulder. "Christ. What else could go sideways today? At least tell me you managed to recover that ... plastic ... doodad Chul-Moo had."

"What? His memory stick, boss?" Mark replied.

Magdalena sighed and nodded emphatically.

"Nah. I turned his room over, good and proper. Just a few clothes and his passport. You know? Random shit."

The fact that Chul-Moo's passport was still in his motel room only served to strengthen Max's story, or at least its plausibility. If the kid had made a hasty return to Korea, he would have needed his passport. The situation was looking grim, and with every passing moment, the odds of finding Chul-Moo alive were dwindling.

"And what about eyewitnesses?" Magdalena asked.

"Uh, well ... there weren't really any," Max replied.

"And what *exactly* do you mean by that?"

"There were a couple of men, a father and son, I presume. They were in cabin five, down at the end. Last I saw, they left a couple of hours before everything went down. Haven't seen them since."

With all the grace of a newborn giraffe, Magdalena took a few hesitant steps toward cabin five before abruptly returning to tower over The Cockatoo Inn's manager, her red open-toe pumps utterly unsuited for the unforgiving asphalt beneath her feet.

"Do these familial fuckers have names?" she asked.

"The father and son, you mean? Uh, it was something French-sounding," Max replied, leaning on his rifle, the barrel lining up perfectly with his lower jaw. "His surname might've started with an 'L'. Uh, like 'Lebref', or 'Lebron', maybe? It was new to my ear."

The name was Lefebvre. Cyrille Matis Lefebvre.

Magdalena turned to Mark and asked, "Have we upset any Frenchmen of late? Well, aside from the sommelier at that rather lacklustre nouveau chic bistro in Mermaid Waters. Honestly, what sort of heathen would pair a full-bodied wine like a Cabernet Sauvignon with Salmon Meunière?"

"Uh, yeah. It was a fuckin' crime, boss," Mark replied.

"Indeed. So? How are we tracking with them?"

"Tracking with *who*, boss? The French?"

"Yes. As in, persons of the Parisian persuasion."

Magdalena's enforcer shook his head. "No issues that I can recall," he replied. "I highly doubt a Frenchman would have the balls for something like this. Kicking in doors? Kidnapping? That's as bold as brass. Besides, one look at the 'Great White Hunter' here, and they would've crapped themselves." He gestured at Max's rifle, still standing upright by its owner's side, the barrel still pointed precariously at his person. "Bloody hell, Sleazeball. Where *did* you find that relic?"

"It belonged to my grandfather," Max replied.

"Oh, you don't fuckin' say?" Mark chuckled.

"Yeah, why? Got some sort of problem with it?"

"Nah … I'm sure it does the job, especially if you've got a fondness for period pieces from the Boer War. Just sayin', if you ever find yourself in the market for something manufactured this century, give us a bell, yeah. I'll hook you up with a contact of mine."

If there was not already a healthy dose of scepticism surrounding Max's tale of marksmanship on the fleeing kidnapper's vehicle, even a quick glance at the weapon in question only deepened those doubts. With its weathered patina, which seemed to scream of a life rougher than Keith Richards' ever had, the rifle looked like it would crumble at the mere suggestion of a good spit and polish.

"What's the likelihood that this father and son are the same individuals who kidnapped Chul-Moo?" Magdalena asked. "They check in, the Korean checks out. Seems … suspicious."

"Nah, I'm certain it wasn't them," Max replied.

"Really? How certain can one be in near darkness?"

"It was a completely different car, for starters."

Max's immediate dismissal of the guests in cabin five only served to aggravate the surly loan shark.

"Perhaps they swapped vehicles?" she suggested.

Max shook his head. "Even if they had, the guy who kicked in the cabin door was a weedy little shit." He gestured, his hand hovering around five feet ten. "The two from cabin five … don't know what's in the water where they're from, but they were both built like brick shithouses. Solid units, about Mark's size. Even the old bloke."

"Hmm. And you are certain they haven't returned?"

Max nodded firmly, his frustration mounting.

Magdalena exchanged a glance with her enforcer, her eyes narrowing as she processed the myriad of possibilities.

"Very well," Magdalena replied, her tone unnervingly calm as she surveyed the empty car park. Then, without warning, she kicked the stock of the hunting rifle. The weapon discharged with a sharp *CRACK!*, the blast ripping through the air, followed by a puff of white smoke. In an instant, Max's head erupted in a grotesque shower of blood and brain matter. His lifeless body collapsed onto the asphalt with a sickening thud. The gore covered Magdalena like a sudden rainstorm, the warm claret mist soaking her from head to toe. She stood motionless, her face speckled with blood, her ears still ringing from the deafening crack of the shot. Her expression remained unreadable, her steely composure hiding any trace of the emotions that might have stirred within her. She drank in the aftermath, the silence settling over the scene as the violence lingered in the air.

"Fuckin' hell!" Mark roared in absolute disbelief.

Unfazed by the chaotic tableau unfolding before her, Magdalena sighed and calmly reached into her suit pocket, producing a purple monogrammed handkerchief. With an almost imperceptible tremble, she wiped the remnants of Max's cranial residue from her face. As the puddle of gore continued to gush from the void where the manager's head once resided, the glistening crimson caught the beams of the floodlights, creating an alluring juxtaposition of horror and beauty that was almost impossible to deny.

"How'd you know it was gonna fire when ya kicked it?"

"What makes you think I did?" Magdalena replied.

Donald and Cyrille, men of contrasting demeanour, had been waiting for a good half hour, eagerly expecting their target's return from wherever he had abruptly vanished. Inside the dimly lit interior of BLACK, they stood at the edge of the polished bar, tapping their fingers restlessly and exchanging glances with each passing minute. Donald's agitation was palpable; he shifted his weight from one foot to the other, his hearing aid switched off, eyes darting around the room as if searching for an escape. In contrast, Cyrille remained relatively composed, his gaze immersed in the pulsating crowd, yearning to blend in with the ordinary patrons who remained blissfully unaware of the name 'Mark Campbell'.

"Clocked that bloke over there yet?" Donald said.

He nodded in the general direction of the dance floor, attempting to draw Cyrille's attention to a specific individual. Curiosity piqued, Cyrille covertly glanced over his shoulder. He spotted the unsavoury figure, with his heavily bandaged face, engaged in a hushed conversation with a group of equally dubious-looking young men. They stood in a dimly lit corner near the toilets, exchanging furtive glances and whispers that seemed laden with an air of secrecy. Unless head wounds and bloody bandages were all the rage with the youth these days, Donald could only have been talking about Neville, BLACK's resident dealer of narcotics.

"Yeah, I see him? What of it?" Cyrille asked.

"So, you haven't noticed?" Donald replied in disbelief.

"Haven't noticed what?" Cyrille replied.

"He's been dealin' right under our noses, lad."

"What? Drugs?" Cyrille asked, genuinely puzzled.

"No, dealing cards, you friggin' turkey." Donald rolled his eyes as he readjusted himself. "Watch this prick go about his business for a while. Every ten minutes or so, he ducks off into the gents. Then, like clockwork, he's back out a minute later, as smooth as silk."

Cyrille shrugged. "Maybe he's got the shits?"

"Diarrhoea, gonorrhoea. Whatever this creepy-looking prick has, he's got a bad dose. Just keep an eye on him."

The two men moved to a secluded corner of the nightclub. Hidden in the shadows, they became silent observers of Neville's every move. They scrutinised each subtle gesture and flicker of expression with unwavering attention, determined to uncover the method in this methhead's madness. Despite lingering questions about Campbell's whereabouts, the diversion offered a brief respite, filling the otherwise yawning void left by the man-mountain's absence.

"Tell me this prick ain't dealing," Donald said.

"So what if he is, Don?" Cyrille replied.

"Use your brain, lad. No owner worth their salt lets a lowlife deal on their premises, at least not without taking a cut. And it's not like this clown is incon-fucking-spicuous, is he? Someone up the food chain's gotta be getting a taste."

Once again, the dealer made a few cryptic gestures before disentangling himself from his clientele, just as Donald had predicted. With an air of nonchalance, he strutted toward the men's restroom like he was the cock of the walk. Cyrille watched the scene unfold, quietly impressed by Donald's uncanny knack for reading a room.

"Stay put, lad," Donald said, leaving their hiding spot.

"Uh, okay. Where are you going?" Cyrille replied.

"Me? I'm off to see a man about a dog."

Donald entered the bathroom and, by a stroke of luck, collided headlong with the dealer, who was exiting the stalls wearing a shiteating grin. Despite the masculine silhouette on the door, this was unmistakably one of those trendy unisex bathrooms that had become popular in upscale circles. There were no traditional urinals, only a row of five cubicle stalls and an equal number of sinks. Behind them stretched a large one-way mirror, enhanced by a serene cascading water feature. It was a clever design, letting patrons keep one eye on the dance floor while washing their hands, all the while preserving what little dignity they had to begin with. Unfortunately for the dealer, the bathroom's design offered no protection when confronted by the grey-haired giant. Donald was formidable in the most ordinary of circumstances, but he seemed even more so as he suddenly appeared, seemingly out of thin air, bathed in eerie blue UV light that accentuated every wrinkle and crevice on his world-weary face.

"Oi! Watch where you're goin'," Donald said as the pair shuffled past one another, eyes meeting for a split second, neither wanting to be *that bloke* who hovered too close in the shitters.

The dealer's expression flickered with recognition, like a distant memory breaking through some chemically induced haze.

"Hey, you look really fuckin' familiar," he scoffed.

The dealer froze in his tracks, his crooked finger pointing accusingly at Donald, as the two men squared off in the middle of the bathroom. The air was heavy with the pungent scent of body odour and urine, punctuated by a faint, lingering aroma of industrial-grade floor cleaner. They stood there, trapped in what appeared to be a chance encounter, engaged in the all-too-familiar game of 'do I know you?'. It took a moment for the few remaining synapses in Neville's recently tenderised frontal cortex to fire before it finally clicked.

"Yeah, I've seen you before," he said, grinning like an idiot, his rotten yellow teeth glowing like the missing urinals in this fancy unisex hellhole. "Didn't you used to be on the telly?"

"Me? Nah. You've got the wrong bloke," Donald said.

"Bullshit. I definitely know ya from somewhere."

"Eh, dunno, mate. Maybe I rogered your mum once?"

The dealer chuckled and wheezed out a breath.

"Wait … you're that gangster, right? Jimmy's uncle … from down Melbourne way. Saw you on the news the other night," he said, smirking. "Yeah … I'd recognise that mug anywhere."

Donald had been in the Sunshine State less than twenty-four hours, and now some poor man's Boris Karloff was about to clock him. "I ain't who you think I am," he said, peeking under the toilet stalls for the telltale sign of occupancy: shoes. The coast was clear. "And if I were, I'd suggest, for the sake of what's left of your health, you forget you ever saw hide nor hair of me. Got it?"

Unaware of Donald's bathroom escapade, Cyrille leaned against the bar, deep in conversation with the blond, well-dressed stranger he had noticed outside earlier. Up close, the man's enigmatic charm was impossible to ignore. Neon lights painted their faces in a soft glow as they leaned in, trying to carve out a private bubble amidst the chaos. The stranger cradled one of Pablo's vibrant blue cocktails, fingers drumming the rim in time with the bass, while the pair traded the usual nightclub small talk in shouted staccato. With little else to go on, Cyrille chalked the man's lively disposition up to whatever BLACK's resident dealer had been slinging from his makeshift bathroom office, like some mummified Arthur Fonzarelli.

"Go clubbing with grandpa often?" the young man asked playfully, leaning in close enough to catch a whiff of Cyrille's cologne.

Cyrille looked momentarily puzzled. "I'm sorry?"

"Grandpa. The old guy you came in with."

"Oh, you mean Don?" Cyrille chuckled.

"Sure. If that's what he's calling himself tonight."

Cyrille shook his head, trying to suppress a smile.

Amused, the young man persisted. "So, what's the story? If he's not your grandfather, what is he then? Your sugar daddy? Or do you just enjoy hanging around with old fogies?"

The kind of old fogey mean enough to drop a bouncer like it was a bad habit. Cyrille signalled Pablo for another drink, a mischievous grin playing on his lips.

"It's kind of a long story," he replied.

"Well, you've got until I finish this," the blond said with a wink, nodding at his cocktail. "And it's Rory, by the way."

"You named your drink 'Rory'?" Cyrille quipped.

The pair grinned and swapped introductions, briefly juggling their glasses before a firm handshake. The nightclub throbbed around them, loud and relentless, yet Cyrille stayed sharp, eyes flicking for any sign of the elusive Mark Campbell.

"Alright then, big boy, lay it on me," Rory said.

Cyrille cocked his head. "Lay what on you?"

"That story you promised. I don't have all night."

"Oh. Uh ... where do I start?" Cyrille replied, a hint of sadness touching his chiselled features as he scanned the crowd. "My mum died when I was young. Really young. Collapsed at the doctor's office during my one-week checkup. Blood clots in her lungs, or something like that. That's when Don and his wife, Denise, came along. She volunteered at the school tuckshop ... I guess she must've heard about what happened to Mum. She had Don set my old man up with a job. Nothing fancy, just driving, but better than being on the dole with three kids. They looked out for us. Had us over for Christmas lunch, babysat us after school. You know the old saying, 'Never judge a book by its cover'? Well, that's Don." He nodded, his voice softening. "He might fly off the handle sometimes, but he's really just a big softie once you get to know him. He's a good bloke, honest."

"Pretty good with his fists, too," Rory added.

"Eh, forget about outside. That big Islander got a bit too ... touchy. Don gets jumpy when strangers lay hands on him."

Rory pursed his lips and offered a nervous smile. The memory of Fijian Bob's shellacking was still fresh, but the allure of the handsome stranger was stronger. Before he could press on, the conversation derailed as a gaggle of inebriated thirty-somethings on a hens night stormed past in a blur of pink dresses, chardonnay breath, and wobbly stilettos. The parade of poor decisions made no secret of their efforts to capture the men's attention, but Cyrille and Rory feigned obliviousness, leaving the bride-to-be pouting in their wake.

"So, tell me more about your mum," Rory said, once all that remained of the interruption was a trail of sequins and shame. "Shit. Am I prying too much? Tell me if I am," he added, cheeks flushed.

Cyrille shrugged, letting the prying continue.

Amidst the warm summer night, Detective Gamble knelt beside a hastily dug hole in the ground, bathed in the harsh glow of the car's headlights. His sweat-slicked face gleamed in the artificial illumination as he shovelled dirt out of the shallow grave, each clump landing with a soft thud onto a growing pile nearby. The surrounding landscape, veiled in the stark beams of the car's lights, took on an eerie, almost surreal quality, far removed from the quietude of the bushland setting. With every laboured breath, Gamble's chest heaved, and he could feel the weight of both the soil and his grim duty pressing down upon him. This was a sombre task, one that had led him to this desolate spot in the dead of night, where he played the dual roles of police detective and gravedigger, burying yet another sordid secret beneath the stark, sun-bleached soil of the Queensland bush.

"This is crap," Gamble huffed, wiping sweat from his brow with a dirty sleeve. "If you're going to have me dig a grave, Mick, the least you could've done was pick a spot where I can dig more than a foot down. It's nothing but tree roots and river rock."

Hughes observed the scene with amusement as his partner extracted another sizeable rock from the hole. Gamble displayed it to him with a theatrical flair, as if it were a geological curiosity, before dramatically hurtling it into the inky darkness.

"And what's your bloody point?" Hughes replied.

"It's impossible to dig, Sarge. That's my point."

"Pfft. What did I say to you when I threw ya that shovel, Barry? What were my exact words? I know I'm pretty loose with the Queen's English, but I distinctly recall askin' you to dig me a 'shallow' grave. Did I not?" Hughes asked, his tone dripping with sarcasm.

"Yes. I heard you, but—" Gamble began.

"I didn't ask you to tunnel your way to China, did I?" Hughes interrupted. "Nah. And I definitely don't recall asking you to excavate the fossilised remains of a Tyrannosaurus-fucking-Rex!"

"Right. I understand that, Mick, but—"

"Jesus, I'd have thought the concept of a shallow grave was pretty self-explanatory, especially for a bloke on the Force as long as you," Hughes said, shaking his head. "Now quit your whingin', mate, and help me get this Korean outta the boot. Another hour in this heat and he'll have a pong strong enough to knock a blowfly backwards."

Gamble tossed the fold-up shovel to the ground with a familiar *clang* and stepped out of the hole. By the strict definition of the Oxford English Dictionary, it was still technically a hole, at least until someone deposited a body into it. The ambiguity surrounding its perceived depth, or rather the lack thereof, was another story altogether. He walked over to his partner, who was staring at the lifeless Chul-Moo, his eyes locked on the motionless form before him. After a tense moment, during which Gamble hoped his partner might show an ounce of remorse or contrition, Hughes simply shrugged and went about the grim task of disposing of the evidence.

"You take the top half, Barry. I'll handle the rest," Hughes instructed. As directed, Gamble dusted himself off and approached the car's boot. He firmly gripped Chul-Moo's arms while Hughes secured the legs. "And remember to bend your knees. Worker's comp isn't going to cover us for ... uh, extracurricular activities," Hughes said with a smirk for emphasis.

The detectives painstakingly shuffled their way toward the grave, the dry grass *crunching* underfoot with each laborious step. Only a couple of metres from the grave, another distinct sound pierced the night: the ringing of a mobile phone.

"Whose fuckin' phone is that?" Hughes asked.

"That'd be yours, Sarge," Gamble replied.

Hughes surveyed the area angrily before dropping his portion of the corpse to the ground, the jarring effect causing his colleague at the other end to respond in kind. "Definitely sounds like mine," Hughes muttered as he dashed to the back seat of the car, chasing the tail of a hard rock ringtone. He scanned the vehicle frantically, searching for the telltale backlight from his mobile phone. It continued ringing relentlessly. Then, at last, he spotted a faint glow emanating from the floor just behind the driver's seat. Hughes reached down, snatched the phone, and scrutinised the display, attempting to discern the caller's identity. "It's that—" Hughes began, just as the mobile phone ceased ringing. "Shit!" he exclaimed.

"Who was trying to call you?" Gamble asked.

"That footballin' fuckface," Hughes said.

"Why would he be chasing you at this hour?"

"Probably at the behest of old Vinegar Tits, no doubt."

Hughes slid his mobile phone back into his pocket and ventured into the inky darkness, rummaging through the undergrowth. His partner shot him a questioning look, clearly wondering why he was not returning Mark Campbell's call.

"Where are you going, Sarge?" his partner enquired.

There was no audible response.

"You *are* going to call him back, right?"

Hughes reappeared, holding a hefty, flat stone from a nearby patch of grass, which bore a suspicious resemblance to the rock Gamble had flung out of the grave only moments ago.

"What?" Hughes replied, feigning ignorance.

"Are you going to call Campbell back?"

"Of course I will, Barry. I'll just loiter here, having a chat on the old dog and bone, right next to a freshly dug grave with a deceased Korean kid at my feet. Priorities, Barry. Priorities."

Hughes knelt beside Chul-Moo's awkwardly sprawled corpse and positioned the stone beneath the lifeless right hand. Gamble could not help but wonder what bizarre ritual was about to take place.

"Okay, come and stand on this," Hughes said.

"On what? His arm?" Gamble asked, confused.

"No, *on mine*, numbnuts. Of course I meant his."

Gamble, perplexed but choosing compliance over provoking his partner's ire, placed his size thirteen imitation leather dress shoe on Chul-Moo's arm, resting it midway between wrist and elbow.

"Nah, slide your trotter up a touch," Hughes said.

His colleague shifted his boot along the arm.

"Yeah, just like that, Baz. Now hold still," Hughes said, snatching up the shovel. He lined up the blade with Chul-Moo's thumb and hoisted it overhead. He held it there a heartbeat longer, eyes locked on Gamble's, letting the silence thrum with anticipation.

"Oh, Christ. Please don't tell me you're about to do what I think you're about to do, Sarge. Please," Gamble muttered.

"Alright then, mate. I won't," Hughes replied.

The shovel blade tore through the Korean's thumb, smashing into the rock beneath with a loud, reverberating *CLANK!* of metal. The strike sliced through bone and all, like a hot knife through butter. The force was so great that the digit flew off and landed a good metre away beside a tuft of grass. Hughes' face contained the ghost of a smile, pride at the skill and accuracy of the amputation. Gamble's expression, however, was one of sheer disgust. Still, he had to admit it was a brilliant shot. Hughes retrieved Chul-Moo's thumb and, with a playful shout of "Think quick!" tossed it in his colleague's direction. Gamble, equal parts unimpressed and unprepared, juggled the thumb momentarily before recovering at the very last second for what could only be described as a competent silly-point catch.

"What the bloody hell, Mick?" Gamble said.

"Now, before you start bellyaching, fat boy, there's a method to my madness," Hughes began. "That thumb in your hot little hand? We're gonna run its print through every law enforcement database we can lay our grubby mits on. And cast wide. I'm talkin' NAFIS, AFIS, IAFIS ... hell, even those Gallagher pricks from Oasis, if need be."

Gamble just stared at the severed thumb in his palm.

"Right now, we've got nothing on this kid. Chances are he's just some dork from the local uni, but who knows? Could turn out he's the Korean Scarface. It's better safe than sorry," Hughes concluded, tossing the shovel onto the dirt pile with freakish accuracy.

Before his partner could snap out of his trance, Hughes grabbed Chul-Moo's body and dragged it to the edge of the grave. With a nonchalant shove of his foot, he sent it tumbling into the void. The corpse hit the base with a *thud*, sending a plume of dry, sun-baked earth skyward, the soil still thirsting from the long summer heat.

"Now bag that thumb, yeah," the detective sergeant instructed as he walked away from the scene, scrolling through the missed calls on his mobile phone. "And then get started on filling that hole too."

"What, aren't you going to help?" Gamble asked.

He was fairly certain he already knew the answer.

Gwangju, Jeollado Provence, South Korea.

In the heart of the bustling city, three imposing jopok stood in the dimly lit office of their boss, Yoon, awaiting his instructions with equal parts respect and apprehension. The air was thick with tension as his steely gaze bore through the trio's foreheads with laser-like precision, emphasising the gravity of the still unfolding situation. The leader of the jopok, a diminutive, androgynous figure known only as 'Butterfly', stood immaculately dressed in a tailored black suit, reflective aviator sunglasses, and short, slicked-back hair. Butterfly appeared to epitomise style over substance, but to those with an ounce of awareness, their impeccable presentation and air of confidence hinted at something formidable bubbling beneath the surface of that serene, zen-like exterior.

"And what news of my brother?" Butterfly asked.

"Chul-Moo? Presumed missing," Yoon replied.

Butterfly broke eye contact and paced the room before eventually falling back into line. "I knew these Australians were not to be trusted. This Magdalena Black, she has disrespected the family. Not only that, she has disrespected you, Yoon. She believes that simply because she is thousands of kilometres away, she can double-cross us with no possibility of recourse."

There was a booming fit of laughter from 'Mr Tooth', a commanding figure who filled the room like a throbbing exclamation mark. With his gakdoogi hairstyle and black silk shirt with the sleeves rolled up to showcase his countless tattoos, Mr Tooth's appearance painted a portrait of a man who was not only part of the Korean underworld and its minutia but was absolutely balls-deep in it.

"What do you find so amusing?" Butterfly asked.

Mr Tooth shrugged his broad shoulders. "Australians," he replied, his deep voice resonating with authority. "Should we have expected anything less from a penal colony?"

"*Former* ... penal colony," Yoon corrected him.

Mr Tooth sighed and bowed his head apologetically.

"Regardless," the mob boss continued, "do not allow such beliefs to cloud your judgement. If this was, as we suspect, a common kidnapping, then we should keep all avenues of civil discourse open until we receive a ransom demand for Chul-Moo. Then, and only then, should we consider any form of retribution."

"And if that fails to eventuate?" Butterfly asked.

"Then retribution will be certain," Yoon replied.

Butterfly grinned with satisfaction as the last member of the trio, the ever-silent 'Bul-Gae', stirred like a creature awakening from slumber. Rumour had it that the jovial drinker had his tongue taken from him after a dalliance with a fellow jopok's mistress. Regardless, the short, squat figure stood there, awaiting orders, wheezing, his long wizard-like beard bobbing with each lungful of air.

"So why summon us, Yoon?" Butterfly asked.

"Because I require three capable volunteers with current passports," Yoon replied firmly. "And I need them on the next flight to Brisbane, Australia, departing Seoul in the morning. It is about time the rest of the family paid a visit to this Magdalena Black character."

The trio nodded respectfully in response.

Detective Gamble reluctantly dropped Chul-Moo's severed thumb into a plastic evidence bag, fully aware that these things were meant for proper crime scenes, not for cleaning up the rot festering inside their own ranks. Meanwhile, Detective Hughes was on his mobile phone with Mark Campbell, his voice thick with disbelief.

"Really? You've got to be shittin' me," Hughes said. "A couple of blokes just rocked up, shoved him in the boot, and buggered off? And you have absolutely no clue who they were? Jesus. There aren't normally that many kidnappings around here, mate, but whoever pulled that stunt must've had balls the size of watermelons."

Hughes signalled to Gamble to halt his macabre task.

"So, what's this missin' fella of yours look like anyhow?" he asked, strolling over to the partially filled grave. Mark described his man in meticulous detail, and Hughes repeated each detail to his partner, his expression growing more concerned by the second. "Korean ... with black shoulder-length hair? Early twenties?" Hughes shook his head in disbelief, then fixed a stern gaze on Gamble. Each green tick was another nail in their respective coffins. "Wearing a black T-shirt ... with *who* on it? Oh, that karate bloke from the movies?"

Gamble knelt beside the grave and gently brushed the dirt from Chul-Moo's torso. There it was, Bruce Lee, mid-pose from *Enter the Dragon*, staring up at him. He gave his partner a slow, grim nod. No words needed. Things had taken an even darker turn.

"Uh, can't say that we've come across anyone matchin' that description," Hughes replied, rubbing at his forehead as a migraine started to build. "And who was he anyway? An exchange student or something?" Hughes pressed for more details, knowing that someone like Mark Campbell would never willingly reveal more than absolutely necessary. "Oh, none of my fuckin' business? Right. Well, just make sure Miss Black knows we'll keep our eyes peeled, yeah?"

Hughes ended the call and stood there for a few seconds, his frustration simmering like an unwatched pot. What in the world had they gotten themselves into? For the first time in a long time, the detective sergeant looked truly concerned, almost defeated, with any remaining colour draining from his already pale, freckled complexion.

"Barry ... I think we're fucked," he muttered.

Donald and Cyrille, weary of waiting for the elusive Mark Campbell, decided to call it a night. Their relentless pursuit of Jimmy's alleged killer had brought them this far, but Campbell would keep, at least for the time being. After all, Rome was not built in a day, and neither was the blood-soaked, serpentine path to vengeance. As they exited the nightclub, they passed Fijian Bob, still bearing the scars of their earlier altercation, evident by the bandaged wrist and ruby-red tissue plugs jammed into the nostrils of his busted nose. Despite the obvious discomfort, he persevered in his regular duties, patiently waiting for an audience with the nightclub's head of security, a highly sought-after ex-footballer by the name of Mark Campbell.

"Glad to be out of that shithole. The music was givin' me a headache," Donald stated, locking eyes with his former sparring partner in passing. Stepping onto the footpath, the two men weaved through the eager crowd of patrons on their way down the grimy, dimly lit street to their rental car parked at the end of the block. Out of earshot of the club, Cyrille's curiosity finally got the better of him.

"So what happened back there, Don?" he asked.

"Huh? Back where, lad?" Donald replied.

"Back when you nicked off to the men's toilet?"

Donald chuckled. "Ever had a turd that wouldn't flush? Imagine that," he said with a grin. "Only on a grander scale."

Cyrille cocked his head, uncertain what to make of that nugget of information. The pair walked on in silence, unaware that tension and hubbub were thickening behind them like billowing smoke.

"Tell me what *really* happened," Cyrille pressed.

"Er, well, let's just say that after a bit of, uh, percussive persuasion, our dealer spilled his guts on Magdalena Black. What she's into, the joker she runs with. The lot. Lock, stock, and fuckin' barrel."

Cyrille did a double-take. "Magdalena Black?" he said. The conversation faltered as they gingerly sidestepped what looked like a freshly minted liquid laugh splattered across the foot-path like an urban Jackson Pollock. "As in, the same Magdalena Black who puts the BLACK on that marquee back there?"

Donald nodded. "One and the same."

"But ... I thought we were chasing Campbell?"

"Yes and no," Donald replied, confusing his colleague. "The bloke from the gun store alluded to something interesting when we were talkin' to him. And Tutankhamen back there confirmed it. Campbell works for Black. And guess what? Black just happens to be one of the top villains around here. So, yeah? Logic dictates that if we find this Magdalena Black, we also find Mark Campbell."

Cyrille took a moment to cogitate over the old codger's reasoning. For the most part, it seemed sound, and right now, they lacked any other leads to fall back on. "Alright, so now what?" he enquired.

"We kill 'em both," Donald replied unflinchingly.

"We kill them both?" Cyrille repeated.

"What? Is there a bloody echo out here?"

"I'm not, uh, really following you, Don."

Donald shook his head. "Doesn't take a Rhodes Scholar to fill in the blanks, lad. Black is the lynchpin holdin' all of this together. Aside from being a loan shark, word is she dabbles in drugs too. Drugs, Cyrille. There's a reason that fucker with a head like a beaten favourite was slingin' gear so blatantly inside that club tonight. She sanctions it. You can't tell me a broad with as many fingers in as many pies as Magdalena Black wouldn't know what's going on inside her own joint."

"But how's that explain Jimmy?" Cyrille asked.

"Well, didn't he get clipped nearby?"

In fact, they were so close to the spot where Donald's nephew had been gunned down it was practically within spitting distance.

"All things considered, my educated guess is that Black ordered the hit," Donald continued. "And yes, Cyrille, before you start firing off twenty questions, I've got no idea why. Spin the bloody wheel, yeah? Watch it land on any of a million reasons these rock apes off each other on the regular. Dealing on her patch? Giving the club a bad rep? Christ, maybe they even killed him for a giggle."

As the men ambled along, tossing around half-formed ideas, muffled voices rose from somewhere behind them, steadily growing louder, as if someone were desperate to get their attention.

"I dunno," Cyrille replied. "I'm not saying you're wrong, Don. But I reckon we're about to stir up a hornet's nest if we go after this Magdalena Black, especially here on her own turf."

"Why? Scared all of a sudden, lad?" Donald quipped.

"Nah," Cyrille replied. "We're not back home, is all."

Donald shot his offsider a dark look and kept walking, the comment lingering until a response burst from his lips like an incendiary scatter of buckshot, unbidden and forceful.

"Right. That's the second fuckin' time," he said.

"Second time for what, Don?" Cyrille asked.

"The second time that remark's slipped out of your cock-holster. That we're not in Melbourne anymore. You said the same back at Jimmy's place too. What's up your arse today, lad? Don't reckon I can handle these soft Queensland pricks? Look around. This place is crawling with nothing but Walter Mittys and plastic gangsters. Small fish in an even smaller fucking pond. Trust me, lad, this sunny, surfed-out shithole doesn't faze me in the slightest."

"Huh? I wasn't trying to be smart, Don."

While he meant no offence, Cyrille was still dirty about being ripped away from Rory in the haste to flee the mess that Donald had left in BLACK's toilet. As the pair bickered down the street toward their rental car, distant voices mingled with the pulsating thuds of electronic music, echoing like war drums on the sweltering night. An unsettling tension was building. The locals were growing restless, yet Donald and Cyrille remained so wrapped up in their own drama that they failed to notice the tonal shift around them.

"I don't get how you're so certain this loan shark's involved?" Cyrille asked with a hint of scepticism. "You tune-up one dealer in the dunnies and suddenly you've got it all sussed?"

"Can't a bloke have an epiphany?" Donald replied.

"A friggin' *what* now?" Cyrille asked, puzzled.

"An epiphany, lad. A moment of sudden and great realisation," Donald clarified. "And you want to know how I figured it out? I figured it out because I've played it out. I've been on the other end of that gun more times than you've been on the end of a piece of skirt. All signs point to Black having ordered the hit on Jimmy for dealing on her patch. Mark Campbell was simply the triggerman."

A silent shrug of uncertainty hung in the air.

"Look, I won't sugarcoat this, Cyrille, but idiots like my nephew usually end up copping a bullet because it's the shortest path between two points. The smart money's always on paint-by-numbers villainy. Don't go hunting for a conspiracy where there isn't one."

As they finally reached their rental, an immediate sense of unease washed over them. The body sat noticeably lower to the ground than when they had parked it, as if an invisible, immense weight had descended upon it. It took a moment, but Cyrille was the first to spot the glaring issue. "What was that about conspiracies, Don?" he remarked, pointing out the problem. Donald cast his eyes downward and discovered that all four of the car's tyres had been slashed, not merely punctured, but brutally butchered, as if someone had derived some sort of sadistic, almost personal satisfaction from the act.

They scanned the area for the culprits on the off chance that they had been foolish or ballsy enough to hang around. Perhaps this was retaliation for their less-than-friendly entrance, or maybe it was the handiwork of a group of bored kids looking to get their jollies. Regardless, one thing was clear: the odds of getting roadside assistance at this time of night, in this part of the city, were somewhere between fuck-all and none.

"Well, that puts a dampener on things," Donald said.

Cyrille looked at his colleague, puzzled.

"I was going to suggest that we do some recon on this Magdalena Black before we pay her a visit. My mate in the shitters reckons she's got a flash penthouse just off the main drag. Somewhere overlooking the beach. How many penthouses overlooking the beach can there be on the Gold Coast?"

Donald's sarcasm went straight over Cyrille's head. Instead, his partner glanced at his wristwatch and let out a yawn wider than a hippopotamus pulling an all-nighter.

"Interrupting your beauty sleep, am I?" Donald asked.

"Well, it is getting kind of late, Don. Maybe we ought to come at this fresh in the morning?" Cyrille suggested. He glanced around, recalling the taxi rank he had spotted earlier on the drive in. Pointing down the street, he added, "I'm certain there was a taxi rank around the corner from here. Let's just take one back to the motel, get a good night's sleep, and I'll call the rental company in the morning."

Donald grumbled, "Bah, taxis are a rip-off."

Cyrille raised an eyebrow. "What? You're going to walk all the way back to the motel because you're tight?"

Unbeknown to either man, trouble was brewing outside the nightclub. Neville, the resident drug dealer, had stumbled out the front door, accompanied by three menacing figures with faces like thunder. The dealer gestured wildly toward Donald and Cyrille, his shouted accusations barely audible from half a block away, but likely something to the effect of, "That's the fucker who bashed me!" This rallying cry caught the attention of Fijian Bob, along with every aspiring cage fighter and wannabe tough guy south of Paradise Point. The growing mob surged, ready to descend upon the unsuspecting pair of Melburnians. Fortunately, before Donald could get too far into his rant about taxi drivers and their inability to find their own arseholes with a torch and a hand mirror, let alone their destination, Cyrille happened to glance over his shoulder and notice the impending tumbleweed of shit rolling their way.

"Um ... uh. Hey, Don?" Cyrille said.

Donald was still mid-rant. "The driver had one of those GPS units and a bloody road atlas, and he still couldn't find the hotel! And it was just down the bloody road! Aren't they supposed to sit a test or something to prove they know how to get around the city?"

"Oi, Don!" Cyrille shouted into Donald's good ear.

"What?" Donald replied, irritation creeping into his voice.

"Uh ... you might want to check your six."

The Diamond glanced over his shoulder and spotted the mob closing in. Their faces were twisted with fury, like rabid villagers hunting Frankenstein's monster. All that was missing were pitchforks and flaming torches. He snorted in disdain, turned away, and kept walking. Not a hint of fear touched his usual stoic demeanour.

"All right, lad," he said, cool as the proverbial cucumber. "If you insist on takin' a taxi, then you can bloody pay for it."

Cyrille chuckled. "It'd be my pleasure, Don."

Both men quickened their pace toward the taxi rank.

Chapter Fifteen

The Satisfying Warmth of Revenge

The Hackston Tavern, the following morning.

Jack returned from his trip to the corner store, clutching a newspaper under one arm and a bottle of milk under the other. This early morning ritual was as predictable as a Swiss timepiece, his means of seeking respite from the establishment's constant demands, if only for a moment. As he ascended the stairs to their shared flat above, he noticed the sound of early morning activity emanating from what passed as the kitchen, a pleasant departure from the usual soundtrack of Hung's chainsaw-like snoring. Hung, their habitual late riser, was rarely seen before eight o'clock in the morning. Jack checked his wristwatch; it was six-thirteen. In good spirits after dodging the wrath of a certain Gold Coast loan shark, Jack could not help but chuckle and ask, "Did you shit the bed, Hung?" There was no response, only the sound of more rattling and the unmistakable aroma of cooking eggs filling the air. Jack entered the kitchen through the lounge room and immediately noticed two figures, one more than he had expected. Hung was hunched over the stovetop, egg flipper in hand, clad only in red boxer shorts and a novelty apron that read, 'May I recommend the sausage?'. The second figure was none other than the elusive Mark Campbell, seated at the table, idly toying with a plate of yellow goop that, to a keen observer, might appear to be overcooked scrambled eggs.

"Mornin', sweetheart," Mark said with a wry grin.

"Uh, what's this all about?" Jack replied.

"You know, early bird gettin' the worm and that."

If Campbell was here exuding his usual charisma, it was a safe bet that his employer was also lurking nearby. Jack scanned the immediate area once more but found nothing, except for a second untouched plate of eggs on the table. The loan shark was probably off rummaging through their pile of dirty jocks or engaging in some other equally distasteful activity. A woman as elegant as Magdalena Black was sure to have a few unconventional proclivities hidden among the skeletons in her designer-clothes-filled closet.

"You okay, Hung?" Jack enquired. He looked rattled, and Jack could hardly blame him, considering the wake-up service.

"I'm, uh ... fine, I guess," Hung replied.

"You sure?" Jack sought further assurance.

"Yeah. Still not sure what they want though, they just sort of barged in and started turning the flat over."

Jack raised an eyebrow and surveyed the room once more. To the untrained eye, it was almost impossible to distinguish whether the current mess resulted from Magdalena's henchman turning the flat over or if the flat had already been in disarray before their arrival. Sadly, it was the latter. Hung's response, however, left little doubt about the intended recipient of the orphaned breakfast.

Suddenly, the nearby toilet flushed. After a brief delay, Magdalena emerged from the bathroom, slipping a small bottle of hand sanitiser into her handbag. Her expression painted a picture of a woman who was clearly dissatisfied with her time spent in the bathroom of two thirty-something bachelors who rarely had the inclination to clean it.

"Magdalena," Jack said with a nod of recognition.

"The Prodigal Son has returned ... and from the corner store of all places," Magdalena replied, her smirking lips delivering what she assumed was a witty biblical reference. "And here we thought that you might have absconded during the night."

"Uh, right? So, what's all this in aid of?" Jack asked.

"Are you familiar with the parable of the Prodigal Son?"

"Well, that kind of depends," Jack replied.

"Mmm. Depends on what, exactly?"

"On whether you're familiar with the parable of 'unlawful entry with intent'?" Jack placed his shopping on the table. "So, what are you chasing, Magdalena? And be specific. I figured running your little errand yesterday would've bought us at least a week until you came chasing another repayment."

Magdalena ran a finger across the table and grimaced. "No, no, no. We are not here to service any loans. Nothing of the sort," she said. "We were simply in the vicinity and thought we would drop in for a spot of, ah, breakfast."

"Yeah, I kinda doubt that," Jack replied.

The only reasons that would lure Magdalena Black down from her ivory tower in the clouds and into the slums were to collect debts, fuck somebody over, or have her muscle put a bullet in somebody's forehead, though not necessarily in that order. Magdalena brushed past Jack and settled in front of the unclaimed plate of scrambled eggs. She cast a cursory glance at the unappetising breakfast offering, her expression contorting with disgust as she promptly pushed the plate away. Her unyielding gaze locked onto Jack, who met her eyes with a slight tilt of his head, anticipating further explanation. However, no words were exchanged, not unless she had acquired telepathy on the down-low since their last encounter.

"Not to say that we don't, ah, delight in early morning visits" Jack began, "but as you may or may not appreciate, a bloke gets a little concerned when Magdalena Black and her shaved Silverback gorilla start makin' house calls at" he checked his wristwatch for dramatic effect, "a touch after sparrow's fart."

Magdalena smiled and gestured to the empty chairs at the table. Hung exchanged a concerned glance with Jack, and after a confirming nod, he reluctantly took a seat opposite the loan shark. Jack, however, stood his ground. He was not about to budge without some sort of explanation for the intrusion.

"I suggest you take a seat," Magdalena said.

Jack persisted in refusing the invitation.

"Do not presume for one moment that there is any illusion of choice here, Jack. Take a seat before Mark grabs that vacant chair over there and shoves it up your back passage, sideways."

Mark cracked his knuckles and rose from his seat, eyes blazing, ready to enforce Magdalena's will. Jack, after considering his options, finally yielded and sat down wearily at the table beside Hung, unable to resist Mark's persuasive approach to interior decorating. As the two men locked eyes in a silent standoff, the loan shark surveyed the room, perhaps contemplating if this was how the other half, about which she had heard so much, lived.

"So? Where is he?" Magdalena asked, out of nowhere and with absolutely no context. "Somebody, somewhere, seems to have got wind of where our Korean friend was staying."

"You mean Chul-Moo?" Hung asked.

"Is he missing or something?" Jack followed up.

Magdalena sat in complete silence. Dressed entirely in black and as sombre as a cancer diagnosis, her appearance gave the impression she was attending a funeral. Naturally, the men turned their attention to her enforcer, who sat across the table, his expression simmering with anger as he nodded in confirmation.

"You've got to be joking, right?" Jack said.

"Does it sound like I am angling to deliver a punchline, Jack?" Magdalena shifted in her chair. "Only a handful of people knew about Chul-Moo's existence. Even fewer were aware that he was staying at The Cockatoo Inn. I knew. This big bastard sitting across from me knew. And by sheer necessity, you two buffoons knew."

"That's four by my count, boss," Mark said.

"Yes, four. Brilliant arithmetic," Magdalena replied with a hint of incredulity, rolling her eyes at the overgrown toddler. "Actually, come to think of it, all the people who knew about our arrangement, and who are still breathing, happen to be located in this very kitchen."

"What about the manager?" Hung asked innocently.

"You mean Maximilian?" Magdalena replied.

"Yeah. That guy knew all about Chul-Moo."

"Good Lord. Allow me to repeat myself for the logically impaired among us. All the people who are *still breathing* happen to be located in this very kitchen. Read between the lines."

"So ... what, he's dead?" Hung replied.

Magdalena sighed at the seemingly foolish question and turned her attention to Jack, initiating her interrogation. "Who are you working for? You must be working for somebody. You hardly strike me as the empire-building type, Jack." She gave Hung a quick once-over with pitying eyes. "And, well, the less said about your moronic friend in the novelty apron here, the better."

"What are you on about?" Jack replied.

"Are you working for one of the Sammys?"

"Sammy who? I don't know any bloody Sammys."

"Hmm. How about those dogs from Cabramatta, then?" Magdalena asked, pointing an accusatory finger in the direction of said moronic friend in the novelty apron. "Your business associate here, Harold, appears to be of that, ah, ethnic persuasion, is he not?"

Jack was growing increasingly uncomfortable with the way things were unfolding, especially with the glaring accusations Magdalena Black was throwing around. If they were indeed on the payroll of the Vietnamese crime syndicates, it was clear they were doing a terrible job, considering they barely had two brass razoos to rub together.

"Neither of us has a clue what you're talking about," Jack replied. "We dropped Chul-Moo off at the motel, exactly as you asked. No deviations. How would we know what happened to him after that? We're not clairvoyant. The manager would've been the last person who had anything to do with him, not us."

"Seems somewhat convenient, blaming a dead man."

"Well, we didn't make him that way, did we?"

Jack raised a very pertinent point.

"Perhaps you are merely opportunists then?" Magdalena continued, brushing off the allegation with ease. "You wanted the information for yourself? Auction it off to the highest bidder? Plenty of powerful, well-connected people would jump at the chance to get their hands on that storage gizmo."

The recent flood of revelations overwhelmed Jack.

"Huh? What friggin' information?" he asked.

"The information that you so brazenly stole, Jack."

"Bullshit. We haven't stolen a bloody thing."

Magdalena turned to address Mark. "Have you ever heard a bigger load of twaddle in your life?" The enforcer shook his head as his boss turned back to address Jack and Hung. "And you know how I know that's twaddle? Before Max 'departed', he informed me that two men in balaclavas snatched Chul-Moo from his cabin and drove off. *Two men*. You and your friend here constitute two men, if only by the slimmest of margins." Magdalena tapped her cherry-red fingernails on the kitchen table. "As luck would have it, one kidnapper was of slight build. Actually, I believe the term 'weedy shit' was used. Hmm. And when I think 'weedy shits', well, see Exhibit A," she said, pointing at the diminutive Hung.

"Wait, somebody kidnapped him?" Jack asked.

"Well, you tell me, Jack," Magdalena replied.

"What? How many times do I need to say it? We don't know anything about … anything? You burst in here ranting about kidnappings and information and … gizmos? We don't have the foggiest idea what you're talking about. Hung and I came straight back *here* after we dropped Chul-Moo off, and we haven't left since. Just ask … " Jack paused, refraining from dropping his niece's name. "If you don't believe us, look around. There aren't any Koreans here, Magdalena! None."

"Don't worry, I already took a gander," Mark replied.

Jack rose from his seat, sensing that Magdalena's relentless questioning had devolved into little more than a circle-jerk of baseless accusations. It was time to throw the circuit breaker.

"In a hurry to be somewhere?" the loan shark asked.

"I've gotta run and grab the door," Jack replied.

"Huh? I didn't hear a buzzer," Mark said.

"Nah, just need to show a couple of arseholes out."

Magdalena shook her head and gazed up at the yellowed, cigarette-stained ceiling, her voice laced with frustration. "And here I thought you had grasped the ramifications of Chul-Moo not showing up for the money transfer this morning," she said.

"That sounds like a *not us* problem," Jack replied.

"Not entirely," Magdalena responded. "I might be able to stall Chul-Moo's counterparts for a few hours, but eventually, his handlers in Korea will realise that he's missing." There was a flicker of concern on the loan shark's otherwise stoic face. "And when they do, well, any torment I inflict upon you and your friend here will pale in comparison to what they will mete out upon yours truly."

Magdalena flicked her hand at Mark so subtly Jack might have missed it if he had not been paying attention. Before anyone could react, Mark lunged across the table, landing a sucker-punch square on Hung's head. Hung went flying off his chair, crashing onto the linoleum with enough force to rattle the cupboards. Jack, never one to back down, charged headlong at Mark. Despite the ex-footballer's thirty kilos of extra muscle and four-inch height advantage, the two men locked into a furious grapple, swinging haymakers with all the precision of a State of Origin brawl. A maniacal grin spread across Mark's face as he threw a volley of punishing lefts and rights. Muscle memory had kicked in: that big bastard was in his element.

And as fast as the fists started flying, they stopped.

Mark's superior reach had erased any advantage Jack had in speed or agility. In a final flurry, Mark switched from old-school brawling to something more suited to an over-60's self-defence class and drove a knee straight into Jack's groin. Jack doubled over, a guttural cry tearing from his throat and sending a shiver through the nether regions of every male in the room. With his opponent writhing, Mark grabbed Jack by the collar like a nightclub bouncer and hurled him across the kitchen, slamming him violently into the wall.

And just as the brawl reached its inevitable climax, Magdalena started a slow clap. Sharp. Mocking. Dangerous.

"Nice try, Jack," she said. "Worthy of an A for effort."

With Hung lying semi-conscious on the floor and Jack now halfway there, writhing in agony as he clutched his neither regions, Mark lumbered over to the kitchen sink. He opened the cupboard beneath it and rummaged through the assortment of cleaning products and household sundries. Eventually, his face lit up with a sense of elation as he retrieved a bottle of methylated spirits.

"Metho's flammable, right?" he asked.

"Does it have a little red symbol on the bottle? The one with a flame that says 'flammable'?" Magdalena replied sarcastically.

Mark examined the label and nodded.

"Then yes, Mark, it's flammable."

The enforcer struggled with the childproof lid for a moment before finally opening the bottle. He then started pouring the contents over Hung, who was still dazed and sprawled out on the kitchen floor. Hung did his best to shield his face from the pungent liquid.

"What the fuck are you doing?" Jack groaned.

Magdalena rose from her seat and took a few steps back, distancing herself from the unfolding chemistry lesson. Mark retrieved a disposable plastic lighter from his jeans pocket and looked at his employer, seeking confirmation for what he was about to do. Magdalena nodded to give the go-ahead. With a push of Mark's thumb, the lighter ignited. The flame flickered faintly as he glanced at Magdalena one last time for a final confirmation. The loan shark nodded again, giving the green light, and Mark raised the lighter.

"Get away from him," Jack interjected from the floor, desperation and pain evident in his voice in equal measure. "We don't know what happened to Chul-Moo! We dropped him off at the motel. I chatted with the manager for a while, then we left. That's it. Maybe ... hell, who knows? Maybe somebody followed us from the club?"

"Followed you? Unlikely," Magdalena replied.

"It ... it's the truth," Hung chimed in, still seeing stars.

There was a lingering silence as the loan shark contemplated her next move. She motioned to Mark to kill the flame before reaching into her purse for a compact, opening it, and examining her complexion; glamorous yet marked by the passage of time, like a former beauty who had ventured too close to the sun. After a quick lipstick touch-up, she stashed her paraphernalia into her handbag with a sigh that conveyed the weight of the world. "Three," Magdalena said, holding up the requisite number of fingers for the men to see. "You have until the count of three to tell me the truth, Jack. Extend me the courtesy of a little honesty, otherwise Mark here will flambé your friend without a second thought."

"What do you want me to fuckin' say?" Jack replied.

"One," the loan shark said, lowering a digit.

Jack got to his knees and began crawling across the floor to protect his friend, like a soldier throwing himself on a grenade to absorb the brunt of the explosion. Before he could cover more than a few centimetres, Mark delivered a swift kick to his ribs. The blow was sharp and precise, sending Jack crashing back to the ground with a gasp of pain, leaving him breathless.

"Two. Come on, Jack, I expected a lot more."

"It's the truth, Miss Black!" Hung pleaded.

When a person was soaked in flammable liquid and someone threatened to introduce a naked flame, the odds of ending up a scorch mark on scuffed linoleum were better than even. The situation was dire, worsening by the second. Jack still could not make head nor tail of it. Why would Magdalena Black want to torch two of her "best" customers? Best, of course, being entirely subjective. And then there was the pesky matter of the missing Korean.

"That's three," Magdalena said calmly, then turned her back and began walking away amidst a chorus of appeals.

This was the cue for her henchman to proceed.

Mark ignited the lighter, and for a moment, he watched the flame dance merrily, transfixed by its beauty. However, the moment was short-lived. Resolute in his grim task, Mark cocked his wrist, ready to toss the lighter at Hung. But suddenly, the flame went out. Mark cursed under his breath as he shook the lighter and attempted to ignite it again, to no avail. Another shake, another attempt. But there was still nothing, not even a faint spark of hope. Magdalena came to a sudden halt. She had expected to hear the agonising wails of a man consumed by flames and to feel the satisfying warmth of revenge. To her dismay, neither of these horrors unfolded. She turned around slowly, her face a mask of menacing fury.

"What the hell happened?" Magdalena asked.

"Uh, the lighter's empty, boss," Mark replied.

Magdalena snatched the offending item from Mark's hand and shook it furiously before attempting to ignite it without success. "Just my luck," she growled under her breath. Her enforcer scanned the room and lumbered over to the kitchen drawers beside the oven, opening the leftmost one in search of another lighter. "I suppose neither of you happen to have a spare, do you?" Magdalena quipped. Jack and Hung remained deathly silent as Mark's search yielded no results. What were the odds of that? Magdalena shook her head in disbelief and, without uttering a word, tossed the spent cigarette lighter onto the middle of the kitchen table, almost as if she was inviting Jack and Hung to keep it as a good luck charm.

"Talk about a fluky pair of cunts," Mark said, sliding a hand to the firearm tucked in his waistband. "How about I just shoot 'em, Maggie?" he said, fingering the trigger like it was his date at the school formal afterparty. "We break some shit, put a few slugs in the wall. The usual. Then, get that pair of bent coppers of yours to spin it as a ... I dunno, a botched home invasion."

"Wait. Hold your damn horses," Magdalena said.

Disappointment flickered across Mark's face.

Magdalena paced the cramped kitchen, weighing her options. Jack and Hung's refusal to spill Chul-Moo's whereabouts meant one of two things: they were innocent, or unnervingly disciplined. Her money was on the latter, but killing them now would only multiply her problems. Keeping them alive worked in her favour, at least until *somebody*, hell, *anybody*, led her to the missing hacker.

"Hmm. Perhaps I was a bit, ah ... hasty," she said.

"Oh? You don't bloody say?" Jack replied.

Magdalena shook her head. "Sarcasm does not suit you, Mister Perkins," she said. "Now listen carefully. I have a proposition. And this is not a 'take it or leave it' kind of deal. It is more of a 'take it or leave a corpse' proposition. I suggest you heed my words: I want Chul-Moo returned unharmed by lunchtime."

"That's twelve o'clock, fuckfaces," Mark added.

Jack slapped the floor with his palm of his hand.

"Jesus, we already told you—" he began.

"Who said you could speak?" Magdalena replied. "In exchange for returning Chul-Moo, I will, regrettably, spare your pathetic lives. On one condition: you sign over the deed to this establishment to me. Sign it over, and then consider relocating elsewhere, perhaps to South America, because you two are *persona non grata* around here." Those two simple words, 'in exchange', made Jack shudder. The current owners of The Hackston were about to either find themselves further entrenched in Magdalena's servitude, without a livelihood, or worse, six feet under. "And should Chul-Moo remain missing, or either of you go missing, Mark here will hunt you down and terminate you with extreme prejudice. Dead. Gone. Fucked. And better yet, before your bodies are even cold in the ground, I'll make it my prerogative to raze this shithole to the ground, with that pretty niece of yours still inside. Am I crystal clear?"

"You absolute cunt," Jack uttered under his breath.

"Oi! What did you fuckin' say?" Mark asked.

The man-mountain had heard every word, but he could not resist goading Jack for his own amusement.

"You heard me, Mark. Leave Charlie out of it."

"Ah, perhaps we have finally found Jack's Kryptonite?" Magdalena smirked. "Your niece is a spirited young thing. It would be a shame if her uncle's hubris put her in any sort of danger." She glanced at her wristwatch. "So, Jack, twelve o'clock. That gives you and your friend, what? Four hours and forty-five minutes to return my Korean."

Chapter Sixteen

Long Shots and Bad Luck

Surfers Paradise Police Complex, later that morning.

Detective Mick Hughes sat hunched over his desk, his head buried in his hands, the weight of exhaustion bearing down on him. Despite being less than two hours into his official shift, his corner desk resembled more of a rolling battleground than a place of procedure and order. A mountain of partially read case files, with creased corners and dog-eared pages, lay buried beneath a heap of discarded facsimiles, printouts and disposable coffee cups. Amid the chaos, a photo of his wife and children lay overturned, its broken frame serving as a makeshift paperweight. While the world slept, Hughes had been burning the midnight oil, wrestling with the identity of the kid buried in a shallow grave on the outskirts of the city.

"It's coming through," Gamble said as he leaned against a filing cabinet beside the shared fax machine. His head tilted as he read the incoming correspondence between the rhythmic buzzing and whirring. "Looks like the beginnings of their department header."

"Right. Wake me when it's done," Hughes replied.

"You sure I can't grab you a coffee, Sarge?"

Hughes clutched his stomach. "Christ, no," he said. "Any more of that swill from the canteen and I'm gonna be as backed up as the M1 on a Friday arvo. Just stay put, yeah. Keep your eyes on that fax machine like a good little public servant while I give mine a rest."

Had it been any other morning, the senior detective would have been full of piss and vinegar, or more accurately, coffee and bravado. A first-grade sadist, he took delight in feigning bright-eyed enthusiasm just to needle his more nocturnally inclined colleagues, despite being anything but a mythical 'morning person' himself. But not today. Amazing how a dead Korean and a severe lack of sleep could strip the shine off even the most well-practised facade.

Gamble examined the incoming fax and sighed.

"You're not going to like this, Sarge," he said.

"Oh, really? Well, spit it out then, fat boy."

The sight of the two detectives, their voices barely more than whispers, engrossed in conversation while awaiting the results of a fax, stirred the curiosity of their nearby colleagues. Heads peeked over desk partitions. Hushed murmurs of intrigue spread through the office. It was a curious sight, considering that Hughes had rarely shown this much dedication to a case in, well, forever.

"Which one do you want first?" Gamble asked.

"What are you on about?" Hughes replied.

"Do you want the good news or the bad news first?" Judging from the many years he had known his partner, Gamble leaned toward delivering the latter first. Hughes remained silent. "The bad news, Sarge, is that the kid appears to be a cleanskin," he said. "At least according to my contact at Interpol."

"What? So, his prints aren't in any databases?"

"That's what it's beginning to look like."

"Fuck me sideways. So, what's the good news?"

"Well ... the kid appears to be a cleanskin."

The term *cleanskin* referred to someone with no prior run-ins with law enforcement. For Hughes and Gamble, the fact that Chul-Moo's file had never crossed their desk was a definite advantage. It significantly lowered the chances of other agencies, ones far better resourced and with a jurisdictional advantage, being on his trail. Yet something did not sit right with the senior detective, and it was not just the seven coffees he had consumed overnight.

"Why would Sleezeball go to so much effort to rescue a nobody from a snatch and grab?" Hughes lowered his voice a few decibels. "Normally that fat prick wouldn't even bother gettin' out of his own way, but last night he was all tooled-up and ready to rock. Why? He had to have been *somebody*, Barry. Some agency is bound to have a file on this kid. Prints, name, address. Anything. He sure as shit wasn't in town to grab a couple of happy snaps with a koala."

"Perhaps Conrad was telling the truth, Sarge?"

"That'd be a bloody first," Hughes replied.

"He did say he was from overseas," Gamble added.

It was a valid point. No local in their right mind would willingly stay at a place like The Cockatoo Inn, at least not unless they were there to get discreetly ploughed, or they had lost a sizeable bet.

"Time to pivot," Hughes said. "Keep runnin' with that international angle, yeah. Get on the blower to a few of the consulates around here, see what sort of juicy details you can pry out of 'em."

"Any specific jurisdictions?" Gamble asked.

"How should I know, Baz? Do I look like the bloody Asian Organised Crime Squad?" Hughes replied, cursing under his breath as he ran a hand through his ginger hair. As a man averse to foreign cultures, and culture in general, the detective regarded anyone of that 'persuasion' to be indistinguishable from one another. "Japan, China, whatever. All I know is that out there somewhere, in this big Wide World of fuckin' Sports, a mum'll be missing their baby boy."

Hung sat quietly at the kitchen table, showered and changed since his encounter with Magdalena Black. Jack, having finished mopping up the last of the methylated spirits, set the mop and bucket in the corner. He took a seat opposite Hung, nudging aside the bottle of milk that still occupied the centre of the table. Neither man had spoken since the ordeal. What was there to say? Chul-Moo had been kidnapped, their livelihood was in jeopardy, and they had escaped with their lives only thanks to a faulty disposable cigarette lighter.

Things were hardly coming up roses for Jack and Hung.

"Care if I smoke?" Jack asked out of the blue.

Hung chuckled and gave a casual shrug. Jack took it as consent to pull a tattered packet of cigarettes from his pocket, a well-travelled relic with more creases than a working girl's bed-sheets. He sifted through its contents, unearthing three loose cigarettes of uncertain age. Each looked as though it had sur-vived a few close calls. He chose the least battered of the trio and held it between the middle and index fingers of his left hand. Jack rarely smoked, the crumpled packet from his bedside table proof enough, but something about the silence in the room made him reach for one now. It felt like the kind of day where the rules went out the window. Hung, who would usually give him grief about his "dirty little habit", stayed quiet. Perhaps he knew as well as Jack that this might be his last cigarette.

"What the hell have I dragged you into?" Jack asked.

"Me? You haven't dragged *me* into anything."

"Well, it's really starting to feel like it, mate."

"No, we're in this together, Jack. Fifty-fifty."

Hung's sentiment, while equal parts noble and saccharine, was, in terms of contract law, entirely correct. Both of their names were on the property title, and that meant they were equally on the hook for whatever came next. Jack nodded, lost in thought, and raised the battered cigarette to his lips before realising he had no way to light it. Irritated, he rose from his chair, then remembered Mark's cigarette lighter on the table. He picked it up, turning it over in his hand, and decided that getting a flame out of it would be about as much of a miracle as either of them making it out of the Gold Coast alive.

"Reckon it's been worth it?" Jack mumbled, the cigarette jutting from the corner of his mouth like a modern-day Humphrey Bogart as he swept his hand to take in The Hackston. "You know, almost dying for a rundown shithole that can barely pull a handful of pissheads on a good day?"

Jack already knew what Hung's answer would be.

"Hell no," Hung said, resolute. "But there's no way I'm signing The Hackston over to Magdalena Black either. Not after all the effort we've put into this place, Jack. Not to her. Not to anyone." He paused, locking eyes with his friend and business partner. "You know better than anyone what my childhood was like. How my parents came to Australia with nothing but the clothes on their backs, raising three kids on the pittance they earned selling vegetables at the local market."

"That I do," Jack replied. "I lost count of the number of times Miss McCready sent you home from school with a pair of shoes out of lost property after yours had a blowout."

"Five times," Hung replied nonchalantly.

"What? You're still keeping score, even now?"

Hung nodded. "Poverty has a way of cementing your memories," he began. "And don't worry, Jack, I'll never forget the times you used to slip me one of your cheese and pickle sandwiches at lunch when we were doing it tough."

"Heh. I forgot about the old C&P sangas," Jack replied.

"Mmm. They were pretty damn good, hey?"

The men indulged in a much-needed moment of levity as they unexpectedly veered down memory lane. How had a pair of carefree kids, once sharing lunches on the playground, become entangled in the intricate web of the criminal underworld? The privilege of age was supposed to bestow wisdom, not plunge a person into the clutches of loan sharks and the looming spectre of death incarnate.

"My point is," Hung continued, "when my parents passed, I sunk every cent of my inheritance into this place. Everything. So, no, Jack. The Hackston might not be worth getting killed over, but there's no way I'm just going to hand it over either. Stuff that. I would rather raze this entire place to the ground before I ever gave anything away to … to that … " Hung trailed off in search of a fitting descriptor.

One that likely rhymed with 'mucking runt'.

Jack nodded in agreement, knowing that Hung's prudish sensibilities would never allow him to drop the dreaded C-word. In dire need of a lungful of carcinogens, Jack tapped the cigarette lighter on the table as if to rouse its Promethean potential. Bingo! It worked on the first try. He could only chuckle at the happenstance of it. Hung, on the other hand, stared at the naked flame and shook his head, realising he was possibly one extra thumb flick away from performing an impromptu rendition of the Jerry Lee Lewis classic 'Great Balls of Fire', wearing little more than his boxers and a novelty apron.

"I've got to say, Hung, I'm liking this new backbone of yours," Jack said, cigarette hanging from his lips as he pulled in a long, indulgent drag, like getting back with an old flame you should never have left. "But let's be honest ... we're up Shit Creek, minus a paddle, and down a Korean. Still, I'm not rolling over either. Not because of someone else's cock-up. What was that Max clown even doing?"

He took another long drag. "You know what? The more I think about it, the more ... nah. Forget it. Sounds ridiculous."

"Whatever it is, Jack, just say it," Hung replied.

"Alright. What if Chul-Moo was never kidnapped?"

Hung narrowed his eyes, sensing Jack was about to pull him into something stupid. "But Maggie told us he was."

"Yeah, that's the story. But what if he wasn't?"

"What? Are you implying it was some sort of ruse?"

Jack nodded. "Well, that's one way of putting it. 'Bullshit' is another. Like, just think about it, Hung. We owed Maggie a heap of money and then suddenly, outta the blue, she comes to us with a time-sensitive proposition to ferry a kid from the airport, no questions asked?" He leaned in closer, as if the walls had suddenly sprouted ears. "What if it was all a lie? A setup. My gut tells me this is some sort of scam to, ah, I dunno ... to wrestle The Hackston from us."

Magdalena Black did have a reputation for sinister deeds.

"But why would she want this place?" Hung asked.

"Why not? Why's the sky blue, mate?"

Hung took a moment to ponder his friend's words.

"Hear me out, yeah," Jack continued. "Black gets one of her Asian mates to play tourist for a few hours, all while a couple of unsuspecting fools, namely us, take him on a grand tour of the Goldie," he explained, punctuating his words with a long drag on his cigarette as he laid out the ruse like a conspiracy theorist with a bone. "Fast-forward to the next morning, and Maggie and her henchman burst in here with some amateur theatrics about said Asian mate disappearing overnight. Then, Bob's your uncle. You've now got two broke fellas indebted to her for something money can't replace, and the only item of value they own is ... well, take a wild guess."

That being The Hackston, for anyone playing at home.

"So ... Chul-Moo isn't really missing?" Hung asked.

"Eh. Your guess is as good as mine," Jack replied.

Without the aid of god-like omniscience, all Jack knew for certain was that neither of them should trust Magdalena Black as far as they could throw her. And in the case of Hung, with his limited upper body strength, that was not very far at all.

"Okay. So let's just go to the police then," Hung said.

"Nah," Jack replied. "Crims don't rise to Magdalena Black's level of infamy without a few local coppers in their perfumed pockets."

"Then we take it outside the Gold Coast."

"To Brisbane? Nah. Still too close for comfort."

With a little over four hours remaining until the deadline, someone had to come up with a plan, and chances were that someone would be Jack Perkins. He scanned the flat's tacky sixties decor, seeking inspiration, his mind buzzing with intricate schemes. Few of them were logistically feasible, let alone likely to pass the self-imposed 'will-it-get-us-killed' test. Jack's eyes eventually came to rest on the old Bakelite rotary telephone on the kitchen counter. Perhaps it was time to start with the basics and channel a bit of his inner Sam Spade.

"I reckon we're best to hedge our bets," Jack began. "Treat it like those debates we used to do in English class. One of us assumes that this Chul-Moo kid was real, and that someone kidnapped him. The other works on the assumption that the story's bullshit." Hung nodded pensively, keen to hear about this fresh new Pandora's box his partner was about to open. "I need you to focus on the legit angle, yeah. That means gettin' on the telephone and calling anyone who might deal with the missing or injured. I'm talking local hospitals, homeless shelters, morgues. Whatever makes sense."

"And what am I supposed to say?" Hung asked.

"Tell them you're a relative or something," Jack said. "Ask if anyone matching Chul-Moo's description has come through recently. If he wasn't kidnapped, maybe he ended up in an emergency department somewhere. I know it's a long shot, Hung, but honestly, that's about all we've got right now ... long shots and bad luck."

As soon as the words left his mouth, Jack realised that his faith in Hung's ability to think on his feet might have been grossly misplaced. But what other choice did they have right now? It was not as if Hung was shotgunning out ideas at a thousand rounds per minute.

"Uh, okay. And what about you?" Hung asked.

"Me? Well, while you're busy letting your fingers do the walking, I'm going to take a drive over to The Cockatoo Inn," Jack said. "I want to see if this so-called manager, Max, is still alive. I know it's a bit of a hike, but it should be able to corroborate Magdalena's story."

"Okay, and *if* her story checks out?" Hung asked.

"That's when Plan B kicks in," Jack replied.

"Boy, oh boy. And what's this Plan B exactly?"

"That's where we plan on being as far away from this pub as humanly possible. That's the only fallback we've got."

Jack checked his wristwatch and cursed under his breath. With no chance of being in two places at once, opening The Hackston today was out of the question. Putting his niece anywhere near the pub only increased the risk of collateral damage if things went south. Wincing at the lingering pain in his ribs, courtesy of Mark Campbell's size thirteen boot, Jack rose carefully from his seat and went to the notepad by the telephone. He tore off a page and, as Hung watched, puzzled, grabbed a nearby pen and scrawled a hasty note.

"Tape this to the door while you're at it," Jack said. "And get onto Charlie. Give her a heads-up that we won't be opening."

The note read: Closed until further notice.

"But ... won't she suspect something?" he asked.

"Charlie already suspects there is plenty wrong around here," Jack said as he stubbed out the last of his cigarette on the milk bottle, which had been sweating on the kitchen table ever since he brought it back from the corner store. The cigarette made a satisfying *hiss* as the orange-red glow faded to a fatalistic shade of black. "Either way, assuming you want to live to see another sunrise, it's unlikely that telling a white lie to my niece will be the least unsavoury thing we do today."

Brisbane International Airport.

The Gwangju Three emerged from the terminal, shielding their eyes from the intense Queensland sunlight and the dazzling reflections off the steel and glass surroundings. While accustomed to the sun in their native South Korea, coincidentally the same sun worshipped throughout Australia, the radiance here felt starker and more unforgiving than back home. Butterfly, the leader of the trio, donned mirrored aviators and surveyed the travellers milling around the entrance. In comparison, the gangsters were like monotone anachronisms. Clad from head to toe in their signature black attire, the trio looked more suited for a wake than leisurely exploration. Their true purpose, however, transcended the usual touristy palaver. They were here to unravel the mystery of Chul-Moo's disappearance, with the name 'Magdalena Black' at the forefront of their minds.

Chapter Seventeen

Exotic Price Tags

Jack Perkins pulled into The Cockatoo Inn's car park, bringing his Datsun to a stop outside the motel's demountable office. He lingered in the driver's seat, letting the engine idle as he drew on his last cigarette. Despite the hour, an eerie stillness hung over the complex. There were no vehicles in the car park and no guests, at least none that he could see. He was alone, left with his thoughts. They had been running wild ever since the drive from The Hackston, as he mulled over how things might play out when or if he confronted the motel's manager, Max Stedkole. And of course, assuming Max was still alive was a mighty big 'if', especially given Magdalena Black's recent hints that he might already be on the wrong side of the grass.

Regardless, Jack needed a lead, a confession, *anything*. The only way he and Hung were going to survive this ordeal was by either tracking down Chul-Moo or gathering enough evidence that Magdalena's involvement was a cunning scheme to steal their pub. There was no in-between. Unfortunately, the grim truth eluded them: the Korean's corpse lay in a shallow grave just off the highway, less than ten minutes from where Jack sat. Had he known this, he would already have been on the blower, booking a flight to some non-extradition country, preferably one with a welcoming climate.

Word was, Brazil was lovely this time of year.

Amidst the deafening, almost mocking laughter of a nearby kookaburra, Jack drew his cigarette down to the filter and flicked the butt out the window with a sigh of frustration. He paused, reflecting on his decision to return to the motel, before climbing out of the car and heading toward cabin three with a growing sense of trepidation.

As he crossed the car park, gravel *crunching* underfoot, the first anomaly in this life-and-death game of 'Spot the Difference' revealed itself: a faint boot print just off centre from the doorknob. Despite an obvious attempt to erase it, the scuff remained visible at the right angle. Jack stopped to examine the door. On closer inspection, the hinges and striker plate showed clear signs of stress, as if someone or something had struck the door hard and fast, followed by what he could only assume was a hasty, makeshift DIY.

Jack was no forensics expert, merely a publican with a tenth-grade education, but it was reasonable to assume someone had gained entry using the old 'size-nine skeleton key'. All things considered, the theory that Chul-Moo had been kidnapped was looking more plausible by the second. Jack scanned the area for witnesses and realised he was going to have to grow a pair and go inside.

Entering cabin three would offer the definitive answer to Chul-Moo's fate. Or, at the very least, definitive enough to influence Jack and Hung's actions in the coming hours. Every fibre of Jack's being dreaded confronting the reality. Right now, the kid, like Schrodinger's cat, was simultaneously both alive and dead while unobserved inside that closed cabin. However, this was more than a laugh for a bunch of university students wanting to get as stiff as a board over quantum superposition. For Jack, knowing the Korean's fate meant having to choose a side. And choosing a side inevitably meant setting in motion a plan that could cost them their lives.

"Here goes nothing," Jack muttered as he turned the doorknob. To his surprise, the door was unlocked, as if inviting him inside to witness the macabre tableau. His heart pounded like a jackhammer, and his breath hitched. He stole one last glance over his shoulder and, against his better judgement, nudged the door open.

With steel in his resolve, he entered cabin three.

The first thing to hit Jack was the smell. Gone was the lingering, musty odour of stale air and mould, replaced instead by the pungent scent of cleaning products. Not only did it smell clean, the cabin itself was immaculate: a neatly made bed with fresh linen, towels hanging in the bathroom, and tiny bottles of shampoo. More importantly, it was devoid of any belongings. The cabin was cleaner than it had ever been, almost *too clean*. There was no way this was the work of The Cockatoo Inn's manager, Max. Unbeknown to Jack, Magdalena Black's right-hand man had not always been a professional footballer. Mark had also worked as a porter at one of Sydney's upscale hotels and had stripped and triple-sheeted more beds in his time than Jack would have had hot dinners.

Cleanliness aside, there was no sign of Chul-Moo.

With an even greater sense of hopelessness, Jack exited the cabin and made the long trek back across to the manager's office at the end of the complex. Passing the first couple of cabins, Jack made a less-than-subtle attempt to peer through the windows. Despite there being no visible signs of life, he hoped that maybe one of them had some activity inside: a blaring television, lights on, *anything* at all. Given The Cockatoo Inn's reputation for clandestine rendezvous, it was likely that something was transpiring in one of these cabins, whether or not Jack desired to witness such transpiration.

Jack approached the office and *rapped* on the door.

"Hey, Max. It's Jack Perkins," he called out.

Silence greeted him. He *knocked* again.

"I was, ah, here yesterday. We dropped off the Asian kid for Maggie," he said. "You remember Maggie, right? Magdalena Black. The woman who you so, uh, eloquently compared to one of those little fish that swim up the eye of your diddle."

Again, there was no response. No movement behind the door, no crunch of corn chips, no echo of a television. It was as if Max had vanished off the face of the earth. Jack stared at the door, frozen, unsure what to do next. There was no Chul-Moo. No Max. There had to be a connection between the two? He tried the doorknob again, hoping for a lucky break, only to find it locked. In a last-ditch attempt, he peered through the window. Shapes and objects emerged in the darkened room, all vaguely familiar from his mental map of the office. What Jack could not have known was that the man called 'Sleazeball' lay sprawled on the floor beside his desk, his antique rifle nearby, a silent hint at self-harm.

Jack returned to his car, a gnawing restlessness clawing at him. The drive from the Gold Coast had been fruitless, yielding more questions than answers. What was he missing? As he opened the door, ready to leave with his metaphorical tail between his legs, he took one last look back at The Cockatoo Inn. Out of nowhere, a subtle shift in the air made the hair on the back of his neck stand up. An inexplicable pull emanated from the cabin at the rear of the complex, a silent beckoning that resonated deep within him, like a siren luring a sailor toward perilous shores.

He froze, running a hand across his stubbled chin. Hell, he had already come this far. What harm was there in taking a second look?

With a renewed sense of purpose, Jack turned back, drawn by the unspoken promise that cabin five held the key to the missing Korean. At the very least, he was going to shit-in his daily step count traipsing across the car park, though any supposed health benefits were moot if a bullet found its way into his frontal cortex.

As the cabin came into view, an eerie stillness settled over the scene, hinting at yet another possible dead end. The structure exuded mundane uniformity, indistinguishable from its neighbours, save for the pair of dirty jocks tossed on the roof of cabin two and the battered door of its adjacent neighbour. Jack scrutinised the fibro shoebox, teetering on the edge of surrender. Just as he was about to add another regrettable choice to his growing catalogue, he caught a subtle variance: a nearly imperceptible flicker of movement behind the window. Instincts on high alert, he fixed his gaze on the source. The sun-bleached yellow curtains swayed with delicate grace, performing a clandestine dance between shadow and light.

Perhaps there was more here than met the eye.

Upon closer inspection, Jack made out the unmistakable silhouettes of at least one, maybe two, figures inside. This was the breakthrough he had been waiting for. Proceeding with caution, he approached the front door and *tapped lightly*, underestimating the hollow resonance of the timber. When that produced no reaction, he *rapped* more assertively with his knuckles. At first, there was silence, then a hushed exchange of words, accompanied by the faint rustle of a newspaper. Finally came the sound of approaching footsteps and the distinct *click* of a lock.

The door of cabin five cracked open, revealing Cyrille's chiselled European features, his brow furrowed at the early-morning disturbance. After giving Jack a quick once-over, he scrunched his face and said, "Whatever the fuck you're selling, champ, we aren't buying," before trying to shut the door.

One thing was certain: this was not Chul-Moo.

"Hold up!" Jack said, jamming his hand in the doorframe before Cyrille could close it. "I need to ask you something."

In hindsight, plunging his hand into the door of a complete stranger, especially one who was a roided-up gangster, was just another addition to Jack Perkins' catalogue of regrettable choices. But what other options did he have? Time was ticking, and he needed to uncover the identity of the second silhouette.

"Chul-Moo! You in there, mate?" Jack yelled.

Cyrille growled at the appendage. "You've got until the count of five," he said. "If your hand's still on that door when I'm done, you're gonna be wearing your arsehole for a necklace. Hear me?"

As Cyrille began his countdown, the bodybuilder's broad shoulders thwarted Jack's attempts to peer through the gap in the door. Could the second silhouette have really belonged to Chul-Moo? "Five!" And if so, what were the chances that Jack could take this Neanderthal alone? The safe money was on somewhere between Buckley's and none. "Four!" Jack went all-in and tried to pry the door open, as politely as possible, if such a thing existed. The act proved futile as Cyrille grinned back at Jack like an attack dog, effortlessly matching his strength and intensity. "Three!" Truth be told, this was the most adrenaline-fuelled thing that had happened to the young bloke since he arrived in Queensland. Sure, Cyrille could have wrestled the door away from the would-be intruder with ease, but where was the fun in that? "Two!" Cyrille almost wanted to let the stranger's little stunt play out, if only to put the 'prize' in the colloquial expression 'play stupid games, win stupid prizes'. "One!" Almost. Anything to break the monotony of plying a grumpy pensioner with tea and biscuits.

"What's going on?" a voice asked from the depths.

"Nothing," Cyrille replied. "It's under control."

Undeterred, Jack attempted to appeal to the disembodied voice behind the golem. "Do you remember me?" he asked, hopeful for any response. "I was here yesterday afternoon, dropping off, uh, a friend of mine. A young Korean guy, about twenty years old. Black shoulder-length hair. He was wearing long pants and a T-shirt with Bruce Lee on the front."

"Bruce Lee? The karate guy?" Cyrille asked.

A wave of movement surged from the rear of the cabin, and abruptly, the door swung open. Jack found himself face to face with a colossal man adorned in a flannel dressing gown, holding a cup of steaming hot tea in his massive paw. Jack took a step back, awestruck, like a termite gazing up at a towering eucalyptus. "What do you want, lad?" Donald boomed. Jack fell silent, his brain in fifth gear while his mouth seemed stuck in neutral. "Well? Don't stand there like a stunned mullet."

Some individuals radiated a larger-than-life presence that demanded attention, whether through their warmth and charisma or, conversely, an unspoken dominance that shaped the space, leaving an enduring impression on those in their midst. Humphrey Bogart had it. John Wayne personified it. And Donald Jacobsen, well, he devoured it for breakfast and casually shat it out by lunchtime. After all, there was a reason he carried a fearsome moniker like 'The Diamond' instead of 'The Marshmallow'.

"Uh ... g'day," Jack began, stuttering and stammering, "I was trying to, uh, tell your, ah, son, that I was here yesterday with a friend of mine. A young Korean guy, staying up in cabin three." Jack pointed toward said cabin. "I was supposed to pick him up this morning, but he doesn't seem to be in his room. I was just wondering if either of you saw him leave or noticed anything strange last night?"

Donald glanced in that direction. "Cabin three?"

"Yeah, the one just in the middle there."

There were five cabins, and this was number five. Logic dictated that cabin three was naturally going to be the one in the middle.

"Not that it's any of your, eh, concern, but the young blood and I were out till all hours last night. Sight-seeing," Donald replied. "Let me guess, you two star-crossed lovers had a tiff?"

"Uh, well … no. He's just … a friend," Jack replied.

"Wait, so you aren't a couple of woolly moofs?"

"No. Like I said already, he's just a friend of mine."

"Well, whatever you do with a young Asian bloke in the privacy of some rundown motel out in the sticks is your own business," Donald replied with a grin. "Now, as the Vicar whispered to the altar boy: 'kindly slip your digits out of my passage, lad, and fuck off'."

Jack yanked his hand back just as the door *slammed* shut.

Jarrah 'The Pom' O'Sullivan, proprietor of The Exchange, observed a group of walk-ins as they perused the shelves of his father's vault-cum-armoury. If he were not already risk averse prior to yesterday's misadventure, The Pom was now packing a concealed firearm snug at the small of his back, with at least a couple of spares stashed within arm's reach. Gone were his shoulder-length locks and carefree smile; his long black hair was pulled into a samurai-style topknot, his face expressionless, and a tan bulletproof vest covered his vital organs. He had the fashion sense of a man who had no intention of getting bent over a second time. By all rights, Jarrah should have been dead. His continued existence was not a testament to his skill, his gift of gab, or even blind luck; it was solely because of the benevolence of one Donald 'The Diamond' Jacobsen.

As he looked on with eagle-like intensity, he considered posing the obvious question before succumbing to temptation. "Is someone planning on starting World War Three or something?" Jarrah asked, his nerves evident. "I'm only asking because, well ... I'm not usually one to stick my bib in, but my old man owned this place for twenty-odd years, and I don't recall it ever buzzing like this."

The group continued to peruse some of the more exotic stock in silence. Stock that would not have looked out of place in a Sylvester Stallone film: rocket launchers, Vietnam-era flamethrowers, and massive belt-fed machine guns. Implements of death and destruction designed to send a message, and more often than not, that message simply screamed 'FUCKING DIE, YOU COMMIE PRICK!' in a slurred, almost unintelligible, American accent.

"Knives?" one customer asked, breaking the silence.

That customer was none other than Butterfly, the androgynous ball of quiet rage, searching the shelves for that one last piece of kit missing from the gangster's lethal shopping list.

"Cutlery? Down on the end," Jarrah replied.

As directed, Butterfly walked to the end of the row, their eyes lighting up upon discovering an assortment of bayonets, shurikens, and throwing knives. Bombastic trinkets of teenage curiosity confiscated by Australian Customs that regularly found their way onto the shelves of questionable establishments, sporting what could only be described as unquestionable markups. After perusing the selection with all the enthusiasm of a kid in a candy store, Butterfly finally spotted what they were looking for and let out a faint, almost imperceptible squeal of delight: an otherwise rare display of emotion from the typically stoic leader.

"How much money do you require?" Butterfly asked.

"To do what? Exist comfortably?" Jarrah replied.

It was too early in the day to entertain life's profound questions, especially when presented in broken English by shady-looking characters. But then again, when were prim and proper, law-abiding citizens the typical demographic for black-market gunrunners?

"No, how much to complete the transaction?"

"To buy all ... of that? You serious?" Jarrah replied.

He scoffed and cast an eye over Butterfly's colleagues, both of whom looked ready to wreak havoc: the formidable Mr Tooth wielded a full-sized Israeli Uzi, while the squat, wizard-like Bul-Gae shouldered a massive M60 belt-fed machine gun. Their thousand-yard stares and unfazed demeanours suggested that this was probably not their first B&S Ball. They looked like stone-cold killers. And if a war were brewing on the Gold Coast, then Jarrah had little doubt that The Gwangju Three were here to finish it. But to answer Butterfly's question, exotic weapons demanded exotic price tags. Considering the scarcity and collector's status of these big boy's toys, coupled with their dubious legality, the running total was somewhere up there with the cost of a second-hand sports car. And that was before factoring in ammunition, which, in and of itself, was about as rare and in-demand as a wet nurse with three teats.

Jarrah raised an eyebrow. "Bugger me. Did you leave the fourth Horseman out front watering the nags?" he asked. "Before you leave, do a bloke a favour and slip me the postcode of where this little soiree is goin' down. I'll promise to give the joint a wide berth for the next, I dunno ... dozen or so lifetimes."

Teetering on the brink of developing a conscience, Jarrah found himself caught between the moral quandary of thwarting a potential terrorist attack and the lucrative act of moving some merchandise. Should he do his patriotic duty and report it? After all, as the slogan went: 'If you see something, say something'. Except in his case, it was not merely a clear-cut matter of seeing something; he was balls-deep in the process of selling firearms and ammunition to a group of foreign nationals. Jarrah eventually gave in to the devil's tempting whisper and began crunching numbers. But before he could spit out a ballpark figure, he was beaten to the punch.

"Would two hundred be adequate?" Butterfly asked.

"What? Two hundred dollars?" Jarrah replied.

"Two hundred thousand Australian dollars."

With Butterfly's offer hanging in the air, Bul-Gae placed the machine gun at his feet and disappeared, only to reappear a moment later with the briefcase that he had brought with him. Jarrah broke character and chuckled under his breath. Had they really been walking around the Gold Coast with a generic black briefcase full of money? The idea seemed so hackneyed that Jarrah had not even given the item a second thought, especially after his portable metal detector confirmed an absence of any objects of the shooty or stabby variety inside. Intrigued and amused in equal measure, he smiled like an imbecile as Bul-Gae set the briefcase on a nearby shelf and unlocked it with an audible *click* that echoed throughout the vault.

Two hundred thousand dollars was no paltry sum. It was more than enough to settle his father's outstanding debts, repair the water-damaged roof at The Exchange, and give his mother a little breathing room to visit family in Darwin. More importantly, it meant Jarrah could finally shed the burden of pretending to be some hardnut underworld gangster. No more faffing about flogging guns or keeping up appearances. He could reclaim his life. Hell, maybe even put his Master's in Chemical Engineering to proper use at last.

"Any chance I could, uh, see it?" Jarrah asked.

"See what, exactly?" Butterfly replied.

"You know? The colour of your conviction."

Butterfly nodded and gestured toward the briefcase.

With a myriad of life-changing possibilities floating around in his head, Jarrah abandoned his typically security-conscious facade and practically skipped to the nearby shelf. All he could see was the light at the end of the tunnel. He stopped and steeled himself before opening the briefcase. However, as the lid reached its halfway point, Jarrah realised that the soothing light at the end of the tunnel was just a freight train coming his way; the briefcase was empty.

Before Jarrah could reach for his firearm, a weapon he lacked the intestinal fortitude to use, Mr Tooth wrapped the Uzi's shoulder strap around his throat and hoisted him into the air like a sack of meat.

Defeated, Jack leaned against the bonnet of his Datsun, eyes closed, his mind sifting through the events of the last few days. Why did he get involved with Magdalena Black? How had it all gone so wrong? And, just as importantly, why did he waste his last cigarette on the drive over? He opened his eyes and retrieved the mobile phone from his pocket. As Jack scrolled through his contact list, he hovered over the name 'Charlie Watson'. He knew he owed his niece a proper explanation. Something tangible, rather than whatever nonsense Hung had fed her. But, as with most things in Jack's life, he was adhering to the philosophy of never put off until tomorrow what you can put off until the day after tomorrow.

With less than three hours until the deadline and another lengthy drive back into the city ahead of him, Jack disposed of a listless sigh and continued scrolling through his contacts. It was time to break the news to his friend and business partner. He landed on Hung's name and, with a press of a button, waited patiently for the call to connect. The line emitted a peculiar sequence of tones before settling into the engaged signal. Engaged was bad. In fact, engaged was terrible. If Hung was still playing telephone tag, that invariably meant that Chul-Moo was still missing. And if Chul-Moo was still missing, well, it was safe to say that Jack and Hung were proper fucked.

"I guess our luck was bound to run out eventually," Jack declared with a touch of finality, slipping the phone into his pocket. "Here's hoping the afterlife doesn't serve Victoria Bitter."

Lacking the desire to make that long and lonely drive back to The Hackston, Jack decided that now was the perfect time for a little introspection. After all, despite the ensuing chaos, the day had unfolded in exceptional serenity. The radiant Queensland sun bathed everything in its golden glow, and a cool, gentle breeze engaged in a delightful dance, coaxing the trees to sway with a cheerful grace. If Jack were of the fatalistic persuasion, he might almost argue that today was as good a day as any to die. To hell with it. Feeling a sudden surge of recklessness, Jack opted for something completely out of character and climbed onto the bonnet of his beloved vehicle. That was how confident he was that he would not be around to worry about the paintwork. And if he was, buffing out a few scratches would be the equivalent of stubbing a big toe after winning the lottery.

Before Jack could fully embrace the tranquillity, his phone rang. He retrieved the buzzing brick from his pocket and eyed the caller ID before answering. At least somebody wanted to speak to him.

"Jack, it's Hung. Any luck?" the voice enquired.

"Luck? Have you forgotten who you're talking to?" Jack replied, followed by a lengthy pause long enough to drive a truck through. While his silence should have sufficed, he figured it was best to elaborate. "Looks like the door of his cabin's been kicked in, and the place cleaned out. I mean, like, professionally cleaned. Spotless. Cleaner than when we dropped him off yesterday ... not that it was a very high bar to begin with."

"So, he was definitely kidnapped?" Hung asked.

"It's looking that way," Jack replied, his eyes tracking a skink as it darted across the car park. "And whoever did it went to a lot of effort to make it seem like he was never here."

"Oh, is that what the manager said?" Hung asked.

"You mean Max?" Jack checked his wristwatch, the futility plain on his face. "I haven't seen hide nor hair of that fat prick, either. And you know what's weirder still? It's nearing checkout time, and this place is emptier than a midweek Yahoo Serious film festival."

"Sure he doesn't work the night shift?" Hung offered.

Jack glanced back at the demountable-style office over his shoulder. It looked just as vacant as it had the last time he checked. Hell, if Max was hiding in there, in a space barely bigger than a shipping container, he could have given Osama Bin Laden a run for his money as the reigning Hide and Seek World Champion.

"Something tells me the only shift Max'll be pulling around here is the graveyard shift," Jack said, somewhat cryptically.

"Huh? Isn't that what I just said?" Hung replied.

"No, I mean, if we're gonna extract any information out of Max, we're probably gonna need to whip out a Ouija board." There was a lull as the cogs slowly turned in Hung's head. It was at this point that Jack laid it out for his friend. "Christ. He's probably friggin' dead, mate!" Jack exclaimed. "My money's on Magdalena having offed him. It wasn't like she was exactly subtle about the whole thing."

"What? Like, *dead* dead?" Hung replied.

"Dead … as in, I dunno, deceased. Kicked the bucket. Uh, expired. The big sleep. Hell, I wouldn't be surprised if Max was buried out in that bushland over the road here. Just like we're gonna be if we don't find this Chul-Moo kid in the next couple of hours."

Jack was only off by a few metres. Regardless, it was only a matter of time before a guest grew curious about the stench wafting from the manager's office, inevitably leading to Max being written off as yet another middle-aged male suicide statistic.

"Actually, I tell a lie. This place isn't completely empty," Jack confessed. "I ran into an oldie and, well, someone I presume was his son, staying a couple of cabins down."

Jack gazed into the distance from his perch on the bonnet of his car, soaking in the surroundings like some bad-boy rocker from an eighties music video. On the horizon, he spotted movement, something that looked like a vehicle heading his way down the highway. He shifted position to get a better look and wondered if it was the mysterious clean-up crew returning to finish the job.

"And before you ask, neither of them were up for a chinwag. At least not with me. Claimed they were out all night and saw nothing. So yeah, this whole thing's been a bust."

The pair lingered in silence, unsure of their next move. Jack's gamble on revisiting The Cockatoo Inn had turned up nothing. No leads. No smoking gun. No hope. Just confirmation of what they already knew: Chul-Moo was missing.

"Tell me you fared better, mate?" Jack asked.

"Me? I made a dozen calls. Every one a dead end," Hung replied, frustration creeping into his voice. "I tried everywhere you suggested. Consulates, hospitals, even morgues. Nothing. Do you know how hard it is to reach someone at a morgue?"

"No, but I feel like you're about to tell me."

"Yeah. It's next to bloody impossible, Jack."

"Wait? So nobody was *dying* to answer your call?"

Hung groaned. "Absolutely hilarious," he began. "And after all of that, I didn't find out a damn thing. It was either twenty questions, or they flat out refused to speak to me."

The distant speck Jack had been tracking on the horizon quickly took shape. It was a boxy grey vehicle bearing a familiar logo, heading south toward the Gold Coast. He squinted in the mid-morning glare, struggling to focus. Then it came into view with unmistakable clarity: an armoured truck. The kind used to haul cash from banks, ATMs and, conveniently, the pokie machines at public bars. As it rolled past, the grizzled guard riding shotgun fixed Jack with a long, piercing stare from behind mirrored sunglasses. It was the kind of look sharp enough to make even an innocent man feel like a fugitive. And then it clicked. A crooked smile tugged at Jack's face as the seed of an idea took root. It might just be their way out. Or, at the very least, a parting shot at Magdalena Black's empire.

"Uh, are you still there, Jack?" Hung asked.

"Yeah," Jack replied. "Just sit tight, alright? Keep calling around. I've got a few things to take care of, then I'll be back."

"What could you possibly have better to do?"

"I'm in need of a little retail therapy," Jack said.

Chapter Eighteen

Fight or Flight

Hung Van Thanh clenched the butter knife with determination, his fingers coiled around the handle, as the mechanical *click* of the front door lock sliced through the eerie stillness of the flat. Was it Jack who had been out of communication for longer than was comfortable? Or perhaps it was Frankenstein's monster, aka Mark Campbell, returning to finish the job? Every nerve in Hung's body tingled with anticipation, ready for any eventuality, be it friend or foe. The air bristled with uncertainty as the door creaked open and heavy footsteps drew near. The footsteps grew louder until the familiar face of Jack Perkins poked through the kitchenette door, his eyes scanning the room, trying to decipher his friend's intentions. Both men locked eyes as Hung let out a sigh of relief, loosening his grip on the butter knife and placing it back on the kitchen table.

"Sorry. I thought you were ... her," Hung said.

"Thought I was who?" Jack asked. "Magdalena?"

Hung nodded his head in the affirmative.

"Surely the absence of cloven feet and stench of brimstone should have been a giveaway," Jack replied, eyeing the weapon of mass degustation as he entered the room carrying a nondescript shopping bag. "And what if I were the Angel of the Bottomless Abyss? What did you plan on doing with that butter knife? Have everyone hold hands while you jam it into the nearest power point and take 'em out with a lethal dose of electric boogaloo?"

Hung's eyes narrowed as he noticed the bag in Jack's hand. The sight triggered an instant surge of anger within him, realising that valuable time had been pissed-away on non-essential pursuits. With a stern expression, Hung confronted Jack, frustration evident in his voice as he questioned the wisdom of his recent shopping spree.

"At least somebody was here holding the fort," he said.

"And what's that supposed to mean?" Jack asked.

"It means that we're in the fight of our lives, and you decide to spend your last moments doing ... what?"

Without a word, Jack shot Hung a searing look as he dumped the contents of the shopping bag onto the table in front of him. The items, at first glance, lacked any cohesive theme, leaving Hung perplexed and, perhaps, even more agitated by Jack's apparent lack of urgency about the unfolding situation. Before Hung could ask the obvious question, Jack picked up each item and displayed it to his colleague, accounting for them aloud in his finest local twang.

"Tape," he began, revealing a roll of ordinary, thick, grey duct tape. "Masks," he presented two children's party masks: one shaped like a cartoon pig, the other a sheep. "Paint." Jack held up a can of black spray paint. "Sports bag," he showcased a large red sports bag. "And the pièce de résistance," Jack concluded by posing with a couple of toy water pistols that looked relatively authentic, if not for the fact they were bright green and of the plastic persuasion.

Hung took a moment to peruse the arrangement on the kitchen table, still none the wiser about how they applied to the situation at hand. It seemed like some sort of joke, almost as if

Jack had simultaneously raided a hardware store and a novelty gift shop.

"There. You asked what I was up to," Jack said.

"What, losing your mind in real time?" Hung replied.

"Oh, I'm sorry, Hung. Did I interrupt your regularly scheduled session of coming up with absolutely bugger all?" Jack fired back, taking a step back and leaning against the kitchen sink, ready to field the inevitable barrage of questions. And given the frosty reception to his haul of goodies, there were undoubtedly going to be a few. "When I was at the motel just before, I was sitting there, figuring we were five different ways of fucked. And then I spotted it, the answer coming over the horizon." Hung sighed and took a seat at the table. It sounded as if Jack had something brewing. "Magdalena Black won't hesitate to finish what she started, regardless of the outcome, yeah? If the bitch wants us dead, she'll have us dead. She's got the money and the resources to make it happen." Jack clicked his fingers to emphasise the point. "Face it, Hung. Best-case scenario, we spend the rest of our lives looking over our shoulders."

"And what's the worst-case, Jack?" Hung asked.

"I think we both know the answer to that one."

If that was Jack's idea of a rousing pep talk, it was no surprise they found themselves in the volatile predicament they were in.

"Okay. So what's your brilliant plan?" Hung asked.

"We do the unexpected," Jack replied.

"Oh, like what? Talk to the police?"

"Better still. We turn the tables on Maggie."

Hung screwed up his face, the kind of look you would expect from someone silently asking, "What the fuck does that even mean?"

"Remember the giant safe in Magdalena's penthouse?" Jack continued. "We've been to her place three, maybe four times, and it's never locked. Never. And, shit, there's got to be close to a million in cash inside, easy. And that's not counting the jewellery and whatever else she's got stashed in there."

It was a stroke of luck that Hung was already sitting down before Jack unveiled his plan. Otherwise, he might have keeled over in disbelief. What Jack was about to propose sounded like a suicide mission, wrapped in an impossibility, bundled inside a long shot.

"Wait up? Am I still asleep?" Hung asked.

"If you are, you have some messed-up dreams."

Or some relatively mundane nightmares.

"Let me make sure I have this right," Hung began. "Your grand plan for getting us out of this mess involves ... boy, I can barely say it with a straight face ... you want to rob Magdalena Black?" he asked. "The same Magdalena Black that you admitted only moments ago would kill us without hesitation?"

Hung's words dangled in the ether like a man at the end of a noose. He waited for Jack's punchline. And waited. A good five seconds passed, and Jack's expression did not change. Either the man was a brilliant actor, or he was dead serious.

"You're not joking, are you?" Hung said at last.

Jack met his gaze and nodded in silence.

"Think about it. Magdalena wants Chul-Moo back, right?" he said. The lingering stench of methylated spirits in the air served as an unspoken reminder of what was driving everyone's favourite loan shark. "So, let's give her what she wants."

"But we don't have what she wants, Jack!"

"We both know that. But Magdalena doesn't, does she? Or at the very least, she's not convinced we weren't involved. Otherwise, we'd already be cactus." Jack paused, uncertain if the idea would sound remotely intelligent when said out loud, but pressed on anyway. "Here's what I'm thinking: we pretend to be the kidnappers."

Hung dropped his head into his hands and groaned.

"Just hear me out, yeah?" Jack pressed. "We call Maggie and put on a funny voice ... tell her we've got her Korean and we're chasing a ransom. Something big, but not ridiculous. Just small enough for her to dip into petty cash. Say, I dunno ... half a million?" A sly grin crept across his face. "And here's the clever bit. We, the supposed kidnappers, give her one condition: we want the exchange to go down out in the sticks. Somewhere on the city outskirts. Take away her home ground advantage."

"And when she realises it's us?" Hung asked.

"Eh, that's neither here nor there, man."

"I dunno. That's pretty *here*, if you ask me," Hung replied, realising where Jack was going with his harebrained scheme. "Let me guess? You're about to suggest that *you* ... and, by extension, *me* ... do something idiotic. Namely, rob Magdalena's penthouse while she's off on some wild goose chase?"

Jack cocked his head. After a moment of contemplation, he nodded in acceptance, as if a revelation had dawned upon him.

"Shit, you might be onto something there," he said.

"Huh? Onto what, exactly?" Hung asked.

"Our economy-class ticket out of this shitshow."

"What? Robbing her penthouse wasn't the plan?"

"Nah. I was gonna suggest a good old-fashioned stick-up. But hitting her penthouse instead? That's a stroke of genius."

"Genius? Are you friggin' nuts, Jack? I was joking!"

"Joke or not, mate, it's still the best idea we've had."

Hung rose from his seat and paced the kitchen, wrestling with the sheer audacity of Jack's plan. Or was it *his* plan now? Either way, it was not just risky. It was a headfirst dive into outright lunacy. Hell, it was not even a plan at all, just a half-baked scheme born from a throwaway remark. Jack watched him closely, looking for a sign, some flicker of agreement, as the weight of the proposal settled thick in the air. When none came, Jack checked his wristwatch.

"Well, I don't know about you, Hung, but I don't intend on standing around here with my thumb up my clacker waiting for Maggie to show," Jack said. "But I get it. If you want out, just say the word. We can split what's left of the money. You go your way. I go mine. I wouldn't hold it against you." He paused and looked Hung in the eye, making sure he understood the stakes. There was a flicker of recognition, something that cut through his usual naivety. "Either way, we've got a couple of hours until Maggie comes knocking. So, if you want a seat at the big boy's table, Hung, I need an answer now."

Hung cackled nervously, almost manically, as if possessed by the same reckless idiocy that had landed them in this mess in the first place. He took a breath, steadied himself, and carried on.

"And what choice do I have, Jack?" Hung asked.

"Choices? Mate, I just gave you at least two."

"No, Jack. I mean, how'd it even come to this?" Hung snapped, frustration pouring off him. "We didn't lose track of Chul-Moo. We did exactly what we were told … drove him from point A to point B. That was it. Job done. Now, I don't know about you, but I'm very much not okay with being punished for someone else's stuff-up."

Hung was right, but reasoning with Magdalena Black was a lost cause. Her wounded pride left no room for restitution or compromise. All that remained was a relentless pursuit of her pound of flesh, with no concern for whose hairy rear end it came from.

Jack stood there, arms folded, waiting for Hung's verdict on the madness he had just pitched like it came bundled with a set of complimentary steak knives and a one-way ticket to prison.

Hung blinked. Looked at the table. Then at Jack.

"You forgot the grappling hooks," he said.

"Huh? Grappling hooks?" Jack frowned.

"You know," Hung said, like it was obvious. "Like the ones in those late-night SBS ninja flicks."

"Okay ... and we need those *why*, exactly?"

Hung gave a sigh so deep it could have come with subtitles. "For grappling, obviously." He gestured to the ceiling. "How else would you get anywhere near Magdalena's penthouse? Last I checked, Jack, 'penthouse' usually means top floor. You know? Way up in the clouds, where schmucks like us don't belong."

A grin tugged at the corner of Jack's mouth. Hung had said *us*. Just a tiny word, almost throwaway, but Jack clung to it like a lifeline. For the first time in hours, a flicker of hope stirred.

"So, you want in on this heist, then?" Jack asked.

Hung shrugged. "Well, it was *my* idea, after all."

Detectives Mick Hughes and Barry Gamble found refuge in the corner of the bustling police station canteen, their hushed conversation blending with the low hum of activity around them. As they claimed this secluded spot, the canteen reached its midpoint capacity, a dynamic mix of on-duty officers and civilian staff concluding their morning shifts while others geared up for impending duties. The aroma of freshly brewed coffee mingled with the clatter of cutlery and sporadic conversation, creating an ambience that mirrored the ebb and flow of the station's daily routine.

"What a complete waste of time," Gamble said.

"Meh. Don't be so defeatist," Hughes replied.

"Defeatist? No, I consider myself a realist," Gamble retorted, pursing his lips as he pushed his salad around his plate, regretting the decision to opt for a healthier option. "We spent all morning trying to ID some kid who turned out to be cleaner than a greyhound's dinner bowl. Tell me how that wasn't a waste of time?"

"Perhaps it was, Barry. Perhaps it wasn't."

Given the circumstances, it appeared to be a rather non-committal response from someone munching on a ham and cheese toastie at ten in the morning. It was not as if Hughes' wishy-washy answer stemmed from hubris, nor did he have an abundance of hot leads to chase up. Or any leads, for that matter. Gamble pressed on, hoping to pluck even the slightest relevance from the response.

"Uh, I'm not really following, Sarge," he said.

"It means the kid's a closed loop," Hughes replied, locking eyes with his partner. "Namely, he won't be popping up on anyone's radar. And I can only speak for myself here, Barry, but that helps me sleep a lot easier knowing there's a lesser chance of some rando shiving me while I'm catching forty winks." Leaning in closer, he lowered his voice, preparing to utter a name that, if heard by their colleagues, would immediately arouse interest. "As it stands, we oughta hope and pray that Magdalena Black doesn't find out we iced this Korean fella of hers. Otherwise, our lives are going to get unnecessarily uncomfortable around here. And I'm not talking about 'getting a massage from your mother-in-law' levels of uncomfortable. I'm talking 'pineapple suppository up the jacksie' uncomfortable."

The detectives fell silent as their eyes tracked a group of uniformed officers ambling past their table, engaged in animated gesticulations and tones that seemed vaguely sports-related.

Hughes screwed up his face and waited until they were long gone before hopping back on his original train of thought.

"The smart move would be to give up on trying to ID this prick," he continued, waving his half-eaten toastie under Gamble's nose. "Instead, remember the basics of the job, yeah? Put the emphasis back on the 'why', not just on the 'who'." He scanned the canteen to ensure they were not being watched before reaching into his leather jacket, palming something, and discreetly placing it underneath a napkin on the table. Cocking his head toward his colleague to attract his attention, Gamble took the cue and lifted the napkin. It was the device they had retrieved from Chul-Moo. "I've got a hunch that doodad is our 'why'," Hughes said, before retrieving the USB and returning it to his pocket. "Granted, Campbell wasn't exactly forthcoming on that subject last night, especially with all that effin' and a jeffin' he was doing, but I got the distinct impression their Korean fella must've been carrying something important on his person."

"And you think *that's* the something?" Gamble asked.

"That little device? Sure," Hughes replied.

"Uh, okay. But we still don't know what it is?"

"Maybe so, but I reckon it's a piece in a larger puzzle," Hughes said, patting his pocket. "Either way, it got me thinking. So much so, I called The Pom when you nipped-off to the shitter before."

Gamble cocked an eyebrow, unaware of how industrious his partner had been in his absence, instead of his usual ritual of swearing at inanimate objects like the office fax machine.

"What did Jarrah have to say?" he asked.

"Nothing much," Hughes replied.

"What? He didn't know what it was either?"

"Nah, the prick wasn't answering. But if my hunch is correct, there's more to that … *thing* … than meets the eye, Barry. Who knows, maybe we missed something? It's not like we got to carry out a thorough sweep of that cabin."

A grimace crept across his partner's face as Gamble scanned the immediate space. With flashbacks of last night's snatch and grab still vivid in his mind, he could sense the perilous direction his partner's thoughts were heading.

"Don't say what I think you're about to, Mick."

"Oh? And what would that be, Barry?"

"You want to return to the scene of the crime?"

"Well, sure. It sounds bad when you put it like that."

Cyrille perched on the edge of his bed in cabin five, bathed in the dim glow of a bedside lamp. The telephone receiver rested firmly against his ear as he conversed with Tanya, a cheerful customer service representative from the car rental company. The worn-out bedsprings creaked beneath the weight of his muscular frame, unintentionally adding a symphony to the frustrating discussion about their vehicle, still sitting abandoned near BLACK.

"Two business days?" he asked, turning toward Donald with a perplexed expression. "Christ, it's only four slashed tyres. It's not like they need to drop in a brand-new engine."

What Cyrille had neglected to mention was the uncertain state of the vehicle after their swift departure from an angry mob. A mob not only infuriated by the old man beating seven shades out of Fijian Bob, but also by the club's resident dealer, who already seemed six-sevenths of the way there. At best, the rental was no longer fit for purpose. At worst, it had been stripped and torched, its parts scattered across the furthest reaches of the Gold Coast. Either way, there was bugger all chance of Cyrille getting his deposit back.

He held the receiver against his chest and relayed the conversation to Donald, who was dealing with his own problems as he wrestled with the signal on the cabin's ancient television.

"Lady on the phone says it'll be at least another couple of days before they can send us a replacement," Cyrille said.

With more prison time under his belt than he was comfortable admitting, The Diamond was confident he could handle two more days cooped up in this shitbox of a motel. His offsider, however, did not share the same enthusiasm for self-flagellation and was already suffering withdrawals from life back in the land of laneways and lattes. It had only been some forty-eight hours since Cyrille had last set foot in a gym, and already his body was yearning to chase the pump and the heady rush of endorphins that came with it.

"So, what do you want to do?" Cyrille asked.

"*Do?* Nothing at all, lad," Donald replied.

"What? We're just going to sit here all week?"

"If that's what it takes, Cyrille. Two days, two weeks, it doesn't matter. We're not leaving this cunt of a state until this Black sheila and her lackey get what's coming to them," Donald said, taking a break from giving the side of the television a bit of unsolicited, open-palmed persuasion. "But don't tell the piece on the phone that. Hit her up for a discount. Play up the whole inconvenience. You know what they say: if you don't ask, you don't get."

Amidst the dimly lit, beer-soaked ambience of The Hackston, where the air hung heavy with the acrid scent of stale hops and aerosol paint, Jack assumed a poised stance in front of a fold-up table draped in the day's newsprint still unread from this morning's encounter. In Jack's hand, a can of matte black spray paint, its nozzle poised to unleash a transformative touch. Atop the surface, two toy water pistols lay in anticipation. With a measured rhythm, Jack worked his craft, each stroke of paint a calculated gesture that elevated these plastic playthings into instruments of menace. The space resonated with a blend of determination and intrigue as Jack artfully shaped these makeshift weapons, turning The Hackston from a public bar into his own personal clandestine workshop.

At least, that was how Jack built it up in his head. In reality, it was simply a thirty-something man painting a couple of children's water pistols in a poorly ventilated space.

"Reckon these will fool anyone?" Hung asked.

"They're just gonna have to," Jack replied.

As Jack went about adding the final flourishes, Hung leaned over and examined the weapons in closer detail. His casual side-eye in Jack's direction conveyed the scepticism of a man unconvinced by the near-finished product.

"How many guns have you seen?" Hung asked.

"Like, close up, you mean?" Jack replied.

"Real ones. In museums ... wherever."

"That piece of artillery Maggie's mate has been flashing around looked pretty damn real to me," Jack said. "Besides, they don't need to look real, mate. Haven't you worked that out? They just need to look *real enough* under the right circumstances."

Hung took another look and pondered the specific circumstances that might make a couple of water pistols appear real. Perhaps if a person were in a pitch-black room during a power outage, in the middle of a total eclipse, blindfolded. Jack glanced at Hung and sensed the dissatisfaction with his handiwork, compelling him to do something he knew he would regret: seeking Hung's advice.

"And what would you do differently?" he asked.

"Have you thought about dry brushing?" Hung replied without missing a beat. It was delivered with the same evangelical tone as a Bible-basher knocking on one's door and asking if they had heard about our Lord and Saviour.

"Sorry? Do I have a *dry what?*" Jack asked.

"No, dry brushing," Hung replied.

"You say that as if I'm expected to know what it is?"

"It's a painting technique hobbyists use," Hung continued. "You load a brush with a little gun metal grey paint, then remove most of it and, like, gently sweep the residual over the raised surfaces." Hung delicately mimed a brushing motion on his palm. "You know, to enhance the textures and highlight its details. It's incredibly effective for bringing out the topography of the surfaces like, ah, the handle part and that ... holey bit where the bullets come out."

"The topography of the surfaces? Fuck me."

Jack's incredulous look shifted to one of pity as he remembered Hung had spent far too many hours painting plastic figurines instead of going outside and living his life. Not that there was anything inherently wrong with painting plastic figurines.

"We don't have time for any fancy stuff," Jack said.

"But you know what I mean, right?" Hung replied.

Jack nodded and checked the clock on the wall before setting the spray can on the table. They had less than two hours left until Magdalena Black's big swinging dick came crashing down. He took a shallow breath, the air now fettered with paint fumes, before giving the weapons a last inspection. Hung had a point. They were not the most realistic representation of a firearm, but who knows, maybe in the right light and at the right angle, they might just pass muster. The truth of the matter was that they were merely a last resort. With any luck, robbing Magdalena's penthouse was going to be a walk in the park.

At least, that was what Jack was hoping for.

Hung stepped away from the arts and crafts table and wandered around the front bar, lost in nostalgia. The flickering lights cast long shadows across the worn timber countertop, where decades of spilled drinks and countless elbows had left their mark, a testament to bygone eras. With over a century of history within its walls, Hung recognised that he and Jack were merely blips in the colourful story of The Hackston Tavern. And like all blips, they would soon be corrected, as all temporary interruptions eventually were.

"I can't believe I'm about to ask this," Hung said.

"Hmm. Ask what, mate?" Jack replied.

"What's the plan ... you know, *after* the plan?"

"After we waltz out of Magdalena Black's penthouse with a shitload of cash, you mean?" Jack replied, looking up from his handiwork. "I've been wondering how long it would take for you to ask." He reached into his pocket and produced a folded travel brochure, now complete with black fingerprints from the sticky tar-like paint. "Take a squiz at that," Jack said as he handed it over.

Hung studied it for a moment, his eyes furrowed.

The brochure had the words 'South America' in prominent gold lettering across the top, in size thirty-six font. It was impossible to miss. It was accompanied by the customary image of a local outside the ruins of Machu Picchu, armed with a smile that felt warm and inviting. However, the smile belied the fact that, deep down, they could probably do without a bunch of beer-swilling yobbos trampling their culturally significant sites for the sake of a few dollars.

"What the heck's in South America?" Hung asked.

"South Americans," Jack replied nonchalantly.

Hung groaned and tossed the brochure onto the table.

"Okay. But ... we can't even speak Spanish, Jack."

"Eh, I'm sure we'll *el-picko it up-o*, amigo."

"And what happens to your niece in all this?"

"Magdalena won't touch Charlie. Worst case, she tells Black everything she knows, which is nothing. At least, nothing that connects us to South America. The girl's an innocent in all this." There was a twinge of regret in Jack's voice. "Don't worry, I'll find some way to make it up to her."

Hung let the idea rattle around in his skull like a stray .22 round. It was batshit crazy, yet he found himself drawn to it. What other choices did he have? Outside of Jack, he had no real friends to speak of, and what immediate family he had left did not deserve to bear the burden of a wanted man. They all had their own lives, dreams, and, most importantly, children to protect. Hung had only himself, and there was no way he could face this alone. Like Jack said, this was fight or flight, and amid all the insanity, fleeing felt like the only sane option. But one burning question stood out above the rest.

"Assuming we flee the country?" Hung began. "Boy, I can't believe I'm even contemplating this. What happens to The Hackston?"

Jack reached into another pocket and pulled out Mark's cigarette lighter. He held it aloft for Hung to see before placing it on the table in front of him, as if it were the missing piece of the equation.

Chapter Nineteen

Korean Finger Candy

Magdalena Black sat in her penthouse office, her back turned to her enforcer, Mark Campbell. Her gaze was fixed on an oil painting hanging on the wall, a captivating depiction of Venice, Italy. The scene portrayed a classic fondamenta with wrought-iron railings, interspersed with columns of Istrian stone, while two gondolas rested in the foreground. Magdalena longed to be back there, sitting on Fondamenta della Misericordia, sipping a Campari Spritz, and making doe eyes at anything with long legs and a pulse.

Lost in thought, Magdalena envisaged the shitstorm that was about to land on her doorstep. She did not know when or how, but as predictably as night followed day, the South Koreans would retaliate once Chul-Moo failed to make contact for their arranged meeting.

"You alright, Maggie?" Mark asked, attempting to elicit some form of response from the seemingly absent figure.

Magdalena remained silent in contemplation, intensifying Mark's unease as he studied his employer. The typical aura of confidence and bravado that she normally exuded was con-spicuously absent. It was a disconcerting sight, Magdalena lost and vulnerable. Unexpectedly, the cordless telephone on her desk pierced the silence with an insistent ringing. *Ring! Ring! Ring!* The sound seemed almost taunting, a disembodied voice mocking the loan shark.

Mark's gaze shifted from Magdalena to the ringing telephone. "Want me to get that?" he asked as the device vibrated on the desktop. The air in the room crackled with tension as he approached the telephone, his giant paw hesitating above the receiver.

"No! Do not touch it," Magdalena replied.

"Uh, okay. Are you certain, boss?" Mark asked.

"Very. It will probably be our Korean friends."

The telephone continued to breakdance on the desk, spewing its polyphonic wall of noise, much to Magdalena's ire. Curiosity eventually got the better of Mark, and he placed his hand on it, bringing it to a sudden halt to eye the caller ID. "It's a local number," he announced, his voice carrying a mix of curiosity and caution as he looked at his employer for guidance. Before any guidance came, the ringing stopped almost as abruptly as it had started.

"Whatever you need, Maggie, name it," Mark said.

The loan shark swivelled in her chair, opened the bottom desk drawer, and retrieved a bottle of Scotch whisky and two crystal tumblers. With a satisfying *pop* of the cork stopper, she took a moment to savour the aroma before carefully pouring two glasses. Mark licked his lips in anticipation, the amber nectar holding the promise of a distraction from impending uncertainties.

"I need Chul-Moo returned, unharmed," Magdalena replied, raising her glass to Mark before downing the contents in one swift gulp. As Mark leaned forward to grab the other, she snatched it away with a sharp *clink* of her long, manicured nails and tossed it back like a seasoned alcoholic. Defeated by the gesture, Mark slid his hands into the pockets of his leather jacket, the movement slow and resigned.

"What do you want me to say, boss?" Mark asked.

"Anything, you giant galoot! Say anything."

"Um, I dunno. We turned over every crack den, meth lab, and knocking shop in the city, Maggie. God's honest. Nobody knew anything about this Chul-Moo … and even less about who might've grabbed him. Fact is, we're outta cages to rattle."

Magdalena filled her glass with another glug of Scotch whisky and downed it in one smooth motion. The crystal tumbler barely had time to grace the surface of the desk before she moved to line up another round, dismissing any consideration for sobriety. Mark, recognising the impending self-destruction, served as a circuit breaker, intervening with an honest, albeit direct, statement.

"Maybe we came in too hot, boss," he said.

"*Hot?* What are you implying?" Magdalena asked.

"Ain't implyin' nothing, Maggie. I'm just saying, everyone who knew about this Korean deal is dead, or … eh, soon to be."

Before Magdalena could respond, a faint ringing echoed from outside the office, followed by a pause and the sound of a one-sided conversation. The loan shark and her enforcer exchanged puzzled glances, trying to make sense of the interruption. Eventually, they shrugged it off, dismissing it as Becky simply taking a call from one of her layabout girlfriends. As Mark had hoped, it was enough to redirect Magdalena's attention to matters unrelated to alcohol poisoning.

"Are you confident in your assessment?" she asked.

"That we turned up sweet fuck all? I suppose so," Mark replied with a shrug, scratching his crotch in a blatant acknowledgement that their dead ends had only led to more dead ends. The impending meeting with the Koreans loomed ever closer, and excuses had become a luxury they could no longer afford.

"You know what to do, then," Magdalena said.

"Uh, do I, boss?" Mark replied, puzzled.

The loan shark sighed. "Round up a couple of meatheads from the payroll," she began. "And as soon as the clock strikes twelve, head to The Hackston and extract anything of value from Jack and his little friend. And for the record, I couldn't care less about the methods you use: blowtorch to the feet, a power drill to the knees, bolt cutters. Dealer's choice, Mark. Plumb the depths of creativity. And when you're done having your fun, I expect one of two outcomes: Chul-Moo returned *alive*, or the deed to that pub of theirs," the loan shark added firmly, her tone leaving no room for negotiation.

"I reckon I can manage that," Mark replied.

"Oh, and this should go without saying, but I want you to make sure those fuckers never interfere in my affairs again."

Mark smirked knowingly as Becky's one-sided conversation grew louder, until she finally stepped into the office, two parts flustered, one part puzzled, a burner phone clutched in her hand. She wore an almost see-through green top and the tightest cut-off denim shorts imaginable. Mark could not help but steal a discreet glance as she leaned across him to pass the phone to Magdalena.

"Um ... someone wants to speak to you," she said.

As Hung sank low into the passenger seat of Jack's Datsun, parked on the sun-bleached street opposite Magdalena's penthouse just off the beach, he tried to stay unnoticed amid the oblivious throngs passing by. A glance in the rear-view mirror revealed a chaotic back seat, strewn with suitcases and assorted items, a testament to their frantic attempt to pack up their lives in under twenty minutes. Peering out the passenger-side window, Hung took in the cityscape, its jutting spires of steel and glass rising between sand and surf. Though he had never fully embraced the glitzy, laid-back surfer lifestyle of the Gold Coast, a pang of nostalgia washed over him. He knew he would miss it enough to regret his decision to flee, but not as much as he would miss the prospect of collecting a bullet to the head courtesy of Magdalena's henchman Mark Campbell.

Across the road, Jack leaned against the weathered public payphone, his body taut with the weight of the conversation. "You don't know me, but I've got somethin' important of yours. And if you want him back alive, you'll listen up," he murmured. Despite the high-stakes game of chicken, there was an edge of absurdity in his tone as he tried to disguise his voice. It almost teetered on comical, a stark contrast to the seriousness of the situation. "How about we meet somewhere out of the way? Two o'clock. No cops. No guns. Just you and a hundred grand. The kid for the cash."

Magdalena listened intently through the receiver.

"Who is this?" she asked, eventually.

"That's, uh ... not important," came the reply.

The loan shark's senses heightened as she sought to decipher the unfolding farce. Every background sound, pause, and nuance in the caller's voice was filed-away in her brain for later analysis.

"Your name *is* of importance," Magdalena began. "You see, you have me at a disadvantage. *You* know who *I* am, yet you remain a mystery to me. How should I address you?"

"Huh? What do you mean?" Jack replied.

"Your name, imbecile. I presume you have one."

Jack hesitated, uncertain about how to respond. What should have been a routine ransom demand was already drowning in an absurd amount of banter. According to every two-bit Hollywood thriller he had seen, this should have been the moment where Jack laid out the terms and abruptly ended the call, not shooting the breeze like a couple of pensioners at the RSL.

"My name? It's ... uh ... John," he said.

At least he had the sense not to say 'Jack'.

"Well, 'Uh ... John', I know one thing for certain: you're no professional, let alone somebody that has even had a passing brush with professionalism," Magdalena replied. "Any kidnapper worth their salt would know to disguise their voice with a modulator, or ... perhaps ... anything, as opposed to whatever is transpiring here."

"Shut up. Stop changing the subject," Jack said.

"Hardly. I was making a simple observation."

"Yeah? Then keep your observations to yourself."

Between the disjointed back-and-forth and ludicrous voice acting, Jack drew peculiar glances from anyone within earshot, particularly the group of bikini-clad teenagers lingering nearby, evidently waiting to use the payphone. He broke eye contact and turned his back to the group, head in hand, silently hoping they would bugger off.

"Hmm. Your voice sounds familiar," Magdalena said, her tone laced with amusement. "Wait, I have it. Is that you, Jack?"

"What? No," he replied unconvincingly.

"Jack Perkins, from The Hackston Tavern?"

There was a pause as the Jack Perkins in question retrieved his testicles from his throat. Their fledgling crime caper had barely stumbled out of the starting block, and already the pair of publicans had been made. Jack *slammed* his hand against the side of the payphone, scrambling to come up with anything to throw the loan shark off the scent. "Do you want Chul-Moo back or not?" he asked, almost entirely dropping the ridiculous voice in his fit of pique. "Let's cut the shit, Maggie? We meet at two o'clock, somewhere quiet and out of the way. One hundred grand, cash, and you'll see your Korean mate again. And no funny business either, otherwise we'll be out of there faster than a pollie on a promise."

Contemplation hung heavily amidst the hustle and bustle.

"So? Are you in, Miss Black? If the answer's 'no', we're happy to slit the kid's throat and let you deal with the fallout."

Silence settled on the other end of the line as Magdalena discussed the proposal with her enforcer, intermittent syllables slipping through her hand clasped over the receiver. Jack or not, Magdalena knew she had to entertain these demands if there was any hope of retrieving Chul-Moo and preventing conflict with the Koreans, even if it meant conceding to a pair of idiots.

"Where do you wish to meet?" she asked.

Detectives Mick Hughes and Barry Gamble made their way through the police station's rear car park at a measured pace, heading straight for their faithful Commodore. Normally, it would have been parked closer to the action, but the grimy blue bullet sponge had to be concealed as far away from prying eyes as possible, at least until Hughes had one of his shady panel-beater mates patch up the newly acquired 'speed holes' in their squad car. For now, Hughes' makeshift solution of some spackle and a few strips of grey duct tape was all that stood between them and the curiosity of the collective of bald, white *Top Gear*-watching fanatics from Fleet Services. Those blokes were very particular about their vehicles, and even more particular about the condition in which said vehicles were returned.

"I still don't see the point," Gamble said, his brow furrowed as he tried to dissuade his partner from the foolhardy decision to return to The Cockatoo Inn. "Why do we even need to do anything at all, Sarge? From the way Campbell was talking,

Black doesn't even suspect we were involved with, uh … well, you know what?"

"Huh? No, I don't know what," Hughes replied.

"With … uh, what happened last night?"

Hughes brushed off the statement with a sharp shrug. The senior sergeant's focus remained fixed on The Cockatoo Inn, so much so that it caused his jaw to clench with determination. There was no way he was going to be talked out of returning, regardless of whatever attempted argument Gamble might pull out of his rear.

"You won't change my mind, Barry," he said.

"Am I really that obvious, Sarge?"

"Just a bit," Hughes replied. "Maybe it's a hunch, instinct, being old school. Call it what you want, big boy, but I can't shake the feeling that we missed something back there."

"Maybe so, but stop and think about it," Gamble replied as he brought the pace to an almost crawl, hoping to drive his objection home. "Has anybody pointed any fingers in our direction? Has anybody come looking for us? No, so why stick our heads on the chopping block again? Heck, we're practically home free."

Hughes scowled and grabbed his partner's shoulder, spinning him like a top in his grey suit. "Home free? How about bein' debt free?" he asked firmly, as the two men had an impromptu deep and meaningful in the middle of the car park. "Dunno about you, but I'm not here to fuck spiders. I'm trying to bolster my nest egg … and maybe even yours too, lardarse, if you'd quit busting my balls constantly."

"Typical. Always out to make a quick buck."

"Bloody oath," Hughes replied. "And there's plenty to be made. Enough to add an extra zero at the end of the old retirement fund. But first, we've just gotta figure out what that doodad was that we swiped, and second, how we can use it for our financial gain.”

In Hughes’ mind, wherever there was a will, there was a payday. However, the only zeroes he was likely to add to the end of anything were to the percentage chance of being killed by Magdalena Black. That, or Cop Killer Bill running them through in the Woodford exercise yard. After all, a couple of ex-coppers in the clink were about as popular as a vegan at a barbecue.

“F-fu ... fuck it all, right?” Gamble said, taking a few paces away to clear his head before turning back to give his partner a piece of his mind. “What choice do I have? You’ll just do whatever it is you want to do. This whole ‘stuff the consequences’ bullcrap is getting old, Mick. There’s a reason you don’t have many friends around here. And I’ll tell you now, you’re on thin ice with the few you have left.”

Hughes waited for his partner to stop talking.

“Are you done with your little tantie, mate?” he asked rhetorically. “You’ve got a point, though. Maggie hasn’t fingered us for this missing Asian kid. From what Campbell was sayin’, it sounds like she’s already got a couple of dipshits on the hook for that.”

“Uh, really? Who?” Gamble asked.

“Dunno. But I’d hate to be in their pluggers.”

The realisation that a couple of innocent people might face the consequences for their actions struck Gamble like a punch to the gut, compounding the look of unease already etched on his face.

“Cheer up,” Hughes said, noticing the expression.

“But ... how can you just—” Gamble began.

“Their misfortune is our favour,” Hughes replied with a grin. “And because of that, we’re offered something rare in this life: a second chance. We get another crack at that motel, yeah? Eliminate all evidence connecting us to that kid. Not only that, but it also means we can have a proper poke around. If old mate had more of those devices with him, maybe they're still in that cabin somewhere. They're pretty tiny ... a bit like your pecker, Barry. One could have gotten kicked under the bed in all the commotion. Who knows?"

The detectives grappled with their differences. Hughes, fuelled by nagging intuition, felt an urgency that clashed with his partner's cautious approach. For a seasoned officer like Gamble, though, there were enough holes in Hughes' logic to drive their squad car through. The biggest one was simple: why return to the scene of a crime? As far as both men knew, nobody had reported an incident last night. The only others aware of the kidnapping were Magdalena, her henchman, and The Cockatoo Inn's manager. And speaking of Max, would he not grow suspicious if a couple of detectives suddenly showed up unannounced for a stickybeak?

The men continued toward their car without a word, but the sensation of a plastic evidence bag scratching against the inside of Gamble's jacket pocket, like a rat clawing its way out of a carcass, reminded him there were more pressing matters.

"On the subject of, ah, eliminating evidence," Gamble began in hushed tones as he patted his jacket pocket. "What do you want me to do with, uh ... *it*? It's beginning to stink, Sarge."

"What are you on about?" Hughes replied.

Gamble sighed and animatedly wiggled his thumb.

"Christ, you're still lugging that around?" The senior sergeant chuckled, leaning against the passenger door and nudging his aviators down the bridge of his nose. "I figured you'd flushed it once we lifted the prints." His partner looked at him with disdain. "Toss it in the boot for now. I'm sure the feral piggies out Sleazeball's way would love to chow down on a bit of KFC ... Korean Finger Candy."

Gamble grimaced and popped the boot of the Commodore, covertly removing the evidence bag from his pocket. His eye caught one of the patched bullet holes, and as his gaze naturally wandered down to a faint purple splatter of dried blood that Hughes had missed cleaning up, he quickly realised that Crime Scene would have an absolute field day in there. With a flick of the wrist, he tossed the bag into the boot of the car, mumbling a quick prayer under his breath. It was a testament that you could take the boy out of the Catholic school, but you could not take the Catholic school out of the boy.

Chapter Twenty

Graham Newton

Jack and Hung sat tense amid the city's restless hum, eyes darting between the Datsun's dashboard clock and the exit to the car park beneath Magdalena Black's apartment complex. Fifty minutes remained until the staged rendezvous between Magdalena and Chul-Moo's 'kidnappers'. Fifty minutes until their fates were sealed. The two hapless publicans waited, nerves frayed, for the loan shark to make her move. Of course, it hardly took a crystal ball to predict what came next: Magdalena's bloody, bullet-riddled vengeance.

Still, between their little smoke-and-mirrors trick and whatever retaliation Magdalena might cook up, the hope was simple: cause enough chaos to carve out a sliver of opportunity. Just enough time to move while the enemy was distracted. At least, that was the plan. As they settled in for what they hoped would be a short-lived stakeout, Jack ran through the heist's ground rules one last time.

"First things first," he began. "And I can't stress this enough ... no violence. Second, in and out, no mucking about. And last but not least, whatever you do, stick to the codenames. Got it?"

Hung shot Jack an incredulous look as he absently picked at the zipper of the red sports bag sitting on his lap, trying to distract himself from the overwhelming wave of nervous energy he felt. After all, it was not every day that someone had the chance to pop their crime cherry by committing armed robbery on a notorious loan shark.

"What's the problem now?" Jack asked with a sigh.

"Uh, it's not really that important," Hung replied.

"Come on. Spit it out, for Christ's sake."

"Okay. They just sound ... kind of ridiculous."

"What? The codenames?" Jack said, shrugging. "Mate, I don't give a rat's what you think of 'em. Just remember ... up there, there's no Jack and Hung." He pointed to the top of the structure. "We don't exist. We're gone. It's only 'Graham' and 'Bert', yeah?"

"Sure. Whatever you say, Bert," Hung muttered.

Adopting the monikers of Australia's most beloved comedy duo for an armed robbery should have been simple enough. But Jack had not accounted for the bruised egos that surfaced when one of the participants refused to accept their place in the internal hierarchy.

"What? No, I'm Graham, *you're* Bert," Jack said.

"Hold on, why are *you* Graham?" Hung replied.

"Because everyone knows Bert was just a sidekick!"

Before they could finish bickering, Magdalena's BMW emerged from the underground car park and crossed the street. Jack instinctively leaned over and shoved Hung's head down, waiting until she passed. With any luck, neither of them had clocked the car. A blue Datsun stood out like a sore thumb on the glitzy streets of the Gold Coast, especially when parked across from a multimillion-dollar apartment complex.

Jack was the first to exit the elevator, stepping into a neatly furnished alcove just outside Magdalena's suite, perched twenty-three storeys above the city. Beyond the nearby window stretched a sweeping panorama of golden sand, sunlit surf, and glittering ocean. It was the kind of postcard-perfect view that made the Gold Coast famous. Jack allowed himself only a second to take it in before tearing his gaze away.

He scanned the area for any surveillance, but nothing caught his eye. From past visits, Jack could not recall seeing any cameras, aside from the video intercom mounted beside the front door. Then again, he had never visited with the sole intention of robbing the joint. Still, the lack of security struck him as odd, especially for a penthouse owned by someone in a line of work that seldom encouraged an open-door policy. Regardless, he took it as a green light and gave a nod toward the elevator, silently urging his partner to follow.

Hung burst out of the elevator, the red sports bag slung over his shoulder, as if he were leading the charge of the Light Horse at Beersheba. With swift, mercurial movements, he positioned himself against a column near the front door, every nerve on edge from the surge of adrenaline. Fumbling into the bag, his hands trembling with anticipation, he retrieved one of the masks Jack had purchased. Ironically, it was the sheep. He slipped it over his face before delving back into the bag, retrieving the pair of water pistols. The weapons looked surprisingly authentic, except for, as Hung had so eloquently put it, the 'little hole where the bullets came out'.

"Ready to rock and roll, Bert?" Jack whispered.

Hung responded with a swift thumbs-up, his demeanour exuding an unmistakable readiness to, indeed, rock and roll as he leaned against the column, water pistols held akimbo in front of his body. Whatever nervousness Hung had before, it had now dissipated, and he was completely in a 'fuck around and find out' mindset.

In fact, it was downright disconcerting.

Jack took a deep breath, feeling the weight of anticipation fuelling his pounding heart. With precious seconds slipping away, it was now do or die. Glancing at the buzzer on the intercom, he skipped it, instead opting to *rap his knuckles* against the door. He waited. Nothing. He *knocked* again, louder. Pausing, Jack strained his ears for any signs of life from inside the apartment. There was a faint waft of electronic garble, possibly from a television, but he could not be certain. Surely Magdalena's live-in lover was inside? And that was not even wishful thinking. It needed to be a reality. After all, this was the part of their plan that had not been fully fleshed out.

"What happens if she's not in?" Hung asked.

"Then we're proper fucked," Jack replied.

The men waited, steeped in uncertainty, until the intercom crackled to life and shattered the silence. Jack flinched, prompting a quiet chuckle from Hung, as both turned their attention to the speaker. A pause followed, thick with static, as if the voice on the other end was still deciding whether to respond at all.

"What do you want?" Becky asked, eventually.

"Oh, it's … um … " Jack stumbled, trying to recall his codename as he fingered the green intercom button. "It's, ah, Graham. Graham Newton. I'm here to see Miss Black."

Becky took a moment to observe Jack's body language on the one-way monitor beside the penthouse's reinforced front door. Although the image was grainy and somewhat washed-out due to the intensity of the midday sun over Jack's shoulder, she could discern enough to sense his obvious nervous energy. With a furrowed brow, she leaned in closer to examine the monitor, her curiosity piqued.

"Graham? You aren't a cop, are you?" Becky asked.

"No. What makes you say that?" Jack replied.

"Because if you are, and I ask whether you're a cop, you're supposed to tell me, right?" Becky said, her eyes fixed on Jack's reaction, searching for any obvious tells. "It's, like, the law or something? You can't trick a person into committing a crime."

Jack parsed the comment, trying to make sense of it.

"Uh, I'm not sure that's *a thing*," he replied.

"It's definitely *a thing*," Becky said.

"Nah. There's no way that could be a thing."

Jack suspected that Magdalena's companion had immersed herself in one too many Hollywood films between her retail therapy sessions, leisurely weed smoking, and lounging about wearing less than a naturist on laundry day. All fine pastimes for a young lady pursuing a full-time career as a gangster's moll, but hardly anything worth celebrating if one were hoping for an honest career.

"I'm ninety percent certain it's not *a thing*," he continued, still dubious of the proposition. "Think about it. Imagine if crims just went around accusing everyone of being a copper, like it was some sort of 'Get Out Of Jail Free' card? It'd make undercover cops redundant. They'd be gettin' rumbled on the regular."

"Still, there's a chance it's *a thing*, right?"

Jack stepped away from the intercom and ran a hand through his hair, the universal sign for trying not to lose one's shit in a major way. Instead of smoothly talking his way inside Magdalena's penthouse, they were wasting precious time locked in a roundabout discussion about police entrapment. There was no Plan B. Jack and Hung needed to get inside and pull off the heist before the loan shark and her henchman arrived at the meet, uncovering their deception and putting them in serious jeopardy. Jack groaned, then composed himself before walking back over to the intercom.

"Anyway, cop or not, you're outta luck," Becky said.

"What do you mean?" Jack asked, feigning ignorance.

"It means that Mark's not here. Neither's Maggie," Becky replied, her patience now about as thin as a single-ply square of public restroom toilet paper. "Oh, and for the record, Maggie doesn't appreciate strangers dropping by unannounced. So, if you don't mind, I suggest you bounce, yeah?"

"But, uh ... what about the—" Jack began.

"Are you deaf?" Becky replied. "Maggie. *Isn't.* Here."

After confirming that Becky was indeed alone, the men now needed to come up with a plausible pretence to get inside. Jack took a moment to collect his thoughts and glanced across at Hung, hoping for a lifeline or a glimmer of ingenuity to salvage their precarious situation. Still with his guns akimbo against the column, Hung's response was underwhelming: a shrug and an inscrutable expression hidden behind the absurdity of the sheep mask. It was as if they were both trapped in a surreal nightmare, where even the simplest task had become an insurmountable challenge.

"Hey! Did you hear me? Clear off," Becky said.

Jack's mind raced as the spectre of inevitable failure pressed down on him like an unrelenting weight. Standing there, his finger hovering above the intercom button, it finally struck him like a dodgy service station pie. What was the one thing that a loan shark coveted above all else? The almighty dollar.

"I heard you. It's just ... well, I didn't really want to be saying this out here, but I've got a sizeable wad of cash for Miss Black," Jack began, stepping off camera and grabbing the red sports bag from Hung. He returned, waving it in front of the intercom. "She was pretty adamant she wanted it by lunch. And hell, I'll be damned if I didn't hold up my end of the deal."

Jack cast his line out into the raging waters, waiting for a nibble. There was a momentary silence, presumably as Becky pondered the best strategy for dealing with her unwanted visitor.

"Okay. And what do you need from me?" she asked.

"A little sympathy," Jack replied, knowing he now had Becky hook, line, and sinker. "I don't wanna be lugging all this cash back across town, to be perfectly Francis. And judging by this big, bugger-off door and intercom thing you've got, well, I don't need to tell you about all the shady pricks gettin' around. Look, let's just do this now? You seem like a nice girl … I wouldn't want Miss Black's money going walkabout on your watch."

Becky accepted that 'Graham' had raised a valid point.

"Ugh, wait there a second," she replied with a sigh.

The duo was taken aback by what seemed like a stroke of good fortune. However, as they waited, seconds stretched into minutes, and anxiety crept in. They exchanged worried glances, pondering Becky's lengthy absence. Jack glanced at his wristwatch; forty-one minutes until the deadline, and time was slipping away rapidly. Despite the possibility that Becky might never return, Jack refused to stand around idly. He signalled to his partner to pass him one of the water pistols. Hung nodded and attempted to toss a gun to Jack. To their surprise, it would not budge. For some inexplicable reason, the weapon seemed to be glued to his palm. Hung muttered a string of G-rated profanities, sounding more like a frustrated toddler than a functioning adult, as he frantically tried to dislodge the weapon.

"What the hell are you doing?" Jack asked.

"It's ... stuck ... to my hand," Hung replied.

"Huh? What do you mean, it's bloody stuck?"

Hung tried again to shake the weapon free, but to no avail. "Must've been that cheap spray paint you bought," he replied, panic welling in his voice. "The guns were probably still tacky when I took them out of the bag just before." He gave another shake. "See? This is precisely why I told you to wait an hour between coats!"

Jack scowled and leaned across the void, attempting to pry the pistol from Hung's grip. Hung let out a muffled *hiss* from beneath his mask as he recoiled in pain, trying to suppress any noise that might give them away. Despite Jack's efforts, the water pistol refused to budge, at least not without taking a few layers of skin with it.

"Christ, it's like a Three Stooges movie with you lately," Jack muttered. "Shit. Okay, just follow my—" He paused mid-sentence, sensing movement from behind the door.

Becky examined the monitor with bewilderment as 'Graham' gestured and ranted, seemingly to no one. Despite drug-addled customers being commonplace in a loan shark's line of work, after all, even junkies needed to borrow money, few lacked the suicidal tendency to show up at said loan shark's home and knock on their front door. Even fewer dared to try it a second time. Fortunately, on such occasions, the menacing presence of the Russian-made AK-47 assault rifle in Becky's hand, courtesy of The Pom's father, Irish, usually gave these troublemakers a less-than-subtle hint to leave.

"Graham? You still out there?" Becky asked.

It was a redundant question, given that she had been watching him for a good thirty seconds, but she asked nonetheless, hoping it might snap him out of whatever the hell he was doing. If 'Graham' did indeed have money for Magdalena, it would have been remiss of Becky not to collect it. After all, allowing even one of these reprobates to skip a repayment could set an undesirable precedent.

"Yeah, I'm still out here," Jack replied.

Becky unlocked the front door, then used her spare hand to push it open just enough to peer through, ensuring her body mass remained behind cover. "Alright. I want you to open the door gently, and toss the bag inside," she instructed, taking a few steps back. Her AK-47 was pointed at the doorway, ready to ventilate anyone foolish enough to step through the threshold. Little did Jack and Hung know, Magdalena Black made sure all her live-in lovers underwent extensive firearms training with a former-commando buddy of hers, affectionately known as 'Tripod'. In Magdalena's words, if they 'couldn't root and couldn't shoot', they got given the boot.

The would-be robbers exchanged glances, a silent understanding passing between them. With a nod from Jack, Hung prepared to make his move. "Okay, I'll toss it in," Jack announced as he slowly pushed the door open, creating a clear path for Hung to enter.

Hung counted to three under his breath.

CRUNCH! With all the force his skinny little leg could muster, Hung kicked open the door and charged inside, guns held out in front of him, resembling some sort of poor man's Vietnamese action hero. With his pig mask now in place, Jack moved to follow Hung through the door, ready to execute their daring heist. However, Hung's sudden halt caught Jack off guard, freezing him in his tracks.

Hung Van Thanh, meet Becky.

Becky, meet Hung Van Thanh.

Hung Van Thanh, meet Becky's AK-47.

Introductions complete, Hung eyed Becky's rifle, now pointed straight at his chest, then glanced down at the two painted water pistols in his hands and back at her Russian crowd-pleaser.

Chambered for a 7.62x39 mm round travelling at roughly seven hundred metres per second, with enough muzzle energy to redecorate a room in shades of claret, Becky's Eastern Bloc AK-47 had all the subtlety of performing brain surgery with a machete.

Conversely, chambered with one hundred millilitres of the finest Adam's ale, siphoned directly from the lead-lined pipes of The Hackston, with a range of three metres and a muzzle energy of ... well, Hung barely gave a shit by this point ... his own pride and joy amounted to a dollar-store plastic water pistol.

Either way, Becky had no way of discerning whether Hung's weapons were authentic. To her, standing in the dimly lit entrance with them pointed at her face, they looked about as convincing as the queue outside of Centrelink on a Monday morning.

"Crumbs!" Hung said under his breath.

"Oh, shit!" Becky said under her breath.

Hung reacted instinctively, diving inside the penthouse a split-second before Becky unleashed a three-round burst from her rifle. *BOOM! BOOM! BOOM!* The thunderous volley reverberated throughout the floor, each blast like a cannon firing in a confined space, rattling the very walls and furnishings. The force of the gunfire was staggering, shattering the reinforced door over Hung's shoulder and sending clouds of grey plaster swirling from the adjoining alcove. In shock, Hung scrambled across the floor, propelled by a mix of adrenaline and sheer survival instinct. It was do or die. He lunged at the smoking barrel of her weapon, striking Becky on the hip and sending her sprawling before she could pull the trigger again, her body crashing to the ground with a resounding *thud*.

Jack could do nothing but reel back in terror. The sound of each shot was like a physical blow to his senses, causing him to clutch his ears as the crack of the rounds felt agonisingly close. As the ringing in his ears subsided and he regained his composure, he caught wind of the commotion and peered around the corner, his heart pounding in his chest as he witnessed the chaotic scene unfolding before him. Without a moment's hesitation, Jack charged into the fray, a surge of determination propelling him forward. He wrested the rifle away from Becky's grasp, the weight of the weapon unfamiliar and unwieldy in his hands. Seizing it by the barrel, he raised it above his head, a brief pause punctuating the moment before he brought the butt of the gun crashing down onto the side of her head.

The blow rendered Becky limp and seemingly lifeless.

"Jesus … fuck … I didn't mean to … " Jack said, mortified at the possibility of having killed the blonde surfer chick behind the door. He tossed the assault rifle onto the floor, or as gently as one should toss a loaded assault rifle, and hastened to check her pulse. The beats came slow and shallow. Becky appeared to be alive, albeit with a headache that would rival demolishing a carton of bottom-shelf tequila once she came to.

Relief washed over Jack in an awesome wave.

Nearby, Hung's chest heaved as if he had just completed a marathon. Grateful to draw another breath, he collapsed beside Becky, his gaze fixed on the ceiling. With the acrid smell of cordite still lingering in the air, Hung could not shake the sobering realisation that he was likely a bee's dick away from certain death.

Jack took advantage of the lull to explore deeper into Magdalena's penthouse, scanning the surroundings before returning to grab the sports bag from the doorway. "We've got about ten minutes until the downstairs neighbour figures out Maggie wasn't simultaneously uncorking three bottles of Pinot Noir Sparkling Rosé up here," he began, as he rifled through the bag, searching for something specific. "Then, if we're lucky, we might have another ten until the cops show, yeah? And I'm talkin' SWAT. Real blokes with real guns. None of this plastic fantastic. So, once you unpucker your sphincter, Hung, go make yourself useful," he instructed, tossing the roll of duct tape to his partner. However, with both hands occupied by the water pistols and his vision obscured by the mask, Hung fumbled, and the tape smacked him right in the face.

Jack sighed and shook his head in disbelief.

Chapter Twenty-One

Rubber Glove Enthusiasts

The Cockatoo Inn.

Magdalena Black's BMW glided into the car park, its engine purring softly as Mark Campbell brought it to a halt in a discreet spot behind the manager's office. Their arrival was no coincidence; Jack's instructions had led them here. The motel, selected as the rendezvous point for Black and Chul-Moo's fictional kidnappers, was ideal for its seclusion. In truth, it was the first location that came to Jack's mind during his farcical ransom call, but it placed Magdalena far enough from the Gold Coast for him and Hung to carry out their heist. That, and it was the location from where the Korean had vanished, making it familiar ground for all involved.

As the engine fell silent, Mark and Fijian Bob exited the vehicle, the latter still sporting a bandaged nose and wrist from a scuffle the night before. Magdalena remained inside, awaiting the all-clear. "Keep an eye on her," Mark instructed his offsider, stretching his legs as he moved toward a secure vantage point at the edge of the demountable. The silence at The Cockatoo Inn had grown into an unsettling presence, more profound and eerie than ever, with no signs of life to pierce its stillness. Even the wind seemed reluctant to disturb the stagnant air that hung over the deserted motel. After a few moments of uneventful observation, Mark returned. "I reckon we got the drop on 'em," he declared, slapping the car's roof with confidence.

Magdalena checked her makeup in the rear-view mirror before exiting the vehicle, having swapped her high heels for more practical leather loafers since her previous visit. She scanned her surroundings, then exchanged a determined look with Mark. Without skipping a beat, he promptly popped open the boot, revealing an array of firearms and a sleek titanium briefcase nestled inside. "You there," she began, casting a discerning eye over Fijian Bob's formidable presence.

"Me?" Fijian Bob replied in his booming voice.

"Yes, you. The, uh, Polynesian fellow?"

"I'm Melanesian," he corrected.

"I beg your pardon?" Magdalena asked.

"The name's Bob, Miss Black. And I'm Melanesian," he stated in a matter-of-fact tone. "We indigenous Fijian folks are usually classified as ethnically Melanesian, you know, despite our ... uh ... social structure being more aligned with ... eh, Polynesian culture."

Magdalena pursed her lips and nodded. It was, she mused, the most coherent thing any of the nightclub's resident door-bitches had ever uttered in polite conversation.

"Melanesian. Forgive me," she replied, correcting herself. "So, with that settled, are we done with the anthropology lecture, Bob? Or shall we continue to loiter in the middle of Bumfuck, Nowhere, staring lovingly into a car boot filled with enough hardware to give a redneck an erection? And if your answer is anything aside from the obligatory 'please continue', then I suggest you reacquaint yourself with the name of the individual who signs your cheques."

"Sorry, ma'am. Please continue," Fijian Bob said.

The man knew on which side his bread was buttered.

"Fantastic. Now, grab a firearm and sweep the perimeter. You know, like they do in Hollywood films," Magdalena instructed, waiting for the bouncer's acknowledgement. The hulking giant blinked vacantly at her. "I assume you are familiar with the concept of a 'perimeter', Bob? Perimeters are usually classified as the boundary of a two-dimensional space," she added, with a blend of sarcasm and belligerence. "As in, the boundary of this godforsaken shithole of a motel."

The bouncer offered no reply, his silence a polite yet pointed response that, in true Islander fashion, spoke volumes. Before he turned to leave, he sensed his boss had more on her mind and braced himself for another round of reprimand.

"Oh, and Bob?" Magdalena added.

"Yes, Miss Black?" Fijian Bob replied.

"Please do so in a stealthy manner," the loan shark said, checking her designer wristwatch. "I appreciate we may be early, but if Chul-Moo's kidnappers are already here lying in wait, I have little desire to draw their attention to our presence. Stealth is imperative. Remember: this is a violent, blood-soaked ambush, not a bean-flicking session at the local Blue Light Disco."

Stealth was a long shot with the Fijian's towering frame and brick-shithouse build. But they had no alternatives. He was the only muscle available on short notice, and with six mouths to feed and a now-busted wrist, Mark had taken pity on him, throwing him any gig that looked even vaguely like a payday.

Fijian Bob nodded, then turned to walk away.

"Oi!," Mark began, "Aren't you forgettin' something?"

The bouncer stopped abruptly, his hangdog eyes shifting between Mark and Magdalena, his expression unreadable. Mark snapped his fingers, directing Fijian Bob's attention to the boot of the car with a pointed gesture. Like a chastised puppy, Bob sidled up to the vehicle and grabbed a loaded shotgun. With deliberate strides, he moved behind the building, his swagger betraying a man who rarely, if ever, felt any sense of urgency.

Detectives Mick Hughes and Barry Gamble were next to arrive at The Cockatoo Inn, unaware that the loan shark and her cronies were lurking behind the office demountable like a pack of awkward teenagers sneaking a durry between classes. Dispensing with any pretence of subtlety, Hughes instructed his partner to park their bullet-riddled Commodore right outside cabin three. The bold move suggested they were not expecting any resistance from the motel's rather portly manager, Max Stedkole, as they prepared to search Chul-Moo's cabin for clues. Bitter experience had taught them that Max had either headed for the hills or was already buried somewhere beneath one, a typical fate for those who dared to cross ruthless crime figures like Magdalena Black and her ilk.

"You sure about this, Sarge?" Gamble asked.

"Am I sure about what?" Hughes replied.

"Going back inside. I know what's done is done, Mick, but where's this going to end?" Gamble said, his hand hovering over the key in the ignition as he questioned the wisdom of returning to the scene of a crime, especially one they had committed themselves. "Look, it's almost lunchtime. How about we just, uh, turn around? Forget all about this. There's a servo ten minutes down the highway that does a decent steak and bacon pie. Homemade. Maybe we should grab something, you know? Stop and re-evaluate our options."

Hughes glared at his partner, a look so potent it could have brought a fully grown African elephant to its knees.

"It's always food with you, isn't it?" he replied.

"Well, no. Maybe I … uh … no," Gamble stammered.

"Jesus H. Christ. Don't sound too convincing."

"What I'm getting at is, we need to use common sense. What happens if we find something in there? Then what? Do we go through this entire roller coaster again?" Gamble switched off the ignition with a sigh, knowing full well that his partner would not leave without combing over every millimetre of that cabin. "Has it even sunk in that we killed a kid last night, Mick? We've done some really questionable things over the years, but we c-c-crossed a line at murder."

"Bah. It was involuntary manslaughter at best."

"And thirty years in high-security, at worst."

Hughes hissed and shook his head, his eyes scanning the area for any witnesses. In one fluid motion, he drew his service revolver from its holster, the metallic *click* of the clasp echoing softly. Gamble's heart raced as he watched, paralysed and unsure whether he should reach for his own. Hughes fixed his partner with an intense gaze, the weight of his emotions palpable even behind his aviators. Slowly and deliberately, he removed the sunglasses with his spare hand, tossing them onto the dashboard with a sense of finality.

Gamble let out an audible sigh of relief.

"Sorry, Baz," Hughes said, his tone dead serious. "But there's no use dancin' around it. We're balls-deep in this caper. If we pull out now, like your daddy should've, then the last twenty-four hours would've been for nothing."

"I get that. But, uh, what about—" Gamble began.

"Shut ya pie hole, big boy. No excuses."

Gamble slumped in the driver's seat of the squad car, his partner's words rattling around in his skull like a marble in a spray can. He just wanted the day to end, to get away from Mick and all his dodgy extracurricular activities before he did something else that would keep him awake at night. What he really wanted was some news about his transfer to the Child

Protection Unit Anything to put some distance between himself and his senior sergeant.

"Whatever. Let's just get this done," he said.

Silence filled Magdalena's office, broken only by the soft hum of the ducted air conditioning overhead. The priceless artwork and first-edition books lining the room went un-admired, their significance overshadowed by the olive-green safe embedded in the wall behind the loan shark's desk. In one corner, Becky sat slouched in a high-back leather office chair, unconscious, her body tightly bound with coils of grey duct tape. Her head hung to the side, blonde hair cascading over her face, concealing the outline of a rifle butt on her tanned skin. Yet, even in that vulnerable state, Becky's posture held a defiance: a silent testament to her refusal to surrender.

Hung entered the room, hands held aloft. "See, they're gone," he said, his palms now free of the water pistols but stained with an unsightly black smudge, the skin raw and pink. "I told you nail polish remover would do the trick. Thank you, Mr Jansen's sixth-grade chemistry!"

As his words echoed through the room, Hung's gaze fell on his partner, slumped on the floor with his back against the safe. This was a far cry from what he had envisioned when he returned from the guest en-suite: Jack, busier than a cucumber in a convent, rifling through wads of cash like a man possessed. Instead, Jack sat there, motionless, teetering on the verge of a nervous breakdown.

"Jack?" Hung said, his voice tinged with confusion as he noticed the open sports bag on the desk, its emptiness begging for an explanation. When none came, he ran a hand through his jet-black hair, scanning the room. "Did we get the money?" he pressed.

Jack finally spoke. "We certainly got ... *something*."

"And by that you mean, uh, what exactly?"

With a heavy sigh, Jack rose to his feet and gathered his composure before approaching the safe. Feigning a smile for his partner, he grasped the handle, noting its stiffness and weight as he turned it. A sharp *click* echoed in the room as the door creaked open, revealing its contents.

Or, more precisely, the absence of any.

"Means, the only thing we got was fucked, mate."

Hung's heart sank as he approached the safe, his eyes widening and fingers trembling as he sifted through the scattered paperwork inside. Receipts, invoices, and an instruction manual for an elliptical cross trainer. Each document mocked him with its insignificance. The realisation that they had narrowly escaped being gunned down by a blonde with an AK-47, only to find Magdalena's safe empty of anything of value, sent shockwaves through his body.

"Is this ... a joke?" he eventually asked.

"A joke? Does it look like I'm amused?" Jack replied. "No. This ain't a joke. This is an absolute shemozzle."

"But ... there was money in here two days ago?"

"Yeah, *was* being the operative word."

As Hung's mind raced, the enormity of their predicament sinking in, he looked at Jack, searching for a glimmer of a plan in his partner's eyes. Jack, ever the pragmatist, was considerably further along in the Five Stages of Grief, drifting somewhere between depression and acceptance. He took a moment to glance at the nearby clock. By his calculation, they had about twenty minutes until Magdalena's ransom exchange at The Cockatoo

Inn, and if they were lucky, another ten until she twigged it was a setup.

"Don't start panicking, Hung, we need to keep our shit together," Jack said, his voice steady despite the chaos. "We've got to take stock. Figure out our next move before Maggie gets back."

"Next move? Are you serious?" Hung replied.

"Sure. There has to be a next move, right?"

Hung scoffed. "Our only move now is to get out of here," he said, swallowing hard as he stepped away from the safe. The ticking clock in his head grew louder with each passing second. This was no longer just a botched heist; it had become a fight for survival.

"We've got time, Hung, trust me," Jack said.

"Time? Did you suddenly develop brain damage?"

Jack raised an index finger to put a pin in the conversation and pressed a hand to his ear, as if listening for something. "You hear that, mate? Surfer girl here discharged a cannon in a residential high-rise, and yet ... nothing. Not even a whisper. Hell, everywhere within a five-block radius should be swarming with cops, sirens blaring, tasers set to stun. But listen ... it's Simon and Garfunkel out there."

"So? What good is time, Jack? There's no cash!"

For once, Hung made complete sense. Jack let out a guttural growl and approached Becky, who was still bound to the chair in the corner. He shook her shoulders, trying to rouse her. At first, she was unresponsive, her body limp and lifeless. After a few tense moments, a faint flicker appeared in her blue eyes. She blinked sluggishly, a pained moan escaping her lips as she regained consciousness. Disoriented, Becky's gaze darted around the room as she struggled to piece together the nightmare she had awoken to.

"Where's the money?" Jack barked, his voice thick with fury. It was a side of him Hung had never seen before.

"Wh-wha ... money?" Becky replied groggily.

"The money from that safe there? Where is it?"

Becky winced as the words reverberated through her skull like a relentless drumbeat, each pulse intensifying the dull ache and making it harder to focus. The room swam in and out of view, the harsh light amplifying her discomfort as she tried to make out the brown-haired figure standing before her. Instinctively, she thrashed in the chair, only to realise she was bound by layers of duct tape.

Escape seemed almost entirely off the table.

She took a deep breath, forcing herself to stay calm as the haze cleared. Fractured memories surged: a conversation at the door, animal masks, a searing burst of pain, a blinding flash of light ... then, nothing. Just a black void. It felt like being pummelled by a massive wave, dragged under by its force, only to be hurled back to the surface, disoriented and gasping for clarity. The difference being the ocean never left a girl questioning its purpose, or why she was bound to an office chair with the mother of all headaches. Before Becky could even ask what in sweet Jumping Jehoshaphat was going on, Jack wheeled her over to the safe, spinning her around to ensure she had a full view before resuming his interrogation.

"Where's the friggin' money?" he repeated.

With those four words, everything fell into place: this was no crime of opportunity but a deliberate robbery. Fantastic. A nervous chuckle escaped Becky's lips, swiftly spiralling into manic laughter that echoed sharply through the room.

Jack scowled. "What's so damn funny, Blondie?"

"Nothing," Becky replied with a smirk.

"Really? So, what's all the cackling about?"

Becky's smirk widened as she blew a stray strand of hair from her face. "Guess you must've missed the memo, huh? Um, okay. Dunno how to break this to you, champ," she said, locking eyes with Jack and letting the silence stretch. "It's all gone," she finally continued, savouring the tension. "The cash, the gear, the guns … the fun. Everything! Gone."

"Gone?" Hung asked, leaning over Jack's shoulder.

"Yeah, gone. As in … not here. Vanished."

Jack cursed under his breath and stepped away, seething with fury at the realisation that all the risk had been for nothing. Worse still, any hope of a semi-comfortable life on the run had crumbled to dust. He paced the room, his eyes scanning the space, anger boiling inside him like a raging fire. Magdalena's office reminded him of that often-quoted line from *The Rime of the Ancient Mariner*: "Water, water, everywhere, nor any drop to drink". But instead of an endless ocean, Jack was surrounded by the relentless excess of a criminal empire, and try as he might, there was no way he could flip an Arthur Streeton landscape for a stack of fifties in the short time they had before fleeing the country. After all, cash was king, and right now, Jack and Hung were nothing but a couple of court jesters.

Sick to his stomach, Jack stopped pacing like a caged animal and perched on the edge of the loan shark's desk, wondering what to do next. From the corner of his eye, his gaze settled on Becky's confiscated AK-47, propped against the far wall. Jack studied the weapon for longer than any psychiatrist would consider healthy. Though he had no intention of resorting to his baser instincts, the sight of the Russian-made boomstick stirred something primal within him. Becky recognised the look instantly. She knew it was in her best interest to give up an answer or risk giving up the ghost.

"Maggie got spooked," she began, drawing Jack back in like a siren luring sailors onto the rocks. "She took a phone call a couple of days back ... out on the balcony. After that, she went fully paranoid. Secret meetings ... out all hours with Mark. If I hadn't already known the call was some tip-off about a search warrant or something, I'd have thought she was, you know, screwing around on me."

"She got a tip-off? From who?" Jack asked.

"I dunno. One of her cop friends, I guess."

"Bullshit. Magdalena Black doesn't have *friends*."

"Well, someone spooked her enough to clean house."

Jack's eyebrows shot up. "Clean house?"

"What, did you really think Maggie would leave her loot lying around for the cops?" Becky replied, her sass cutting through the tension. "Not unless you're talking about that pile of rupiah we brought back from Bali last month, sitting in the bowl on the kitchen bench." Jack and Hung exchanged looks of disbelief. "Oh? Is that what you were expecting when you burst in here? An easy payday? Because if that's the case, you're even stupider than I thought ... uh, Graham, was it? If that's even, like, your real name."

Cyrille peered out the yellowed curtains of cabin five, his curiosity piqued by the sound of a vehicle pulling into the complex. For a fleeting moment, he hoped it was the car rental company delivering their replacement ride, offering a chance to escape his claustrophobic confines. But deep down, he knew it was just wishful thinking. The scene outside grew more intriguing as two middle-aged men stepped out of a battered blue sedan. One was short and poorly dressed in a faux leather jacket and a garish Hawaiian shirt; the other was tall and solid, equally ill-dressed, but attempting to salvage some semblance of respectability in an ill-fitting grey suit and a crooked black tie. Cyrille scoffed under his breath. If either of these clowns worked for the car rental company, then he was a monkey's uncle.

"Hey, Don, come look at this," he whispered.

As the mystery men pottered around the rear of their sedan, locked in an animated discussion over what appeared to be a pair of rubber gloves, Cyrille's focus shifted to the police-issued revolver on the hip of Miami Vice.

Cyrille's newfound acquaintances were on the job.

"Don!" he called again, gesturing for his colleague to join him at the window. But The Diamond remained oblivious. With his hearing aid out, he sat nursing yet another cup of tea, absorbed in yesterday's newspaper, since, for some inexplicable reason, today's edition had never arrived.

"Hey, Don!" Cyrille repeated, raising his voice in a last-ditch effort to grab his attention.

Donald caught enough of Cyrille's urgency the second time around to put down the newspaper and coax his rusty bones out of the chair. Hearing aid now in, he shuffled over to the window, intrigued by Cyrille's insistence. He stuffed his reading glasses into his shirt pocket and took a moment to size up the individuals outside.

"Yeah, two blokes. What of 'em?" he asked.

"I've got a feeling they're cops," Cyrille replied.

Donald observed the pair for a while longer, scrutinising their every move. "Eh, well, they certainly aren't with the Fashion Police, lad. If the Fashion Police ever caught up with these two clowns, they'd probably kick the shit out of them," he said with a smirk. "What makes you think they're cops anyhow? Who's to say they aren't just two fellas looking to get, uh, frisky off the highway somewhere?"

"Huh? What are you implying, Don?"

"Well, I don't know if you've done the arithmetic, but this isn't exactly the place for the mister and missus and their two-point-four. It's more for the, ah, mister and mister ... if you catch my drift."

The pair of dirty Reg Grundies strewn on the roof of cabin two should have driven that point home by now.

"Whatever, Don. Just scope the short fella."

"The one with hair redder than a hangover piss?"

"Yeah, him," Cyrille replied. "He's strapped."

"Strapped?" Donald asked, giving his partner an amused look before turning his attention back to the men loitering outside cabin three. They were clearly up to something. Something that, judging by their jittery energy and their choice of accessories, namely rubber gloves, was about to unfold inside.

"Reckon they're looking for us?" Cyrille asked.

"Hmm. And why would that be, lad?"

"Well, we haven't exactly kept a low profile."

Donald chuckled, placing a hand on Cyrille's shoulder. "Well, whatever they are, they definitely aren't Feds, lad. Their clobber is far too cheap for that," he said. "My bet? They're just garden-variety Dick Tracys. Or, judging by what they're about to get up to in that cabin there, maybe a couple of rubber glove enthusiasts."

Ready to confront whatever awaited behind the door of cabin three, Hughes felt his heart thumping in his chest. He nudged the door open with a gloved hand and immediately froze, surprised by what he saw. To the detectives' chagrin, Chul-Moo's room was now empty, pristine, and spotless. It was a stark contrast to Hughes' earlier view through the eyeholes of his balaclava. Back then, the room had looked lived in, with belongings scattered about and sheets rumpled on the bed. Now, everything was neatly in place, almost as if no one had ever been there. Someone had clearly taken the time to clean up. Was it the manager? Maybe. The cleaner? Doubtful, considering the state of the rest of the place and the lack of any hired help.

A nondescript white rental van barrelled down the highway, blending seamlessly with the swarm of tradies' vehicles bouncing from one cash-in-hand job to the next. Inside, the Gwangju Three argued heatedly in their native tongue, their sharp voices slicing through the tension. The van's interior was a chaotic mess of fast-food wrappers, crumpled maps, and empty bottles, the result of hours spent driving in circles. In the passenger seat, Butterfly furrowed their brow as they wrestled with a street directory, unaware that they were hopelessly lost in the no-man's-land between Brisbane and the Gold Coast.

"Why must everything be so 'big' here?" they snapped, pointing at the map with exasperation. "Big landmarks, big everything: kangaroos, pineapples, peanuts. Big deal."

Mr Tooth, whose bulky frame devoured what space remained in the front cabin, leaned forward in the driver's seat and squinted at an approaching road sign. "Being bombastic is an Australian obsession," he rumbled, his deep voice reverberating through the van. "However, unless that map of yours has a 'Big Crocodile' on it, it is of little use in helping us find Chul-Moo."

Butterfly shot Mr Tooth a sharp sidelong glance as the trio continued on their journey down the highway in silence.

"I think you meant 'cockatoo'," Butterfly finally said.

"That is what I said," Mr Tooth replied, unfazed.

"No, you said 'crocodile'," Butterfly corrected.

"Then you misheard," Mr Tooth insisted calmly.

With the giant's words still ringing in their ears, the van passed yet another sign boasting about an oversized landmark, making Butterfly's original point even more valid. From the back seat, Bul-Gae, silent but ever expressive, leaned forward and mimed a bird gliding through the air, his hands fluttering gracefully, like wings. Mr Tooth caught the gesture in the rear-view mirror, meeting Bul-Gae's playful smirk. His irritation softened momentarily, overshadowed by the mute's unshakeable charm. With a grunt, Mr Tooth turned his focus back to the road. "My point stands. Unless this 'Cockatoo Inn' is marked on that map, we are wasting precious time."

As Hughes and Gamble stood in the doorway of cabin three, their eyes fixed on its unexpectedly pristine condition, Magdalena, Mark, and Fijian Bob materialised behind them with guns drawn. The detectives remained blissfully unaware until the loan shark's sharp throat-clearing shattered the silence. Startled, the pair turned slowly, their hands instinctively rising as they saw the weapons trained on them. Hughes' expression shifted from confidence to unease, his mind racing to make sense of this sudden turn of events.

"Well, well, well," Magdalena began, tutting as if she were a disapproving headmistress. "If it isn't Senior Sergeant Michael Hughes and his bashful sidekick ... ?"

"Gamble, ma'am," the man in question replied.

"Ah, yes, Sergeant Gamble," Magdalena hissed, her eyes lingering on his pudgy exterior. "As in, 'it must be a gamble squeezing yourself into that cheap, off-the-rack suit each morning'? Forgive me. Normally, I am above reproach with name association." Gamble nodded as if he had just granted her forgiveness, though it was clear Magdalena could not have given a frog's freckle either way. "Anyhow, it seems you two have been rather industrious. And here I was thinking you lacked the intestinal fortitude to cross me."

"Cross you? How's that?" Hughes asked.

"Really, Michael? You want to play innocent?"

"Me? I'm not playin' anything, Miss Black."

"So that's your natural state of being, then?" Magdalena quipped. "Well, let me spell it out for you. You've been poking the bear, Sergeant. And now the bear's in a right fucking mood."

The detectives approached Magdalena and her henchmen cautiously, their movements deliberate and measured as they tried to defuse the situation. There was no point in reaching for their revolvers; three against two on the draw was literal suicide.

"No closer. So, where is he?" Magdalena demanded.

"Where's who?" Hughes replied, playing dumb.

"Chul-Moo, the Korean you and your portly friend abducted from this very motel last night," Magdalena continued, her voice primed with scorn. "The same Korean I am supposed to be paying a ransom for. *That* Chul-Moo."

Hughes tried to muster a convincing look of shock at the allegation, his mind scrambling to work out how Magdalena had clocked their involvement in Chul-Moo's disappearance. That was no lucky guess. He had to change tack and fire up the old Mick Hughes bullshit offensive, though even he doubted whether his silver tongue could save them now.

"Seems like we might have our wires crossed, Miss Black," he began, his eyes flicking to Mark's distinctive handgun, momentarily pulling his focus away from explaining why they were outside the missing Korean's cabin. "I'm not exactly sure what you think's happening here, but it's nothing suss, God's honest. We were just … responding to a callout," he managed.

This new information piqued Magdalena's curiosity.

"A callout? And pray tell, for what?" she asked.

"Nothing to cream your slacks over. Just an anonymous tip-off about … " Hughes trailed off, snapping his fingers as if waiting for his partner to jump in with a lifeline.

"A … ah … Type 2B?" Gamble offered.

"Exactly, a classic Type 2B," Hughes confirmed.

"A Type 2B?" Magdalena repeated, eyebrow raised.

There was a pregnant pause, with only those brave and literate enough contemplating whether to make the obvious Shakespeare joke. Mark Campbell ploughed through like a typical Rugby League forward, clearly lacking any of the aforementioned literacy.

"And what's that when it's at home?" he enquired.

"A 2B? Just some joker driving like a lunatic," Hughes explained, gesturing toward the highway that ran past the motel. "Probably another boy racer thinkin' he's the next Peter Brock."

Magdalena gave the detectives a once-over, her eyes searching for any signs of deception. "It seems peculiar to send officers with your seniority on a hooning call. Is that not typically Traffic's domain?" she asked, her tone tinged with suspicion as her gaze shifted to the detectives' vehicle parked nearby.

"Well, we like to share the load," Hughes replied.

"Oh, I bet you pricks do," Mark sniggered.

As Magdalena approached the Commodore, she crouched beside the rear wheel and meticulously inspected the two pieces of grey duct tape haphazardly slapped onto the body. Hughes and Gamble exchanged nervous glances, their unease palpable as they awaited her next move. Intrigued, the loan shark picked at the tape until it peeled away, revealing a light grey putty concealing some kind of damage. She prodded it with a manicured fingernail, noting that it was still malleable and had clearly been applied within the last few hours.

"That's not what it looks like," Hughes said.

The Melburnians continued to peer out the yellowed curtains, their eyes locked on the unfolding scene outside cabin three. What had presumably started as a routine robbery quickly took on the appearance of an ambush. They had taken part in their fair share to know the difference. Without exchanging a word, Donald and Cyrille opted to keep their noses out of it, watching silently in hopes that the situation would resolve itself without drawing further attention from the local authorities. The appeal of a rundown dive like The Cockatoo Inn lay in its anonymity from law enforcement, and the last thing they needed was an impromptu shootout to shatter that illusion.

As tension in the car park mounted, Donald's gaze fixed on a familiar silhouette: the imposing figure of Fijian Bob, the bouncer from BLACK with whom he had clashed the night before. "Well, bugger me sideways," Donald muttered under his breath, shifting his focus to the petite, elegant woman nearby. With her stoic demeanour and nearly all-black attire, she looked as if she had just emerged from the local undertaker's, ready to size up a few new clients. Suddenly, the pieces of the puzzle clicked into place. Unless the Fijian was moonlighting, it was highly likely he was involved in something shady for his employer. And who was his employer? None other than the proprietor of BLACK, Magdalena Black.

"Think we might've hit the jackpot," Donald said.

"How?" Cyrille asked, scanning the scene.

Donald shifted his focus to the final member of the ambush trio: a burly figure clad in a leather jacket and jeans. As he scrutinised the mountain of a man, his gaze fell upon the firearm in the giant's grip: shiny chrome, with a pearl handle. A chill ran down The Diamond's spine as he realised he was face-to-face with his mythical white whale, the bastard responsible for his nephew's death. The revelation struck him like a sledgehammer to the chest. This was no random encounter; fate had delivered Mark Campbell right into his hands. Donald grinned with the calm confidence of an apex predator. What had once been a distant fantasy, revenge imagined from the comfort of his home in Melbourne, now felt tantalisingly close.

"That's the fucker, lad," Donald muttered as he sprang into action, his movements surprisingly swift and purposeful for an old codger. Before Cyrille could fully grasp what was happening, Donald had darted across the cabin to the duffle bag beside the bed. With a mix of curiosity and confusion, Cyrille watched him rummage through it, pulling out the nickel-plated .357 Colt Python he had 'borrowed' from The Pom. As Donald gripped the firearm in his massive hand, a determined glint flickered in his world-weary eyes.

"Who?" Cyrille asked, waiting for a visual.

"The cunt that shot Jimmy! That's who."

The Koreans continued down the highway, the monotony of the barren landscape lulling them into an apprehensive silence. Mr Tooth kept his eyes fixed on the endless stretch of road ahead, while Butterfly stared out the window, lost in thought. Suddenly, something garish caught the driver's eye. A flash of colour just beyond the tree line. He turned his head and spotted a towering, gaudy sign rising out of the scrub like a misplaced relic. 'The Cockatoo Inn', it read in large, faded letters, with a pair of male cartoon cockatoos perched above it, likely an inside joke for the clientele who frequented the place.

Mr Tooth's lips curled into a smirk as he nudged Butterfly and pointed at the sign. "I might have found your big cockatoo," he muttered in Korean, satisfaction lacing his voice. He slowed the van, and the pair regarded the sign with a mix of curiosity and disdain. This was it. They had no idea where Magdalena Black was or what she looked like, but The Cockatoo Inn was Chul-Moo's last known location. And logically, the first place to start their search.

"Remember how to wield one of those monstrosities?" Mr Tooth asked, glancing at Bul-Gae in the rear-view mirror as he gently caressed his M60 machine gun like a lover. Bul-Gae grinned and, as he was known to do, gave an enthusiastic thumbs-up.

Having served as an officer in the Republic of Korea Armed Forces before becoming one of Yoon's trusted jopok, Bul-Gae was no stranger to weapons of this ilk. Hell, if one had to carry a giant, intimidating firearm, this mammoth, gas-operated, air-cooled, belt-fed beast epitomised 'fuck-off-edness'. Affectionately known as 'The Pig' among US servicemen, it looked nastier than a severe case of haemorrhoids and earned its colourful nickname because of its voracious appetite for ammunition. Capable of spitting out five hundred and fifty rounds per minute in the enemy's general direction, the M60 had a fearsome reputation on the battlefield.

Five hundred and fifty rounds per minute.

One hundred rounds on the belt.

Eleven seconds of fully automatic chaos.

Jack's frustration mounted. No matter how many times he rephrased the question or how aggressively he pressed, Becky remained evasive, offering nothing more than vague answers and dismissive shrugs. It was like trying to squeeze blood from a stone, and with each passing second, the ticking of the clock grew louder in Jack's head. "Alright, Blondie, I'm gonna ask this one last time," he said, his voice steady. "And however you choose to answer will determine what's bound to go down next. Am I crystal clear?"

"Like the waves in Bora Bora," Becky replied.

Jack snorted. "Huh? I'm not a surfer."

"Pretty sure she means 'yes'," Hung chimed in.

Becky chuckled and leaned forward in her chair, a smirk playing on her lips. Her blonde hair veiled her eyes as she stared down Jack's, aka Graham's, false bravado. From their brief exchange, she could tell he was all swing and no ding, incapable of hurting a fly, despite the bruise on her face from the rifle butt that suggested otherwise.

"So, where'd Maggie stash it?" Jack pressed.

"Stash what?" Becky shot back, feigning innocence.

"The bloody money from her safe!" he barked.

Becky shifted against the duct tape. "How the hell should I know? Last I checked, I'm not her personal-fucking-assistant."

Jack leaned in. "But you *are* her girlfriend."

"Plaything ... more like. But sure ... still doesn't mean she tells me everything." Becky paused, letting out a dry laugh. "Anyway, make yourselves comfortable. Maggie'll be thrilled to answer your questions in person when she gets back. After all, nothing a fiercely independent woman loves more than getting grilled by a couple of pencil dicks in the comfort of her own home."

"Now it all makes sense," Magdalena said, pressing the duct tape patch back onto the squad car as she rose to stand beside Mark. Fijian Bob, shotgun held haphazardly in his good hand, watched with a mix of puzzlement and mild amusement, as if he were catching the latest twist in a soap opera. "Jack was telling the truth."

"Jack?" Hughes muttered under his breath.

"And to think, Mark, we almost killed his little friend this morning," Magdalena said, a wry smile curling at her lips.

The loan shark chuckled to herself as the group lingered outside cabin three, each silently wondering where the standoff would lead. Mark, his chrome pistol glinting in the midday sun, made a downward gesture, signalling for the detectives to lose their holstered weapons. The detectives exchanged a glance, a silent understanding passing between them: they knew that once their guns hit the asphalt underfoot, their lifeless bodies would soon follow.

"Let me explain, Miss Black," Hughes began.

"Zip it, Detective," Magdalena cut him off sharply.

"Come on ... this has all been one big balls-up."

"No, Michael," she said, her tone cold and final as she pointed a slender, ring-adorned finger at him. "Your opportunity to play the innocent here has well and truly passed." She flicked her gaze toward Mark and gave a nod. "Search the boot."

"What, now?" Mark replied, momentarily distracted.

Mark shrugged and approached the detectives' sedan with caution, his mind racing through a myriad of possibilities. Keeping his gun trained on Hughes and Gamble, the thought haunted him: what if Chul-Moo's body was inside? As he slowly lifted the boot, he braced himself for the worst. His breath caught as the lid opened to reveal ... nothing. Well, nothing besides a couple of plastic evidence bags, an emergency first aid kit, and a box of rubber gloves. The discovery answered one question: why these two were sporting latex, but left a dozen more in the wind.

"No Korean's in here, boss," Mark called out.

Magdalena blinked, incredulous. "Come again?"

"It's empty. Chul-Moo ain't here," Mark repeated.

Magdalena's face fell, or at least as much as her botoxed expression would allow. The defiance that had fuelled her moments earlier drained away, and the fierce light in her eyes faded into weary resignation. For a moment, she stood frozen, her fingers absently twisting the bracelet on her wrist as she searched for something solid in the sudden void. The news hit harder than she had anticipated.

Had Chul-Moo been in that boot, alive or otherwise, she might have been able to steer his employer's fury away from herself and toward the kidnappers. But there was no sign of the Korean. Nothing. Hell, she was not even sure this *was* a ransom exchange, especially given that her newfound prime suspects were missing the one essential ingredient: someone to exchange.

Regardless, Magdalena knew that if she failed to locate the missing hacker before the scheduled wire transfer, an empty boot would be the least of her worries; it was merely the first crack in a dam about to burst and erode the iron grip she held over the criminal empire inherited from her father. More than just a business, it was a legacy. A dynasty built on decades of control, fear, and respect that spanned every corner of the Gold Coast. Her father had built it brick by brick, body by body, with blood, sweat, and ruthless determination. When he passed it down to her, she had sworn never to let it crumble. But pride, as always, comes before a fall. Now, with the Koreans angered, the police circling, and her once-loyal inner circle doubting her, she feared that her father's empire and all she had fought to preserve was slipping through her perfectly manicured fingers.

"You two ignoramuses have caused me no end of trouble," Magdalena sighed, her frustration mounting. "You've just kicked a beehive. And once those bees discover their computer expert is missing, they'll be on the very next flight here and straight up my fanny with a flashlight."

"Shit, they're probably here already," Mark said.

"Uh, don't remind me," Magdalena replied.

"Sorry, boss. But it's almost guaranteed."

"Oh, is it now? Almost guaranteed? So, on top of murdering two police officers, we're also adding 'battling the South Korean mafia' to our little to-do list. Or should I say, *your* to-do list, Mark? After all, that is what I pay you a considerable amount of money for."

Mark shifted uneasily, itching to say something.

"Uh ... yeah, about that, boss ... " he started.

"Here we go. I simply cannot wait to hear this."

"Well, I'm more your 'deal with local thugs' kinda guy. International crime syndicates aren't in my job description."

The loan shark rubbed her temples in slow, deliberate circles, as if trying to knead out the pounding ache behind her eyes. Her slender fingers pressed deeper, betraying the frustration simmering just beneath the surface. After a sharp breath, she dropped her hands and gave her jacket an irritated flick, tugging at the hem and snapping the collar back into place. Her expression hardened, every movement a calculated effort to reclaim her edge. Things were not looking good.

"Listen, you don't have to off us," Hughes pleaded.

"And why is that, Detective?" Magdalena asked.

"Innocence, for starters. Wrong place, wrong time."

Magdalena chuckled, a low, throaty laugh that filled the air. Mark, ever the loyal henchman, echoed her with loud, mocking laughter as he hovered around the boot of the detective's Commodore. He jabbed his gun toward Hughes, an explicit invitation either to keep talking or take his chances with the business end of his firearm.

"Let's work this through?" Hughes interjected.

Gamble pleaded, "Please, Miss Black. I'm begging you. There's got to be a way out of this. I've got a wife and kids."

"Oi! So do I, you fat bastard," Hughes shot back.

What the senior sergeant had conveniently left out was that he was about as popular with his family as a pork chop at a bar mitzvah. But, as the saying goes, never let the facts get in the way of a good story. While the two detectives continued pleading their innocence to his employer, Mark's attention was drawn to a curious sight in the car's boot. In the dim light of the wheel well, he spotted a plastic evidence bag wedged awkwardly. Intrigued, he squinted at it, trying to make out its contents. As he observed the heated exchange between the detectives and Magdalena, he reached in and pulled the bag out for a closer look. Holding it up to the sunlight, the contents initially resembled a piece of flesh-coloured meat. However, after a moment of closer inspection, Mark's eyes widened as he realised what it was, nearly dropping the grisly find onto the ground.

"Jesus! What's this?" Mark shouted, holding it aloft.

"Nothin'," Hughes replied, glancing at his partner.

"Nah. It's more than nothin'," Mark replied.

"Not unless you count my lunch as something."

Mark blinked in disbelief. "Your lunch?"

"Yeah, beef jerky. Gets me through the arvo."

Mark sniffed the bag, his brow furrowing. "Mate, if this is jerky, your butcher's got some serious explaining to do."

Intrigued, Magdalena stepped closer to examine the object retrieved from the squad car. Her eyes widened as recognition dawned. "Is that ... ?" she began, her voice trailing off.

Mark nodded. "Bruce Lee's digit? Yeah."

"Good Lord," Magdalena sighed. "These two knuckle-heads had it all figured out, didn't they? Chop off the Korean's thumb to unlock the USB doodad, then sell off its contents to the highest bidder."

"It's lookin' that way, boss," Mark replied.

Hughes and Gamble exchanged confused glances. Chul-Moo's severed digit unlocked what now?

"Speaking of which, where is it?" Magdalena asked.

"The USB? Um, good question," Mark muttered.

Without missing a beat, Magdalena snapped her fingers, signalling Fijian Bob to move in. The tension thickened as Bob tucked his shotgun under his arm and stepped forward, ready to get all up in the detectives' shit, determined to find the missing piece of the puzzle.

The Korean's van screeched into The Cockatoo Inn's car park, skidding to a halt just metres from the standoff outside cabin three. Before the scent of burning rubber even reached their nostrils, Bul-Gae had slid open the door and levelled his machine gun at Magdalena's crew and the two detectives. He had no idea what they had stumbled upon, but faced with a group of shady characters and drawn guns, his instincts were clear: shoot first, ask questions later. And since Bul-Gae was mute, questions were very much off the table.

As the tension thickened and everyone scrambled to make sense of the chaos, especially with the M60 aimed their way, Mr Tooth lumbered out of the driver's compartment, Uzis akimbo.

"Freeze, you monkeyfuckers!" he bellowed in broken English, flashing a wide, menacing grin. His deep voice reverberated like a rolling thunderclap. Sure, the profanity might have been lost in translation, but the message was unmistakable. Friend or foe, it hardly mattered: none of these pricks were making it onto his Christmas card list.

"Who the hell are these jokers?" Hughes asked.

Magdalena sized them up. "I'm not entirely sure," she said, her eyes narrowing, "but if I had to guess, I would say this is what passes for South Korean charm these days."

With the situation contained, Butterfly stepped out of the van with unhurried grace, seemingly oblivious to, or entirely unconcerned by, the ensuing shitshow. Clad in a tailored black suit and peacoat that fell just past the knees, the androgynous figure exuded an eerie calm. Each step was deliberate, providing a quiet contrast to the chaos swirling around them. The coat seemed entirely unnecessary in the sweltering Australian summer, but that was beside the point. Butterfly's presence commanded attention, and soon enough, all eyes were on them as they approached Fijian Bob, who had paused mid-frisk of Detective Hughes' jacket pockets.

Donald and Cyrille were oblivious to the vanload of new arrivals, or to the fact that they were packing enough artillery to fend off the Japs at Pearl Harbor. Their focus was solely on ending Mark Campbell. As they stood with their backs against the door of cabin five, gripping their guns tightly, they felt their hearts pounding in their chests and adrenaline surging through their veins. Even though The Diamond had buried more crims than a Sicilian undertaker during a Martin Scorsese film festival, the nervous energy never seemed to wane.

"On the count of three, we charge outta that door and unload. For Jimmy, yeah?" Donald said, his voice edged with icy determination. Cyrille nodded, his intensity matching Donald's own. "Outstanding. So, are you ready, lad?"

Cyrille cocked an eyebrow. "Wait, so we go on three?"

"Huh? Right after I say three. Not before."

Cyrille smirked. "Alright, alright, just checking."

The two men exchanged glances, not merely as colleagues, but as if one were imparting final words of wisdom to his child. Donald relaxed momentarily, letting a rare smile pierce his grim exterior as he placed his hand on Cyrille's broad shoulder.

"He would've been proud," Donald said.

"Who, Jimmy?" Cyrille asked.

"No. Your French fuck of a father. That's who."

Cyrille took a moment to process Donald's words, his smile widening, momentarily illuminating his chiselled jawline and European good looks. However, the smile gradually faded as he faced the reality that if they botched this, he might be reunited with his old man sooner than expected ... wherever the hell the French went when they met the big baguette vendor in the sky.

"Let's do this. On the count of three," Donald said.

Cyrille gave a silent nod and closed his eyes.

With that, Donald took a deep breath, his voice steady as he began the countdown. "One ... "

Butterfly tilted their head, watching with detached curiosity as Fijian Bob's large hand fumbled with something hidden inside Detective Hughes' imitation leather jacket. The calmness in Butterfly's gaze stood in stark contrast to Bob's growing unease. His face twisted into a blend of mischief and guilt, like a schoolkid caught mid-prank. He shot a quick, uncertain glance at Mark, silently seeking approval, but Mark's cold, irritated stare gave nothing in return. With a reluctant sigh, Bob relented. Slowly, almost theatrically, he pulled the object from the detective's pocket and held it up for Butterfly to inspect, his hesitation evident.

Butterfly examined the small, unassuming object: a simple lump of black plastic. But then, their breath caught. A flicker of recognition crossed their usually impassive face, and for a moment, the intensity in their eyes softened as a wave of relief washed over them. "Where did you find this?" Butterfly asked, their voice calm, though it betrayed the surge of emotion bubbling beneath the surface.

The object in question was Chul-Moo's USB drive.

Without another word, they stepped back, their movements fluid and graceful. In an instant, two balisong 'butterfly' knives flicked open, the polished steel flashing as the blades spun with hypnotic precision. Magdalena nodded, impressed by the display, unaware that the moniker 'Butterfly' had nothing to do with demeanour. The soft, deadly whisper of the blades slicing through the air heightened the tension. Behind them, Mr Tooth and Bul-Gae mirrored the shift, their weapons now aimed squarely at Fijian Bob, who suddenly felt the full weight of the situation crash down on him.

"Two," Donald counted, his voice sharpened with resolve.

With the Koreans on edge over the discovery of Chul-Moo's USB drive, Mr Tooth's gaze swept methodically across the group, his Uzis poised as the car park Mexican standoff hit its peak. When his eyes landed on Mark Campbell, they sharpened, zeroing in on the evidence bag Mark was half-heartedly trying to conceal. The faint outline of its contents drew Mr Tooth's full attention. With chilling precision, he raised an Uzi, the barrel aimed squarely at Mark's head: an unspoken but unmistakable command. Naturally, Mark, in his typical macho defiance, acted oblivious to the universal language of gun-bound sheepherding, refusing to surrender the bag.

"He's got your kid's thumb in there," Detective Hughes shouted, trying to deflect attention from his own piece of incriminating evidence. "Lurch and Morticia here, they lopped off your mate's digit to get into that ... computer doohickey of his," he added hastily. "We're total innocents, yeah. Just a couple of good-natured blokes in the wrong place at the wrong time. Those are the two you fuckin' want."

Fijian Bob's eyes lit up with visible relief, grateful to be excluded from the dubious shortlist of local villainy. His grip on the shotgun loosened ever so slightly as suspicion shifted away from him. He took a few cautious steps back, silently hoping these arrogant *kaivalagi* would give him a wide berth and wipe each other out in the process.

"Pig's arse! We're not involved," Mark shot back.

"That baggie says otherwise, mate," Hughes retorted.

"As will my solicitor," Magdalena added calmly.

Mr Tooth repeated the gesture to Mark, and once again, the request went ignored. Instinctively, Bul-Gae pulled back the cocking handle on his machine gun, the mechanical *racking* sound serving as a stark reminder that the mute had a hundred little friends of the 7.62mm persuasion and they could all run a hell of a lot faster than Mark. Caught dead to rights, Mark offered an apologetic shrug to Magdalena and complied, lifting the bag to show the Koreans.

Butterfly stepped forward to examine the bag, a wistful sigh escaping them as the grim realisation settled in. "Where is the body?" they asked, their tone disturbingly detached, as if they were reading aloud from a shopping list.

"Whose body?" Mark replied, feigning ignorance.

"The kid missin' a thumb," Hughes interjected.

Butterfly scowled, their eyes flicking to the knives in their hands. Their calm demeanour concealed a dangerous focus as they weighed up which of Mark's major arteries to puncture first. This was no longer just a botched business deal; it was personal, at least for the knife-wielding maniac in black. Nothing anyone could say or do would salvage this monumental clusterfuck. The simple truth was that Chul-Moo was as good as dead, and this ragtag group of locals had both figurative and literal blood on their hands.

With the grim realisation that the only resolution was a swift and brutal response from the Koreans, delivered in a staccato hail of M60 gunfire, the instinct for self-preservation kicked in. Somebody had to draw first blood, and Mark wanted it to be him. Eyes darting like a Spaghetti Western gunslinger, he swung his firearm toward Detective Hughes, who wasted no time returning the favour. The brief distraction was all Hughes' partner, Gamble, needed. His hand shot to his holstered sidearm like a striking cobra, drawing it and aiming squarely at Butterfly. Jolted into action by the sudden spike in tension, Fijian Bob reacted next, awkwardly pointing his shotgun at the nearest non-white person not responsible for signing his paycheques.

Never one to be outdone, Butterfly charged forth and flicked their wrist, a blade catching the sunlight as its tip hovered at Magdalena's throat. It was a pointed reminder that in this deadly game, there were no spectators. Well, except for Bul-Gae, who watched with cold precision, his machine gun sweeping over the ever-evolving standoff.

"You must be Magdalena Black?" Butterfly asked, a grin spreading across their face as they pressed the knife tighter against her throat, the edge biting in just enough to make their point.

"Guilty as charged," Magdalena replied, unflinching. "And who in the merry fuck might you be?"

"The Grim Reaper," Butterfly said with a hint of flair.

"How cute." Magdalena let out a low chuckle. "And here I was expecting you to come wielding a giant scythe ... not a pair of fancy butter knives."

Donald gritted his teeth and braced himself for action.

"Three!" he bellowed. Cyrille flung open the door of cabin five, and without a moment's hesitation, the Melbournians surged outside into the scorching summer sun, guns blazing like Butch Cassidy and the Sundance Kid.

The Cockatoo Inn reverberated with the sound of gunfire, the staccato rhythm of ejected brass casings adding to the chaotic symphony as they *pitter-pattered* onto the asphalt below. The pungent smell of cordite hung heavily in the air, mingling with the screams of anguish and agony that pierced through the chaos. Crumpled bodies clung to life, their blood seeping into the crevices of the pavement, painting a chilling tableau of carnage. Whether driven by revenge, retribution, or sheer happenstance, the force at play seemed to be in a *kill 'em all and let God sort 'em out* kind of mood.

Chapter Twenty-Two

Cause and Effect

Back to where it began: The Hackston Tavern.

Jack Perkins and Hung Van Thanh stood on the precipice of their fates, knowing they had precious little time before Magdalena Black stormed back into the Gold Coast, furious at their ruse after Chul-Moo's kidnappers failed to show. While she had no proof the publicans were responsible for the kidnapping or subsequent ransom demand, only for his delivery to the destination, in the revenge-addled mind of a woman who cared nought about true culpability, she would want to punish someone, anyone, as an outlet for her anger. And what more fitting punishment could she inflict than snatching The Hackston right out from under them?

"Well, time to shit or get off the pot," Jack sighed, eyeing the disposable lighter Mark Campbell had left for them.

"Do we have to?" Hung asked, his voice wavering.

If recent events were any indicator, when faced with certain death, Jack and Hung's choice was usually binary: fight or flight. Flight seemed like a no-brainer; after all, the Datsun was packed, and they had their sights on a sun-soaked paradise with a non-extradition treaty. However, this time they decided to take a very un-Jack-and-Hung-like stand and add a shot of 'fight' into the mix. Torching The Hackston was more than a desperate act of defiance; it was the obliteration of their dreams, livelihoods, and cherished memories. Despite the pub being their sanctuary, their home, there was no way in hell they were going to sit idly by and surrender it to a ruthless bitch like Magdalena. No fucking way. No fucking how.

"You're only *now* asking if we have to do this? What, you've got some genius Plan B stashed away?" Jack shot back.

Hung shook his head. "Nah. I've got nothing."

"I figured as much," Jack said with a grim smile.

The men exchanged a last glance, silently agreeing that they would rather see their pub consumed by flames than let it fall into enemy hands. With a nod, Jack crouched low and brought the flickering flame close to the petrol-soaked floorboards. The liquid shimmered in the dim light, its pungent scent hanging in the air. With a swift motion, he ignited the trail of petrol, and the serpentine blaze raced across the floor with ferocious speed. The flames devoured the flammable material, slithering up the wooden walls and countertop, hungry tongues of fire consuming varnish and paint in seconds. An eerie glow danced and flickered, casting chaotic shadows across the room. The heat intensified, warping the air, causing the metal fixtures to groan and pop. Glass bottles behind the bar exploded, sending shards flying as the inferno claimed them. The aged, dry wood of The Hackston fuelled the flames, causing them to leap ever higher as the pub transformed into a blazing hellscape.

"Time to get a wriggle-on," Jack urged, as the intense heat pushed them back, compelling a retreat from the scene.

"But, Jack? What about—" Hung began.

"This ain't the place for a chinwag, you peanut. Go!"

"But ... don't you want to know what's inside?"

"Oi! Stick a cork in it and move!" Jack replied, hurrying through the front bar with the determination of an Olympic power walker, his prized Humphrey Bogart lithograph tucked under his arm. "And no matter what you do, Hung, don't look back. Regardless of what happens, looking back's only gonna make it sting more."

Amidst the chaos of swirling smoke and crackling flames, Hung exited the rear door moments after Jack and stumbled into The Hackston's car park, coming to an abrupt halt metres from their getaway vehicle. Ignoring his partner's profanity-laden prompts to keep moving, Hung coughed and spluttered, the acrid smoke stinging his throat and filling his lungs. Squatting on his haunches, he struggled to catch his breath, his red eyes fixed on the unfolding horror before him. Teetering on the verge of tears, Hung felt a sense of helplessness wash over him as their dreams crumbled in the inferno's relentless embrace. Without a word, Jack hauled Hung to his feet as the distant wail of approaching sirens pierced the crisp summer air, growing more distinct with each passing moment. There was no time for reminiscing, nostalgia, or for indulging whatever sentiment had gripped Hung. As the authorities drew nearer, Jack's sole focus was to usher his friend into the car before the long arm of the law thwarted their ramshackle plan.

"But ... aren't you ... curious?" Hung spluttered.

"Curious about what?" Jack asked as he directed his partner toward the blue beast. "Curious about how much time we're going to get for attempted arson? Or, better still, curious how many shades of fucked we're gonna be when Magdalena Black, famously known for her compassion, realises we were the ones who botched the armed robbery on her penthouse. I'm sorry, Hung, but the only thing rattling around in my head right now is the desire to get outta Dodge."

Hung glared at Jack with profound exasperation.

"No, about the cardboard boxes," he said.

"Huh? What cardboard boxes?" Jack asked.

"The ones that Campbell stashed in our office."

Jack's blistering pace faltered, if only momentarily. Amidst the chaos involving ruthless loan sharks and kidnapped Koreans, he had completely overlooked the twenty-one nondescript cardboard boxes stacked floor-to-ceiling in their makeshift office. A flicker of curiosity sparked within Jack, though it paled in comparison to the fiery orange flames consuming their pub. Realising this was not the time or place to delve deeper into the thought, he blinked, opened the driver's door of the Datsun, and tossed the lithograph into the back seat with the rest of their worldly possessions.

"Clean your ears out, mate," Jack replied, urging Hung forward as the city's soundtrack escalated into a cacophony of sirens. "In case that mind-splitting wail isn't enough to jog your memory, we're right in the middle of committing a pretty major crime ... or three. So, uh, excuse me if a couple dozen boxes of Maggie's crap going up in smoke isn't exactly at the top of my list of priorities."

Hung brushed off Jack's sarcasm and stumbled toward the Datsun, adrenaline coursing through his veins and his heart pounding so loudly it drowned out all sense of urgency.

"I'm simply saying, *maybe* we should—" he began.

"Just get in the bloody car," Jack replied.

"Hear me out," Hung said as he climbed into the passenger seat and *slammed* the door shut. "Wouldn't it be ... poetic ... if the answer to all our problems had been under our noses the entire time? Like the last act of a Shakespearean play."

If anything, this whole affair was shaping up more like a Greek tragedy than anything The Bard could have squirted out.

"What are you babbling about?" Jack asked.

"The contents of Maggie's safe," Hung replied.

Jack eyed his partner as he turned the key in the ignition, the engine spluttering to life.

"I'm just saying ... what if she stashed all of her ill-gotten gains *here* ... after the tip-off about the search warrant on her penthouse? All her cash, jewellery, and whatever else?"

Jack raised an eyebrow. "You're saying the entire proceeds of Magdalena Black's criminal empire ... lock, stock, and barrel ... have been sitting here, *in our office*, this entire time? All while we've been busy running all over the Goldie like blue-arse flies chauffeuring that Korean kid around?"

Hung nodded and then shrugged at the prospect.

"The *same* office that's now a raging inferno?"

Jack gazed into the fiery chaos unfolding in his rear-view mirror as the gravity of his partner's conspiracy theory dawned on him. Could Magdalena Black have really stashed the contents of her safe at The Hackston? The men shared a fleeting glance. "Nah," they uttered in unison as Jack jammed his foot on the accelerator, the engine roaring to life as they sped away from the scene.

Chapter Twenty-Three

Charlie's

Eighteen months later.
  A mansion somewhere in Brazil.
  Eduardo Ramos da Cruz reclined on a deckchair at the edge of his poolside bar, basking in the glorious warmth of the sun. He flipped through a large notebook filled with barely legible chicken scratch, pausing occasionally to brush the ashen remnants of a fat Cuban cigar from his unbuttoned purple silk shirt. Handsome and well-tanned with shoulder-length grey hair, the former cartel accountant turned bored, fifties-something bourgeois family man liked to keep his eye in while his politician wife was out of town. Fortunately for Eduardo, her most recent jaunt just happened to coincide with the best outdoor drinking weather of the summer, as evidenced by the steady supply of his favourite cocktail, the Caipirinha: a delicious blend of cachaça, sugarcane juice, and lime.
  "Carlos?" he said, with a nudge of his sunglasses.
  The man in question was part of a three-person security team seated at the opposite end of the bar, who, contrary to their employer's choice of libation, sipped small cups of intense, extremely hot coffee while keeping one eye on proceedings and the other on a portable television playing flashy bossa nova music videos on repeat. At first glance, Carlos may have appeared meek and diminutive, but his wiry frame belied a silent power beneath. Honed by decades of bitter experience, the scars map-

ping his body were a clear testament that he was not a man to be fucked with.

"Há algum problema?" he replied in Portuguese.

Eduardo frowned. "English in front of guests, Carlos."

"Desculpe, chefe. Ah … is there a problem?"

"A question for you. Do you happen to know the name of the currency this week?" Eduardo glanced at his 18-karat gold Swiss wristwatch and chuckled. "Considering it is still mid-morning, I doubt those palhaços at the Central Bank have had a chance to, as our guests might say, 'make cocks of themselves' and change it yet."

Carlos raised an eyebrow at the curious question.

"Uh, it is the Brazilian Real," he replied.

"After all this?" Eduardo asked in astonishment.

"Já. I am fairly certain. Why is that, boss?"

"It is a pleasant surprise, that's all." The loan shark placed his cocktail on the decking beside him and went about preparing a fresh cigar for sacrifice to the God of Emphysema. "One day it is the Cruzeiro. The next, the Cruzado. Blink and they rename it to the, ah, Cruzados Novos. And once you have finally gotten used to the new currency, they retire it, only to introduce the Cruzeiro again."

The implication that Brazilians changed their currency as often as they changed their underpants appeared lost on Carlos. Defeated, Eduardo set his cigar down in a nearby ashtray and returned to poring over his notebook with the imagined intensity of Stevie Wonder trying to read a braille copy of *Picture* magazine.

"Okay then," he began. "By the look of my notes here, you two already owe me, what? Twenty-five thousand Reais?"

"Sounds about right," a familiar voice said.

Seated across from their friendly neighbourhood loan shark were none other than Jack Perkins and Hung Van Thanh, looking considerably more relaxed than they had some eighteen months earlier.

It was amazing what a little sunshine could do.

Neither man had a clue what had happened to the smouldering wreckage of their former lives: the pub, Magdalena, her henchman, or even the missing Korean. Aside from a brief news article about a suspicious fire on Hackston Street, there had been no mention of the events that had unfolded and, as far as they knew, no threats of reprisal. While a less paranoid pair might have assumed they were in the clear, Jack and Hung, as two men who had dipped their collective toe into the murky depths of the Gold Coast underworld, understood all too well that the criminal fraternity was highly skilled at covering its tracks. There would be no returning home, at least not in the foreseeable future. And should they ever be foolish enough to err against their better judgement, there was a better-than-average chance they would be walking straight into certain death.

"And how much are you after this time?" Eduardo asked.

"Uh. Another forty thousand, I guess," Jack replied.

The loan shark took a lengthy sip of his cocktail.

"Why not an even fifty, Jack?" he asked.

"Well, we kinda figure forty is enough to get us square with, uh, just about everyone we need to get square with."

What kept Jack up at night was how he had left things with his niece. Charlie was the only truly innocent victim in all the bravado, bullshit and bloodshed, and despite his best efforts to shield her from the darker side of The Hackston, he felt a heavy guilt for dragging her into his mess. Fortunately, life appeared to have worked out for her. A quick internet search for 'Charlotte Watson' turned up a photograph of his niece proudly holding a newly minted Bachelor's Degree in Psychology. The sight gave Jack a rare sense of satisfaction, knowing she was now forging her own path. It reminded him that even if Charlie achieved nothing else in her life, she had already accomplished something meaningful, which was a damn sight more than her uncle had ever managed in all his years.

"We're good for the money," Jack said with a forced smile. "We've got this little shack down by the water. It's like somethin' from a postcard ... you can literally watch the waves rolling in while you sit at the bar and drink cocktails. Oh, and we found the perfect operations manager too. A young local woman by the name of Isabella." Jack and Hung nodded in unison. "We feel like we've got a solid business plan, Eduardo. We just need another injection of capital. You know? Just until peak, ah, 'temporada turística' rolls back around."

Eduardo grinned and chuckled to himself.

"Did I say that right? Tourist season?" Jack asked.

Eduardo nodded. "Já. But your accent needs work."

Jack shot Hung a smug look, as if to suggest he was already halfway to speaking fluent Portuguese and, by extension, blending in as just another 'rich' foreigner playing at being a local.

"And what is this bar called?" Eduardo asked.

"It's called 'Charlie's'" Hung replied. "We're just off—"

Eduardo raised a finger. "Carlos? What is this establishment like?" he asked. "Sell me on it, especially given that I am about to drop another forty-thousand Reais to keep it afloat. How is the atmosphere? The customers? What about the mulheres bonita behind the bar? I want to know if it's worth my time and money."

Carlos shrugged. "What would I know about bars?"

"You must be kidding? You have worked security all around Rio de Janeiro, meu homem. If I were a betting man, which I am, I would guess that you have probably been in more, ah, altercações at bars than I have had Caipirinhas. Eh, and I have had a lot of Caipirinhas, my friend."

Carlos considered the question while he readjusted the weighty submachine gun he had slung over his right shoulder.

"Well, when you put it like that, boss," he began. "I cannot comment on the young lady who works there. But if you want to know what this place is like, well, I guess it is ... how does one say? A 'hole of shit'? The bar is in a bad part of the city, full of pickpockets and peasants. Even the locals know not to step foot there."

The assessment was blunt, yet nevertheless accurate.

Four Caipirinhas deep and basking in the warm mid-morning sun, the loan shark's mind wandered to his upcoming lunch date with his fiery Lebanese mistress. Eduardo took a long drag on his cigar, watching the plume of smoke disappear against the crisp blue sky. "Carlos? Go to the safe and get Jack and his amigo their money," he said, the words laced with a hint of amusement. "After all, how much trouble could they get into over a measly forty-thousand Reais?"

Cue some flashy bossa nova music and roll credits.

About the Author

Jamie C. Richter lives a peaceful existence with his family, dodging Queensland's melanoma-inducing sun, avoiding human interaction, bingeing British panel shows, and pretending the golden age of '90s Australian alt-rock never ended. As far back as he can remember, he always wanted to be a writer. Unfortunately, Jamie had to get a *real* job and ended up spending two decades in the software industry, rather than doing something that brought him joy. These days, he still clings to the wildly optimistic belief that everyone's got one good novel in them. This probably isn't his ... but give it time, he's circling the bastard.

About the Book

Unorganised Crime began life in 2005 as a screenplay submitted to Project Greenlight Australia, the local adaptation of the American reality competition where aspiring filmmakers vied for the chance to direct their film with a $1 million budget. The screenplay performed exceptionally well, earning glowing reviews and landing in the top 20 of the competition. Realistically, that was about as far as it could have gone, given the author's complete lack of camera-ready charisma.

Back then, there were no streaming services hungry for local content, and the Australian film industry was as difficult to break into as it had ever been. As a result, the screenplay was shelved for several years. But that was not where the story ended. Cue a montage in which the author decided to adapt the screenplay into a novel. Over the next two decades, he would occasionally pull the manuscript out of the bottom drawer, tinker with it, and write another draft whenever life quietened down enough to let him.

Now, the finished product is in your hands!

If you enjoyed *Unorganised Crime* and would like more, hopefully not in another twenty years, please leave a review at your favourite online book retailer. With enough noise, the author might just get off his arse a bit sooner next time.